LETTERS NEVER SENT

Letters
Never Sent

SANDRA MORAN

Bink Books
Bedazzled Ink Publishing Company • Fairfield, California

978-1-939562-10-4 paperback
978-1-939562-11-1 ebook

Cover Design
by
TreeHouse Studio

Bink Books
a division of
Bedazzled Ink Publishing Company
Fairfield, California
http://www.bedazzledink.com

For Cherie and Cheryl—who never once doubted

ACKNOWLEDGEMENTS

It's said that you're only as good at the people with whom you surround yourself and in this regard I've been enormously lucky. Much thanks to my friends and family for putting up with my weird schedule. I am thankful for Ashley Fletcher who read, re-read (and sometimes re-read) each and every draft of the manuscript. Thanks also to my beta readers Stephanie Smith, Kathy Belt, Rebecca Maury, Betts Ballard, Nancy Kasting, Rachel Bailey, Nancy Orlich, Kathy Graff, Kathy Harmon, and Mary Shields. Thanks to Jordan Chambers for designing and hosting my website. Thank you to my agents, Denise Marcil and Anne Marie O'Farrell, for their unflagging support and to my editor, C.A. Casey, whose eagle eye and encyclopedic knowledge of the Chicago Manual of Style made the book sing. Huge thanks to Ann McMan who took a chance on a stranger with the caveat that I pay it forward. Finally, a special thank you to my mother, Cherie Moran, who likes to remind me of how she went through fifty-two hours of excruciating labor and gave up her career as an Ice Capades dancer to be my mother, and to Cheryl Pletcher, without whose patience, support, and love none of this would have been possible.

CHAPTER 1
Lawrence, Kansas, 1997

THE RAMBLING VICTORIAN house stood empty and still, a dark mass hunched forward against the illumination of the city. It was strange, Joan realized as she stared into the darkness, to see it and know that Katherine, her mother, wasn't inside—strange and almost surreal. But, if she were honest, she could admit that she was slightly relieved. Still, how awful did it sound that she was relieved that her mother was dead?

Joan placed both hands on the steering wheel and stared thoughtfully out the windshield. She could drive away. She could just as easily go to the Eldridge Hotel and get a room. She could go down into the old smoking lounge and have a drink. She could sit and chat with the other strangers before wandering back through the antique lobby and up to her room. She could deal with all of this later.

Or, her mother's brittle voice intoned in her head, she could shut off the car engine, get her bags out of the trunk, and go inside. There were certain things that had to be done, like them or not, her mother would have lectured. *Strange how the teachings of youth haunt us as adults*, she thought as she forced herself to turn off the engine and pull the key from the ignition. No sense in spending money for a hotel when she had free lodging here. There was a lot of work to do over the next few weeks and it would be better all the way around if she just jumped in tomorrow without having to worry about paying a bill, getting checked out, and driving back across town. Granted, Lawrence wasn't that big, but still, with all the students and people going to work, it just made more sense to stay here. Before she could reconsider, she dropped the keys into her purse, pushed the button to pop the trunk, and opened the car door.

The air was crisp with the sweet woodiness of fall—her favorite season when she had lived here—and she smiled at the sound of dried leaves crunching underfoot as she walked to the back of her car for the suitcase. She grunted as she hauled it out. She had packed far more than she needed for the two weeks, she knew, but experience had shown her that having choices was important when it came to dressing for Kansas fall weather. Warm mornings could turn into cool, or even cold, after-noons without warning.

As she lugged the suitcase up the walkway that led to the porch, she was unprepared for the motion-sensor light that snapped on and bathed her in fluorescent, unforgiving light. She dropped the bag with a loud, "oh."

"Joanie?"

The voice was soft and came from the darkness to her right. It was a scratchy, old woman's voice, and for a moment, Joan crazily thought it was her mother's.

"I was beginning to worry."

Joan blinked against the light as realization set in. It wasn't her mother; it was Mrs. Yoccum, her mother's neighbor and, as far as she knew, her only friend.

She squinted in the direction of Mrs. Yoccum's porch. "Hi, Mrs. Yoccum. I didn't see you there."

"I was waiting for you to make up your mind," Mrs. Yoccum said. "You sat in that car for such a long time."

"I wasn't sure I was ready to go inside," Joan admitted and held up her hand to shade her eyes. She could just make out the shadowy form of the elderly woman sitting on one of her wicker chairs. "How have you been?"

Mrs. Yoccum laughed softly. "Oh, I'm as good as can be expected." She paused. "It's lonely without Kate next door."

Joan nodded. "Well, you know . . ."

"Will you be here long?" Mrs. Yoccum asked.

"Oh, no," Joan said. "Just a couple of weeks. Just long enough to clean out the house and get it ready to go on the market."

"So you'll be selling it, then." Mrs. Yoccum sighed, no doubt concerned that strangers would be moving into the neighborhood— moving in next door to her.

"I will," Joan said. "There's no way Luke and I can take care of it from Chicago. And renting it out would be too much work."

Mrs. Yoccum made a noise in her throat just as the motion-sensor light snapped off, thrusting them back into darkness.

Joan felt slightly disoriented. Spots of white and yellow and pale green floated across the back of her eyes, obscuring her vision. She swayed slightly.

" . . . let me know if you need anything," Mrs. Yoccum was saying.

Joan nodded. She was tired of the conversation already. Her head ached and suddenly, she longed for the safety and solitude of the house. Her mother's house. Her house now.

"Well, I guess I had better get inside," she said after a moment.

Awkwardly, she leaned down to pick up her suitcase. The motion-sensor light snapped on again, but this time she was prepared.

"Good night, Mrs. Yoccum," Joan said and walked the remaining stretch of sidewalk to the porch, where she was once again returned to shadow.

She turned slightly, using the glow of the yard light to sort through her keys for the tarnished brass key worn smooth from use. It slid easily into the lock. She took a deep breath as she turned it and pushed opened the door. Her mother's smell struck her full force—Chanel No. 5 mixed with lemon Pledge and the somewhat acrid smell of recently-activated furnace. She felt like she was seven . . . fourteen . . . nineteen years old.

Joan closed her eyes and allowed herself to be momentarily swallowed by the darkness. She waited several seconds before she extended her hand toward the wall and fumbled for the light. Her fingers found the faceplate and then the switch. She hesitated, flicked her finger upward, and flooded the entryway with light.

It was exactly as it had always been. The narrow wooden stairs on her left with its darkly-polished newel, the umbrella stand with its four umbrellas, the antique mirror to her right, under which stood the narrow table with its arrangement of artificial flowers. She felt as if she should announce herself.

"Silly," she murmured. Still, she hesitated, then finally walked fully into the center of the entryway. To the right was the living room, where, when her father had been alive, she could remember the two of them watching television and lounging on the couch. To the left was her mother's sitting room where, when she wasn't next door visiting Mrs. Yoccum, she sat doing crossword puzzles or writing letters.

Her parents each had their spaces. But when her father had died, her mother laid claim to the living room. It hadn't even been a day after the funeral when her mother asked her to remove the television—a feat that was easier said than done given that the console television was as much a piece of furniture as a means of entertainment. After attempting to push and shove it on her own, she finally commissioned two neighborhood boys to help her move it to the curb.

Now the picture window was the focal point of the room, where her mother had sat in her rocking chair and kept tabs on the activities of the neighborhood. Joan walked to the window and looked out. The light from the room made it impossible to see anything other than her blurred reflection. She stared instead at herself. Her eyes were dark and enormous. And empty. Or was it just a trick of the reflection? She blinked and then turned to look at the rocking chair. She trailed her fingertips lightly over the top rail of the chair's back. The wood was smooth. Cool. Comforting. She nudged it forward with her index finger and watched it rock gently back.

Joan reconsidered her decision to stay at the house. She really wanted a drink. She stood motionless for several seconds, contemplating whether to get back in her car and drive downtown or simply to go upstairs and sleep. It would invariably be better in the morning. Wouldn't it? Finally, with a resigned sigh, she walked back into the entryway, picked up her bag, and climbed the stairs.

THE NEXT MORNING, Joan stood barefoot in the doorway to the living room and stared again at her mother's rocking chair. Sleep had been elusive, and when she had dozed, her dreams had been surreal and only partially-formed. She was surprised to find that she actually missed having Luke next to her—even though his snoring generally annoyed her.

Luke.

Despite the reason for her trip, there was a part of her that had almost been looking forward to this time apart. She needed time to think—time to figure out what she was going to do about her marriage or more to the point, her lack of marriage.

Joan shook her head at the thought. There was nothing wrong with Luke—nothing substantial, anyway. She just didn't love him. She had probably *never* loved him, she had come to realize. Theirs had been a romance of convenience. They had simply fallen into the relationship and had been too lazy to do anything but marry. And honestly, it had seemed like the thing to do at the time. She had secured a good job. She had a nice apartment. It had been time to add a husband to her list of accomplishments. And then children—though in retrospect, she found herself wondering why exactly she had thought that she needed a husband and kids.

The answer was obvious, though she didn't like admitting it. She had done it, in large part, to show her mother that she was her own woman.

"Guess the joke was on me," Joan muttered as she leaned against the door frame, the irony of her situation not lost on her. She hadn't wanted to be like her mother but there was a part of her that knew she was. It was clear in her actions—no matter how she tried to deny it.

Like her mother, Joan had married a man she didn't love. And, like her mother, she had had children that made her feel tethered to a life that felt like someone else's. She thought about the woman she had planned to be as opposed to the woman she had settled for becoming. She was supposed to be a lawyer rather than a paralegal. She was supposed to be living in New York surrounded by eclectic and clever people instead of a living in Chicago and shuttling the kids to their never-ending social events. She was supposed to have torrid love affairs instead of going to bed each night next to a snoring husband.

Was this how her mother had felt? Was that why she had always been so distant and angry? Had she, like Joan, wished she had made different choices? Had she, too, settled? Her mother had never specifically said she didn't love Clyde but she didn't have to. It was obvious. When she was young, Joan had often wondered what had brought them together— why they had married. She'd heard the stories, of course—about her father's strange infatuation with the Henderson sisters. And she knew her mother wasn't her father's first wife—or even his second. She had been the third choice of three sisters.

Joan was struck by the desire to see her parents' wedding photos. They were packed away upstairs, she knew, though where, she wasn't sure. The most probable places would be in the spare room, in her mother's closet or, more than likely, in the attic. She would look, she promised herself. But only after she had some coffee.

In the kitchen, Joan fumbled with the old-fashioned plug-in percolator her mother insisted on using. As she waited through the burbles and gasps for the final wheeze that signified the percolator was finished brewing, she went to the entryway and removed from her purse the folded to-do list she'd put together after talking to the auctioneer. After she inventoried the furniture, she would go through the smaller things like books and clothing. But for now, she just needed to get an idea of the scope of the sale. The task seemed suddenly daunting— especially on an empty stomach.

Joan wandered back into the kitchen and rummaged through the pantry. She had cleaned out the refrigerator when she had been back for the funeral, and all that remained were canned vegetables and tuna fish. She would have to settle for coffee. She searched the cabinet for the biggest mug she could find—a battered mug with Ziggy hanging from a rope encouraging her to "Hang in There, Baby." She rolled her eyes, filled the cup, and wandered back into the front sitting room where, despite her reservations, she allowed herself to settle into Katherine's chair. It was comfortable, and she rocked slowly, enjoying the quiet creak of one of the joints. It felt strange to sit there, but still, she didn't move.

As she sipped, Joan stared out at the leaf-filled yard. It needed to be raked. She knew that her mother typically hired one of the neighbor boys to do it, but the thought of getting outside and working in the crisp autumn air sounded appealing.

"It's probably because I'm dreading the work I need to do in here," she murmured as she finished the last of her coffee and rose to get more.

It was time to start working, she knew. She poured another cup and went to her room to change into jeans and a T-shirt.

Her approach was methodical, beginning with the upstairs and working her way down. She inventoried everything but the contents of her mother's room and finished late in the afternoon. The fact that she hadn't found her mother's pictures suggested they were in her closet—which meant that she had to enter the room she had been avoiding. She sighed, walked back to the foot of the stairs, and looked up at the hallway and the closed door of her mother's bedroom.

"Might as well get it over with," she said and forced herself to again climb the stairs. She reached out for the door knob and was surprised to see her hand tremble. She curled her fingers into a fist and willed them to stop shaking. Her mother's room had always been off-limits and apparently, that restriction still stood despite her death—at least in her mind. She shook her head and resolutely forced her fingers to close around the door knob.

The room was characteristically tidy. Her mother was one to have things always in their place. The bed, in which she had died, was the only thing that seemed out of place. It had been stripped of the sheets and bedspread, leaving only the bare mattress. Joan tried not to stare at the bed and, instead, focused on the task at hand. If the photographs were going to be anywhere, she realized, they would be in the closet. Quickly, she strode across the room and opened the closet door. She was unprepared for the smells. Chanel No. 5. And laundry soap. And the faint hint of herbs from a faded sachet in the back of the closet. It was the smell of her mother and, for a moment, she felt an overwhelming sense of . . . what? Love? Nostalgia? Loss?

She shook her head.

"Stop it," she told herself firmly.

The closet was like the room—organized. Her mother's clothes hung neatly from plastic hangers. Shoe boxes were stacked along one end of the shelf. Old hat boxes were stacked in the middle and at the other end, pushed against the wall, were the boxes Joan had been looking for—the ones she knew contained her mother's pictures. She pushed the clothes to the side and was about to reach up for the boxes when she saw the suitcase. It was small, battered, and shoved against the back of the closet.

She had seen the suitcase only one time before. She had just turned five and it had been well past midnight. She had been on her way to the bathroom when she noticed a thin sliver of light coming from the barely open door of her mother's bedroom. She had crept forward and peeked in. It had been the first time she had ever seen Katherine being someone other than her mother and Joan was fascinated.

Despite the hour, her mother sat on her bed, still fully dressed. Beside her lay the suitcase, its lid thrown back. Though she couldn't see inside, Joan could tell that her mother appeared to be running her fingers over a folded piece of white cloth. She wished she could see what it was, but her mother didn't pull it out or hold it in her hands. She simply touched it. She sat that way, unmoving, for several minutes—so long that Joan became bored and considered going back to bed. But then her mother slid her hand under the fabric and pulled out what looked like a book. Joan leaned closer to the crack and watched as her mother turned away from the suitcase and placed the object in her lap.

It was a box, Joan realized. A dark, polished, wooden box.

She watched in fascination as her mother ran her fingers lightly over its shiny lid. She longed for her mother to open it so she could see what was inside. She tore her eyes from the box to her mother's face when she heard a soft hitch in her breathing. Her mother was crying, but unlike Joan's sloppy, wet sobs that contorted her face when she cried, her mother's face was unchanged except for tears that ran from the inside corners of her eyes down along the sides of her nose.

Joan had never seen this version of her mother, and she felt scared. After what seemed like forever, her mother unfastened the top two buttons on her blouse and pulled out the delicate silver locket she always wore on a thin chain under her clothes. She rubbed it gently with her thumb, opened it, and removed a tiny silver key. Joan had always wondered what was in the locket and had even secretly hoped it contained a tiny picture of her. Despite her disappointment that the thing her mother guarded so closely was a key, perhaps, she thought suddenly, the real treasure was what was *inside* the box. Perhaps that was where her mother kept all the notes and pictures and drawings from Joan.

Her mother slid the key into the lock on the front of the box, turned it, and took a deep breath before opening the lid and staring dully inside. Joan looked from her mother's face, to the box, and back again. Her mother was crying harder now, and Joan shifted in hopes of seeing what was causing the upset. The floorboard beneath her creaked.

Her mother's head snapped up, her eyes puffy and red. Joan froze, pinned by her mother's angry gaze. Her mother placed the box onto the bed next to her, stood, and strode to the door. Joan felt her stomach tighten, and she drew back in fear—torn between wanting to comfort her mother and running from her. She gulped as her mother reached out her hand and pushed the door closed.

The sound of the door latch clicking shut echoed in Joan's memory as she stared at the suitcase. She stooped to pick it up, surprised at how light it was, given that its contents had contained the power to make her mother cry. She set it on the floor next to her, retrieved the boxes of photos, and carried all three down to the dining room table.

She stood, arms crossed, and considered what to do. Her mother wasn't there to stop her from going through it now. She could do whatever she wanted. Her mother was gone. She licked her lips and stared at the suitcase for several more moments. She was going to open it, she knew. Her stomach growled. She realized that she still hadn't eaten.

"Food," she said, relieved to have postponed the decision for a little while longer. "And then I'll deal with this."

JOAN LOCKED THE front door.

"Beautiful day."

She turned, startled, and blinked in the direction of Mrs. Yoccum's voice. The elderly woman sat on her front porch bundled in a thick sweater. A woolen blanket was spread across her lap.

"Hi, Mrs. Yoccum," she said. "It *is* a beautiful day."

"Reminds me of when I was young." Mrs. Yoccum sighed.

Joan smiled and pointed toward her car. "I'm on my way to the grocery store. Is there anything you need while I'm there?"

"No, no. Well, actually . . ." She smiled sweetly. "My son brings me food and everything I need for the week. But your mother used to . . . well." She raised a gnarled hand and gestured for Joan to come closer.

Joan walked across the grass and stood at the foot of the stairs. Mrs. Yoccum leaned forward. This close, Joan could see the cataracts that made Mrs. Yoccum's brown eyes slightly milky.

"Evan Williams," Mrs. Yoccum said in a stage whisper.

Joan frowned, confused. "Who?"

"Evan Williams," Mrs. Yoccum whispered again. "Black Label."

Realization dawned on Joan. She smiled and exhaled. "Oh. Sure."

"The big one," Mrs. Yoccum said. "I could go get it myself, but I'd rather not have to call a taxi just for that. You understand, don't you?"

"Of course," Joan said.

"Your mother was sweet to go get it for me when she was out," Mrs. Yoccum said.

Joan snorted softly. "I don't know as I'd ever call Katherine sweet."

"I know you feel that way, Joanie," Mrs. Yoccum said. "But she had a difficult life. She did the best she could, given the circumstances."

Joan drew her lips into a tight line and nodded. "Well, I should get going. I want to get back before it gets dark."

Mrs. Yoccum nodded and leaned back in her chair. "If I'm not on the porch, I'll leave the door open. Just come on in."

TWO HOURS LATER, Joan sat in her mother's dining room, a half-eaten baguette and an empty can of Campbell's Chunky Chicken Soup pushed to the edge of the table. Around her lay stacks of black-and-white photographs. Some she remembered having seen before, but many were unfamiliar.

She tried to organize them by putting them into piles based on the subjects of the pictures. There were photos of her as a child, pictures of her grandparents and relatives on both sides of the family, and a number of images of people and places she had never seen. She placed the pictures of her mother and father in a separate stack—including the pictures of her father's weddings to her aunts.

She studied the familiar, faded sepia images carefully. Clyde's first wife, Wilma, had been a plain, though not unattractive woman—sturdy with thick, useful-looking arms. She and Katherine had the same eyes. The shot was staged with a young, handsome Clyde standing stiffly behind Wilma, who was seated, her hands in her lap, her crossed ankles tucked almost beneath the chair. She wore a simple dress that opened down the front over a white smock of some sort. The ties hung loosely. Her wavy blonde hair was cut in a pageboy that fell just below her somewhat boxy jaw.

Joan smiled and set the picture to the side.

Next she picked up the pictures from Jeannie's wedding. Unlike the studio portrait from Clyde's first wedding, these had been taken outside. The first picture was just the two of them standing side by side, though Jeannie was slightly turned to show off her dress to the most advantage. Clyde was wearing the same suit as in the previous photo, although it fit differently—tighter. And although his face was again scrubbed, somehow it didn't look as clean as before. He looked tired. Jeannie, however, looked radiant. She wore a white dress and cloche-style veil that flowed into a train just visible down her back. The front had a V-neckline that disappeared into what appeared to be a loose, lacy bodice that segued into a skirt that was hemmed mid-calf. She wore white stockings and white shoes. Her blonde hair was styled in soft waves that fell around her face. She was beautiful.

Joan flipped to the next picture which featured the entire wedding party. The photographer had used a different angle for this shot, and the sunlight had caused everyone to squint—everyone that was, except Jeannie, who grinned in delight for the camera. Next to her was Katherine, her maid of honor—though, to Joan's eye, her mother looked anything but honored. Her expression was one of irritation. Joan did the math. Katherine would have been sixteen or seventeen years old.

Joan returned to the stack of pictures of her parents and realized that there were none from their wedding. She gazed down at the suitcase. Was *that* what was inside?

Joan grabbed the handle and lifted the suitcase onto the table, again surprised by how light it was. Though it must have been expensive at one time, the case was now just scuffed, worn, and somewhat depressing looking. The leather handle was worn smooth and shiny from use. In addition to the button-operated latches, stiff, cracked leather straps buckled in the front. She struggled for several minutes to unbuckle one of them. She went into the kitchen, pulled out several drawers in search of scissors, and found a steak knife that would do the job.

She returned to the dining room and flipped the case onto its side. She pulled the knife across the strap and sawed, ignoring the feeling that her mother would be furious at the desecration. She slid the blade under the strap, cut it the rest of the way, and sawed through the second strap. The scratched and tarnished latches were all that kept the suitcase closed. She brushed her fingertips across the buttons and then used her thumbs to push them to the sides. The latches sprang open. She paused, inhaled, and lifted the lid.

The smell of mothballs wafted upward from the case. Joan sneezed twice and wrinkled her nose. The contents of the suitcase appeared to be neatly-folded women's clothing. A dark skirt and a white blouse, yellowed with age, lay side-by-side on top of the other clothing. She thought back to the night her mother sat touching the white cloth. It must have been this. She reached out her own hand and caressed the blouse. It was cotton. Simply cut. She lifted it out of the case and unfolded it. It was short-sleeved. Tapered. Carefully, she set it aside and picked up the skirt. Her fingers felt something hard beneath it. The box.

She pushed aside the material and saw the shiny dark wood. It was just as she remembered—perhaps even shinier. Carefully, she lifted the box from the suitcase. Inside, something metallic clinked against something else. Curious, she tried to raise the lid, but it was locked. She remembered her mother's locket and the tiny key it contained. She had been buried with it on. The only way to open the box would be to jimmy it. Her mother, she knew, had bobby pins upstairs. She jogged up the stairs, grabbed several pins, and returned to the kitchen.

"Do I leave the plastic tips on?" she wondered aloud and shrugged. "Why not?"

Joan picked up the box and sat in her chair. As she tilted the box upward to catch the best light, she again heard the contents within shift and clink. She frowned, pushed her bangs from her eyes, and inserted the end of the bobby pin into the tiny keyhole. Using the tips of her thumb and forefinger, she delicately jiggled the pin. Nothing happened. *Maybe I should turn it like a key.* She gripped the pin with more force. She twisted. Nothing. She sat back and considered. Maybe she should try a combination of the two maneuvers. Within seconds, the pin turned easily.

"Wow," Joan exhaled, surprised that it had worked.

She leaned forward and placed the box on the table, the bobby pin still protruding from the keyhole. Whatever was in this box had made her mother cry. Her hands trembled as she took a deep breath and lifted the lid.

She blinked at the contents for a few moments, trying to make sense of a puzzling mishmash of items. Keys—to an older car from the looks of it. Theater ticket stubs—also old. A spent bullet case, a battered silver flask, and a thin stack of letters bound up in a green-and-white mesh scarf. She frowned. *This* was what made her mother cry? It seemed odd.

She picked up the keys. The key fob was a stretched, elongated penny—the kind that could be made as a souvenir at just about any carnival or museum. Pressed into the copper was "WORLD'S LARG-EST FOUNTAIN: WORLD'S FAIR CHICAGO 1934." She could tell it wasn't meant to be a key fob, but rather someone had used a nail and a hammer to punch a hole in it so it could be attached to the ring. The three keys, themselves, were less interesting. They were all worn and had the smell of old metal. The smallest was tarnished brass and appeared to be a house key. The other two were to a car—a Chevrolet. She cupped them in her palm. The larger key was likely to the ignition and the slightly smaller one opened the trunk and glove box. She looked back down into the box and trailed her fingertips over the tarnished body of the flask. At one time it probably had been very nice. She picked it up and felt the weight of it. She shook it. Liquid sloshed. She twisted open the top, sniffed, and drew back. Whiskey.

"Whoa," she muttered with a small frown. Her mother didn't drink. And then there was the bullet case. *Why had her mother saved that?* As far as she knew, her parents didn't own a handgun. It was all so odd.

She picked up the packet of letters. The scarf tied around them was made of some kind of gauzy, scratchy material that smelled dusty and old as she carefully untied the knot and freed the letters. The scarf itself was like the ones her mother wore in some of the pictures from the 1950s. It had, at one time, been white, although now it was somewhere between beige and ivory, with a thick green border inset with thinner green bands.

The packet of letters consisted of sealed envelopes. The envelopes were blank and appeared to have never been opened. Joan guessed they had been written by her mother but never mailed. She held one up to the light and could see the faint impression of her mother's bold, but meticulous handwriting. She fanned them out like a hand of cards—seven envelopes, each thick with several sheets of paper.

Joan picked up the oldest-looking one. She was curious to know what was inside but also hesitant to invade her mother's privacy. She laughed softly. Her mother was dead. What did it matter? Before she changed her mind, she grabbed the knife, slid the tip of the blade under the envelope's flap, and slit it neatly open. The paper inside was folded into thirds and looked as though it had been wadded up and then flattened. The tight, clean script was her mother's. The upper right hand corner was dated 1947.

Dearest A~

I'm sitting here at my desk, staring out the window and wondering what you're doing right now. I imagine you lying on a blanket in the park, a book on your stomach, your flask tucked into your pocket for a quick nip. The sun is warm on your face and you're dozing. I would like to pretend that you are dreaming of me, but know that likely enough, that time has passed and now your dreams are of Doris.

I know you said that you have moved on, but I want you to know that I am in love with you. I know it now. I know it without question and if you could just ignore the past—if you could just give me a sign that there is still a chance for us, I would leave my life here and come to you.

Do you ever think about those days when we were together? I do. You were everything to me and now that you're gone—now that you're with her—I don't know as I can live. If I had just gone inside, packed my bag, and put it in your car. If I had just left with you before Clyde came home from the war, none of this would have happened.

I dream of you at night—of your kisses and the warmth of your body. And then I wake next to him snoring beside me. And I hate him. Sometimes I hate you, too. I hate that you have a new life—a life that doesn't include me. Do I sound bitter? Jealous? I am. I am so jealous that sometimes it feels like it's consuming me.

I am in love with you—so deeply in love with you that nothing else matters. I refuse to give up on us because it's clear to me now that you're gone that without you, I'm nothing.

Joan sat back and stared at the letter clutched in her hand. Her mother undoubtedly had written it, though the sentiment and the emotion sounded nothing like the woman she knew. Who was "A"? And what had gone on that they would have . . . she paused, suddenly aware of the date. The date was seven years before she had been conceived, but well after Katherine and her father had married, which meant . . . She gasped. Her mother had been having an affair.

CHAPTER 2
Big Springs, Kansas, 1929

"COME ON, KATIE," Jeannie wailed as she twisted and adjusted her dress. "Stop pouting and come help me. It's my special day, and you're going to ruin it if you don't come and help me."

Without turning to look at her, Katherine nodded from her perch in the window seat. She was watching her father prepare the car that would take them to the church for the wedding. He was dressed in his best suit, hair slicked down, although she noticed, with a small smile, the cowlick at the back of his graying head obstinately standing up. He was cleaning out the inside of the family car, brushing away any dust and dirt that might get on Jeannie's wedding dress. Katherine knew that her father, like the rest of the family, didn't understand why Jeannie had set her sights on Clyde. But they had all realized that she had and accepted—as did Clyde himself—that marriage, especially in light of the pregnancy, was the only option.

As if sensing her gaze, her father looked up at the window and met her eyes. They gazed at each other for several seconds before he raised and lowered his hand. He looked tired, she thought as she returned the wave.

"Katie." Jeannie again cut into her thoughts. "I need your help."

Katherine sighed, cast a final look at her father, and turned her attention to her sister. "You don't really need my help. You just want me to pay attention to you."

"You *should* pay attention to me," Jeannie said. "It's my wedding day. Everybody should pay attention to a girl on her wedding day."

Katherine snorted.

"Just because you're jealous—" Jeannie began.

"Jealous because you intentionally got yourself pregnant so you could force a man who doesn't love you into marrying you?" Katherine said. "Not likely."

"That's not how it happened," Jeannie said.

"Um." Katherine went to stand behind Jeannie and worked on inserting the delicate cloth-covered buttons into the eyelets.

At seventeen, she was already taller and more willowy than her sister. She paused in her buttoning and looked over Jeannie's shoulder at their reflections in the mirror. They looked nothing alike. Jeannie looked like their older sister, Wilma. Small and plump, both Jeannie and Wilma had their mother's wavy blonde hair and rounded face. Katherine was tall—almost too tall, she thought—with curly dark hair and an angular face. The only trait all three sisters shared were their somewhat slanted green eyes—cat's eyes, her father said fondly.

Katherine knew she was plain in comparison to her sisters. Their looks were what women aspired for—rounded and feminine with soft complexions. In comparison, Katherine looked gangly and dark. Her dress hung loosely from her almost bony frame.

"You're too thin," her mother always said. "You need to stop spending all your time reading those books and more time eating. Who's going to want to marry a skinny thing like you?"

"I guess it's a good thing, then, that I don't want to get married," she would answer. It was her stock response.

"You're young," her mother would always retort. "That'll change."

Katherine knew her mother believed that. But in her heart, she knew it wasn't true. She had no desire to remain in Big Springs or to marry Albert Russell or to become a farm wife. She wanted to move to Kansas City or Chicago to work in a store or a factory. She wanted to see people from different places. She wanted to *live*.

"Done?"

Again, Jeannie's voice broke into her thoughts. Katherine jerked to attention and fastened the last few buttons. When finished, she stepped back.

"How do I look?" Jeannie asked.

Something about the way she spoke the words made Katherine raise her gaze to meet Jeannie's eyes in the mirror. Her cheeks were flushed, her green eyes were wide. Despite her claims of happiness, Katherine thought she looked young and scared.

"You look great," she said, surprised at her kind impulse. "You look beautiful. Really."

Jeannie smiled brightly, and then her face sobered. "Do you think Wilma minds?"

"No," Katherine said, softly. "Probably not."

"I guess I just wonder . . . Do you think she's watching us from heaven?" Jeannie asked.

Katherine shrugged and, noticing her sister's worried expression, smiled. "I'm sure she is. And I'm sure she's happy you're taking care of Clyde."

"I do love him," Jeannie said with a happy smile. "I've always loved him. And now he loves me. Only me."

Katherine patted Jeannie's shoulder. "That's great, Jeannie." She glanced at her watch. "We should probably be heading downstairs. Daddy has the car ready, and the sooner we get to the church, the sooner you can become Mrs. Clyde Spencer."

THE CEREMONY HAD taken forever, Katherine thought as the wedding party stood in the hot afternoon sunlight waiting for the photographer to take the picture. She hated having her picture taken anyway—not that it happened all that often. She sighed and scowled as she watched Jeannie preen and flounce and coo over Clyde.

Katherine felt sorry for her brother-in-law. He was, as far as she could tell, a nice man. He had loved her sister, Wilma, for as long as Katherine could remember and had been devastated when she had died. They had all been surprised when he started spending so much time with Jeannie. Or, she amended, Jeannie had started spending so much time with *him*.

Katherine cocked her head. The bright afternoon sunlight made her head hurt—as did the constant hum of people laughing and joking with the bride and groom as the pictures were being taken. It seemed like the entire community gathered for the event. Albert Russell caught her eye and smiled. Katherine knew he would want to claim her attention as soon as the picture taking was over.

"Look over here," the sallow-faced photographer said. "Everyone look over here and smile."

Katherine looked in his direction. Beside her, Jeannie gave her a pinch.

"Smile," she hissed through gritted teeth. "Don't ruin this for me, Katie."

Katherine squinted into the sun and forced her mouth into the semblance of a smile. It was going to be a very long day.

"SO, YOU WANT to go for a ride?" Albert asked Katherine and Evelyn as they stood in the shade of one of the towering oaks that bordered the edge of the church property. He gestured toward Howard Lewis, who was leaning against the car owned by Albert's father, the town's wealthiest resident. "Me and Howie were thinking about going for a ride."

"I can't," Katherine said and gestured toward Jeannie. "Maid of honor and all that. I have to stay."

Albert grinned good-naturedly. "How 'bout I come over after."

Katherine ignored Evelyn, who looked down at her shoes and smiled.

It was common knowledge that Albert was in love with Katherine and that his attempts at courtship were not going as smoothly as he would have liked.

"Can't," Katherine said. "I have to help get her things packed and moved over to Clyde's."

Albert's grin faded slightly. "What about one night this week? We could take a walk . . . or go to Lawrence."

"Maybe," Katherine said.

Albert sighed and leaned forward. "Katie, why are you doing this?"

"You know why," Katherine said.

Albert frowned, but said nothing. She had explained to him many times that she wasn't playing hard to get. She simply didn't want to give him the wrong impression. He wanted to propose, and she wanted to leave Big Springs and move to a large city as soon as she was eighteen. Those plans didn't include a husband.

Evelyn had once asked her why she seemed so uninterested in Albert. "He's nice and funny and handsome. And he's rich."

"He is," Katherine agreed. "He's all those things. And if I were interested in settling down and staying in Big Springs all my life, I'd probably pay him more mind. But, Evie, that's not what I want."

"Albert or Big Springs?" Evelyn had a soft, open face that made her thoughts and emotions entirely readable. Her expression showed that she was genuinely puzzled by Katherine's words.

"Neither," Katherine said.

Evelyn wrinkled her brow.

"Is that bad? To want more than this?" Katherine swept out her hand. "I want to see and do things."

"But how would you get by without a husband?" Evelyn asked. "What would you do?"

"Get a job," Katherine said simply.

Evelyn looked stricken. "Where would you live?"

"I would take a room with a family, I suppose," Katherine said.

"But why? When you could marry Albert and have a family?" Evelyn leaned forward and touched Katherine's arm. "Wouldn't you be lonely?"

"I can always do those things," Katherine said.

"I'm sure Albert would take you to the city if you asked him." Evelyn grabbed Katherine's arm. "Maybe on your honeymoon. You two could go to Kansas City. Or Chicago."

Her eyes were bright with excitement.

"Evie, I don't want to just visit," Katherine said. "I want to *live* there. I want to walk down the streets and see people."

Evelyn shook her head. "I don't know why." She paused thoughtfully. "But you better be careful or Albert will find somebody else."

As Katherine lay in bed that night, Jeannie ensconced at Clyde's, she wondered what was wrong with her that she wanted nothing to do with marriage or children. She thought about Evelyn's reaction. She had been perplexed. Why would someone like Katherine—someone who had the option of getting married to a man like Albert—want to go off by herself to a large city and work at a job?

It was a good question—and one Katherine had asked herself more than once with always the same answer. She simply wanted to have a life different than the one she was expected to have.

With a frustrated sigh, Katherine rolled onto her side and stared at the shadows of trees cast on her wall by the light of the moon. She had never been like the rest of her friends and family. They wanted the safety of their uncomplicated lives, and she wanted . . . What? Travel? Adventure?

"It's not healthy," her mother often said. "This obsession with books and far-off places just makes you want what you can't have. You need to be out with your friends, not filling your head with places you're never gonna see. You're seventeen. You're going to be graduated soon. You should be thinking about settling down with Albert and giving me some grandchildren—not going to Egypt or Paris or wherever it is you think you need to go."

"Mama, please," Katherine had said in exasperation. "I don't want to get married straight off. You know that."

"A woman can't wait too long," her mother had responded, giving her the once-over. "You're young now, and pretty enough, but that'll fade. Wait too long and all the good ones'll be taken."

Jeannie hadn't waited, she thought as she fingered the lace trim on her pillowcase. She had pursued Clyde with the same relentless determination she used for anything she wanted.

"She's ruthless," Katherine had confided to Albert one day after Jeannie had announced that she was pregnant and going to marry Clyde. "I feel sorry for him. The poor guy didn't stand a chance."

They had been walking down the long drive that led to her parent's house, but had stopped to take advantage of the shade provided by a thatch of trees. Albert sat on the top rung of the wooden fence that ran along the gravel drive. Katherine leaned against one of the solid wooden posts. Despite it only being late afternoon, an industrious bullfrog croaked in the distance.

"She may be ruthless, but she loves him," Albert said with a subtle wistfulness in his voice. "She wants to marry him—to start a life with him. You can't blame her for that. It's only natural."

He grinned, and Katherine felt a strange heaviness in her chest because she knew what he was subtly trying to tell her. She looked down at the toes of her shoes. They were dusty, and she had the sudden desire to wipe them clean.

"Just think," he continued. "Once she's married, it's your turn."

"I can't imagine I'll get married anytime soon," she said. "I want to—"

"Go to the city and experience things. I know. But, think about it. Is that really what you think will happen—that you're going to go off to the big city? How are you going to get the money? How will you survive?" He shook his head and grinned down at her. His tone was dismissive. "Nah, you're gonna marry me. And we'll have lots of kids." He paused at her expression and quickly added, "But we'll go to Chicago if you want—just so you can see it."

Katherine felt her stomach contract.

Albert jumped down from the top of the fence and landed lightly in front of her. His shirt sleeves were rolled up to expose smooth, muscular forearms which he crossed over his chest. "Come on. Say the word and I'll propose. You know how much I want to marry you. Hell, everybody does."

"Albert." She paused. His wide, anxious face began its all-too-familiar transition from optimism to angry resignation. "Can't we just wait to have this discussion? I'm still not graduated from school yet. Neither are you."

"I know what I want. But you want something that's not yours to have." He shook his head angrily. "There's something wrong with you, Katie. Most girls—"

"I'm not most girls," she interrupted.

Albert scowled and turned away from her. "I know, dammit. Maybe that's why I love you."

"Can't this wait?" Katherine asked. "Can't we just focus on school and spending time together? We have the rest of our lives to get married and all the rest."

Albert kicked at a tuft of grass but didn't answer. Finally, he sighed and nodded. "I suppose." He stared out over the field at the trees that ran along the distant creek bank.

A hawk wheeled overhead.

"I'm not saying 'never,'" she said finally. "I'm just saying 'not now.'"

Albert jerked his head up, the pleasure and hope so clearly written on his face that Katherine felt guilty as soon as she uttered the words. It was true, she reasoned. She wasn't saying "never." But in her heart, she knew that the sentiment was empty—that she was simply hedging her bet.

"Well, that's something," Albert said, once again happy. "What say we go into Lawrence and see what's going on in the big city?"

She smiled, though she knew it wasn't genuine, and nodded.

"It's all gonna be okay, Katie," he said as he led her back to her parent's house. "You'll see. I'm not giving up." He grinned broadly. "One day you're gonna marry me and I'll be the happiest man alive."

CHAPTER 3
Lawrence, Kansas, 1997

JOAN SET THE letter carefully on the table and drew in a deep breath. "Wow," she breathed.

Joan searched her brain for who "A" could possibly have been. She couldn't recall her mother talking about anyone whose name began with that letter, but still . . . She considered the stack of pictures. Was an image of "A" among them? Surely if she had loved him that much, she would have a picture of him. She was tempted to go through the pictures again. Her mother had often scribbled names and dates on the back.

She looked down at the remaining six letters. Perhaps there were some clues there. She considered how best to read them. Should she do it in order or perhaps begin with the most recent? She fanned them out and studied them. She had begun with the oldest, so she opted to continue sequentially. She picked up the knife and the envelope that looked to be the next oldest just as the telephone rang. She put the letter and the knife on the table and walked into the kitchen. The phone, the one she remembered from her childhood, was a boxy wall unit the color of split pea soup. She lifted the receiver from the silver cradle and raised it to her ear.

"Hello?" she said into the mouthpiece.

"Hey." It was Luke. "How's it going?"

Joan sighed. "It's . . . going. I'm going through everything."

"Well, don't overdo it," he said.

"How are the kids?" she asked. "Have they given you any trouble?"

"Nah," Luke said. "Matty is working on his homework and Sarah is up in her room."

"Good," she said. "You're doing okay as a single parent?"

Luke laughed. "Easy as pie. I was expecting it to be a lot harder from the way you talk about it."

Joan frowned at the comment. "Try doing it all of the time," she muttered.

"Huh?" Luke asked. "I didn't catch that."

"Nothing," Joan said. "Just talking to myself. Did work call?"

"Yeah." Luke sounded distracted. Joan could hear a football game on the television in the background.

"What did they say?" Joan asked.

"Damn!" Luke said.

"What?" Joan asked.

"Green Bay just scored," Luke said. "Great. I've got twenty bucks riding on this game."

"Luke, what did work say?" Joan asked again.

"Oh . . . uh, Bethie called and said your boss said to take as long as you need. He said he would get Bethie and one of the other paralegals to cover your work while you're gone."

Joan nodded, not surprised that Mark would say that, but slightly disappointed that her absence was so easily accommodated.

"So, you're good." Luke paused. "Shit! The Bears fumbled the kickoff."

Joan waited, and when Luke didn't say anything, she knew he was watching the game.

"Okay, well, I'm going to let you go," she said, struggling to keep the irritation out of her voice. "I'm going through some of Mom's stuff so I should probably get back to it."

"Yeah," Luke said, distracted. "Okay, well, we're here so call if you need us."

"I will," Joan said. "Kiss the kids for me."

"Okay," Luke said. "Bye."

Joan opened her mouth to answer and heard the dial tone. He hadn't even waited for her to respond before hanging up. She replaced the receiver and sank down onto the wooden stool under the phone. She stared at the faded curtains that hung limply on the kitchen door and wondered what had happened to her marriage. How had they become so careless of each other? Was this what had happened to Katherine and Clyde? Perhaps that was part of what led Katherine to have her affair with "A." She remembered the letters and returned to the dining room.

"Oldest first," she murmured as she slid back into her chair and picked up the envelope she had set down to answer the phone. She slid the knife under the gummed lip. Years of storage had already done much of the work, and it opened with a dusty crackle. She unfolded the sheets of paper and began to read.

1954

My Darling A~

It's been six months since your death—six months without your laugh or your amazing face. It's as if a light has gone out. Every day I think of you, long for you, wish that I would have been brave enough to be with you. If I had just been stronger, you would still be here. But then, you always were the braver of the two of us. You knew from the beginning.

My life without you is a constant string of activities designed to pass the hours, the days, the months. I get up, make breakfast, clean the house, shop for groceries, prepare meals, walk in the afternoons, and long for the night when I can sink mercifully into sleep. It's only there, my love, that we can be together. You visit me nightly, did you know that? Sometimes we talk. Sometimes we make love. The hardest part is letting go of the dreams the next day and wading through the hours of reality.

I was walking yesterday when in my head I heard our song and it evoked a memory so real, it brought tears to my eyes. You were sitting on that rock and the waves of Lake Michigan were rolling in and out. It sounded like the ocean. Your sleeves were rolled up and you were holding a cigarette and singing. Do you remember that day? You had the worst singing voice in the world, but it was the sweetest sound to my ears. Isn't it amazing how the smallest memories can elicit the strongest emotions?

Please know there is not a day that goes by that I don't regret my life, the decisions I made or the fact that your murder was my fault.

I love you now and forever with all that I am.
K.

Joan stared in disbelief at the last few lines. How could this man's murder possibly have been her mother's fault?

She sat back and rubbed her eyes. It was almost too much to take in. Her mother not only had a lover, but this man had been murdered, and her mother had had something to do with it.

She looked back at the contents of the box. Her mother had written the first letter in 1947. This one was dated 1954, shortly before she had been born. She picked up the next envelope and, without the care she had shown with the other letters, ripped it open. It was dated 1955.

1955
Dearest~

It's been more than a year without you and already it feels like a lifetime. I am so lost without you. I weep when I think about all the time I could have had with you—time that I squandered. I could have had a LIFE with you. And

I threw it away with both hands, running toward something that would never make me happy. I'm ashamed at my wastefulness.

I'm a mother now. It's ironic, isn't it? All I thought I was supposed to be—a wife and a mother—I now am and it makes me miserable. I'm trapped in a prison of my own making. This is my punishment. I see that now.

I rarely sleep now—not because of the baby, but because when I sleep, I dream of you. I dream of your eyes, your smile, your mouth kissing mine. I can feel you making love to me. And then I wake and it's almost too much to bear.

I cannot live without you. More to the point, I don't want to live without you. I think more and more often about ending my life so that we can be together. But I'm too much of a coward even for that. I've made my choices and my punishment is living with them. I have responsibilities. I have a daughter.

You are never far from my thoughts. One day, my love. One day.

K.

Joan winced as she reread the letter. She had not been wanted. Although she had always sensed it, to know that she had been a burden to her mother was something else. She put the letter on the table and shoved the chair back, scraping the wooden floor. She felt the tears burning the backs of her eyes, but held them back.

"Fuck you, *Mother*. You don't deserve my tears." She looked angrily around the room. "I don't even want to be here!" She sighed as some of the anger ebbed out of her. "Do you understand that? I never wanted to be here."

Joan stood, dragged herself into the hall, and yanked open the front door. The evening was chilly. She grabbed her jacket and stepped onto the front porch.

"Bitch," she muttered as she hurried down the steps and along the walk to the sidewalk. She strode toward campus at a brisk pace, her hands shoved into her jacket pockets, her collar turned up against the chill. For several blocks, she stared blindly ahead, lost in her own thoughts.

As her anger cooled, she looked through the illuminated windows at the people inside the houses. Some were watching television, some were eating, and some were doing both. She enjoyed being on the outside looking in. To see such normalcy, such domesticity, calmed her. It reminded her of her own family, though they never seemed to sit down to family dinners anymore. Between Luke's late nights at work and the kids' extracurricular activities, meals were often on the go.

And then there were her own extracurricular activities.

Joan snorted in frustration. She didn't know why she was so shocked to learn that her mother had been having an affair. How was it any different than the one she was involved in with Mark? She shook her head at the memory of Mark kissing her, his dark eyes and dark wavy hair, his hands on her body. She hadn't wanted to get involved with him—at least not at first. But after working with him on cases, spending hours together, she had gotten to know him. And she had liked him. He was smart, attentive, and sensitive—everything that Luke wasn't. And he wanted her. What could be more of an aphrodisiac?

At first, their relationship had been just about sex and mutual attraction. She could admit that. But after several months of furtive meetings at hotels, in cars, or in his office when they could get away with it, it had become more. It had become much more. They had begun to talk of divorcing their spouses and marrying each other—that was until last month when Mark had become distant and vague. Finally he admitted that his wife suspected he was being unfaithful and had threatened to keep him away from his children.

"And you don't think I have the same pressures?" Joan had asked. "You don't think I worry about losing my children over this?"

"You're the mother," Mark had said. "They won't take your children away unless you're a raving lunatic. And even then you're pretty sure of getting custody."

"So, what are you saying?" Joan asked.

"I'm saying that we need to tone it down for a little bit," he said. "Regroup. Figure out a game plan."

"I thought we *had* a game plan," Joan responded.

"A different game plan," he said.

And then, nothing. He began to avoid her at work. And what was once the best part of her day had become the worst. She had been relieved when dealing with her mother's estate had provided an excuse to take a temporary leave of absence. No doubt he had been, too.

But that's because he didn't know, Joan thought morosely. *He doesn't know.*

She breathed heavily as she climbed the long curving hill that started behind the library and wound up to the campus's main thoroughfare, Jayhawk Boulevard. She didn't want to think about the baby growing inside her—or the fact that it was most likely Mark's. She had slept with Luke as soon as she had missed her first period. She had hoped it was close enough to the conception—if it was indeed Mark's—that there wouldn't be any questions regarding parentage. Lord knew they looked somewhat similar. But still.

"Jesus," she breathed as she crested the hill. "I don't remember the hill being this steep." Panting, she stopped, put her hands on her hips, and turned to look down the curving sidewalk. Her thoughts returned to her mother's lover and the letters. The mystery was a nice diversion from her own problems.

"There must be someone I could ask," she said aloud as she turned left and began the familiar walk through campus. As far as she knew, her mother didn't have any close friends aside from Mrs. Yoccum. Her mother's brother, Bud, was still alive but they had been estranged for as long as she could remember. Still, he might have some information. She seemed to remember that he was living in a nursing home in Topeka and that he had Alzheimer's. It wouldn't hurt to call her cousin Barbara and see what she had to say. Maybe Bud had good days. Topeka was only thirty minutes away. Perhaps she could go visit him.

And she should read the rest of the letters. Maybe they could give her some kind of clue as to who "A" was, explain why her mother had made the choices she had, and why she had been so distant and remote.

She reached the Chi Omega fountain that signaled the end of campus. A jogger stopped to let his shaggy, black dog drink, and in glow of the street light, she saw him lift his hand in greeting. She forced herself to smile in return before turning on her heel and heading slowly back in the direction of her mother's house.

JOAN WAS MORE confused than ever by the time she finished reading the fourth and fifth letters dated 1956 and 1957. It appeared Katherine was writing a letter each year. Joan opened the remaining letters and checked the dates. 1958 and 1959.

"I need a chronology," she muttered as she picked up the spiral notebook she had been using for her inventory. She flipped to a fresh page and wrote down known dates, along with her notes.

> *1912—Mom born*
> *1931—Moves to Chicago*
> *1930s—Meets "A" (and begins affair?)*
> *1939—Mom and Dad married*
> *1947—First letter*
> *1954—Second letter (why time lapse?)*
> *1955—I'm born/third letter*
> *1956—Fourth letter*

1957—Fifth letter
1958—Sixth letter
1959—Last letter (why no more?)
1977—Dad died
1997—Mom died

Joan stared at her timeline. Her mother's lover must have been someone she had met while living in Chicago, but who? She thought about the stories she had heard over the years. No one fit the bill. She returned her attention to the dates of the letters. Why, after so much time, did Katherine begin this annual vigil? And why did it suddenly end? She shook her head. None of it made any sense.

"This is getting me nowhere," she murmured finally. "I need to talk to Barbara. Maybe Bud can explain what the hell was going on."

CHAPTER 4
Lawrence, Kansas, 1957

KATHERINE WIPED HER hands on the thin cotton dish towel and surveyed the kitchen. Everything seemed to be in order. There was little she hated more than to get up in the morning and have to do dishes or clean up from the night before. Satisfied, she hung the damp dish towel on the wooden rack, took off her apron, folded it neatly, and placed it in the pantry. She closed the pantry door, snapped off the light, and walked through the darkened house.

She had been dreading it all day, but now it was time.

She climbed the stairs to her room. Joanie had been put to bed around eight o'clock, and she could hear Clyde's deep, rhythmic snore as she passed his door. She smiled as she fantasized about holding a pillow over his face until the snoring stopped. She imagined his face when she removed the pillow. Would it be red or purple? Would his eyes be open or shut?

"Bastard," she said and continued on to her room. She and Clyde hadn't shared a bed since Joan had been born, which was fine by her. She had never loved him, and what fondness she had developed prior to Joan's conception had long since turned into hate—a feeling that she knew was mutual. They were trapped in a prison of their own making— both staying out of necessity and the desire to punish the other.

Katherine had contemplated leaving several times, but she recognized there was no way she could survive. And to divorce, given the circumstances, would be the ultimate embarrassment. So there they were, day after day, year after year. She kept the house, and he made the money. And then there was Joan. Despite everything that had happened, Clyde loved his daughter. And, if she were honest, he was a better parent than she, herself, was. He had wanted Joanie. She had not, and if she were to leave, she would have sole responsibility for the child.

Katherine opened the door to her room and, without turning on the lights, went inside. Almost greedily she allowed herself to be swallowed by the darkness as she remembered other times she had stood in another darkened room—the urgent kisses, the trembling fingers as they unbuttoned whatever dress she was wearing, the feel of every sinew of her body taut with expectation. She leaned back against the door and pressed her fingertips to her lips. Her heart thumped heavily in her chest, and she closed her eyes. Remembering was almost harder than forcing herself to forget.

She stood that way for several minutes, eyes squeezed shut until finally, she forced herself to walk across the room to the small desk and turn on the lamp. It was the same one she'd had when she had lived in Chicago, and its warm, buttery light usually made her feel better. Not on this night. She sagged against the back of the desk chair, weighted down by what she had to do. Finally, when she felt able, she turned, walked to the closet, and removed the battered suitcase from where it was hidden in the back. Carefully, almost reverently, she carried it to the bed.

Three years had passed since she had taken the case, its contents, and her memories and put them in her closet—three years since her happiness had been stolen from her. She trailed her fingertips over the leather straps that buckled on the front and caressed one of the gold buttons that worked the spring-latch closure. She had taken the same suitcase with her when she had gone to Kansas City with every intention of leaving Clyde.

With a sigh, she bent to the task of unbuckling, unclasping, and opening the case. The faint scent of lavender wafted up from the clothes within. With shaking hands, she pressed one hand on the top garment—a white, cotton shirt. It felt cool to her sweaty palm.

She moved her hand below the neatly-folded fabric, pulled out the wooden box she knew would be there, and set it gently on her lap. She caressed the smooth, polished lid. For a second, she remembered the morning she had awakened to find the box sitting on the nightstand.

The note propped up in front of it had read simply, "For You." She had sat up, the sheet covering her nakedness, and lifted the box onto her lap. It was light. She opened the lid. Inside was a delicately-embroidered handkerchief, upon which lay a tooled gold locket on a delicate chain. She gasped. It was beautiful. She gently touched the design on the front—a lily, its bloom open. Carefully, she lifted the locket from the box and held it with the chain draped over her fingers and down the back of her hand. It was warm to her touch. She used her fingernail to release the tiny clasp and opened the locket. Inside was a small key that looked as if it fit the lock on the front of the box and pictures of the two of them taken at the World's Fair. She tipped the key into her hand and studied the tiny images. They had been carefully clipped to fit into the oval cavities of the locket.

Katherine smiled, remembering the day, still feeling the sun shining on their shoulders as they strolled down the fairway. In front of them had been an older couple—the woman with a cane and the man in shirt sleeves rolled up to his elbows.

It had been an amazing day—so much to see and do. And then, later that night after too much sun and drink and excitement, they had kissed. She hadn't expected it at the time, although now, in retrospect, she supposed she had. *It's surprising at how much you know that you don't think you know—or*, she amended, *were scared to know*. That kiss, she recognized now, had changed her, had shown her who she was, even as it had turned her life upside down.

Katherine shook her head, as if to dispel the memories, and pulled the gold locket out of the front of her blouse. It was warm from the heat of her body, and she rubbed the worn back with the fleshy part of her thumb. She inhaled and used her fingernail to press the tiny clasp. Inside was the key to the box and the pictures from so long ago.

"We were so young," she said softly, almost in wonder as she stared into her own much younger face. "We had no idea."

Katherine wanted to weep at the thought of who they had been and what she had lost, but instead, forced herself to the task at hand. She inserted the key into the lock on the front of the box and turned it to the left. The lock disengaged with a tiny click, and she raised the lid. Inside, everything was as she had left it the previous year. And the year before that. And the year before that. There were the car keys, the theater tickets, the bullet casing, and the small stack of letters wrapped in the green-and-white scarf. Last year's letter lay on top.

Katherine touched the scarf and the letters with her fingertips. They were the only way she had now to communicate. She set the still-open box back in the suitcase and walked to the writing table. She had two hours before it was midnight. She pulled out the expensive writing paper and her old fountain pen, sat down, and began to write.

1957

Dearest A~

It's nearing midnight and I've thought about writing this letter all day—both with anticipation and also with dread. I can't believe it's been three years. It seems like both just yesterday and an eternity.

Joan asked me today why I was so angry all the time. I don't think she realized it wasn't anger, but in fact sadness. You wouldn't recognize or like the bitter woman I've become. I don't even like myself. Maybe Joanie is right—I am angry. And I take it out on those around me—especially

*her. I know she's just a girl, but how can I reconcile her birth
with the loss of everything I wanted for my life?*

*You still haunt my dreams and usually, they are lovely in
how mundane they are—the two of us walking or laughing
or reading together. But then I wake and it's agony because
your laughter echoes in my ears and your scent lingers in
my nose. The shadow of your presence is so real, that when I
realize that it was just a dream—that none of it was real—all
I want to do is weep. Oh, how I wish I could summon you
back—somehow manifest you into flesh. But I can't. I can
only pray (not that I believe in God any longer) that one day
we'll be together again. Until that day, you remain my one
true love.*

K.

Katherine re-read the letter. It was no different than the previous ones, she realized—not really. *But then, how many times can you say you're sorry for decisions you've made? How many ways can you express regret? How many ways can you grieve?* Her eyes burned and her throat tightened. She looked at the window and saw her bleary face reflected back. She looked old and tired. She knew the years hadn't been kind to her. Once, she had been attractive, even beautiful some had said. But now she just looked used up.

"No use fussing about the things you can't change," she said, echoing her mother's oft-used saying. And she couldn't change things— she knew that all too well.

She sighed and suddenly became aware of the steady ticking of the clock. It was time. She folded the paper with care and slipped it into the envelope. As the grandfather clock downstairs chimed, she stood, went to her closet, and pulled the hatbox from the back of the top shelf. Back at the desk, she lifted off the lid and removed the bottle of whiskey and two jelly jars that she used only on this night. She unscrewed the cap, poured several fingers-worth into each of the jars and raised one of the glass jars in a toast.

"To you, my love," she said as she blinked back the tears she could no longer stop. She raised the glass to her lips and poured the contents into her mouth. She smiled wryly at the familiar, cauterizing burn as the alcohol made its way from her lips to her throat to her chest and finally, her stomach. She picked up the second jar and held it aloft. "And here's to the day when we're together at last."

She emptied the glass and exhaled sharply. She never drank anymore except on this day, and already she could feel the effects of the whiskey. She contemplated having a third drink, but decided against it. Two was enough, especially with the generosity of her pours. She capped the bottle, put it back in the hatbox, and used her skirt to wipe clean the jelly jars. She placed them next to the bottle and returned the box to the back of her closet shelf. Finally, she sealed the envelope containing the letter and carried it to the bed. The other letters lay in a neat stack tied up with the scarf. Gently, she untied the knot and pulled away the layers of cloth that covered the parcel.

"This is what my life has become," she said as she placed the newest letter on the top of the stack. She sighed deeply and retied it. It was always this way—this organized precision. Write the letter . . . make the toast . . . put the letter in the box . . . lock the box and put the key back in the locket . . . put the box in the suitcase and the suitcase in the back of the closet until next year.

Katherine looked at the clock. It was almost midnight. The day was almost over—not that her grief eased with the passing of the day. Far from it. If anything, the annual observance made things harder. But it was the least she could do.

She walked back to the window and pressed her forehead against the cool glass. Her face was flushed, though from the whiskey or her emotions she wasn't sure. She thought wistfully back to when she was young, before she knew about love and passion and loss and obligation. She leaned back and opened her eyes. Her blurry reflection stared back at her.

"Coward," she spat bitterly. She glared at the reflection, and it glared back, mocking her. She snapped off the lamp. Though the reflection was gone, the recrimination remained.

She stared out into the blackness, her eyes taking in but not registering the skeletal trees devoid of their leaves. Before all of this, fall had always been her favorite season. She loved the smells, the feel, the energy as everyone and everything gave one last big push of activity and life before hunkering down for the winter. She had especially loved the fall in Chicago as she walked down the crowded streets with all the other people suddenly freed from the oppressive heat of summer. There had been an energy—an excitement that appeared when the air finally turned cool.

Chicago. The corners of Katherine's lips rose into a weak smile. She had moved to Chicago in the fall of 1931. That was when her life had begun.

"God damn it," she whispered as she again leaned her head against the cool glass and finally allowed herself to cry. "Why does it have to be so hard?"

CHAPTER 5
Chicago, Illinois, 1932

"NEW GIRL," CLAIRE said softly out of the side of her mouth.

They were standing behind the counter waiting for the two women examining several pairs of gloves to make a decision. Claire jerked her head in the direction of the front of the store, and Katherine, who had been watching the women discuss the merchandise, shifted her attention to the man and woman who stood in the main aisle just outside their department.

Mr. Ansen, the store manager, stood stiffly, bending slightly from the waist as he swept his hand to indicate the various departments. His dark hair gleamed from too much pomade making it look shiny and plastic. He hovered over the woman who was small-framed with brown hair drawn up into a neat bun at the back of her head. Ansen gestured in the direction of the ladies hats and said something. The woman nodded gravely at whatever he was saying, her large, dark eyes scanning the people and merchandise around her. She made eye contact with first Claire and then Katherine, who nodded slightly in silent greeting.

"She's young," Claire said softly out of the side of her mouth.

Katherine nodded. "But at least eighteen if she's working here. And no younger than I was when I started."

Claire tried to suppress her grin. "And look at you now." She raised her eyebrows. "Corrupted beyond belief. All that small town naïveté out the window."

"No thanks to you," Katherine said with a tiny smile.

"You were such a baby," Claire said. "And now you drink and smoke and well . . . I'm not even going to mention Alex."

Katherine stole a glance at Claire's bemused expression. "Please don't." She turned her attention back to the front of the store. Mr. Ansen and the woman were gone.

"CAN YOU SPARE one?"

The voice startled Katherine. She was standing at the corner of Washington and Randolph Streets, enjoying a cigarette and watching the people rush home or to other important destinations. Though they lived

---

in the same rooming house, Claire had gone ahead because Katherine had planned to run errands downtown.

She turned to look at the speaker and was surprised to see the young woman who had been with Mr. Ansen earlier that morning. Up close, she looked even younger, her eyes even larger. And they were brown, she realized—dark brown. She was attractive, though Katherine couldn't decide if she thought she was beautiful or not. The woman gave her a small smile, tipped her head slightly forward, and raised an eyebrow. A cigarette. This woman had asked for a cigarette.

"Of course. I'm sorry. You caught me daydreaming. I was . . ." Katherine laughed self-consciously and flicked her hand. "Never mind." She extended her cigarette case.

The woman delicately plucked one out. "Lucky Strikes." She laughed. "Reach for a Lucky instead of a sweet."

Katherine nodded and held out her lighter. The woman took off one of her dove-colored gloves, spun the flint wheel, and held the cigarette to the flame. The oily smell of naphtha filled the air. She inhaled deeply, held the smoke in her lungs, and slowly exhaled.

"Ah," she said through a cloud of smoke. "Thanks. You have no idea how much I needed that." She handed the lighter back to Katherine and pulled her glove back on.

"Your first day?" Katherine asked as she shoved the lighter back into her handbag and snapped it shut. "I remember mine. It was long."

"The day itself wasn't so bad," the woman said, as she exhaled a second long drag. "It was Ansen who was the pill. He couldn't seem to keep his hands to himself."

She bent forward and extended her hand as if guiding an invisible person. " 'No, after *you*, Miss Bennett.' 'Oh, allow *me*, Miss Bennett.' Ugh. Men get away with so much under the guise of being polite. Have you ever noticed?"

Katherine stared.

"I'm Annie." The woman extended her hand. "Annie Bennett. And you work in the glove department, right?" Her large eyes studied Katherine for several seconds. "And you are . . . ?"

"Oh, I'm sorry." Katherine lightly grasped Annie's hand. "I'm Katherine Henderson."

"Katherine Henderson," Annie said in delight. "What a wonderful name."

Katherine nodded, not sure what it was about her name that was so delightful, but smiled politely at the compliment.

"Waiting for the streetcar?" Annie asked.

Katherine shook her head. "No, I have some things I need to pick up and I wanted to stop by the library and check out a couple of books. And return these." She gestured at the cloth bag at her feet.

Annie took another drag from the cigarette and looked down at the bag. "May I?" she asked through the smoke.

Katherine frowned, not understanding what she was asking.

"Your books," Annie said. "May I see what you're reading?"

"Do you like to read?" Katherine asked.

"I do." Annie laughed a little self-consciously. "I love expanding my mind." She paused. "Have you read *Brave New World*—the new one by Aldous Huxley?"

Katherine shook her head. "No, I haven't. What's it about?"

"It's . . ." Annie paused thoughtfully and took another drag. She flicked the ash off the end of her cigarette and watched as the bits floated away. "It's hard to describe, really. It's set in the future and mass production has become a religion—literally. They're mass producing humans and there are scientists and savages and . . . oh, it's wonderful. But hard to describe. As you can imagine, it's deliciously controversial."

"It sounds . . . interesting," Katherine said.

Annie's grin widened, and she again indicated the bag at Katherine's feet. "So, what sorts of things do you generally read?"

"I like novels," Katherine said, wondering why she felt almost embarrassed at her answer.

"Oh. So, like Brontë and Dickens and all that?" Annie's tone suggested disappointment. She paused and raised the cigarette to her lips. "Please don't tell me you're a romantic, Katherine."

Katherine felt stung. "No. Not in so many words. I mean, yes, I enjoy a good love story, but who doesn't?"

Annie laughed. The sound was light and crystalline in the crisp air. "I don't. They never get it right. Love isn't about flowers and platitudes. It's messy and bloody and . . . well . . ." She waved her cigarette in a circular motion. "It's dramatic, yes, but not remotely like it's depicted in those books with their Mr. Darcy this and Mrs. Graham that."

"You seem awfully young to know so much about what love is and isn't." Katherine tried to smile knowingly—as if she knew something this young woman didn't.

"Oh, you know . . ." Annie assumed a worldly air and laughed. "So, come on, are you going to show me what books you have in your bag, or am I going to have to wait until you're looking the other way and wrench them from your grasp?"

Katherine looked at Annie. Though her tone was playful, she sensed a hint of a challenge beneath her words. "I don't think so." The denial was small, but it made her feel powerful. "I'd prefer to let you think what you want."

Annie studied her for several seconds, her brown eyes suddenly serious. She opened her mouth as if to speak and then shrugged, took a final pull from her cigarette, and dropped it to the pavement. She used the toe of her delicate kid leather shoe to almost viciously grind it out. She exhaled in a long, gray-blue plume and raised her head.

"I will," she said with a small smile. "See you around?"

Katherine nodded tightly, unsure as to what had just happened.

Annie turned to go and stopped. "You know, if you want to read a love story—a realistic love story—you should check out *The Great Gatsby.*" Her tone was conversational, but with a hint of something more serious.

An olive branch? Katherine wondered. She nodded and smiled.

"Anyway, thanks for the Lucky," Annie said as she again turned and walked away.

KATHERINE HURRIED UP the steps of the library, a beautiful building with its classical revival-style façade, but also an imposing building—solid. She tipped her head to study the windows of the fourth floor. Though the library wasn't arresting in the new skyscraper sort of way, it had a steady permanence she appreciated.

She pulled open the heavy bronze-framed doors and stepped into the three-story, vaulted lobby. The white Carrara marble seemed to glow and, as usual, she paused to take it all in. She closed her eyes and listened to the sounds of the building—the echoes of the footfalls; the murmurs of the lowered voices. Something about the building demanded respect. She wished it was earlier in the day—that she could go to the fourth floor reading room and sit at one of the leather-topped desks. There was something she enjoyed about sitting in the dark room, alone with her book, but still in the presence of other people lost in their own worlds.

With a sigh, she climbed the marble staircase to the third floor and her ultimate destination, the General Delivery Room with its leaded-glass Tiffany dome. Regardless of her mood, the colors never ceased to calm her—the way the glass caught the light of the room, darker at the top with signs of the zodiac ringing the center.

She finally turned her gaze to the circulation desk. One of the young women behind the desk gave her a pleasant smile. With a polite nod, Katherine slid her books across the counter to the librarian who glanced at the titles and asked in a low voice, "So, what did you think of it?"

Katherine raised her eyebrows. "I'm sorry?"

The librarian tapped the top book. "*The Greek Coffin Mystery*. What did you think of it?"

"It was . . . good," Katherine admitted. "Not as good as Agatha Christie, but still good."

"I've heard good things about it," the librarian said. "Though, I personally prefer the classics—the romances."

She smiled sweetly, and Katherine thought about her conversation with Annie Bennett. Was this how Annie saw her? She smiled and turned to walk away but paused and turned back. "Where would I find *The Great Gatsby*? I don't know the author."

"F. Scott Fitzgerald. If you can't find it in the card catalogue, ask Nancy." She pointed to a pretty, blonde woman wandering around the maze of card catalogue drawers. "She's the one in the blue dress."

Katherine nodded and went to the card catalogue. The card was easy to find, and she wrote down the information and call number.

"That was quick," the librarian said when Katherine returned to the circulation desk. "Just fill out this form, and we'll get that for you right away."

Katherine nodded and bent her head to the request slip. Once finished, she filled out a second request slip for *Northanger Abbey* and handed both to the librarian.

The librarian smiled, nodded, and placed both slips into one of the capsules that would take her request through the pneumatic tube system to the people in the stacks who would retrieve the books and send them for Katherine to check out.

THE COVER WAS interesting, she thought when the librarian handed her the books—very art deco with an intense pair of woman's eyes and lips superimposed over what appeared to be some sort of country fair. She ran her fingertips over the image as she studied it. She peered more closely at the eyes. The irises were composed of what appeared to be two reclining female nudes.

"Not one of his better ones, I'm afraid," the librarian said as she completed the checkout process.

"It was recommended to me," Katherine said.

"Well," the woman said, "it's not bad. Just different. I think you'll much prefer this one." She tapped the worn copy of *Northanger Abbey*.

"I'm sure I'll enjoy them both," Katherine said as she accepted the books and slid them into her bag.

"They're due in two weeks," the librarian said.

Katherine nodded her thanks, turned, and collided with the woman standing behind her. She dropped her bag and leapt back in surprise. "Oh, I'm so sorry." She stared into the startled eyes of Annie Bennett. "It's you."

"It *is*," Annie said with a grin.

"Are you following me?" Katherine blurted out. She immediately regretted her words.

Annie laughed. "Nothing quite so sinister. You mentioned the library, and it got me thinking that I wanted something new to read. So I decided to come down and check out some books for myself."

She glanced down at the bag, which still lay at Katherine's feet. "So, what did you choose this time?" She scooped up the bag and peered inside before Katherine could stop her. "Ah, *Northanger Abbey*." She looked up and grinned. "Glad to see you're not a romantic." Her tone was playful, but tinged with sarcasm.

Irritated, Katherine reached for the bag, but not before Annie pulled out the second book.

She looked up at Katherine in surprise. "*The Great Gatsby*." She sounded pleased. "I'm surprised."

She smiled—a genuine smile this time—and Katherine felt her cheeks warm, embarrassed to have been caught checking out the book after being prompted by Annie's challenge.

"I'll be anxious to know what you think of it," Annie said. "Maybe we could discuss it when you're finished."

Katherine nodded stiffly, albeit noncommittally. "So, you're here for books." She couldn't believe she said something so stupid.

Annie slid the book back into Katherine's bag and handed it to her. "I am." Her voice held a hint of amusement. She leaned forward. "Care to offer some recommendations?"

Katherine laughed despite herself and glanced at her watch. "I can't. I told Claire I would be home in time for dinner."

Annie looked interested. "Who's Claire?"

"You didn't get to meet her," Katherine said. "She was the other woman in the glove department. She was standing next to me when you and Mr. Ansen came into the department—in the print dress. We live in the same rooming house."

Annie looked thoughtful and smiled. "The older woman with the red, curly hair."

"So . . ." Katherine said after several seconds of awkward silence

"You'd better go," Annie said finally.

"I'd better," Katherine echoed. "So, I guess I'll see you at work."

The humor returned to Annie's eyes, and a smile tugged at the corners of her mouth. "Yes. I believe they'll have me in the shoe department. At least that's what Mr. Ansen said. Stop in and say hello."

"I will." Katherine patted the book bag. "And thank you for the recommendation. I look forward to reading it."

Annie smiled—a full smile this time that reached her eyes. "Well, then," she gave a small wave, "tomorrow, perhaps."

CHAPTER 6
Chicago, Illinois, 1932

SEVERAL WEEKS PASSED before Katherine saw Annie again. She was standing against the side of the Sears building, her collar pulled up around her ears. The wind no longer carried the refreshing snap of autumn, but instead hinted at the sharpness of the coming winter. Despite the cold, she had opted to smoke outside just to get away from everyone.

"Got an extra one of those?"

It was the voice that she had, for some reason, heard in her head several times over the past weeks. Only this time, it wasn't a memory, it was Annie standing in front of her and looking up at her with her serious, dark eyes.

Katherine was surprised to realize she was so much taller than the younger woman. "I do." She extended her cigarette case.

Annie plucked out a cigarette and put it to her mouth. Katherine fumbled in her handbag for her lighter.

"No need." Annie pulled out her own lighter. She turned toward the building, hunched her thin shoulders to block the wind, and spun the flint wheel. She cupped her other hand around the lighter and inhaled deeply as she touched the tip of the cigarette to the flame. When it was lit, she snapped the lighter shut and returned it to the pocket of her coat. "I forgot my cigarettes. Next ones are on me. I promise."

Katherine waved her gloved hand—the one with her own cigarette. "Not necessary."

Annie grinned and inhaled deeply.

They smoked in silence. Katherine found herself studying the crack in the sidewalk. She looked up and saw Annie watching her, a cigarette delicately pinched between her fore and middle fingers.

Annie turned her head slightly and exhaled out of the corner of her mouth. "It's nice to see you."

"You, too," Katherine said and was surprised to realize that it was true.

"So, what did you think of *The Great Gatsby*?" Annie asked.

"It was different than I expected. It was . . ." She searched for the correct word. "Anxious. And sad."

"And you haven't found life to be sad and anxious?" Annie asked, a tiny smile playing on her lips.

"No," Katherine said. "Have you?"

Annie studied her, still smiling, but no longer amused. "Much of the time, yes."

Katherine blinked in surprise.

"But I'm an optimist," Annie continued. "Deep down, at least."

"What do you mean?" Katherine asked.

"I always hold out hope that eventually it will all turn around." Annie shrugged. "So tell me about your friend. Cecile, isn't it?"

"Claire," Katherine said.

"That's right, Claire," Annie said. "Tell me about Claire. How did you become friends?"

"Here," Katherine said. "At work. She took me under her wing and helped me out when I first came to Chicago. I don't know what I would have done without her. It was so different than where I grew up."

Annie took a deep pull from the cigarette. "And where was that?" She exhaled through her nose.

"Big Springs," Katherine said. "Kansas."

"You're from Kansas," Annie said in surprise. "Well, then, Chicago *would* have been a big change for you. Why did you come?"

"I wanted more than my hometown had to offer," Katherine said. "I wanted to do more than settle down, marry, and have children. I didn't want to be a farmer's wife. I wanted to see and do more." She couldn't believe she had said that—and to a stranger no less.

Annie nodded, her eyes never leaving Katherine's face. She held her left arm across her stomach, her right elbow balanced on her left wrist, the cigarette held between her curled fingers.

"I understand. That's part of why I left Arlington Heights. I wanted more than it could offer." She paused. "And I was more than it could handle."

She raised the cigarette to her lips, took a long drag, and dropped it to the concrete where she scratched it out with the toe of her shoe. She exhaled a final cloud of smoke and raised her eyes to meet Katherine's.

"Small towns are no places for women like us. We want too much." She glanced down at her watch. "I have to get back to my post but . . ." She paused. "I'm going to the library after work tonight. Would you care to join me?"

"Yes. I'd love to." Katherine paused at her impulsiveness. "What I mean is that I didn't have time to check out any books after I returned the others and so, yes, I need to go."

"Let's meet at the corner?" Annie asked. "Where I saw you that first day?"

Katherine nodded and snubbed out her own cigarette. Together, they turned, stepped from the shelter of the building, and headed for the entrance to the store.

"SO, WHAT DO *you* like to read?" Katherine asked as they walked down State Street toward the Chicago Public Library building. She wasn't sure what to ask so she focused on their shared interest.

"My tastes are eclectic," Annie said. "Honestly, I read whatever appeals to me at the moment though you probably wouldn't have heard of most of it. I read a lot of books that are banned—or at least are off limits to women. "

"What do you mean?" Katherine asked.

"Oh, you know, books that cause women to question the status quo or that might put ideas into our heads. And then there are books that are sexual in nature—because heaven forbid women realize that they can be sexual creatures with the same freedom as men." She sounded playful, but there was an underlying touch of real anger in her words.

Katherine stopped walking and stared at her in amazement.

"What?" Annie stopped and turned to Katherine. "Oh good lord. Please don't tell me you believe that women aren't sexual creatures?"

"I hadn't considered it, to be quite honest. But I'm not a prude, if that's what you're thinking." She closed her mouth, unused to discussing sexual politics with complete strangers. "I would prefer that we talk about something else."

Annie blinked at her. "Of course. I didn't mean to make you uncomfortable."

"Well, you did," Katherine admitted. "I barely know you."

"True. Completely my fault." Annie grinned. "I promise to keep my opinions and collection of banned books to myself until we know each other better."

"You actually own banned books?" Katherine asked. She knew her tone sounded scandalized.

"Oh yes," Annie said with a mischievous twinkle in her eyes. "Wicked stuff. Nothing but sex."

Katherine stared and took a step back.

Annie put a gloved hand on Katherine's arm and leaned forward. Katherine felt the moist heat of her breath on her cheek.

"You know I'm teasing you, right?" Annie said.

Katherine felt her face flush. Annie had been joking. And she had believed her. "No, I didn't actually."

Annie studied her for several seconds and linked her arm with Katherine's. "I'm cold."

Katherine nodded and continued walking. In less than five minutes, they stood in front of the library. As usual, Katherine looked up at it and smiled. "It's such a beautiful building. I love everything about it—the marble, the Tiffany dome, the reading room." She let her eyes roam the square, pillared façade. She sighed and became aware of Annie's eyes on her. "What?" She felt strangely embarrassed.

"Nothing," Annie said with a small smile. "I just . . . nothing. Let's go in."

They jogged up the steps into the main lobby.

"I'm going to go to the newspaper reading room before I get my books," Annie said. "How about I meet you back here in say . . . thirty minutes?"

Katherine nodded and wondered what Annie was going to do that she didn't want her to see? She wondered what books Annie was going to choose and if she was suggesting the time apart so she could browse without Katherine's scrutiny. She mentally shook her head and felt like an old biddy—a judgmental prude.

Annie touched her lightly on the arm. "You can come with me if you want. I just want to check the *London Times* to see what's going on in Europe and then look at the *New York Times Book Review*."

Katherine smiled, relieved, but tried to pretend as if she hadn't been curious. "That's okay. I'll meet you back here in thirty minutes."

Annie turned toward the newspaper reading room, stopped, and looked back at Katherine. "Where do you live? I live off of Kenzie and sometimes, if it's not too cold, I like to walk home over the bridge. If you live nearby, we could go together."

It was almost, though not quite, a question.

"Wells and Grand," Katherine said.

"Just a couple of blocks from me," Annie said happily. "How about we pick up some bread and cheese and have dinner in my room, and then I'll walk you home?"

Katherine nodded. Claire, she knew, was out with Lenny, so she wouldn't worry if she came home later than usual.

"I'd like that," she said.

"Great," Annie said. "Then I'll see you in a bit."

"SO TELL ME more about this town of yours . . . Big Springs," Annie said as they crossed over the bridge into the Near North section of the city after stopping at a small market for bread and cheese. "It sounds like a hoot."

"It's just a small farm town," Katherine said. "It was a watering stop on the Oregon trail, which is where it gets its name."

The wind off the water was biting, although Annie didn't seem to notice. She had been right, though—her rooming house was only a couple of blocks from her own.

"So you do this a lot?" Katherine asked through numbed lips. "Walk home, I mean?"

"I do," Annie said. "It saves money and it's good to get out and stretch your legs after a day of standing still."

"Which is yours?" Katherine asked.

"The one across from the Merchandise Mart," Annie said. "The four-story one."

"My goodness, you *are* close," Katherine said as they neared the narrow, four-story brick building.

"It's not the best place to live," Annie said. "But it's not the worst. I enjoy it in the summer and, as I walk to work, I've got a great view of the clock tower."

Katherine nodded, relieved when they entered the small entryway of the building and climbed the stairs to Annie's third-floor room.

"Now, I'll warn you. It's not much," Annie said as she opened the door and gestured for Katherine to step inside.

The room was dark, although some light came from the buildings and street lights outside. She stepped into the room and waited for Annie to turn on the light. Instead, Annie walked to a small bureau and lit a kerosene lamp.

"I hope you don't mind," she said as she turned to Katherine. "But I prefer the lamp instead of the overhead light."

Katherine nodded and looked around the large single room. The furnishings were spare—a table with two wooden chairs, a small sofa and coffee table, a couple of shelves and the bed. Annie hadn't seemed to make any attempt to make the room homier. The only decoration appeared to be haphazard stacks of books. In fact, books appeared to be everywhere.

"You really *do* like to read," Katherine said.

"You seem surprised," Annie said as she took off her coat and tossed it on the bed. "Did you think I was just trying to impress you?"

"No. I just . . . didn't expect you to be so . . . ." Katherine shrugged.

"Hungry?" Annie asked.

Katherine looked up from her inspection of the room, and Annie gestured at the food. She seemed amused.

Katherine blinked, wondering what she had missed. "I am." She shrugged off her coat and laid it across the foot of the unmade bed.

She turned back to the small table where Annie had unwrapped the bread and cheese. Annie plucked a knife from a cup of utensils on the table and sawed off several slices.

"Can I do anything?" Katherine asked.

"There's really not room," Annie said with a laugh and pointed the knife at one of the wooden chairs. "Please. Sit." She cut the cheese into neat slices.

The cheese was sharp Wisconsin cheddar. Katherine's mouth watered in anticipation.

"Would you like something to drink?" Annie asked. "I can heat some water for tea or coffee. Or, I have whiskey."

"Whatever you're having is fine," Katherine said.

"I'm having whiskey," Annie said. "Thank God for the end of Prohibition. I'm glad we don't have to wait until December like some of the other cities in the country." She rolled her eyes dramatically. "Jesus."

"Huh," Katherine said, not sure what, or even if, a response was required.

Annie placed the slices of bread and cheese on a plate, set it on the table, and pulled out a bottle of Walker's Canadian Club and two glasses from a cupboard.

"I really can make you some coffee if you'd rather," she said.

"No," Katherine said. "Whiskey is fine."

Annie poured an inch of liquid into each of the glasses and sat down opposite Katherine.

"A toast," she said as she picked up her glass. Katherine lifted her glass. "To new friends."

Katherine smiled and clinked her glass against Annie's. "To new friends."

Annie slid the plate toward Katherine, who picked up a slice of cheese.

Annie took a large bite from her slice of bread and chewed as she studied Katherine. "So, let me list what I know about you. You're from a small town in Kansas. You came to the big city for adventure and excitement. You work in the glove department at Sears & Roebuck and you read mysteries and romance novels."

"That about covers it," Katherine said.

"Oh, Kate, I can't believe that." Annie paused. "I'm sorry. Is it okay to call you Kate? Or do you prefer Katherine? Or Katie?"

"My family calls me Katie." Katherine took a piece of bread. "I began to use my full name when I moved here but I'm okay with any of the three. Claire calls me Kate."

"Ah," Annie said. "Reinvention. That's the beauty of moving someplace new. You can be whomever you want."

"And you?" Katherine asked.

"I've always been an Annie," she said. "Even though it's really my middle name."

"Really?" Katherine asked. "What is your full name?"

"It's pretentious." Annie waved a hand.

"Tell me," Katherine insisted.

"Charlotte Annette Grayson Bennett," Annie said. "Annie."

"You have four names," Katherine said in surprise.

"Uh huh," Annie said around a mouthful of bread and cheese.

Katherine chewed thoughtfully. Charlotte was a nice name, though she couldn't see Annie as a Charlotte. Annie suited her much better.

"What are you thinking?" Annie asked, and Katherine realized she had again been watching her.

"Just about names," Katherine said, feeling her face flush at the scrutiny.

"A rose by any other name," Annie quoted and shrugged. "So do you come from a big family? Do you have a fellow back home?"

"So many questions. My goodness." Katherine smiled, took a swallow of the whiskey, and exhaled sharply as it burned its way to her stomach. She felt much warmer now. "I come from a large family—well, fairly large. I have . . . well, had . . . six brothers and sisters but my oldest sister died giving birth and my other sister, Jeannie, stepped on a rattlesnake nest."

Annie leaned forward and put her hand lightly on top of Katherine's. "I'm sorry. Were you close?"

Katherine shook her head. "No. Wilma was a lot older than me and Jeannie and . . . well, we had different ideas about most things. She married my older sister's widow, Clyde."

"Huh," Annie said thoughtfully. "That's kind of strange, but then I can't imagine being married in the first place, so . . ." She picked up a piece of cheese and bit off the corner. "You?"

Katherine shrugged. "Not really. I've been out with men, but nothing . . . serious."

Annie nodded. "Do you ever see yourself moving back home?"

Katherine considered the question. The subject was an ongoing argument between her and her mother. "I don't. I don't know as there's really much for me there. You?"

Annie shook her head and took another sip from her glass. "I'm not really welcome back home."

"Why?" Katherine asked. "If it's not too personal."

"Actually, I would prefer not to talk about it," Annie said. "It's the past and I would rather talk about the present and the future. Speaking of which, have you seen the work they're doing on Northerly Island? It's going to be an amazing fair. I can't wait for the summer."

"The progress has been pretty astounding," Katherine said, glad for the conversation change. "They say it's going to be beyond belief."

"We should go," Annie said. "You're planning on going, aren't you?"

"Yes," Katherine said. "Claire and I have discussed it a couple of times. The three of us should go together."

"That would be fun, don't you think?" Annie said.

Katherine imagined the three of them going to the World's Fair together and smiled. Annie's presence would certainly add a new element to the experience. She wondered what Claire would think, and then realized she didn't care.

"Actually." She took another sip from her glass. "I think it would."

CHAPTER 7
Chicago, Illinois, 1932

"SO, WHAT ARE you doing for Christmas?" Annie asked one day in early December as they stood in front of the Marshall Field's holiday display windows.

As fall had turned into winter and Claire's relationship with Lenny had become more serious, Katherine had been spending much of her free time with Annie.

Unlike with her friendship with Claire, Katherine quickly realized that spending time with Annie wasn't always easy. Annie's intensity and disregard for societal norms sometimes made her a challenge. But she was also fiercely loyal and honest to a fault—even if what she said seemed hurtful at the time.

"Going home," Katherine said, her eyes still on the dramatic window display. "What about you?"

"Probably stay here," Annie said. "I'm not inclined to see my family."

"Well, that's a shame," Katherine said as she was jostled by two children pushing forward to get a closer look. She watched in irritation as they pressed close to the glass, leaving behind nose and fingerprints. She made a noise of disgust in the back of her throat. Annie laughed.

Katherine looked sideways at her and frowned. "What?"

"Nothing," Annie said, the smile still on her lips. "It's just that your love for children is apparent."

Her amusement irritated Katherine. "So, when are you going to tell me what happened? Why are you estranged from your family?"

Annie's smile faded. "It's not important." She turned and started to walk away.

Katherine grasped Annie's arm. "I'm sorry, Annie. It's just . . . ." She shrugged. "Given how outspoken you are about absolutely everything else in your life, the fact that you're not willing to talk about this suggests it was pretty important."

Annie shrugged, but refused to meet Katherine's gaze.

"Annie." Katherine stepped in front of her. "What happened?"

"They don't approve of me," Annie said in a low tone. "They don't approve of me or the way I live. They've disowned me."

Katherine frowned, confused. "What do you mean? Because of the books?"

"It's more than that," Annie said. "I . . . I just really don't want to talk about it."

"Annie—" Katherine began.

"Please, can we just discuss something else?" Annie faced the window display.

"Well, then, why don't you come home with me for the holidays?" Katherine said after several minutes of silence.

Annie turned, looking surprised at the offer.

"One more won't make a bit of difference," Katherine said. "My brothers will all be there. And my aunts and uncles." She grabbed Annie's arm. "It will be such fun. Say yes."

Annie smiled, but said nothing.

"Come on," Katherine said. "Say yes."

"Are you sure?" Annie asked finally. "I mean, shouldn't you ask your mother if it's all right?"

"It'll be fine," Katherine said. "You'll have such a good time. I'll show you around Big Springs and introduce you to everyone. My family is very traditional with a tree and stockings and an ice skating party on the pond. Everyone from town comes. You'll love it." She grinned.

"It does sound like fun," Annie admitted.

"Then say you'll come," Katherine said. "I won't take no for an answer."

"Well, then, yes. I would love to come home with you for Christmas." Annie hesitated. "Thank you, Kate. You don't know how much I appreciate this."

ALTHOUGH SHE ALREADY knew the answer, Katherine wrote her mother that night and asked if it would be all right for Annie to come for the holidays. Within a week, her mother's reply came in the post.

"My mother said she would love to have you visit," she told Annie as they ate their lunch in the employee break room. "And everyone is excited to meet you."

Annie grinned. "I'm excited, too. Now, remind me of your brothers' names."

"Arnold is the oldest," Katherine began. "He's married to Nancy Jean and they have five kids. We're not close, but a lot of that has to do with our age differences. He farms like my father. Then there's Meyer. He's married to Eleanor. They live in Lawrence and he's a barber. They have three boys. Then there's Bud. He's next oldest. His real name is Harold, but everybody just calls him Bud. He is married to Emily. I'm probably closest to Bud. He's a farmer, too. But he also keeps cattle. They have four kids. And then there's Willie. Willie is a couple of years older than me. He works for the railroad. He's married to Sue, they don't have any children."

"And then there's you," Annie said and laid her hand on Katherine's arm. The only girl."

"The only girl left," Katherine said.

"That's right." Annie took a bite of her sandwich and chewed thoughtfully. "And they were married to the same man."

Katherine nodded. "Yes, but don't mention it when you're around the family. It's a sore subject because Jeannine tricked him into marrying her by pretending to be pregnant and . . ." She paused, searching for words. "It's just better not to bring it up."

Annie nodded.

"The other thing . . ." Katherine said in a rush. "And I know I don't need to say this, but I feel like I should anyway. Please don't tell them about some of the things we do here. They don't understand my life. They wouldn't like knowing that I drink or dance or see boys or, well . . . any of the things we do, really. They wouldn't approve."

"Ah," Annie said knowingly and grinned.

"Don't say it like that," Katherine said, her face warm. "It's not like I'm . . . we're doing anything wrong, they're just small town, provincial people. Kind, but . . . well, you know . . . narrow in their thinking."

Annie frowned. "Maybe this isn't such a good idea. You know how I am."

"It will be fine," Katherine said. "Just follow my lead."

"Has Claire met your family?" Annie took another bite of her sandwich

"No," Katherine said.

Annie smiled, as if pleased.

"Though not for any reason other than she hasn't had the opportunity," Katherine added quickly, unsure why she felt the need to add that fact. "I'd like you to get to know Claire better. You would like her a lot, I think."

"But would she like me?" Annie asked. "I don't think she approves of our friendship."

"Really?" Katherine asked. "Why do you say that?"

"Just the way she looks at me," Annie said.

Katherine shook her head, even though she had noticed the same thing. "Oh, I don't think that's it. She's never said anything like that to me."

Annie shrugged. "Or maybe she's just jealous. You've been spending a lot of time with me lately. Wasn't that time you used to spend with her?"

"Well, yes," Katherine admitted. "But not really that much lately—not since she started going with Lenny."

"Lenny," Annie repeated. "What do you think of him?"

Katherine hesitated. "He's a lot of fun. He laughs a lot."

"Not necessarily a ringing endorsement," Annie said.

"He just drinks a lot," Katherine said. "And when Claire is with him, she does, too. She's just a different person when she's around him."

"Are they sleeping together?" Annie asked.

"Annie," Katherine exclaimed. "That's none of our business."

"So, they are," Annie said. "I'm not surprised."

"So what if they are?" Katherine said.

"Oh, believe me, I don't have a problem with it," Annie said. "If that's what you're into, it's fine by me. Don't judge lest you be judged."

"Judge not, that ye be not judged," Katherine corrected. "Matthew 7:1."

Annie raised her eyebrows. "A student of the Bible. So, you're a Christian?"

"You can't *not* be Christian where I'm from," Katherine said. "Though I'm not as devout as the rest of my family—especially in regard to going to church."

"So, is that why you don't approve of Claire and Lenny?" Annie asked. "Because they're having premarital sex?"

"Annie." Katherine looked fearfully around the room. "Shhh."

"Oh, stop," Annie said. "No one here cares enough to listen to our conversation."

"I just don't like gossiping," Katherine said. "Especially about Claire. She's my friend."

"So that *is* it," Annie said triumphantly, in a lowered voice.

"No." Katherine sat up straighter. "That's not it."

"So, you have no problem with premarital sex?" Annie said.

"You're being argumentative," Katherine said.

"You haven't answered the question," Annie said. She had a strange gleam in her eye.

"If you love someone, I think it's less of a sin than just doing it to do it," Katherine said finally.

"And have you?" Annie asked.

"Annie, that's none—"

"Have you?" Annie persisted.

"Yes," Katherine said. "I have."

Annie blinked twice and sat back, her expression strange and unreadable. "Who? When?" Her tone was suddenly aggressive.

"His name was . . . is . . . Alex, and we dated this past spring and summer," Katherine said. "Not that it's really any of your business."

"What happened?" Annie asked.

"What do you mean?" Katherine asked.

"Why did it end?" Annie asked.

Katherine shrugged and shifted her gaze from Annie's face to the remains of her soup. She waited, hoping that Annie would let it go. She didn't.

"I . . . he . . . we just had different ideas as to where the relationship was going," Katherine said finally. "That's all. Why are you so interested in my love life?"

"So, you ended it?" Annie said.

"In a manner of speaking," Katherine said. "But honestly, I'd rather not discuss it. I can't imagine why this is interesting to you anyway."

"You're my friend," Annie said. "I just want to know you better."

"What about you?" Katherine asked, anxious to steer the conversation away from her. "Are you seeing anyone? Do you date much?"

"I go out," Annie said. "And I've had a couple of relationships. And yes, before you ask, they were sexual."

"I wasn't going to ask," Katherine said quickly and felt herself blush.

"It's okay. I'm not ashamed. I think sexual expression is a God-given right. And I think men are intimidated by that. So they call those of us who are comfortable with our sexuality whores or they suggest that we're immoral. It's ridiculous, really." Annie's voice rose. "If men can have sex without remorse, then we should be able to as well—without judgment or recrimination."

"Annie." Katherine looked around to see if anyone was listening. "People can hear you."

"There's nothing wrong with it," Annie continued adamantly. "I'm sexual, but I'm not easy. I do what I want and with whom. *I'm* the one in control. *I'm* the one making the decisions."

Katherine nodded uneasily, hoping that was the end of the conversation. Annie sat back defiantly, almost as if she expected Katherine to challenge her.

"So . . ." Katherine faltered, unsure of what else to say. She desperately wanted to change the subject. "We'll take the train to Lawrence. And then Bud will come pick us up at the depot."

Annie blinked at her.

"For Christmas," Katherine said. "We'll take the train from here to Lawrence. It will be a good chance for you to see the countryside. Have you ever been to Kansas?" She didn't wait for Annie to respond. "It's nothing like what most people think. It's not flat—at least not my part. There are lots of trees and hills." She hesitated, searching for something else to say. "It's named after the Kansa Indians."

She forced herself to stop speaking.

Annie narrowed her eyes but said nothing.

Katherine sighed, leaned forward, and said in a low voice, "Listen, it's not that I think you're not entitled to your opinion. It's just that I don't think it's appropriate to have these kinds of discussions in the employee break room."

"Okay." Annie leaned forward, mocking Katherine's pose. "I'll stop, but only if you answer one question. What do *you* think? Do women deserve the same rights as men when it comes to sex?"

"Annie," Katherine said in exasperation, "I don't know. I guess . . . yes . . . I think women deserve equal rights. But I'm not sure that anyone, male or female, should be engaging in premarital sex on a habitual basis. It's a sin."

"Funny," Annie said, her voice still low. "I didn't peg you as such a prude."

"I'm not a prude," Katherine exclaimed and slammed her hand down on the table. Occupants of the other tables turned to stare.

Annie grinned. "Please keep your voice down. I have a reputation to think about."

"Oh, shut up," Katherine said angrily.

Still smiling, Annie wadded up the wax paper that had contained her sandwich and, without waiting for Katherine, pushed her chair back from the table and stood.

Katherine looked up, surprised by her sudden movement.

"I'm looking forward to meeting your family," Annie said with a wink. She turned on her heel and walked out of the break room.

"SO, ARE YOU and Lenny getting together tonight?" Katherine asked Claire as they tidied one of the displays left in disarray by last-minute Christmas shoppers.

"We are," Claire said with a broad smile. "Lenny has something special planned for us."

Katherine raised her eyebrows. "Special as in . . . ?"

Claire grinned and shrugged. "Just something romantic."

"I've never seen you like this," Katherine commented. "You're really smitten with this one."

Claire carefully arranged the gloves by color and fanned them so that the fingers looked like a turkey's plumage. Her reluctance to meet Katherine's eyes was confirmation.

"Are you in love with him?" Katherine asked.

Claire shrugged.

"You are, aren't you? Oh my gosh." Katherine leaned forward. "Does he feel the same? Have you talked about it?"

"Of course we haven't talked about it," Claire admitted. "Lenny's swell. And he's fun. But he doesn't like to talk about serious stuff. He's more about action than words if you know what I mean."

"I guess," Katherine said.

"So, what are you doing tonight?" Claire asked. "Spending more time with Annie?"

Katherine looked up sharply. Something about Claire's tone made her think of Annie's comment that Claire didn't like her. She thought about how to broach the subject.

"What do you think of Annie?" she asked.

Claire shrugged. "She's a nice enough kid."

"Do you like her?" Katherine asked.

Claire was silent, very intent on making miniscule adjustments to the gloves on display.

"Claire?" Katherine pressed.

"I don't dislike her," Claire said finally. "I just . . . there's just something off about her—something not quite right."

"What do you mean?" Katherine asked. She heard her own defensive tone.

"She just makes me feel . . . uncomfortable," Claire said. "And you're different after you've spent time with her. I can't explain it."

"I don't think that's the case at all," Katherine said.

"All right," Claire said. "You just asked me what I meant and I was telling you."

"You're different, too," Katherine said. "When you're around Lenny, you're different."

Claire frowned and looked at Katherine with a strange expression. "But that's different, isn't it?"

"What do you mean?" Katherine asked.

"Well, we're a couple, aren't we?" Claire said carefully. "Lenny and me. We're seeing each other."

"So?"

"So, there's an intimacy there that's different than just friendship." Claire touched Katherine's arm. "It's not that I don't like Annie. I just think there's something about her that isn't good for you. She's too outspoken."

"You're outspoken," Katherine said. "And spending time with you has changed me. I never drank before I met you. Or went to bars. Or . . . Alex."

Claire nodded. "You're right. But I always have your best interests at heart. I encouraged you to let go and have fun, but I also tried to take care of you—keep you safe. I don't know as she will. She's more interested in shaking things up. She doesn't care how it appears to others." She squeezed Katherine's hand. "I just don't want to see her pressure you into doing things you're not comfortable with. She's already got you reading those books. Next thing you know—"

"I'm fine," Katherine interrupted. "Really. And besides, I still have you to look after me, don't I? How much trouble could I get into with you around?"

Claire smiled, put her arm around Katherine's shoulders, and squeezed affectionately. "Exactly." She hesitated. "So what say you come out with Lenny and me and meet some of his friends?"

"Oh, Claire, no," Katherine said. "I'm not ready. Not after what happened with Alex."

"I'm not saying that you sleep with any of them," Claire said. "I'm just suggesting that you meet them. Have fun. Get your nose out of a book for a change. You can't hide away forever. So what if it didn't work out with Alex. There are plenty of guys out there who would love to get to know you."

Her expression was so hopeful that Katherine relented. "Let me get through the holidays. Maybe when I get back from Big Springs?"

"All right," Claire said and dropped her arm as two women walked into the department and toward the counter. "But I'm holding you to it."

"I HOPE YOU don't mind sharing a bed," Katherine said as they stepped into the narrow bedroom and set down their luggage. "It's just that everyone is going to be here Christmas Eve and the kids will all be staying over." She smiled. "I promise I don't snore."

"It's fine," Annie said as she turned slowly to survey the room. "So, this is where you grew up. Very nice. Very . . . you. Clean. Simple. Orderly."

"I made so many plans in this room," Katherine said wistfully. She wandered to the window and looked out. "I used to sit here and imagine a life full of glamour and excitement."

"And has it turned out to be what you thought?" Annie asked with an uncharacteristic gentleness that made Katherine smile a little.

"Not as glamorous," Katherine said, still looking out the window.

"A lot harder . . . and more complicated. But satisfying. I could never be happy here. And even though I feel like I work more than I do much else, I'm happy with my life. I like my independence. Had I stayed here, I would have been married by now."

"You're not missing out on anything in that regard," Annie said.

Katherine turned, surprised. "Did it seem like I felt that way? I didn't mean to suggest that if it did. I'm quite satisfied with my life."

"I just meant—" Annie began as Katherine's mother poked her head into the room.

"You girls doing all right?" she asked. "Getting settled in?"

Katherine nodded.

Her mother, Nedda, turned her attention to Annie. "You are such a little thing. We're going to need to fatten you up." She laughed and patted Annie on the shoulder and turned to look again at her daughter. "And you too, Katie. My goodness, you're nothin' but skin and bones."

She shook her head dramatically and turned to Annie. "I keep telling her that men like women with some meat on their bones." She gestured at her own substantial girth. "Course, if she just came home and settled down . . ."

Annie glanced at Katherine, but said nothing.

"Albert was asking about you the other day," Nedda continued. "He wanted to know when you was comin' home. He's going to be at the skating party."

"Oh." Katherine felt slightly uncomfortable having this conversation in front of Annie. "I was telling Annie about the skating party—about how most of the town turns out for it."

She turned and looked around the room for her suitcase, forgetting she had set it down near the bed. She gestured toward the bags.

"We should get settled in," she said to Annie. "And then we'll come down and help with dinner, Mama."

Nedda laughed heartily. "No need to hurry. You girls have to be tired from the trip. Just take your time." She walked to the door and turned to smile at Katherine. "It's nice to have you back, Katie." She left the room.

"Your mother loves you," Annie said as she picked up her case and carried it to the bed.

"Well, of course she does." Katherine laughed. "Even though she sometimes drives me crazy."

"She cares. Not everyone is so lucky." Annie's tone, though soft, was matter-of-fact.

"You're thinking about your mother, aren't you?" Katherine asked. "I'm sorry."

Annie nodded, her lips pressed tightly together. "It's probably for the best." She held up her neatly-folded nightgown and several pairs of underwear. "Where should I put these?"

Katherine studied her tense features and wanted to say something comforting. Nothing came to mind. "In there." She pointed at the dresser. "You take the top two and I'll use the bottom ones."

Annie went to the bureau, pulled open the top drawer, and put the nightgown inside. She returned to the bed and took several other pieces of clothing from her suitcase.

"Annie," Katherine said softly, still wanting to let her know that she understood her sadness.

"Hmm?" Annie didn't look up.

Katherine touched her arm, and Annie froze. "I'm sorry you're sad." She slid her fingers down to grip Annie's hand and squeezed. For several seconds, they stood without moving. Finally, Annie curled her fingers around her hand, squeezed it twice, and let go. Annie cleared her throat and turned back to her clothing.

They unpacked in silence. When they were finished and their suitcases slid under the bed, Katherine turned to Annie.

"So, would you like to have a tour of a real, live working farm?" She kept her tone light.

Annie smiled, and Katherine knew she had made the right decision not to press the issue of Annie's family.

"You know," Annie said. "I have been on a farm before. It's not like I don't know one end of a cow from another."

"Oh, good," Katherine said with a grin as she gestured toward the door. "Then you'll have no problem when we ask you to help with the milking."

Annie laughed, and Katherine knew that her darkness, whatever it had been, had passed.

THE EVENING PASSED quickly. They had decided to wait until the next day to walk around the farm and, instead, went downstairs to help Nedda with dinner. The kitchen was warm and pleasant, thick with the aroma of roasted chicken and freshly-baked bread. When, Lester, Katherine's father, came in, he kissed his wife and daughter, bobbed his head politely in Annie's direction and went to wash his hands.

Dinner was just the four of them. The rest of the family would come on Christmas Eve and stay through Christmas Day, Nedda explained as they sat down and waited for Lester to say grace.

Katherine and Annie were ready for bed by the time they had eaten and helped Nedda with the dishes.

"I can barely keep my eyes open," Katherine said.

Annie nodded. "It was all that good food." She smiled at Nedda.

"I'll have the two of you fattened up in no time." Nedda patted Katherine's arm. "Why don't you two go on up? I'm just going to finish up a little sewing and then I'm off to bed, too. Even your father's done for." She gestured at Lester on the couch, a book open on his lap, his head tipped backward. Soft, rhythmic snores escaped his slightly-parted lips.

Katherine smiled at him. "Are you sure?"

"Go on," Nedda said. "You've had a long day."

Katherine looked at Annie and raised her eyebrows in question. Annie nodded. Katherine went to hug and kiss her mother good night.

"Thank you for including me," Annie said as Katherine stepped back and Nedda pulled her into hug. "You have no idea how much it means to me to be here."

Nedda waved her hand. "I'll wait until after you've met everyone to hold you to that." She laughed. "Now get on up to bed. Both of you."

Annie followed Katherine up the stairs, the old wood creaking and popping as they ascended. The bedroom was dark, and Annie waited as Katherine went to the bureau and turned on the small lamp. Its dim light was reflected in the mirror over the bureau.

"You can use the bath first," Katherine said as she walked to the large, oak chest at the foot of the bed, opened the lid, and rummaged around.

She pulled a thick quilt out of the box and spread it across the bed just as Annie returned from the bath.

Annie wrapped her arms around herself as she shook from the cold. "Which side do you prefer?"

Katherine gave her a surprised look. "Either is fine."

Annie nodded and quickly slipped between the covers.

"I forgot how cold this room gets in the winter," Katherine said when she returned from the bath. She untied the sash of her robe and gestured toward the lamp. "All right to turn this off?"

Annie nodded.

Katherine turned off the light and hurried across the room and climbed into bed. The mattress dipped slightly as she slipped beneath the covers.

"Do you think you'll be warm enough?" she asked. "There are more quilts in that storage chest."

"I think we'll be fine with these once we warm up," Annie said as she pulled a hand out from under the covers and fingered the delicate stitching. "They're beautiful." She rolled her head to look at Katherine. "Did your mother make them?"

"My mother, my grandmother, me," Katherine said. "Remind me tomorrow to show you the one we made for my hope chest."

"Ah, yes, the handsome Prince Albert," Annie said. Katherine couldn't see her face, but she could hear the note of amusement in her voice. "So, I take it he was your . . . ?"

"No, nothing like that," Katherine said quickly. "We . . . well, he wanted to get married. I wanted to move to Chicago."

"And I suppose he's waiting?" Annie said and flipped onto her back. "Pining away for you here in Big Springs until you get tired of the big, bad city?"

"No," Katherine said. "Not at all."

"Huh," Annie said.

Katherine shivered, wishing the sheets would hurry and warm from her body heat.

"Cold?" Annie asked.

"It always takes forever for me to warm up when I go to bed," Katherine said.

"Come lay closer to me," Annie said and, before Katherine could object, she slid her arm under Katherine's pillow.

Katherine stiffened but then, feeling the warmth radiating from Annie's body, slid closer.

"It's okay," Annie murmured. "I won't bite."

"I know," Katherine said. "I'm just not used to . . ."

"What?" Annie asked.

"Sleeping this close to someone," Katherine said. "It feels strange, is all."

"Um," Annie murmured and yawned.

"It's not for you, though, is it?" Katherine asked. Even as she spoke the words, she could hear the slight tone of judgment.

"No, not really," Annie said. Her voice was sleepy.

They lay that way for several minutes before Annie made a soft noise and rolled onto her side, her front facing Katherine, her arm still under her pillow. Her breath was warm on Katherine's chin. She was asleep.

For some reason, the thought made Katherine smile, and she slowed her breathing to match Annie's. As she relaxed, she rolled onto her side, her back to Annie. Annie mumbled something incoherent, draped her arm over Katherine's waist, and pulled herself up against Katherine's back. Katherine stiffened and was about to move Annie's arm when she heard a gargling sound next to her ear. Annie was snoring softly. The incongruity of it struck her as funny, and she laughed, causing the bed to shake. She lay that way for a long time, listening to Annie's soft snores.

Her laughter faded into a smile, and she allowed herself to relax into Annie's warmth and fall into sleep.

"I CAN'T BELIEVE you've never been ice skating," Katherine said as she and Annie trudged along the snow-packed path toward the pond where people were gathering. She carried two pairs of ice skates tied together by the laces. One pair was hers and the other was a pair that Bud had used when he was young.

"Why is that so surprising?" Annie asked. "We don't have ponds like this in Arlington Heights."

Up ahead were several of the young men from town piling sticks and wood together for a bonfire. Other men and boys were hauling wood and brush from the woods that ringed one end of the frozen pond. One of the men, Katherine realized with a start, was Albert.

"So, is it hard?" Annie asked. "Skating, I mean. Is it hard to do?"

"Not really," Katherine said. "It's just balance. I'm sure you'll be great at it."

Annie laughed. It was the unadulterated laugh of a young girl, and Katherine looked at her in surprise. Annie's large eyes sparkled with excitement and her cheeks were ruddy from the cold. She was, Katherine realized, beautiful. The thought made her smile.

"What is it?" Annie asked.

Katherine blinked and shook her head, still smiling. "It's nothing." She linked her arm in Annie's. "You just looked so happy." She squeezed Annie's arm. "I can already tell we'll have to beat the boys away."

Annie raised her hand and gave a dismissive laugh. "All I want is to enjoy this day with you. I want you to teach me how to skate."

"I will," Katherine promised. "And when we get cold, we'll go sit by the bonfire and drink cocoa or coffee."

"Or something a little stronger," Annie said.

"Well," Katherine said thoughtfully, "some of the men might have something . . . and I know the older boys usually have something stashed away. But—"

"No," Annie said with a satisfied grin. "We *will* have something stronger." She reached with her free hand into the pocket of her coat and pulled out a small silver flask. It shone brightly against the red of her mitten.

"Annie," Katherine gasped, though she couldn't help but laugh. "Put that away. If anyone sees—"

"No one's going to see, Kate," Annie said and slipped it back into her pocket. "I'll hide it in my mitten. I just thought it might be a nice little something for our cocoa."

"You're impossible," Katherine said, and Annie laughed.

They walked toward the pond still arm in arm. The snow crunched and squeaked under their shoes. The blades of the ice skates clacked together against Katherine's thigh.

"I may be impossible, but I'm good for you." Annie tilted her head and grinned up at Katherine.

"I don't know about that," Katherine said. "You make me crazy more often than not."

"And that's good for you," Annie said. "Admit it. Kate."

A snowball exploded against Katherine's shoulder.

"Gotcha," a male voice called, followed by a laugh.

Katherine turned, half-angry, half-stunned, until she saw her assailant. "Albert." She grinned. "Oh my gosh. It's good to see you. Mama said you'd be here."

"Where else would I be when I knew you were in town?" he asked as he trotted to her, wrapped her in a hug, and spun her around in circles. "This place is no fun without you here." He set her down and looked into her face. "How is it that you get prettier every time I see you?"

Katherine felt her cheeks warm. "I don't know." She was very aware of Annie's scrutiny.

Albert grinned down at her and shifted his attention to Annie who stood off to the side, eyes narrowed, her expression unreadable.

"Hello," he said, releasing Katherine's waist and extending his gloved hand. "I'm Albert."

"Albert, this is Annie." Katherine gestured toward Annie. "Annie, this is Albert. We grew up together."

"More than that. Katie, here, was the first girl I kissed." He grinned and still stood with his hand out.

"I've heard a lot about you, Albert." Annie paused and then extended her mittened hand to meet his.

Katherine frowned a little at Annie's reluctance to shake his hand.

"Don't believe a word of it," he said with a twinkle in his eye.

"Oh, I don't." Annie's tone, though equally playful, held a touch of something sharper. Katherine flicked her eyes from Albert's face to Annie's and back. He appeared not to notice.

"So, Katie," he said, turning back to Katherine. "We've got the fires all set up, and I'm just going up to the car for some matches but I'd love the chance to catch up."

"Me, too." Katherine glanced down toward the pond. "Is Evelyn down there yet?"

"Not yet," Albert said. "But I know she's on her way."

"Albert, come on!" came a voice from down by the bonfire.

"Gotta go," Albert said and started toward the row of cars at the top of the hill. "But we'll catch up later on, right?"

"Of course," Katherine said. "You can help me teach Annie to skate."

Albert grinned. "I can't wait," he said over his shoulder.

They stood for several seconds and watched him trudge up the hill. Annie turned first and began to walk alone toward the pond. Katherine hurried to catch up.

"He seems nice," Annie said finally.

"He is," Katherine said.

"So, you were his first kiss?"

Katherine laughed. "Yes, but that was ages ago. We were ten."

"And since?" Annie asked.

"Since what?"

"Since you were ten?"

"Well, of course," Katherine said uncomfortable with where this conversation was going. "We saw each other until I moved to Chicago."

"Mmm," Annie said.

"What is it?" Katherine asked.

"Nothing," Annie said.

Katherine nibbled her lower lip. She could tell something was wrong, but chose to let it go. "So, are you ready to learn to skate?"

Annie squinted in the direction of the pond. Several people had changed into their skates and were already on the ice. She frowned. "How do you know it won't crack with so many people on it?"

"You can tell from the color of the ice," Katherine said. "And we've been skating here for as long as I can remember. No one's ever fallen in. It's not that deep of a pond anyway."

Annie didn't answer.

"It'll be fine," Katherine said and linked her arm with Annie's. "Come on and I'll show you how."

"SO, WHAT DO you think?" Katherine asked as she and Annie settled on one of the logs that had been placed close to the bonfire. "Did you have a good time?" Her nose and cheeks were numb from the cold, and she turned her face toward the popping, crackling fire.

"I did. I absolutely did. It was so much fun." Annie laughed in delight.

As it had before, her laugh made Katherine turn to look at her. Annie's dark eyes glowed; her cheeks and nose were reddened. She smiled happily at Katherine and turned to the fire. She closed her eyes and tipped her head back to let the heat bathe her face and neck.

Katherine was again struck by the odd symmetry that resulted in such a pretty face. She traced the line of Annie's profile with her eyes—the straight nose, the rounded cheeks, the graceful lines of her neck and jaw. It was like looking at a stranger, but also someone she knew so well. She remembered how it felt to lay with Annie's arms wrapped around her and her stomach tightened. She wondered why.

Annie opened her eyes and caught Katherine's gaze.

"You'd never know it was your first time skating," Katherine said quickly and faced the fire. "You were great."

"Thanks." Annie tipped her head to the right. "What were you thinking? Just now?"

"Just . . . I don't know." Katherine shrugged. "Enjoying the day."

"Oh," Annie said.

Katherine was aware of Annie's scrutiny. She felt self-conscious and more for a distraction than anything else, she waved to Clyde Spencer who was looking at her as if he were trying to place her. At her greeting, he smiled and waved back.

"Who's that?" Annie asked.

"That," Katherine said with a grin as she met Annie's eyes, "is Clyde Spencer." She leaned closer to Annie and lowered her voice. "The one who—"

"Married both your sisters." Annie peered at Clyde's shadowed face. "Him?"

Clyde stood on the edge of the fire, his collar turned up, his hands shoved in the pockets of his dark brown farm coat. He was talking to Albert and several of the younger men. Occasionally he looked at Annie and Katherine, his wide face thoughtful.

"He looks nice enough," Annie said. "But given what happened to your sisters, it's probably a good thing you're not next in line. The chances of surviving seem slim."

Katherine looked at her to see if she were joking.

Annie grinned. "I'm teasing. But get ready. He's coming over."

Katherine glanced in Clyde's direction and stood quickly to greet him.

"Katie. I heard you was home. Bud said something about it the other day down at the station. It's good to see you, little girl." Clyde grinned and pulled her into his arms for a hug. "Last time I saw you proper you was just a little thing. And now look at you. All growed up."

"I am," Katherine said and stepped back when he put her down. "Um, Clyde, this is my friend, Annie." She grabbed Annie's arm and pulled her forward. "We work together in Chicago. She came to see a hometown Christmas."

Clyde turned his attention to Annie and smiled down at her. "Yer just a little thing, too, aren't ya?" He extended his large, chapped hand. "Nice to meet you."

Annie slipped her hand from her mitten and shook his hand. Her hand looked ridiculously tiny and slender in comparison. He seemed to notice it, too, and quickly, almost apologetically, withdrew his hand.

"Been working on the tractor." He nodded as if this explained everything and returned his attention to Katherine. "I just can't get over how growed up you look. You remind me a lot of Wilma, the way you move and such."

"Thanks, Clyde," Katherine said and caught Annie's smirk out of the corner of her eye. "So, how are you?"

"Not too bad," he said.

The conversation lapsed into silence, and Clyde glanced over his shoulder at the activity on the pond. "Got a good turnout this year." He leaned down. "Seems Albert ain't lost interest. He's been talking about you two all afternoon. Reckon he's working up the nerve to come over and ask you for a skate. Or a walk." He grinned.

From the corner of her eye, Katherine could see Annie stiffen. She was about to ask about Clyde's parents when Albert trotted up to them.

"You were doing great out there," he said to Annie and jerked his head toward Katherine. "But then you had a good teacher." He blushed and cleared his throat. "Would you like to go out for a skate with me?"

Katherine blinked in surprise; the question was directed at Annie.

"I mean, if you don't mind," he said to Katherine.

"No, of course not," she said quickly. "Why would I mind?"

Annie glanced at Katherine and then back at Albert. She, too, seemed surprised. She looked again at Katherine and nodded.

"I'd like that," she said to Albert and extended her hand. "But you'll have to go slow. I'm not very good."

Albert barked a laugh and took her hand. "I'll be very careful." He led her toward the ice.

Clyde watched them go and looked down at Katherine. "Would you like to go out for a skate? I'm not very good, but we could have a fun twirl or two."

"No thanks," Katherine said. "I . . . I just want to sit here by the fire and get warm."

"I could sit with you until your friend gets back," he offered.

"That's all right. But thank you. You're sweet. I think I'll just . . ." She gestured at the log and at the fire.

Clyde nodded, shrugged, and walked away.

"THAT WAS SO much fun," Annie said as they were getting ready for bed.

She had talked about the day nonstop since they had returned, charming Katherine's parents with her descriptions of the skating and the people.

"I had no idea it would be like that," Annie said as she stood near the bed and pulled a brush though her hair. "It was like flying."

"I'm glad you had a nice time," Katherine said, unable to keep her irritation from her voice.

"What's wrong?" Annie asked. "You've been acting strange ever since we left the bonfire."

"Nothing," Katherine said stiffly. "I'm just tired. I'm glad you had a good time."

"And . . . ?" Annie said.

"And . . . nothing." Katherine shrugged.

Annie studied her for several seconds. "Is this because I skated with Albert? Because if it is—"

"This has nothing to do with Albert," Katherine said tightly. "I'm *glad* you skated with him the whole time. You two seemed to be having a gas."

She turned away from Annie and slipped out of her clothing. She pulled on her nightgown and turned. She could feel Annie's gaze and after several moments, forced herself to look up.

Annie was sitting on the bed, the brush clasped loosely in her hands, which lay in her lap. "I'm not interested in Albert, if that's what you think."

"I couldn't care less," Katherine said as she buttoned up the front of her nightgown.

"You're more important to me than he could ever be," Annie said, her voice low.

Something about her tone caused Katherine to pause, and she flicked her gaze at Annie to see that she still was watching her. She felt her face flush, and her heart thumped as Annie laid her brush on the bed, stood, and walked to stand in front of her. Katherine stood, unmoving. After several seconds, Annie reached up and began to secure the remaining buttons at the top of Katherine's nightgown.

"All he did was ask questions about you," she said softly, her eyes focused on the task of sliding the buttons into the holes. "Just in case you were wondering."

"I wasn't," Katherine said, though she knew it was a lie.

"Mm," Annie said with a small smile as she carefully secured the final button at the throat of the nightgown. "And I was worried you were jealous."

She pressed her fingertip against the button, flattening the cloth around the eyelet, and held it there for several seconds before withdrawing her hand.

Katherine shook her head and swallowed.

Annie looked up into her face. "Good." She stepped back. "Because, if anybody has cause for jealousy, it's me."

Katherine frowned. "What do you mean?"

Annie smiled with a sad thoughtfulness in her eyes. "He's completely in love with you. You were all he could talk about. He spent most of his time looking over at you—though you probably already know that since you were staring at us the entire time."

She began to unbutton her blouse, and Katherine looked quickly away, her gaze settling on the lipsticks and face cream that lay on top of her dresser.

"I don't know what you mean," she said, her face hot. It was another lie.

She could hear the rustle of Annie's clothing as she undressed and pulled on her nightgown.

"You can look now," Annie said.

Katherine stared at the wall, willing her cheeks to cool.

"It's all right to be a little jealous."

"What do you mean?" Katherine asked and finally turned to study Annie.

"It's natural," Annie said. "And that I felt it, too, watching the two of you."

"But you know I don't want to be with him," Katherine said.

"That doesn't change how it felt," Annie said simply. "Seeing the two of you together . . . I was envious."

Katherine made a noise that was part exasperation and part irritation. "Well, then you can have him, if that's what you want. I'm not interested."

Annie stared at her for several seconds and laughed.

"What?" Katherine asked. "Why are you laughing?"

Annie shook her head. "It's just . . ." She laughed again. "It's nothing. It's . . . silly. This whole conversation is silly. We're arguing about who doesn't want Albert more."

Katherine stared at her for a moment and laughed.

"I don't want Albert," Annie said. She went back to the bed, sat down, and patted the spot next to her.

Katherine sat down. The mattress dipped under their combined weight. "Well, I don't want him either. And I don't want to live here again. I just . . ." She paused. "I guess I *was* jealous. I'm sorry if I was snippy."

"It's okay. I'm sorry, too." Annie pulled Katherine's hands into her lap. "Friends?"

Katherine smiled and squeezed Annie's fingers. "Friends."

CHAPTER 8
Lawrence, Kansas, 1997

BUD LOOKED NOTHING like Joan had remembered him. Age and dementia had taken their toll, and the once imposing man had become a shrunken husk. He sat in a cushioned wooden chair in front of the window in his room. His daughter, Barbara, sat next to him, her plump hand resting gently on his arm as he stared out at the birds at the feeders. Joan stepped into the room and cleared her throat.

Barbara looked up. "Oh, my gosh. Joanie." She rose. "I would have known you anywhere. You look just like your mom." She pulled Joan into a tight hug. She was much older than Joan had remembered—and much rounder.

"Hi," Joan said when Barbara finally released her.

"I'm so glad you called," Barbara said. "And Daddy's pleased, too. Aren't you Daddy?"

Bud turned and looked up at Joan without recognition.

"It's Joanie, Daddy," Barbara said. "Katie's little girl."

Bud stared into space and blinked several times before he returned his gaze to Joan's face. "No offense, girl, but your mother was a raging bitch."

Barbara hurried to her father and patted him on the shoulder. "Now, Daddy, you know you don't mean that." She turned to Joan and shook her head. "He doesn't mean it."

"I sure as God damn hell *do* mean it. Every time she opened her mouth it was to say something nasty. And the way she treated Clyde." Bud shook his head sadly. "Unforgivable."

Barbara's face grew red, and she opened her mouth to say something. Joan burst out laughing. Barbara blinked and looked from Joan to her father and then back.

"You couldn't be more right, Uncle Bud," Joan said. "Truth be told, I didn't like her much myself most of the time."

Bud raised his shaggy gray eyebrows and studied Joan again. This time, he seemed to know exactly who she was and his assessment of her was almost approving. "She was a shitty mother."

"She could be difficult," Joan said. "Actually, it was my mother I was hoping to talk to you about."

Bud brushed his hand across his stubbled chin and shook his head. "Not much to tell."

"Well, actually that might not be true," Joan said. "I've found some old letters and I was hoping to ask you about some things that happened when she was younger—after she and Dad got married."

Bud looked down at the table and back up at Joan. "Why do you want to bring all this back up? It ain't gonna change nothin'."

"I'm going through Mom's stuff," Joan said as she sat in the chair abandoned by Barbara. "There are some things I really need to know—things I need to understand." She swallowed. "I think my mother was having an affair. I think she had been seeing someone in Chicago."

"Oh, she was having an affair all right." Bud sneered. "We didn't know what was goin' on until it was too late."

"Can you tell me what happened?" Joan asked. "You're the only one left who knows." She slid her hand across the table to touch the papery back of his hand. "Please."

Bud slowly shook his head. Joan waited.

"It's nothin' but grief," Bud said. "You'd best leave it alone."

"I can't," Joan said. "You don't understand."

"No," he said sharply. "*You* don't understand. This ain't something you want to be dragging back up. Just let it stay in the past where it belongs."

"Who was 'A'?" Joan asked. Her tone was defiant, bullying, and she was more than aware of the fact that she sounded like her mother.

Bud frowned and raised his eyes to meet hers.

"The man my mother was having an affair with . . . his name began with 'A' didn't it? And the reason she was so bitter and nasty was because of him, wasn't it? Because he died and she was stuck here." She felt suddenly furious. "Tell me."

Bud and Barbara flinched at the ferocity of her words.

"It's not that simple," Bud said finally and sighed. "There's a lot more to it."

"So tell me," Joan said.

"No." He craned his head to look up at Barbara, who still stood with her hands on his shoulder. "I'm tired. I want to rest."

Barbara looked from her father to Joan. "Look, Joanie, I think you'd better go."

"But . . . no—"

Bud held up a gnarled hand. "I'm tired. Come back some other time."

Joan gave Barbara an imploring look. Barbara shrugged sympathetically.

Joan sighed in resignation. "What about later this week? Please, Uncle

Bud. I'm sorry I got upset. I just need to know what happened. How did 'A' die?"

Bud's face grew pale. "What did you say?"

"I asked how 'A' died," Joan repeated. "I know he died. And I know my mother felt responsible."

"She was responsible," Bud said. "And that's all I'm gonna say." He turned back to the window. "Now leave."

"Can I come back later in the week?" Joan asked.

Bud didn't reply.

"Let me talk to him," Barbara whispered as she pulled Joan into a goodbye hug. "I'll call you later and tell you when." She turned back to her father. "Now, Daddy, let's get you into bed."

When she saw that nothing more could be accomplished, Joan walked out of the room.

"SO, IT SOUNDS like a productive day," Luke said later that night.

"Yes and no," Joan said as she wound the phone cord around her index finger. "How are the kids?"

"Good," Luke said. "Busy. Sarah is with a friend at the mall. Oh, and Matty says there is a bake sale thing for the soccer team and you were down to make something?"

"Shit . . . yeah, I did," Joan said. "There's a brownie mix in the pantry. And there should be eggs in the fridge."

"I don't have time to make brownies," Luke said. "I've been running the kids everywhere and need to do some things for work."

"Well, I don't know what to tell you," Joan said irritably. "I can't come home so you're just going to have to make the brownies."

"Couldn't we just stop by the grocery store and buy some?" he asked. "It would be a lot faster."

"And twice as expensive," Joan said. "Not to mention that the point of a bake sale is to bake things to sell. If people wanted to buy grocery store cookies, they'd just do that."

"You know most people don't even eat the crap they buy at those things," Luke said. "You don't know who's touched it or if some kid put their nose boogers in it."

"That's not the point, Luke." Joan felt the familiar irritation rise in her throat, and she had to force herself to bite back a nasty retort.

"Yeah, okay," he said in a tone that sounded more like a petulant child than an adult.

The silence went on for so long, Joan wondered if he was still on the line.

"Luke?" she asked finally.

"Yeah," he said.

"I'm sorry I snapped," she said. "This is just dredging up a lot of emotional stuff for me."

"It's okay," he said. "Hey listen, I gotta go."

He's punishing me. Instead of calling him out on it, she simply sighed. "Sure. So, bye?"

"Yeah," he said. "We'll talk later."

"Asshole," she muttered as she considered ripping the phone off of the wall and throwing it across the kitchen. Instead, she closed her eyes and gently placed the receiver back in its cradle.

She leaned her head back against the wall. Through the kitchen window, she could see into Mrs. Yoccum's backyard. The afternoon sun slanted through the yellow- and rust-colored leaves of the massive oak that had grown to span both properties. She remembered how she and Mrs. Yoccum's son, Jason, used to climb into the tree to escape their mothers. The back door to Mrs. Yoccum's house swung open, and Mrs. Yoccum slowly descended the stairs. Cradled in both hands was a clear plastic bag full of bird seed. She carefully moved around the yard filling the various feeders.

Joan knew she needed to work on the inventory, but she instead wandered aimlessly through the house. Twenty minutes later, she found herself back in the dining room standing over the polished wooden box and its strange assortment of objects.

She touched the gauzy material of the scarf. The letters she had read were stacked, in order of date, on the corner of the table. A part of her felt guilty for reading them. Clearly, they hadn't been meant for anyone but "A." But, she rationalized, how else could she figure out the identity of her mother's lover? And, she admitted to herself, who was she kidding? She *wanted* to read the letters.

Justified in her actions, she picked up the sixth letter. It was dated 1958 and began much like the others.

> *My Dearest~*
>
> *I spent most of yesterday preparing myself emotionally for today. I have come to both anticipate and dread this anniversary.*
>
> *Today, I thought about the ring you bought me from that antique store on La Salle. I had been looking at it in the shop window. And later that week, you snuck back and bought it. I was devastated when I learned that someone had purchased it. And then, on that Sunday morning, I woke to find you, your*

head propped up on one elbow, looking down at me. You always looked so adorable in the morning. And you kissed me on the bridge of my nose. Just that. And then you slipped the ring on my finger. You didn't say a word. You just slipped it on my finger and smiled. In that one moment, I felt more wedded to you than I ever have to Clyde.

Joanie is four now. Even now I can tell she's going to be a challenge to raise. She questions everything I say and does everything she can to rebel against what is expected of her. She reminds me of what I imagine you were like when you were young.

I know I sound like a broken record, but I miss you, my darling. All I have are memories and even those are beginning to fade. Now I get only snippets—remembrances of your skin, your smell, your mouth. God, how I loved your mouth and the sensation of it as you explored my body.

Joan blushed as she read the words, unable to imagine her mother in the throes of passion and unwilling to finish the letter. She winced and shook her head to dispel the image only to find it replaced by a flash of her and Mark—his eyes, his dark skin, the tiny hairs on the backs of his fingers, the way he caressed her.

Joan closed her eyes and pressed her fingertips to the lids. She had been avoiding it for weeks but at some point she was going to have to figure out what to do. Mark was out of the picture. And even though she had toyed with the idea of telling him about the pregnancy, what good would come from it? At this point, she wasn't even sure she wanted him to leave his wife. And then there was Luke. She hadn't told him about the pregnancy either though she had slept with him soon enough after that he wouldn't question the parentage.

It's not about them, she reminded herself. It was about what *she* wanted. That was part of why she had come to Lawrence—to figure out what she wanted to do. There was an abortion clinic in Wichita. She could go down there, have the procedure, and be back the next day. Or she could go to Kansas City. Hell, she could have had it done in Chicago, but somehow that seemed too close to home.

"Not now," she muttered, willing herself not to think about the situation just yet.

She picked up the letter and returned to the description of the ring. Had there been a proposal of some sort? If so, she should add it to her list. There was no date given, but it would have had to have occurred in Chicago. She made a note to check for antique shops on La Salle during the 1930s.

"Damn it," she muttered. "I need to find a way to get Bud to tell me what he knows."

She flipped to the back page of her notebook and stared at Barbara's telephone number. It wouldn't hurt to call, if for no other reason than to offer an apology for what had happened earlier. She walked into the kitchen, lifted the receiver, and dialed.

"Barbara," she said when her cousin answered. "Hi, it's me. Joanie."

"Hi, Joanie," Barbara said. She sounded cautious.

"Listen, I just wanted to apologize about today," Joan said. "I didn't mean to lose it like that. It's just . . . there's so much about my mother that I'm realizing I don't know. And I think he's the only person who does—the only one who was there and can tell me."

"I know," Barbara said. "But are you *sure* you really want to know everything? Maybe it's just best to leave it alone—remember her as she was."

Barbara's tone suggested that she knew more than she was telling her. Joan frowned and sank onto the stool. She leaned her forehead against the wall. "What do you know?"

Barbara sighed. "I don't even know if any of it is true. Daddy talks a lot when he's not in his right mind. He says . . . crazy things."

"What has he said about Mother?" Joan asked. "Barbara, I need to know."

"He went downhill after you left," Barbara said. "He seemed to think I was Mama. He kept talking about how Aunt Katie was a whore, how she cheated on Clyde and she deserved what she got—that both of them did."

"Both?" Joan asked. "Mom and 'A'?"

"I don't know," Barbara said.

"Was there anything else?" Joan asked.

The other end of the phone line was silent.

"What?" Joan asked. "What did he say?"

"Keep in mind that he gets confused," Barbara said. "He makes up things all the time—says things that aren't true. He sees shows on television and later thinks they happened to him. The other day he was talking about going to Korea and getting his toe shot off. He wasn't even in Korea."

"What did he say, Barbara?" Joan asked.

Barbara sighed. "He said he and your dad killed someone. Your mother's lover."

"*What?*" Joan asked.

"It's probably just something he saw on television," Barbara said.

"Tell me exactly what he said," Joan said. "Did he mention a name?"

Barbara sighed again. "He didn't say a name. He just kept saying 'that son-of-a-bitch.' He thought I was Mama, and he seemed to think he had just gotten back from Clyde's. He said over and over that he didn't want to be involved in that nasty business. That's what he called it—nasty business. That's all I know."

"I'd like to talk to him again," Joan said.

"I know," Barbara said. "But, I don't think that's a good idea. He doesn't want to talk about it. And you know how stubborn those Hendersons can be. How about I see what I can do to convince him?"

Joan sighed. It was better than nothing. "Thanks, Barb."

"No problem, sweetie," Barbara said. "Listen, I've got to go, but I'll call if he says anything else. Okay? Bye."

She hung up before Joan could say anything else.

"Damnit," Joan said softly and replaced the receiver. "Doesn't anyone politely end phone conversations anymore?"

CHAPTER 9
Chicago, Illinois, 1933

"I DON'T KNOW why you invited her along," Claire said as they walked to Annie's rooming house.

Katherine gave her a puzzled look. "She's my friend."

"She's just so . . . I don't know . . . loud and unpredictable," Claire said. "She seems to go out of her way to make everyone else feel uncomfortable."

"It's not that," Katherine said. "She's just young. And she's got a lot of spirit. That's all."

"Something about her is just not right. And it doesn't have anything to do with age or spiritedness. It's . . . I don't know." Claire shrugged and shook her head.

"We don't have to like each other's friends," Katherine said and added almost defiantly, "I don't much care for Lenny, but I still spend time with you two."

"Not all that much anymore," Claire said. "And anyway, that's different. Lenny and I are a couple. We're going to get married someday."

"Uh huh," Katherine said.

Claire abruptly stopped walking. Katherine stopped, turned, and, after a second, walked back to where Claire stood.

"What's that supposed to mean?" Claire asked.

Katherine chewed on her lower lip for a moment before meeting Claire's eyes. "I just don't know if Lenny is as," she paused as she searched for the right word, "committed as you are."

Claire's eyes flashed with indignation. "Why would you say that?"

Katherine shrugged, wishing they weren't having this conversation where everyone could see and hear it. "He just seems to be more into having fun than being serious."

"He *is* fun," Claire said. "And that's part of why I like him. He doesn't take things too seriously."

"And that's why I like Annie," Katherine said. "She *does* take things seriously."

"Too seriously if you ask me," Claire said and kept walking.

"And what's *that* supposed to mean?" Katherine asked, intentionally using Claire's own words. She walked quickly to catch up with her.

"She just seems a little too serious," Claire repeated. "Or too . . . intense is maybe a better word. She just seems like an unlikely friend for you to have."

Katherine shook her head. "I don't think that at all. She challenges me."

"Just be careful *how* she challenges you," Claire said in a low voice. She sighed deeply, almost dramatically, and faced Katherine. "She seems to have ulterior motives if you ask me. And I don't want you to be hurt or . . . anything."

"Hurt how?" Katherine asked even as she wasn't sure she wanted to hear the answer.

Claire looked down at the sidewalk for several seconds and raised her gaze to meet Katherine's. She seemed to be deciding whether or not to say something. "Just . . . I think you should be careful. I think her interest in you is—"

"There you are," a loud voice interrupted.

They looked up to see Annie hurrying toward them. She was wearing a green-and-white print dress with a wide green belt. On her head was a white straw hat.

"I was wondering where you were so I decided to take a chance this is the route you'd use and meet you halfway." Annie was breathing heavily. Tiny beads of perspiration glistened on her upper lip and on the bridge of her nose. "It's going to be a warm one." She smiled. "Are you . . . ?" She lapsed into silence, her gaze bouncing from Claire to Katherine and back. "What's wrong?"

"Nothing," Katherine said and smiled at Claire. "Right?"

"No, nothing," Claire said quickly. "We were just disagreeing on the best way to get to the fairgrounds."

"Oh, well, that's easy. We should take the trolleybus and get off at the main entrance. We want to walk down the Avenue of Flags, don't we?" Annie laughed.

"That's what Claire said." Katherine smiled.

Claire smiled back as if nothing had happened.

If anything, Katherine thought, *she looks a little relieved at the interruption.*

"SO, ARE YOU excited?" Annie asked as they stepped off the streetcar.

"I am," Claire said with a smile. "Although they've been working on all of this for so long that it almost seems normal to look out across the water and see all these buildings. It's a shame they will just tear it down afterward."

"I think it's wonderful," Katherine said with an excited laugh. "I've never seen anything like it before. There are going to be so many things to see and do."

"A little different than the Big Springs County Fair?" Annie asked in a teasing voice.

"It's actually called the Douglas County Free Fair," Katherine said saucily.

"It's an unfair comparison," Claire said in Katherine's defense.

"I know it's an unfair comparison," Annie said. "I was just teasing. You knew that didn't you, Kate?"

Katherine nodded and laid a hand on Claire's arm to let her know that she recognized and appreciated the gesture, but that her defense was unnecessary. She smiled at Claire. "So, Claire, what should we do first?"

Claire raised her hands to adjust her hat. Like Annie, she was wearing a light summer dress and hat. She squinted into the sunlight and gestured at the Avenue of Flags. "I suppose we should start here and work our way along."

They gazed at the two lines of gracefully billowing red flags and began to walk down the boulevard. Around them, tourists and Chicagoans alike wandered along staring at the almost unbelievable assemblage of sights and sounds. At the end of the Avenue of Flags stood the Sears & Roebuck Building. Like all the structures, it seemed to gleam with modernity. Towering over the rest of the buildings the 227-foot thermometer stood in the distance.

"Oh my god," Katherine breathed. "The colors are fantastic." She pointed to a blue building topped by a gray dome and flanked by three very tall, curved fans. Nearby was a bright red building built in the Chinese style with a peaked golden pagoda roof. Everywhere were buildings accented in startling shades of green and blue and yellow. "It's like a strange, unbelievable dream."

They wandered through the crowd as if half-asleep, overwhelmed by the grandeur. Everywhere people were stopping to gawk at buildings or displays. As they walked, Katherine could hear people talking about the Chrysler Motors Building or the glass tower of automobiles or the Wonder Bread Display. On the first lagoon, people were being shuttled around on lifeboats.

"We should go on the Sky Ride," Annie said as they passed under a section of the complicated cable network upon which the cars moved. "It's all that anyone's talking about."

"Ugh, but look at the line to ride it." Claire craned her neck to look up the lattice scaffolding to the cables upon which bullet-shaped cars full of people dangled. "Besides, it's awfully high up, don't you think? I have to wonder if it's entirely safe."

"I heard one man say it was 628 feet high," Annie said.

"Claire is afraid of heights," Katherine said. "You should have seen her face when we went up to the roof of our building last year to watch the Fourth of July fireworks."

"I was all right until we got close to the edge." Claire looked at Katherine and Annie. "You two should go, though."

"And leave you?" Katherine said. "Never."

"What about that?" Annie pointed to a red building with a dome painted to look like a globe. In the alcove above the entrance, two dinosaurs stood on either side of a huge ape pounding its chest while the dinosaurs' tails swung back and forth. The lettering above the creatures read, "The World a Million Years Ago."

"Oh, my goodness. We should." Katherine looked around. "Do we need tickets?"

Annie looked at Claire, who shrugged.

"We should find out," Katherine said. "And I want to go to the Midway, too. They have rides. A woman at work was talking about the red serpent ride."

"We will do whatever your heart desires," Annie said.

Katherine smiled happily until she caught Claire's look. "We should do something that we all would enjoy. Claire?"

"I'd like to find the Hiram Walker Whiskey building," Claire said. "I've heard you get samples and I could do with a little taste."

Annie grinned and took Claire's arm. Katherine noticed that Claire neither pulled away nor leaned into her as Annie locked elbows. Rather, she stood stiffly, tolerating the gesture.

"That sounds like a great idea," Annie said as she extended her other elbow to Katherine so they could link arms as well. "I think a drink or two would loosen us all up a little."

After several samples from the Hiram Walker exhibit, they ventured back to the midway, talking more freely and pointing out displays to each other. Katherine smiled when Claire laughed at something Annie had said. The awkwardness between the two had disappeared and rather than join in, Katherine decided to let them get to know each other better. She stopped in front of the serpent ride and watched as people climbed aboard the roller coaster. It rushed past with a rattling, clunking rush of wind and screams. She felt a light touch on the lower part of her back. She started and turned to see Annie standing next to her.

"Where's Claire?" Katherine asked loudly as she craned her neck to look in the direction Claire and Annie had been standing.

"She ran into some friends," Annie yelled back. "They're going to look around and maybe meet up with us later."

Katherine scowled. "Lenny, by any chance?"

Annie nodded.

Katherine snorted and turned back to the roller coaster on its second loop around the track.

"What's wrong?" Annie asked once the train had roared past.

It's nothing." Katherine shook her head. "We were just having a conversation this morning about Lenny and . . ." She had been about to say "and you" but stopped herself. She shrugged.

"You don't like him, do you?" Annie said it more as a statement than a question.

Katherine pressed her lips together, turned her head to look at Annie. After several seconds, she grudgingly nodded. "Not much." She turned her attention back to the ride and opened her purse for her cigarettes. "Want one?" she asked as she opened the case.

"No thanks," Annie said and reached into her own purse. "Want some of this?"

Katherine looked up from lighting her cigarette. Annie held the same flask she had brought with them to the ice skating party. She looked from the tarnished silver flask to Annie's impish smile and back.

"You're incorrigible," she said with a laugh. "I was going to say that I can't believe you brought this, but actually, it doesn't surprise me in the least." She held out her hand for the flask, handed Annie her cigarette, and faced the roller coaster. With her back to the crowd, Katherine raised it to her lips. It wasn't the same quality that they had been served at the Hiram Walker exhibit, but it still tasted good.

"Take another for good measure," Annie said loudly in her ear. Katherine turned her head and looked down at Annie who had leaned close. Annie grinned and lifted Katherine's cigarette to her lips. "And then I have a surprise for you."

Katherine looked at her bemused. "Why do those words coming from you frighten me?"

"Probably for good reason," Annie said as she took a deep pull from the cigarette. "But trust me, this will be fun."

Katherine took another gulp of whiskey and handed the flask back to Annie, who didn't bother to turn away from the crowd as she raised it to her lips and took a large swallow. Daintily, she wiped the corner of her mouth with her bare index finger.

"Should have worn gloves," she said.

"It's too hot to wear gloves," Katherine said as she studied Annie's dress. The fabric was a light summer blend, unlike Katherine's own cotton dress which clung heavily to her body in the heat. "It's too hot for whiskey."

"Well, I can take care of that. Let's get a lemonade." Annie pointed to a nearby drinks vendor.

They walked to the stand and ordered two drinks. The cold liquid tasted deliciously tart and sweet on Katherine's tongue. She smiled and laughed as Annie surreptitiously removed her flask and added healthy shots of whiskey to each of their drinks.

"Annie," she said in a half-amused, half-chastising tone. "You're going to get me drunk."

"Good," Annie said. "You need to get drunk more often. It frees the soul. And besides, I think you're going to need it for this next adventure."

"Ah, yes," Katherine said. "You have a surprise."

"I do," Annie said. "Follow me."

They walked for several minutes until they reached a building with life-sized pictures of a beautiful blonde woman, her body hidden mostly from view by large, white ostrich-feather fans.

"Sally Rand?" Katherine gasped. "Oh, Annie, we can't go in there."

Annie laughed. "Of course we can. Our money is as good as anyone else's."

"That's not the point," Katherine said.

"So, what's the point?" Annie placed her free hand on her hip and looked indignantly at Katherine.

"The point," Katherine hissed, "is that Sally Rand is a burlesque dancer. It's indecent."

"Oh, stop," Annie said. "She's a performer who does illusion. I have it on very good authority that she's not really nude. She wears a bodysuit."

"What do you mean 'a bodysuit'?" Katherine asked.

"A flesh-colored suit that covers her body," Annie said. "It makes her look naked, but she's not. And she moves the fans so quickly, you only *think* you see nudity."

"And where did you hear this?" Katherine asked.

"Her cousin is a friend of mine," Annie said.

"Her cousin?" Katherine asked. "How do you know her cousin?"

"It's a long story," Annie said and blushed. "She's from Hickory County, Missouri."

"Who?" Katherine asked. "Your friend or Sally Rand?"

"Well, both, actually," Annie said. "Bobbie—and Sally's for that matter—real last name is Beck."

Katherine looked up at the building and the show displays. "I don't know. It's not really—"

"Oh, come on," Annie said and pulled her toward the building. "Someday you'll be proud to be able to say you saw Sally Rand's fan dance at the Chicago World's Fair."

KATHERINE HAD TO admit to Annie as they walked home that evening, she had been right. "It really was tasteful." She squeezed Annie's arm, which was linked with hers despite the sticky heat. "And scandalous." She hummed softly to herself. "Are you *sure* she wasn't nude?"

"I'm sure," Annie said.

They walked in silence for several minutes, and Katherine was aware that they both swayed somewhat. They had been drinking whiskey in their lemonades most of the day, and between the heat, the excitement, and the alcohol, she was feeling more than a little intoxicated.

"I think, Miss Bennett," she said matter-of-factly, "I am drunk."

Annie laughed. "Well, then it's a good thing that we're home."

"Huh?" Katherine asked dumbly and looked around at the buildings. They were standing in front of the Merchandise Mart. Across the street was Annie's rooming house.

"We're home," Annie said. "Well, my home at least. Want to come up for a bit? Sober up before you head home?"

Katherine blinked and considered the offer. If she went home, she would only be alone in her hot room. She nodded. "Why not."

"I have a fan," Annie said. "We can wet a cloth and put it over the front of it. It helps cut the heat."

They crossed the street, and Annie unlocked the large, wooden outer door. It swung open and, as usual, Katherine smelled the decades of cooked dinners, aging building, and human occupation. The entryway and stairwell were stuffy as they climbed the stairs to Annie's floor. She opened the door to her room and gestured for Katherine to enter.

"Would you like a drink?" Annie asked as she closed the door behind her. "I have whiskey."

"I think I've had quite enough whiskey for one day," Katherine said and walked to look out the window at the darkening street. "But a glass of water would be nice if you have it."

Annie rummaged for something on one of the shelves and turned back to Katherine. She held a pitcher in one hand and a box of matches in the other. "I need to run downstairs for some water." She pushed the matches into Katherine's hands. "Why don't you light some candles or the lamp? And turn on the fan. I'll go wet the cloth."

Katherine nodded and slid open the box of matches. She heard the door close behind her and the sound of Annie's footsteps in the hall and, more faintly, on the stairs. Outside, the evening had turned a dusky blue-gray, and she stood, mesmerized by the people on the street below. A man and a woman talked. Several boys tossed something back and forth. She didn't realize until she heard the door open and close behind her that she had been standing in the same position for several minutes.

Embarrassed, she pulled one of the matches out of the box and went to strike it. Her fingers, clumsy from the whiskey, lost their grasp on the thin piece of wood and the match fell to the floor. She bent to pick it up and, as she rose, banged her head on the corner of the table.

She cursed, and Annie rushed to her side.

"Are you all right?" she asked and took the matches from Katherine's hand.

Quickly she took another match from the box, lit the candle, and tipped Katherine's face down and to the side, frowning as she examined the small cut on her temple.

"Maybe it *is* a good thing we're switching to water," she said as she walked to the closet and returned with a washcloth. She dipped just a corner into the pitcher of water and pressed the cloth to Katherine's cut.

"It's not bad," she said as she gently dabbed it against the wound. "But you're probably going to have a headache."

Annie cupped Katherine's jaw with her other hand and steadied her head. Katherine felt the cool fingertips on her face and closed her eyes. Her body swayed just a little. She opened them to find Annie looking intently at her. As always seemed to happen when Annie stood that close and looked at her that way, Katherine felt odd. Her pulse thumped faster. Suddenly, the room seemed too small.

Katherine stared back, unable to look away. "I . . ."

Annie lowered the hand holding the cloth, though her other hand remained on Katherine's jaw. She continued to stare into Katherine's eyes, her breathing light and shallow. Slowly, she leaned closer. Katherine could feel her soft breath on her cheek. It smelled faintly sweet—like fresh tobacco and bourbon.

Katherine pulled slightly back. "What . . ." she started to say, but realized she didn't know what she had been about to ask.

They gazed at each other. Annie leaned forward, arched slightly up on her toes, and touched her lips to Katherine's.

It wasn't even really a kiss, Katherine thought abstractedly. It was just a soft, fleeting brush of the lips. She inhaled sharply as she felt the rush of blood in her head, in her cheeks, in her lips. She had been expecting it, she realized. She had perhaps even wanted it to happen. She blinked, and Annie, whose face was still only inches from her own, seemed to understand. Her lashes seemed impossibly long as she closed her eyes and pulled Katherine's head down. This time, the kiss was less tentative.

Katherine tipped her head to the side and opened her mouth. She felt Annie's lower lip between her own. She felt Annie's fingertips on the sides of her face, on her jaw, pulling her face lightly forward. She breathed heavily through her nose and made a small sound in the back of her throat—a soft, plaintive moan. Annie increased the pressure of her lips.

"No," Katherine said suddenly as she comprehended what was happening and pulled away. She took two steps backward, her legs trembling. Annie looked stunned. "I can't . . . I'm not . . . I'm sorry."

"Kate," Annie said helplessly. "I . . ."

"You don't understand," Katherine said, shaking her head and holding her hands out protectively in front of her. "I am not like . . . that."

Annie frowned but didn't reply.

"It was just the moment," Katherine said. "We had too much to drink. It didn't mean anything."

Annie blinked and seemed to consider what to say next. "It did to me."

"Annie, don't do this," Katherine said.

"I'm sorry, but it did." Annie stepped forward, and Katherine stepped back. "I wasn't planning this, Kate. But I'm not sorry that I did it. I've wanted to kiss you from the first moment I saw you—the day Ansen gave me the tour of the store and you were standing behind the counter next to Claire. Do you remember?"

Katherine felt herself blushed. She *did* remember. She remembered seeing Annie—remembered her awareness of her gaze. Had she sensed this connection even then? Had she somehow encouraged it?

"I'm not interested in women," she said, quickly. "I like you, and I'm flattered but I'm not—"

"I think you are," Annie interrupted.

"You're wrong," Katherine said, aware of the flush in her cheeks. Her tone was harsher than she had intended. "I need to go."

"Stay," Annie insisted. "Please. Stay. I won't do that again. I swear, it just happened."

"I need to go." Katherine raised her hand to her temple. She winced slightly. "My head. I need to take care of my head."

Annie grabbed Katherine's hand. "Kate, please. We need to talk about this."

"No." Katherine pulled her hand away. "I need to get home. I've had too much to drink and my head hurts. I need to go home and sleep. Besides, we have work tomorrow."

"I don't want this to hurt our friendship," Annie said.

"It won't," Katherine said quickly. All she wanted was to get out of Annie's room and be outside. She picked up her purse and rushed out the door.

THE HUMIDITY OF the afternoon was just beginning to give way to the cool of the evening as Katherine rushed from Annie's building and hurried along the sidewalk. Her thoughts were fractured and jumbled. Annie had kissed her. But Annie was high-spirited and aggressive. Her behavior was often shocking. What was more upsetting to Katherine was how she, herself, had reacted. Not only hadn't she stopped Annie, she had kissed her back. And, until she realized what she was doing, she had enjoyed it.

Katherine pressed her fingertips to her lips. They felt swollen and strangely sensitive. She had a flash of Annie's impossibly long eyelashes brushing against her cheek as she closed her eyes and kissed her the second time. It had felt good.

But it isn't supposed to feel good, Katherine thought wildly. What had happened was appalling. It was unnatural. *Wasn't it?* She felt sick as she imagined what her friends would say—what her family would say. Was this what Claire had been trying to tell her? In any event, she needed to put an end to it.

As she walked, she considered her options. She could pretend it hadn't happened—that she had had too much to drink and didn't remember it. She could simply blame it on the whiskey and make clear that such a thing could never happen again. Or, she could distance herself from Annie, let the friendship lapse into mere acquaintanceship and try to never let something like that happen again.

With a sigh, she opened the door to her building and climbed the stairs to the floor she shared with Claire and two other women.

Claire opened her door and popped her head out. "Hey, kiddo. You're home earlier than I expected. I would have thought you and Annie would still be at it."

Katherine felt herself flush. "I had to call it a night. The fair, the heat . . . it was all too much." She gestured at Claire's nightgown. "Why aren't you with Lenny?"

Claire waved a hand. "He and the boys were going to get blasted, so I decided to come home. Work tomorrow." She smiled and leaned forward to get a closer look at Katherine's face. "Are you sure you're all right?" She noticed the cut on Katherine's temple. "What happened to your head? Did you fall?"

Grateful for the diversion, Katherine nodded. "Too much heat." She touched her chin. "I dropped something and when I stood up, I hit my head. It's nothing really."

Claire stepped fully into the hall and placed her hand on Katherine's forehead. It felt cool against Katherine's flushed skin. She left it there for several seconds and nodded gravely.

"You do feel warm," she said and peered into Katherine's face. "Perhaps we spent too much time outside today." Her expression softened. "Why don't you go get ready for bed, maybe take a cool bath."

Katherine nodded, grateful for the kindness. She walked toward her room and stopped, aware of Claire watching her, and turned to her. "I know I don't say this enough, but thank you for being such a great friend. You always have looked out for me and I appreciate it. I really don't know what I would have done all this time without you here. I don't tell you enough how much I value you and our friendship. Thank you."

Claire blinked in surprise, then smiled. "You're feverish. And you're talking nonsense. Go get your things, and I'll draw you a cool bath. That and a good night's rest will fix you right up."

MUCH LATER, KATHERINE lay in her bed and stared at the ceiling, noticing, not for the first time, that the plaster had a slender crack that extended from the wall to the light fixture. The night was proving to be a sleepless one full of recriminations and a giddy awareness of something she couldn't identify.

Over and over she replayed the events of the evening—the kiss, her hurried exit, the combination of exhilaration and anxiety she had felt as she walked home. What, she wondered for the hundredth time, was she going to do when she saw Annie at work in just a few hours? What would she say? How should she act? She had already considered feigning sickness but decided that would accomplish nothing but delay the inevitable. They should meet this head on. They had had too much to drink. The kiss had meant nothing. She would greet Annie as if nothing had happened. And if Annie pressed the issue, well, she would deal with that then.

Even as she thought it, though, she raised her hand to her lips. They still felt sensitive. She lightly brushed her fingertips across her lower lip—much as Annie had done with that first kiss. Just a light, brief press of flesh on flesh. And then she stopped, shocked; she should feel disgust. She *did* feel disgust. She moved her hand up to her forehead, to cover and rub her eyes. This was ridiculous. She needed to get up, get ready, and meet Claire so they could take the streetcar to work. Still, she lay there until she heard a gentle knock on the door and a soft voice.

"Kate?"

It was Claire, checking on her.

"Yes," Katherine said as she pushed the covers aside and got out of bed. "Just a moment." She grabbed her robe, thrust her arms into the sleeves, and knotted the sash as she walked to the door and opened it.

Claire peeked in. "How are you doing? Better?"

"Much," Katherine said and forced herself to smile ruefully. "Though it appears as if I've overslept."

Claire peered at her. "You look like hell. Are you sure you're all right?"

"Yes, yes," Katherine said. "I'm just running a little behind. Give me twenty minutes?"

Claire nodded. "But if you can be ready in fifteen, we might be able to stop for some bread at that little bakery on the corner. You look like you could use a little something in your stomach."

"Good idea," Katherine said with more enthusiasm than she felt. "I'll meet you out front."

ANNIE WAS WAITING for them outside the department store. She smiled tentatively as they approached. She looked as if she hadn't slept well either.

"Hello, hello," Claire said in greeting. "That was quite the day yesterday, wasn't it?"

Annie nodded and turned her attention to Katherine. Though she was still smiling, her eyes were worried.

She's waiting to see how I play it, Katherine thought.

"It was a lot to take in," Annie agreed. "So, did you both sleep well after so much sun and excitement?"

"I did, but I'm not sure about poor Kate," Claire said and inclined her head toward Katherine. "She was feeling feverish last night."

Annie's eyes jumped from Claire to Katherine. "Oh. That's too bad. Is everything . . . all right?"

Katherine knew what she was asking. She hesitated almost imperceptibly and nodded.

"I'm much better," she said with a tight smile. "I don't know what came over me but it wasn't anything that a little rest couldn't cure. Probably a little too much to drink. I don't remember half of what we did or saw."

Annie nodded slowly, thoughtfully. "I'm glad."

Katherine was aware of Claire watching the exchange. She thought about Claire's aborted warning the previous day and felt embarrassed. She knew without a doubt now what Claire had been trying to tell her. She turned with exaggerated nonchalance to her and sighed dramatically.

"Why is it that the work week drags by, but our days off go so quickly there isn't even a chance to enjoy them properly?"

Claire laughed. "I don't know. But if we don't hurry up and get inside, we won't have to worry about our work week because we won't have jobs."

KATHERINE WALKED DOWN the hall from the employee lockers to the large double doors that separated the public and employee spaces and saw Annie. *She must be on her break*, she thought as Annie walked toward her.

Katherine hesitated.

"Just going back on?" Annie asked.

"Yes," Katherine said.

They shuffled their feet in an awkward silence.

"About last night—"

"We should talk—"

They spoke at once and stopped.

Katherine closed her eyes and shook her head. She sighed and placed a hand on Annie's arm. "Let me."

Annie pressed her lips together and nodded.

"I think we had a bit of a misunderstanding last night. Too much excitement . . . too much time in the heat . . . way too much to drink." Katherine shrugged. "It was just a strange set of circumstances that I think we should write off as a mistake."

Her speech delivered, she waited for Annie to agree.

"I don't want to write it off," Annie said finally. "And I'm not going to pretend it didn't happen. It did."

"I'm not saying it didn't happen," Katherine said. "What I'm saying is that it was a mistake—two friends who," she shrugged, "became overwhelmed by closeness."

"Overwhelmed by closeness," Annie repeated. "Maybe for you, but I wanted to kiss you."

Katherine blinked, unsure how to respond. "So, you're . . ."

"A lesbian?" Annie supplied. "Yes, I suppose I am."

Katherine recoiled. "Well, I'm not. I like men." She felt almost panicked. "And what happened last night cannot happen again. It *won't* happen again. We're friends, nothing more."

Annie looked up at her, her dark eyes large and serious. "It will happen again," she said in a low and soft voice. "Maybe not anytime soon, but it will."

Katherine started to protest but Annie held up a slender hand.

"You seem to forget that you kissed me, too," she said.

Katherine felt herself blush, the heat spreading through her chest and arms. "It won't happen again."

Annie blinked and exhaled sharply, eyes full of hurt. "Fine."

Katherine's anger faded. "Annie. I want to be your friend. I just—"

"All right," Annie said softly. "I understand."

Katherine reached again for Annie's hand and stopped herself. "Just friends."

"Sure. Just friends." Annie raised her eyes to meet Katherine's and shifted her gaze to look down the hallway to the break room. The awkward silence stretched.

"Well," she said finally, "I need to go to my locker before my break is over. See you later?"

She smiled, and Katherine felt sad and relieved.

"Yes," she said tiredly. "Later."

CHAPTER 10
Chicago, Illinois, 1933

OVER THE WEEKS that followed, Katherine saw very little of Annie. For the most part it was a relief because it gave her time to think about what had happened that night after the fair. Her initial fear had been that she had wanted the kiss to occur. But the more she thought about it, the more she concluded that she hadn't. It had just been the closeness of their friendship that had confused the situation. And the fact that she returned the kiss was simply an instinctual response to being kissed. She had just reacted. The important thing was to make sure that it didn't happen again.

The few times she had seen Annie lately, had either been at work or just in passing when she arrived or left with Claire. Annie, for her part, seemed to be taking earlier streetcars or, more likely, walking. And, much to Katherine's relief, when they saw each other, the conversations were short and superficial. Everything was fine as far as Katherine was concerned. Claire seemed to see things differently.

"Annie's been acting odd, don't you think?" she asked one evening as they rode the streetcar home.

Katherine feigned surprise. "Odd? What do you mean?"

Claire shrugged. "I don't know. Distant. Like something is on her mind. You don't suppose something's wrong, do you?"

Katherine looked out the window. They were traveling over the river. Ahead and to her right was the Central Office Building with its red brick façade and stately clock tower. On the docks below, sweaty men were loading and unloading pallets. She wondered if it was less muggy by the water.

"Kate?"

She started. "Sorry?"

"I said, you don't suppose something's wrong, do you?" Claire said. "With Annie? Have you noticed how thin and pale she's gotten?"

"Oh, I'm sure she's fine," Katherine said quickly. "Just struggling with this heat like the rest of us."

"Has she said anything to you?" Claire asked. "I know you two are close. If she were to confide in anyone, it would be you."

"We're not *that* close," Katherine said quickly. She continued to stare out the window. "I mean, we spend time together, of course, but she and I . . . well, we don't talk about personal matters. Not really. In that respect we barely know each other."

She felt guilty for the lie—as if by saying it, she was betraying Annie. But still, she didn't want Claire—or anyone for that matter—to suspect just how close they had become.

"Umm," Claire said.

"I would have thought you would be glad," Katherine said. "I know you don't necessarily like her."

"It's not that I don't like her," Claire said. "I simply question her influence on you. And, if I'm going to be perfectly honest, I was worried that she was interested in something other than just friendship, if you know what I mean."

Katherine could feel Claire looking at her. She felt the heat of a flush rising from her chest to her neck and to her face. Her ears felt hot. Did she appear guilty? She fought the desire to fan herself and considered how to react.

"Well, I never got that impression from her," she said finally.

They rode on for several minutes in silence, and Katherine could tell Claire wanted to say more.

"It's so hot," Katherine said and waved her hand in front of her face. "I feel sweaty and hot all the time. I barely slept at all last night." She turned her head from the window and met Claire's gaze.

"It has been hot," Claire agreed. She hesitated. "Did something happen between you two? An argument?"

"No," Katherine said quickly. "Why would you think that?"

Claire shrugged. "You just seem to be cool to each other."

Cool, Katherine thought. *Well, yes, she supposed they had been cool.* After their conversation in the hall, she had gone out of her way to make sure their encounters were brief and always in the company of other people.

"No, not at all," she said. "It's just been a busy couple of weeks."

The streetcar was nearing their stop, and Katherine inclined her head to indicate that they needed to get off. Claire nodded and rearranged the purse and small bag she used to carry her lunch. Claire was dropping the topic for the moment, but Katherine sensed that the conversation was far from over.

TWO DAYS LATER, Katherine opened the metal door of her locker to slide her purse inside and noticed a square bundle wrapped in butcher block paper and bound with thick cotton string. Two women stood chatting nearby, neither paying attention as Katherine pulled out the package. It was heavy and nondescript. She stared at it for several seconds, certain it was from Annie. It had to be. Who else would leave her an anonymous gift?

With trembling fingers, she untied the string and peeled back the paper. It was a book, of course, simply bound with a light brown cover. She turned it over to see the title. *The Well of Loneliness.* Her heart thudded loudly in her ears as she flipped open the cover. It had been published in 1928, so it was a recent book. She glanced to the side and was relieved to see that the other women had left the break room. She was alone.

She read quickly through the author's note. The book appeared to be about British female ambulance drivers during World War I. She frowned. This wasn't a subject she was particularly interested in, so why would Annie give her a book on the subject? It wasn't a library book so it must be from Annie's own collection. She ignored that her break was over and flipped to the first chapter.

The story began with a description of an English manor house and its lady, Anne Morton. Katherine puzzled over this. Anne? Annie? Was *that* the connection? She was tempted to read further, but knew she had to return to work. Carefully, she re-wrapped the book, returned it to the locker, and closed the door. Despite feeling anxious, she realized that she also felt oddly excited to have this contact with Annie. She had been careful to keep a distance between them, but if she were honest, she missed her friend. She missed the closeness, the laughter, the . . . well, she might as well say it . . . the intimacy. The fact that Annie had left the book for her suggested that Annie missed her, too.

She caught Annie's eye as she returned to the glove counter and felt a strange nervousness sweep over her body. She had, she realized, intentionally walked past the shoe department—something she hadn't done in weeks. Annie nodded a hello, but gave no sign of anything other than polite recognition. Katherine smiled in return and continued to her post.

Claire glanced at her and stopped to peer more closely. "You okay?"

"Of course, why?" Katherine busied herself with straightening the display.

"You were late getting back from your lunch and you look flushed." Claire shrugged. "Just checking."

"It's this heat," Katherine said.

"I know," Claire said. "Last night I finally got up at about three and wet down my old nightgown and sat in the window with the fan going just to cool down. I didn't care who might have seen."

"Well, we have the fall to look forward to. It's only," she ticked off the days in her head, "two-and-a-half months away."

Claire laughed and then quickly sobered as she noticed Mr. Ansen striding toward them, the light bouncing off his slicked-back hair.

"Ladies," he said in greeting as he stopped in front of the counter.

"Mr. Ansen," they said in unison.

He smiled curtly and turned to survey the department. Out of the corner of her eye, Katherine could see that one of the round table displays was disorderly. His gaze fell immediately on the table.

"Ladies," Mr. Ansen said and pointed to the display. "I know that our change in philosophy might be somewhat complicated, but as I noted in the employee meeting last month, the corporate mind-set of Sears & Roebuck has evolved. No longer are you merely cashiers, but in fact, saleswomen. It is your job to keep the glove department looking tidy and appealing—both for the women who come to buy gloves for themselves and more importantly, for the men who are buying gifts. Need I remind you about General Wood's new retail plan?"

They shook their heads. Claire surreptitiously nudged Katherine's foot beneath the counter.

Ansen clasped his hands in front of himself, midway between stomach and chest and said in a patient voice, "If we are to continue to be a retail leader—especially in these hard times—it's essential to present ourselves as knowledgeable, efficient, and," he looked again at the disordered display, "tidy. We are no longer a mail-order company. Appearance is everything."

He paused, as if considering which other corporate catch-phrases he could use to illustrate his point.

"We understand, Mr. Ansen," Claire said quickly. "And we're eager to be a part of such an exciting . . . endeavor."

"Good." He pointed first at Katherine and then the round table. "Please see to that display."

LATER THAT EVENING, after supper with Claire and a slow walk down Grand Avenue, Katherine sat on her bed with the paper-wrapped book in her lap. She had snuck the package into her bag when she and Claire were collecting their things to go home and even as she tried to forget it was there, all the way home she was aware of its presence amongst the rest of her things.

It has to be from Annie, she thought as she studied the packaging. Who else would give her a book? And the title, *The Well of Loneliness* . . . was she trying to send Katherine a message? She thought again about the kiss and felt the familiar tingle in the pit of her stomach. None of what was happening made sense. She stared down at the package and nibbled on the skin along the edge of her thumbnail. *You're being ridiculous,* she told herself. *What are you waiting for? It's a book, nothing more.*

Decision made, she tugged at the hastily retied string. It came loose with little resistance. She pulled the paper away and studied the cover again before flipping it open and turning to the first page. The type was small and neat. She took a deep breath and began to read.

She put the book down with trembling hands at nearly midnight. The story—at least what she had read thus far—was nothing like she had expected. It had begun with the love affair and life of a Victorian couple and the birth of their first child. The story took a strange turn, though, when the expected baby boy turned out to be a girl. For a number of reasons, the couple went ahead and called the little girl Stephen and, as she grew, indulged her adventurous and headstrong personality. While that turn of events had surprised Katherine, they were nothing compared to the shock she experienced when Stephen developed romantic feelings for the house maid, began to wear masculine clothes and later, fell in love with an American woman married to one of her neighbors.

Katherine's heart raced. This, she realized, was Annie's message. She took a deep breath. The story was unsettling. But, at the same time, it made her feel . . . How *did* it make her feel? It had to be one of Annie's banned books. It was, without a doubt, controversial.

Katherine stood and paced the room. She was tired and her head hurt. She wanted to sleep—to shut out the thoughts that were racing through her brain—but she knew she would not be able to rest until she spoke with Annie.

She looked at her alarm clock. It was twelve-fifteen. She considered the propriety of going now to Annie's rooming house and confronting her. But what would she say? What was there to say? Would she accuse her of leaving the book? Of pushing her perversions on her? Of . . . what? She shook her head. She didn't know what she was thinking. She needed to calm down. Perhaps Claire was still up. But what would she tell her? How could she explain the situation without *explaining* the situation?

No, Katherine thought, *it would be better to simply go to bed—to try to sleep.* But that, she knew, was impossible. Her eyes fell on the book. If she couldn't sleep, she could at least read. And when it was finished, she could . . . what? Give it back? Tell her why it was inappropriate to have given it to her in the first place?

She didn't want to read the rest of the book. But also, if she were being honest with herself, she did. She had part of a bottle of whiskey hidden in the back of her closet. Perhaps a nip would help her sleep. Or, at least, perhaps it would give her the courage to finish the book and decide what to do.

Six hours later, the novel was finished and the whiskey was signifi-
cantly diminished. Katherine felt numb, though from the alcohol or the
book, she wasn't sure. She had sipped and smoked as she read. The
whiskey had made it easier to take in the story that had gone from
scandalously bad to worse. The relationship—if you wanted to call it
that—with the American had ended badly. Stephen's perversions were
exposed by the American who was fearful of being exposed herself.
Stephen went to London, wrote a successful novel, and then moved to
Paris where she continued to write and seclude herself from society.
When World War I broke out, she joined an ambulance unit and
eventually fell in love with another driver named Mary. Although they
lived together after the war, this relationship, too, ended badly when
Stephen pretended to have an affair with yet *another* woman in an
attempt to push Mary into the arms of a man named Martin.

Katherine was stunned. It was an appalling story. And depressing.
And unnatural. She could see why this book must have been banned. She
walked to the window. The sky was just beginning to lighten. In different
circumstances, it was one of her favorite times of the day. But after
having not slept, after having too much whiskey, and after reading that
story, the coming dawn did little to inspire her.

Katherine folded her arms closer to her body and pressed her wrists
against her ribs. She was at a loss as to what to do—how to respond? Or
should she not respond? Which would be the better route? Should she
confront Annie? To do so would make clear once and for all that she
wasn't interested—that she wasn't like Annie. Or Stephen. Or any of the
characters in the book. She turned to stare at the offending volume. She
wanted it out of her sight.

"I'll return it," she said. Her voice was raw from fatigue and the
whiskey. "Today. Without a word. I'll simply hand it back to her. Or
perhaps put it in her locker."

She contemplated her options. To simply hand it coldly back to Annie
would certainly get the point across. But what if Annie made a scene? It
was better not to do it in public, she decided, though she didn't want to
return it in private either. Who knew where that would lead? No, putting
it in Annie's locker was the best choice.

Katherine considered what she should write.

> *Dear Annie:*
> *Thank you for the book but I'm not interested . . .*

No, she didn't want that sentiment on paper. Even unsigned it
suggested too much.

Dear Annie:
I read the book you loaned me and would appreciate in the
future if you . . .

Katherine frowned. Still the wrong tone.

Dear Annie:
Please . . .

In her mind, she saw a blank sheet of paper with the single word scrawled in black ink. Please . . . what? She had no idea what she wanted to say. Perhaps a letter was unnecessary. Just the return of the book with no acknowledgement or discussion would suffice. By saying nothing, perhaps she was saying everything. And, really, hadn't everything already been said? She should simply rewrap the book, put it in Annie's locker, and pretend the whole thing hadn't happened.

Katherine turned back to the window. She needed to pull herself together. She grabbed her cigarettes. There were only a couple left. She pulled one out of the case, pressed it to her lips, and picked up her lighter. The hand that held the flame trembled. *Nerves,* she thought as she took a long, unladylike drag, held the smoke deeply in her lungs, and exhaled slowly. The sky was still lighter. She looked down at her watch and sighed. It was almost time to get ready for work. She would need a lot of coffee this morning. And more cigarettes.

She smoked in silence for several minutes before snubbing the cigarette in the amber-colored glass ashtray and turning to the desk. She rubbed her eyes, took a deep breath, and picked up the book.

KATHERINE GLANCED AROUND the nearly-empty department. It had been a slow morning with only a couple of customers and even those were more interested in looking at the displays than actually buying anything. Two women lingered near the larger of the two round displays, their heads bent together as they fingered the gloves. The taller of the two said something that must have been amusing because both women laughed. The shorter woman touched the other woman's arm in a way that was almost intimate, Katherine thought. She frowned. Were they . . . ? Could they be . . . ? She closed her eyes and shook her head. It was the book. It had corrupted her thoughts. She needed to rid herself of it.

Lips pressed together, Katherine turned to Claire, who was bent over a box looking for a replacement for the size-six gloves they had sold the day before. She was humming "Isn't it Romantic" as she worked.

Katherine took a deep breath. *Now was as good a time as any.* "Claire. Could you cover for me? I need to go to the ladies room. I think I may have started my period."

Claire straightened and turned to Katherine. "Of course." She lowered her voice. "Do you need anything? I think I have everything in my locker if you need it."

Katherine shook her head. "I should be fine. I try to make sure I have something when it gets close—you know, just in case."

Claire nodded and patted Katherine's arm. "I'll cover here. Oh, and I have some aspirin if you need it. It's in my purse in my locker."

THE EMPLOYEE ROOM was empty when Katherine entered. This was the time of day when she knew she would be least likely to run into anyone. She walked quickly to the wall of lockers, opened the one with her name on it, and removed the bag containing the book. She had carefully rewrapped it, using the same paper in which it had been delivered. The package felt heavy in her hands. The fear of being caught caused her pulse to throb in her temples, accentuating the headache that stemmed from a likely combination of whiskey, lack of sleep, and nerves. She made a mental note to get the aspirin out of Claire's purse.

Katherine glanced over her shoulder to ensure she was still alone and scanned the lockers, looking for Annie's name. Originally, the attempt had been made to alphabetize. But with people coming and going, the system had become a mishmash of intermingled letters. Annie Bennett's locker was located between Esther Stephenson and Maurice Talbot on the second-to-bottom row.

Katherine stooped, pulled open the metal door, and slid the book into the locker. She began to close the door.

"What are you doing?"

Annie, of course.

Katherine closed her eyes and sighed. Annie must have seen Katherine leave the glove department and left her own post to see what was wrong.

"I'm returning your book to you," Katherine said as she straightened, though still facing the lockers.

"Which book?" Annie asked. "If I'm correct, you have several of my books."

"Which book?" Katherine spat out. "What do you mean *which book*? Which book do you think?"

She spun to face Annie who stood just inside the closed employee room door. She was wearing a dove-gray dress and her arms were crossed defiantly across her stomach. She looked thinner than usual, Katherine noted. And paler. She looked as if she had been sleeping no better than Katherine had herself.

Annie's lips were pressed together although one corner of her mouth twitched. "I don't know what you're talking about."

Katherine stared at her and was suddenly furious. "Don't you? Did you think I wouldn't know? Sneaking it into my locker that way? What were you trying to do with that lurid trash? Did you think that by getting me to read about it I would change my mind?"

Annie smirked. "Me think she doth protest too much."

"What?" Katherine spat.

"You heard me," Annie said.

Katherine glared at Annie, who calmly stared back. "I think I've made clear to you—"

"That you're not interested," Annie said. "I know. That you're not like that. I know that, too. But tell me you didn't read the book. Tell me you weren't compelled to read it, despite your abhorrence of me . . . of what I am. You seem to know enough about what it contains to pretend to be disgusted."

Katherine scowled at her and shook her head in protest. "How dare you—"

"You can protest all you want, Kate. You can say we're just friends, that what you read in that book was appalling to your sensibilities," Annie said quietly, calmly. "Fine. But you know as well as I do that's not the case."

"You took advantage of me," Katherine protested.

"You kissed me back," Annie countered.

"You don't know what you're talking about," Katherine snapped.

"Don't I?" Annie strode up to Katherine and stood too close in front of her.

Katherine pressed herself flat against the lockers. She could feel Annie's heat and thought she was going to kiss her again. She waited, heart pounding, but Annie just looked at her.

"It didn't mean anything," Katherine said almost defiantly.

"You can convince yourself of whatever you need to sleep at night." Annie leaned forward and raised herself so her mouth was close to Katherine's ear. "You can think what you want, but I did not take advantage of you." She turned and walked out the door.

ANOTHER SLEEPLESS NIGHT, Katherine thought as she lay on her bed and stared at the now familiar cracks in the ceiling. She had thrown off the covers and lay in her nightgown, her arms and legs splayed across the bed. It was too humid to sleep—not that her mind would slow down long enough to allow her the luxury. She wondered, briefly, idly, if Annie were sleeping. Or was she lying in her narrow bed, smoking a cigarette, and replaying the events in the break room as well.

Katherine thought about what had happened—about the confrontation and Annie's words. "You can protest all you want, Kate. You can say we're just friends, that what you read in that book was appalling to your sensibilities. Fine. But you know as well as I do that's not the case."

She *had* been appalled by the book. She hadn't wanted to read it. Not really. Or had she? a little voice in the back of her brain chided.

"You kissed me back," Annie had said.

She had been right. Katherine *had* kissed her back. But it had been a reflex. That's what you do when someone kisses you, she reminded herself. You kiss them back. She had kissed plenty of men and most of them had meant nothing. How was this kiss any different? But even as she asked herself the question, she felt a pressure in her chest and knew that if she were honest, it had been different.

"It didn't mean anything," she had said.

"You can convince yourself of whatever you need to sleep at night," Annie had responded.

Oh, but that was the irony, Katherine thought. She wasn't sleeping— hadn't slept well in weeks.

It was amazing how one moment's indiscretion, a single minute, could change everything. In the blink of an eye, Katherine had lost a dear friend and begun to question everything she thought she knew about herself. She had always been different. She hadn't wanted to stay in Big Springs. She hadn't wanted to marry. She hadn't wanted to follow the route that had been prescribed for her. But did that make her one of *those* women.

Katherine had seen plenty of them in their neighborhood. Not only was Near North Chicago an artistic enclave but also it was the main rooming-house section of the city for single men and women. She had seen several women strolling along in pants or the more extreme, in men's clothing. She had viewed them as a curiosity, nothing more. They had never appealed to her. They were frightening. But Annie was nothing like them. She didn't swagger or act like a man. She was forthright and bold, yes . . . but not masculine. So, how could it be that she was a . . . she didn't even want to think the word.

Irritably, she rolled onto her side. For weeks she had tried to pretend the kiss hadn't happened—tried to erase it from her memory. But the closeness of Annie's body today as she had stepped forward and the familiar mix of lavender and body lotion, had brought it all back. Her stomach knotted and her heart beat faster as she recalled the firm softness of Annie's lips. She felt again the soft grip on her shoulders and remembered Annie's face tilting upward, her eyes closed with those impossibly long eyelashes. She jerked awake. She had been dozing.

"I need to put an end to this once and for all," she murmured and flopped onto her back. And the best way to do that would be to clear Annie out of her life. Once she had rid herself of that influence, these thoughts would disappear. She would start with the books.

It felt good to have a plan, Katherine thought as she got out of bed and pulled on her summer robe. She crossed the room quickly, switched on the lamp next to the bookcase, and studied the titles. Annie was right— she did have several of her books. Methodically, she pulled them off the shelf. All in all, there were seven. She set them on the table and scanned the room. Annie had a bad habit of forgetting things, and Katherine saw several of her possessions—an umbrella, a lighter, and a fountain pen. She quickly gathered them up and set them on top of the books.

It was Saturday. As soon as it was appropriate, she would put everything in a bag and take it to Annie. It would simply be a case of knocking on the door, returning her things to her, and explaining that she had thought about it and that their friendship was too difficult right now. She would be polite, to the point, and then leave. Problem solved.

Several hours later as she stood outside Annie's door, she began to question whether or not her plan was such a good idea. Perhaps she should just leave the bag in the hallway outside the door. That would express her sentiments, wouldn't it? Everything that needed to be expressed had been said the other day, hadn't it? The less contact the better. She bent to place the bag against the door when it suddenly swung open.

"Kate?"

Katherine looked up, stricken and embarrassed to have been caught. She quickly straightened.

Annie was in her robe, her hair down and sleep tousled. Beside her stood a tall, dark-haired woman in street clothes. They both stared at her. Annie glanced briefly at the woman and returned her gaze to Katherine, her forehead puckered in a tiny frown.

"I've come to return your books," Katherine said weakly.

Annie nodded, but didn't speak.

The woman smirked. "I was just leaving," she said to Katherine and turned to Annie. "You know where to find me."

Katherine watched as she leaned forward and kissed Annie lightly on the lips. Annie blushed and nodded, but didn't say anything. The woman looked at Annie for a moment longer before shouldering past Katherine and disappearing down the stairs.

"I was just returning your books," Katherine repeated.

"Come in," Annie said.

Katherine shook her head. "I can't. I have to be . . . to meet . . ." She paused, looked toward the stairs, and back at Annie. "Who was that woman?"

Annie sighed, glanced down the empty hallway, and gestured for Katherine to come inside. "Please just come in. I don't want to disturb the neighbors."

Katherine stepped into the room.

Annie closed the door behind them and went to the middle of the room. "Would you like some coffee? Or tea? I think I have some tea somewhere."

Katherine put the bag containing the books on the table. She noticed the empty whisky bottle, the glasses rimmed with lipstick, the full ashtray, and the disheveled bed. She realized that this woman had been here all night. She was suddenly angry.

"Who was that woman?" she asked again, surprised as she felt a surge of something that felt absurdly like jealousy.

Annie looked uncomfortable. "She's a friend." She turned to pour coffee into two cups.

"A friend?" Katherine said tightly. "Is that all?"

Annie turned in surprise. "Why does it matter?"

"It doesn't," Katherine said in a dismissive tone. "It's just that if you're going to flaunt your—"

"If I'm not mistaken," Annie said, "you came here, to my home, unannounced. I would hardly call that flaunting anything."

Katherine stared and said almost defensively, "I just came to return your things."

"So you said," Annie said. "Thank you."

Katherine blinked, unsure how to respond but still fully aware of the anger making her temples throb.

"Is there something you want to say?" Annie asked finally, a small smile playing on her lips.

"No," Katherine said, "it's nothing."

"Really?" Annie asked. "Because you seem bothered by the fact that Margie was here."

"I'm not." Katherine stared at her as she tried to hold in her anger.

Annie nodded.

"I'm not. I just find it odd that you profess your . . . that you kissed me and then . . ." Katherine shrugged.

"But you're not interested in me as anything more than a friend," Annie said.

"No, I'm not."

"And the fact that we kissed meant nothing to you—did nothing for you."

"No, it didn't," Katherine said.

Annie stepped close enough that Katherine could smell the faded scent of her perfume, the stale residue of whisky, and something earthier. Katherine forced herself not to back away.

"So then why do you care who that was?" Annie asked softly and held out one of the coffee cups.

"I don't," Katherine murmured, accepting the cup and looking away.

"Mm," Annie murmured as she stepped back. The sound had a smugness to it that irritated Katherine. Annie's expression, when Katherine finally met her gaze, echoed the sentiment.

"I'm not like you," Katherine protested. "You seem to think that I wanted you to kiss me. But I didn't. And anyway, one kiss doesn't mean anything. It doesn't make me . . ."

Annie crossed her arms and smirked. The gesture made Katherine suddenly furious. How *dare* Annie stand there making judgments about her when she knew nothing about who she was or what she wanted?

"I'm leaving." Katherine slammed down the cup, not caring that the liquid sloshed over the rim and onto the table. "I just came to return your things and to tell you to leave me alone. I've done that, now."

"Fine," Annie said.

Katherine raised one hand as if to make a point and then dropped it to her side. Her head pounded. The room was too small, too warm. She needed to leave. She took several steps to the door. Annie grasped her wrist. Katherine spun around. Annie slid her hand up around Katherine's neck, pulled her face roughly down, and kissed her—insistent and thorough, unlike the gentle and hesitant first kiss. Annie's lips and tongue explored Katherine's. Katherine trembled as Annie tightened her grip on her neck and pressed herself into her with surprising strength. Katherine let herself lean into Annie's embrace. The kiss was as good as before. Better. The word rang like an alarm in her brain—better. No, it couldn't be. It wasn't.

"Stop." Katherine panted and stepped back. She staggered slightly, as did Annie. They were breathing heavily, and Annie looked as conflicted as Katherine felt. She sucked her bottom lip into her mouth as they stared at each other.

"I need to go," Katherine said numbly.

"We need to talk about this," Annie said.

"There's nothing to talk about," Katherine said as she raised a shaky finger to her swollen lips. "If I find more of your things, I'll just leave them in your locker at work."

Blindly, she turned and stumbled for the door.

CHAPTER 11
Lawrence, Kansas, 1997

JOAN LEANED BACK in her chair and sighed deeply. She had read all but one letter and found that she was no closer to understanding what had happened with her mother and "A" than she had been after reading the first letter. With a small frown, she brushed a strand of hair from in front of her eyes, tucked it behind her ear, and looked down at her list of notes.

"I need a drink," she murmured as she tapped her pen on the pad of paper.

She looked at her watch. It was almost eight o'clock. Surely liquor stores were open in Lawrence until at least ten. But did she really want to go out for just a bottle of wine? *And*, she thought, *I really shouldn't be drinking anyway*. Not with the baby. But she was probably going to get rid of it anyway, wasn't she? Her mind stopped for a moment. Well, wasn't she? She shook her head. Too much thinking was not good.

"Focus on the list," she said. "And if it doesn't pass, then you can go get something."

Joan looked back down at her notes. None of it made sense. She wished for the hundredth time that Bud would simply tell her what he knew—or at least shed some light on her mother's life during the years in question. She tossed her pen onto the table and wearily rubbed her eyes. All she could glean from the letters was that her mother had had an affair that began in Chicago when she worked at Sears in the 1930s. She had gone to the Chicago World's Fair with "A" who apparently liked to read, smoked, was a terrible singer, bought her a ring she had admired in an antique shop, and was an amazing lover. She again thought of Mark and the way his strong hands had stroked her body. And look where that had gotten her. She stroked her stomach. Had her mother considered an abortion?

"She would have been happier," she murmured. "She could have run away with 'A' and read books and lived happily ever after."

But she hadn't. Katherine had stayed with Clyde, given birth to their daughter, and seemed to have, in many ways, regretted her life choices until the day she died. She had fulfilled her obligations even though her heart was broken. Why?

Joan pushed the chair away from the table and wandered into the darkened living room. She knew she needed to work on her inventory of the house and figure out what to do with her mother's things, but instead, she sank heavily into her mother's rocking chair and stared out the window. How often had her mother sat there, enveloped in darkness, watching the comings and goings of her neighbors? There was so much she realized yet again that she didn't know about her mother. In her mind, Katherine had always been a somewhat cold and aloof person incapable of loving anyone or anything. But nothing could have been farther from the truth. Clearly, her mother had been a woman who not only loved, but loved deeply and passionately—a woman who had made hard decisions and endured the consequences of those decisions. Was that what Joan, herself, had to look forward to?

The ringing of the telephone shook her out of her reverie. She waited for the machine to pick up before remembering that her mother hadn't believed in answering machines. "If someone really wants to talk to me, they can just call back," she said every time Joan suggested she invest in one. The memory made her smile.

She stood, walked back into the kitchen, and picked up the receiver. "Hello?"

"Hi." It was Luke. "We just got back from pizza and the kids wanted to say good night."

Joan smiled, surprised at his consideration. "Thanks. How are things there?"

"Okay," he said. "Chicago plays at home this weekend so it should be a good game."

"Oh," Joan said and wondered how that was an answer, but chose not to pursue it. "So, outside of sports, how are things?"

"Good," Luke said and then hesitated. "So, when are you coming back? Any idea?"

The newness of being Mr. Mom had clearly worn off. Joan realized he hadn't called so the kids could say good night, but rather so he could find out when she was going to come home.

"It's probably going to be at least a couple of weeks," she said, not knowing if that was the case, but wanting to torment him with the possibility of having sole responsibility for the kids and the house for as long as possible.

"Oh. Really? Because I was thinking—"

"I talked to Uncle Bud," she said quickly, not waiting for him to tell her that she needed to come home sooner rather than later.

"Oh yeah?" he asked, clearly uninterested. "How was that?"

"Interesting," Joan said. "He has good days and bad. I guess on the bad days, he tells all sorts of strange stories. In fact, he told Barbara that my—"

"Hey, Sarah's standing right here," Luke interrupted. "She wants to say 'hi.'"

Joan heard the phone being handed off.

"Hi, Mommy," Sarah said. "I miss you."

"Hi, sweetie," Joan said. "I miss you, too."

"When are you coming home?" Sarah asked.

"I don't know," Joan said. "There's a lot to do here with Grandma's stuff."

"Can I come there?" Sarah asked. "Dad's no fun."

Joan laughed softly. "No, sweetheart. I'm sorry, but I've got lots of work I'm doing here and you have school."

Sarah sighed dramatically.

"But I'll tell you what," Joan said. "When I get back, we'll go out for some girl time. Just you and me. How's that?"

"Good," Sarah said, the pout still in her voice.

"So, are you being good?" Joan asked. "How's school?"

"It's okay," Sarah said. "Jennifer Fraser told everyone her parents are getting divorced because her mom likes other girls."

"Oh," Joan said, unsure how she should react to that information.

"Yeah," Sarah continued. "Tessa and Dawn made fun of her, but I think it's okay. You know?"

"Yeah," Joan replied.

"So, can I go to Jennifer's house for a sleep-over?" Sarah asked. "She invited me, Leslie, and Sara H."

"You'll need to ask your father," Joan said.

"He said to ask you," Sarah said.

"Well, he and I will talk about it, but I don't see why not," Joan said. "When's the sleep-over?"

"Friday night," Sarah said.

"Okay," Joan said. "So, how are other things?"

"Good," Sarah said.

Joan waited for more and, when she realized no additional information was forthcoming, opened her mouth to ask another question.

"Hey, Mom, I've got to go."

"Okay, sweetie," Joan said. "Well, I love you. Have a good day at school tomorrow."

"I will," Sarah said. "Love you, too."

Joan waited for her to hand the phone back to Luke, but after several seconds of silence, realized that her daughter had hung up. She stood, receiver in hand, as she considered what to do. She could call back but the idea of talking to Luke made her change her mind. Instead, she replaced the receiver and walked back into the living room. Beneath her weight, several of the floorboards creaked. She stopped and rocked on one of the loudest. After deciding that it was just old wood rather than something that needed to be replaced, she continued on to the large picture window and sank into her mother's chair. Without really seeing, she gazed out the window for several minutes and then leaned her head back and closed her eyes.

She jumped at a knock on the front door. She must have dozed off.

"Joanie? Are you there?"

It was Mrs. Yoccum.

Joan went to the door and flipped on the porch light. Mrs. Yoccum, blinking against the sudden burst of light, stood on the porch—a tiny form in jeans, a bulky University of Kansas sweatshirt, and a blue, nylon windbreaker.

"Hi Mrs. Yoccum," Joan said as she pulled open the door, wondering, even as she asked, how her mother's neighbor navigated the steps in the near darkness. "Is everything all right?"

"Oh, yes, dear. I just . . ." Mrs. Yoccum shrugged. "I just wanted some company. I wasn't sure you were here, though, what with all the lights off. But then, I thought to myself, think how often Kate did that same thing. Like mother like daughter, eh?"

She laughed. The sound was light and musical, and for just a moment, Joan could imagine her as a young woman. She smiled and flipped on the entryway light.

"Company would be nice," she said and stepped back to allow Mrs. Yoccum to enter. "Come in."

Slowly and carefully, Mrs. Yoccum stepped over the threshold and into the entryway. She glanced around and up the stairs to the shadowed second floor.

"How is the packing going?" she asked.

"I'm making some headway," Joan said. "Would you like to sit in the living room?"

Mrs. Yoccum peered into the darkened room and smiled.

"I would. Your mother and I used to sit in the living room near the window. She would light some candles, and we would sit and talk." She paused and looked up into Joan's face. "I love the light they cast—even with my poor old eyes."

Joan smiled. "I think I can find some if you'd like."

Mrs. Yoccum removed her jacket and hung it over the back of Katherine's chair. "I think you'll find them in the bottom drawer of that sideboard."

Joan blinked, saddened to realize that Mrs. Yoccum knew her mother's house better than she did. Dutifully, she went into the dining room and pulled open the bottom drawer. Inside were several candles, holders, and matches.

"You were right," she called as she chose several of the largest and lit the curled, burnt wicks. She walked slowly and carefully into the living room, holding the candles before her, their flames bent back by the forward motion. She set them down on the table and pulled a chair forward. She sat across from Mrs. Yoccum who smiled into the candlelight.

"It just seems so much more romantic," she said thoughtfully before raising her gaze to meet Joan's. "Not in the love sense. More in the fanciful sense—like everything is wrapped in a cloak of unreality."

Joan nodded.

"Your mother used to say that," Mrs. Yoccum added.

Despite herself, Joan made a noise of derision, and Mrs. Yoccum smiled. "Oh, I know you think she was cold and hard, but she wasn't. She was just damaged."

"What do you mean?" Joan asked and leaned forward. It hadn't occurred to her, but her mother and Mrs. Yoccum had been close friends for decades. Joan and Mrs. Yoccum's son, Jason, had played together when they were children. Perhaps Mrs. Yoccum could answer her questions.

"She was damaged by life," Mrs. Yoccum said. "It can make a person bitter."

Joan frowned and waited for Mrs. Yoccum to continue. When she didn't, she said, "I know Mom didn't love Dad."

Mrs. Yoccum looked up but still said nothing.

"And I think it was because she was in love with someone else," Joan said. "Did she ever talk to you about her life when she lived in Chicago? In the '30s?"

Mrs. Yoccum studied her for several seconds before nodding slowly. "She did."

"Was there someone there?" Joan asked quickly. "Someone whose name began with the letter 'A'?"

"Why are you asking all these questions?" Mrs. Yoccum asked.

Joan took a deep breath and pressed on. "I know Mom was having an affair while she was married to Dad. I also know that she didn't want me—that she didn't want to have a child."

Mrs. Yoccum frowned slightly. "How do you figure that?"

"I found a box," Joan said. "A wooden box with sealed letters. Wrapped in a scarf."

Mrs. Yoccum looked startled. "Letters?"

"Yes," Joan said quickly. "Love letters. Addressed to a man she only identifies with his first initial. 'A.'"

Mrs. Yoccum sat slowly back in her chair.

"I know I probably shouldn't have read them," Joan continued. "But Mom's gone and they seemed important. Do you know who 'A' is? Can you tell me what happened?"

Mrs. Yoccum stared past Joan into one of the dark corners of the room. After several long seconds, she sighed deeply. "You have to appreciate the fact that Kate didn't want to marry your father. She only did it to save her reputation—and perhaps to get even." She shook her head sadly and returned her attention to Joan. "So much had gone wrong. After what happened with Claire . . . well, in a lot of ways, that was the turning point."

Joan frowned. "Who is Claire?"

"Claire was a woman who worked with your mother at Sears," Mrs. Yoccum said. "She took care of Kate when she first moved to Chicago." She laughed. "Got her into some trouble, too, I expect, but she took care of her. She showed Kate how to have fun."

"What do you mean?" Joan asked, unable to imagine her mother being playful.

"Your mother led a sheltered life," Mrs. Yoccum said. "She grew up during Prohibition and moved to Chicago during the Depression. She was one of a million single girls who moved to the big cities searching for excitement. She didn't know a soul. Claire took care of her, helped her find a decent place to live, introduced her to people."

"So, Claire . . . I guess I don't understand," Joan said and shook her head. "What does this have to do with 'A'?"

"What happened to Claire made your mother understand what was important in life," Mrs. Yoccum said.

"What do you mean?'" Joan asked. "What happened to Claire?"

"It's such a long story," Mrs. Yoccum said, her voice suddenly weary. "And it's one that I promised your mother I'd never tell you."

"Why?" Joan asked.

Mrs. Yoccum stared into a candle for several seconds. She sighed but still didn't speak.

"Mrs. Yoccum, she's not here anymore and this is something I need to know. Please."

"I'm sorry, Joanie, but I can't," Mrs. Yoccum said.

Joan sighed in frustration and rubbed at her eyes. "So, what *can* you tell me? Why did my mother marry my father instead of this other guy?"

"It's just so complicated, dear," Mrs. Yoccum said. "The abridged version is that Kate married your father because she was hurt and angry and scared."

"I don't understand," Joan said again.

Mrs. Yoccum sighed. "I know you don't. Let's just say that there were circumstances in Chicago that resulted in your mother coming home. And she married your father because he was," she shrugged, "safe. He always had a thing for the Henderson girls . . . Wilma . . . Jeannie . . . Kate. You know that."

Joan nodded.

"He had his sights set on your mama long before she knew it," Mrs. Yoccum continued. "But Clyde was smart. He knew she didn't love him. But he convinced her that they could have a marriage of convenience. And Kate was so heartbroken that she agreed. She didn't realize that he actually *was* in love with her."

Joan nodded thoughtfully. "When you say heartbroken . . . do you mean 'A' broke her heart?"

"In a way," Mrs. Yoccum said.

"But at some point they reconciled," Joan said. "It says as much in her letters."

"They did." Mrs. Yoccum nodded. "But there was no way she could have resisted. It takes a strong person to deny their true love. And your mother wasn't that person."

"So, when did they pick back up?" Joan asked.

"When your father went away to the shipyards during the war," Mrs. Yoccum said.

"World War II," Joan said.

Mrs. Yoccum nodded.

"But how?" Joan asked. "My mother was here then. She stayed at the homestead in Big Springs. She took in a boarder for money."

"Yes," Mrs. Yoccum said.

"So he came here?" Joan said.

Mrs. Yoccum nodded.

"During the war," Joan said thoughtfully. "And continued after. Until she got pregnant with me?" She paused, running the dates in her head. "Did it end because of me?"

"No," Mrs. Yoccum said. "It ended before that. But that didn't matter to your father. When he found out about the affair, he was furious."

"So, why didn't she leave him?" Joan asked.

Mrs. Yoccum raised her thin shoulders in a slight shrug. "She got pregnant with you."

Joan frowned. "Pregnant by my father?"

"Yes," Mrs. Yoccum said.

"*After* he found out about the affair," Joan said. "So he knew she had cheated on him. He knew she was in love with someone else. But they were . . . intimate?" She shook her head. "That doesn't make sense."

The image of sleeping with Luke immediately after realizing she was pregnant with Mark's child popped into Joan's mind, and she felt her face flush. She was glad for the dim lighting. She shifted uncomfortably.

Mrs. Yoccum, for her part, said nothing and, finally, almost guiltily, Joan forced herself to meet her gaze. Her features were cast in shadows, and Joan couldn't see her expression though she could sense she was waiting for her to take the next logical step. Though she didn't want to, she felt like she had to ask the next question.

"My father *is* my father, correct?" she asked.

"Yes," Mrs. Yoccum said softly.

"So they had sex," she said.

"Yes," Mrs. Yoccum said again.

"After he found out about the affair," Joan pressed.

Mrs. Yoccum nodded. "The day he found out."

Joan narrowed her eyes. "What do you mean? Did she do it to convince him the affair was over or . . . what? Was it make-up sex?"

Mrs. Yoccum returned her gaze to the candle.

"Mrs. Yoccum, please tell me," Joan said.

"He . . ." Mrs. Yoccum hung her head and slowly shook it. "Keep in mind he secretly loved your mother."

Sudden realization flooded Joan, making her feel sick and weak. Her pulse thudded in her temples. She trembled and inhaled sharply. "Oh my god, it wasn't just sex, was it? She didn't have sex with him to make up or to keep him. She didn't want to have sex with him at all."

Mrs. Yoccum swallowed and studied her with kind eyes. She touched Joan's knee with a gnarled hand. "Sweetheart—"

"He forced her," Joan said. "Didn't he?"

"Joanie," Mrs. Yoccum said softly. "You have to understand."

"Oh, I understand, all right," Joan said, angry, appalled, and conflicted at the same time. "No wonder she hated me."

"There's no excuse for what he did," Mrs. Yoccum said. "He spent all those years in love with her, waiting for her to love him, too. When he found out it would never happen—when he found out *why* it would never happen—it sent him into a rage. I don't even think he knew what he was doing."

Joan wildly shook her head. "Oh, I think he knew what he was doing."

She remembered some of the late night arguments between her parents. She remembered, too, her father's temper and the sting of his belt when he spanked her for indiscretions.

"He raped her," Joan said dully, almost to herself. Understanding flooded her. "No wonder she hated me."

"Your mother didn't hate you," Mrs. Yoccum said quickly. "She hated your father and what he did to her—what he took from her . . . but she never hated you."

Joan suddenly remembered what Barbara had said about her father talking about helping to cover up a murder. Could they have had something to do with the death of "A"? She wanted to ask if Mrs. Yoccum knew anything about it, but realized that she probably wouldn't divulge any more than she already had.

They sat in silence.

"Well," Mrs. Yoccum said finally and pushed herself to her feet. "I'd better be getting home."

Joan rose awkwardly, still stunned by what she had learned but wanting to know more.

"Could we talk again?" she asked as Mrs. Yoccum shrugged into her jacket, the satiny nylon making a *sczhing* sound. "Maybe tomorrow?"

"Maybe later," Mrs. Yoccum said. "But I've really told you all I can without breaking my promise to your mother. Besides, you've got a lot going on right now. This can wait."

"No," Joan said. "I'm not sure it can."

"Well," Mrs. Yoccum said, touching Joan's arm. "When you reach my age, you realize what a waiting game life really is. Seems we're always waiting for something."

They walked in silence to the door.

"Let me walk you home," Joan said as she flipped on the porch light and turned to look for her shoes.

"No, dear," Mrs. Yoccum said. "But thank you."

Joan watched as Mrs. Yoccum made her careful way down the steps and along the sidewalk to her own yard. The motion-sensor light snapped on, illuminating her path up her own front steps and into her house. She waved before going inside and pushing the door closed behind her.

With a sigh, Joan turned off the porch light, locked the door, and wandered back into the candlelit living room. She felt numb, overwhelmed at what she had learned and furious at her father. Though they might not have considered it rape back then, that's exactly what it was. And it now made sense why her mother had resented her. And it made sense why she had hated her father so much. But why, if she had reconciled with "A" had she stayed with Clyde? None of it made sense.

Joan sank back down into her mother's chair and stared at the flame of the candles, mesmerized by the way they danced and swayed. She again touched her stomach and thought about the unwanted baby growing inside her. She was almost certain she was going to Wichita for an abortion. Had Katherine considered the same thing? Had it even been an option?

Perhaps, Joan thought dully, her mother should have had an abortion. Perhaps she would have been happier if she had. Life was all about choices. And she had a choice she had been avoiding making.

"Soon," she promised herself. "Soon."

CHAPTER 12
Chicago, Illinois, 1933

KATHERINE CROUCHED AMIDST the rows of wooden card catalog cases and flipped through the slender drawer of neatly-typed note cards. The librarian had assured her that the book she was looking for, *As I Lay Dying,* would be listed here but she hadn't had any luck finding the correct call number.

"Damn it," she muttered as she pushed the cards back and began to go through them again. "Why do they have to make it so—ah ha." She triumphantly located the card in question. She turned slightly, picked up the request slip, and, using her knee as a desk, began to copy down the call number. She heard the soft clearing of a throat and craned her head up and froze. Annie. Katherine's heart thumped faster and her stomach tightened. She slid the drawer closed, stood upright, and started to walk away.

"Kate," Annie whispered. "Please."

Katherine wasn't sure what she expected, but the utterance of that single word, "please," stopped her. She stood for several seconds, her back still to Annie. Her chest rose and fell rapidly as she tried to catch her breath.

"Just . . ." Annie paused. "Just please hear me out."

Katherine turned and met Annie's gaze and was shocked by what she saw. Annie's eyes were as large and dark as ever. But the glimmer of amusement, as if she were inwardly laughing at her own private joke was gone, and they now looked haggard, the delicate skin beneath them smudged with purplish shadows.

"Are you following me?" Katherine hissed and looked around to see if anyone was watching them. "What are you doing here?"

Annie frowned. "I came to check out some books. And then I saw you." She looked at Katherine. "We need to talk."

"I really can't," Katherine said and looked down at her watch. "I'm actually just leaving. I have to meet—"

"This is ridiculous," Annie hissed. "You've been avoiding me for weeks now. Why?"

Katherine jerked her eyes to meet Annie's which were no longer simply tired, but also angry. "You know why."

Her voice was louder than she had intended, and she glanced around to see if anyone had heard her. Thankfully, the library seemed to be fairly empty.

"Look," she continued in a softer voice. "I understand that you're a . . . a . . ." She faltered. "But I'm not. And I don't like the way you look at me. I don't like the way it makes me feel."

Annie nodded solemnly, much as she had the first time Katherine had seen her standing with Mr. Ansen, nodding at something he was saying to her. Her expression was unreadable.

"Annie," Katherine began, her voice gentler. "I like you. But only as a friend. That's all it will ever be."

"But—" Annie began.

Katherine held up a hand. "That's all it will ever be."

Annie gazed at her for long moment, her expression pained. She blinked and nodded. "I understand. But what about our friendship?"

Katherine sighed and looked instead at the librarian seated at the circulation desk. She didn't know what to say. A part of her was drawn to Annie—as a friend, she clarified to herself. She enjoyed their time together—felt as if they shared a common intellect. But there was an equally large part of her that was scared of what she would be opening herself up to by remaining connected to Annie.

"We're still friends," she said finally. "But you have to promise that what happened before can never happen again. And you also need to agree that when we spend time together, it will be in the company of others or in public places."

She stole a glance at Annie. She looked elated and disappointed at the same time but swallowed and slowly nodded acquiescence.

"And I need your word that we will not talk about . . ." Katherine searched for how best to phrase it. Nothing came to mind. "About what happened ever again."

Annie nodded and stuck out her hand. Katherine stared down at it, noticing the long fingers, the narrow, upturned palm. She remembered those fingers on her jaw, gently guiding her face as Annie had intensified their kiss. She blinked away the memory and glanced at Annie's face. Her eyes registered amusement at Katherine's reaction—amusement and an unspoken challenge. Katherine jerked her chin defiantly and extended her own hand. Annie grasped it firmly. Her hand was warm and dry. Katherine knew hers was moist and perhaps a little clammy.

Annie laughed.

"What?" Katherine asked sharply, wondering if Annie was amused by her nervousness.

"Nothing," Annie said with a small shake of the head.

"Tell me," Katherine insisted.

Annie pressed her lips together. She shook her head again. "It's nothing." She glanced down at their still-joined hands.

"I don't believe you," Katherine said as she, too, looked at their hands and quickly pulled hers away.

Annie sighed. "I was just making a promise to myself and laughing at the incongruity of it."

"And that was . . . ?" Katherine asked even as she wondered why she was being so insistent. She knew she was treading on dangerous ground and even as she didn't want to hear what Annie had to say, she knew the larger part of her did. She felt Annie's eyes studying her and, after a moment, met her gaze. She was unprepared for the jolt of . . . what? She didn't know what to call it. Excitement? Nervousness? Giddiness? She blinked, though she was unable to look away.

"I promised myself," Annie said finally, her voice soft, her eyes locked on Katherine's, "that next time, you would come to me."

Katherine jerked backward as if she had been struck. "Didn't we just agree not to discuss that?"

"We did," Annie said. "But you insisted on knowing what I was thinking. You can't have it both ways, Kate."

"This isn't going to work," Katherine said with exasperation and took a step backward. "Clearly this can't work." She looked down at the slip that now was crumpled in her hand. She had forgotten she even held it.

"Kate—" Annie said and reached out as if to touch her.

Katherine slapped her hand away. "Please leave me alone. If you really consider me a friend, just leave me alone."

She turned and walked quickly away.

KATHERINE WAS SITTING in her room later that evening when she was startled by the soft knock on her door.

"Kate? You in there?"

It was Claire. Katherine set the book she was reading on the table, rose, and went to the door. As she reached for the handle, she heard Claire's exaggerated whisper again.

"Kate. Are you—?" Claire blinked, startled when Katherine opened the door. "You're here."

Katherine smiled and stepped back to allow her to enter the room. "Of course I'm here. Where else would I be?"

Claire started to answer, shook her head, and smiled. As she stepped into the room, Katherine saw her face in the light. Her eyes were red and swollen as if she had been crying.

Katherine's smile faded into a frown. "Claire, what is it? What's wrong?"

Claire wandered around the room, her back to Katherine. She stopped at the table and idly picked up the book Katherine had been reading. "*Alice's Adventures in Wonderland.* Did you bring this from home?"

Rather than answer, Katherine closed the door and went to Claire. She tipped her head downward and touched Claire's upper arm. "What's wrong?"

Still not looking up, Claire shrugged, dropped her head, and hunched her shoulders. Katherine put a hand on her back, but said nothing. After several seconds, Claire shuddered, and Katherine realized she was crying. Carefully, she turned Claire and pulled her into her arms. The sobs became louder and more violent. The low keening that came from deep in her body was jagged and raw.

"Shhh," Katherine murmured. "Shhh. It's going to be all right. Whatever it is, it will be all right."

"No . . . it . . . won't," Claire cried, her words uttered between ragged sobs. "It won't."

"Is it Lenny?" Katherine asked. She felt, rather than saw, Claire's nod. "Did you two have a fight?" Again, Claire nodded.

"Oh, sweetie, just give it a couple of days," Katherine said. "It will all come out in the wash."

"It . . . won't," Claire hiccupped. "It won't."

"Whatever it is, it can't be that bad," Katherine said.

Rather than reassure her, the words seemed to make Claire cry harder. "Oh, Kate." She gulped. "If you only knew."

"Knew what?" Katherine asked. "What is it?"

I'm . . .." Claire took a deep breath and straightened. She raised her eyes to meet Katherine's. They were bleak, sorrowful. "Oh, Kate. I'm pregnant."

Despite herself, Katherine gasped. Tears spilled from Claire's eyes.

"How?" Katherine asked.

"How do you think?" Claire asked miserably.

"But, I mean, I thought you were careful," Katherine said.

"We are. Well, most of the time. He always pulls out before . . .." She sniffed. "But there were a couple of times . . . Oh, Kate, what am I going to do?"

"Pulled out?" Katherine said. "Why didn't he use . . . ?" Although she wasn't as worldly as Claire, she understood that the only way to prevent something like this was to use a condom.

"He doesn't like them," Claire said as she again sniffed and used the back of her hand to wipe her nose. "He says they make it harder for him to feel anything."

"But Claire—" Katherine began.

"I know, I know," Claire said and inhaled deeply. She looked past Katherine to a spot on the wall and slowly let out the air in her lungs, her cheeks puffing out in a way that at any other time would be funny.

Katherine simply watched her, waiting for a fresh round of tears.

"Shhh," she said as Claire's body shook with more sobs. "It's going to be all right."

"No it won't," Claire said. "You don't understand. Lenny is furious. He says I'm trying to trap him—to make him marry me. He says . . . I have to get rid of it."

"Claire," Katherine said, shocked. "You're not going to, are you?"

"I don't know," she cried miserably. "I don't want a baby—not alone. And he made it clear he won't help. Oh, Kate, I barely make enough to take care of myself. I just . . . I can't have it."

"You could go to one of those homes," Katherine said. "For unwed mothers. You could have it and then give it to an orphanage."

Claire pulled back to stare bleakly at Katherine. Her eyes were red and watery. Her nose was runny. Her chin quivered as she tried to speak. "I couldn't do that. Besides, if I have it I'll lose Lenny for good."

"Lose him?" Katherine exploded. "Who cares? Any man who acts like this after what he has refused to do isn't worth your time."

"You don't understand," Claire said. "I love him. I can't be without him."

"I thought you didn't want to get serious," Katherine said. "I thought you said you liked him because he was fun and carefree. What happened to that?"

"I love him," Claire said, simply. "I can't lose him."

She stared pleadingly into Katherine's eyes.

At a loss as to how she should respond, Katherine shook her head and gave a helpless shrug. "I don't know what to say. What do you need me to say?"

"I don't know," Claire said. "I . . . I don't know."

Katherine could feel fresh tears seep through her blouse and wet her skin. Gently, she stroked Claire's hair. They stood for a long time until Claire's sobs subsided.

"I need a favor," Claire said.

Katherine tensed. She knew Claire felt it, too.

"I can't do this alone," Claire said. "I need you to go with me when I have it done." She grasp Katherine's wrist and squeezed it tightly.

"I–" Katherine began.

"Please, Kate," Claire whispered. Her eyes were pleading. "Lenny says he knows of a doctor who can do it."

"Claire . . ."

"He's going to pay for it," Claire said quickly.

"Pay for it?" Katherine exclaimed. "He needs to go with you. He's the one who got you in this mess."

Claire dropped her gaze to her hand gripping Katherine's wrist. "He said he would, except that he's not good in those sorts of situations. He doesn't like blood or seeing women cry."

"Uh huh," Katherine said and pressed her lips together in irritation.

"Please say you'll come with me," Claire said as she shook with new sobs. "I don't think I'll be able to do this alone."

Katherine sighed and pulled Claire almost roughly against her. As Claire sobbed, she watched their blurred reflection in the window. She wondered briefly, what Annie would do in this type of situation? Likely, she would go find Lenny and do to him what they did to the bulls back in Big Springs. The thought made her smile even as she rocked Claire gently.

"Shhh," she murmured. "Of course I'll go with you. If that's what you decide to do, I'll go with you."

Her words seemed to cause Claire to cry harder.

"I'm going to go to hell," Claire said. "But I can't keep it."

"How long have you known?" Katherine asked. "Are you sure?"

"I'm sure," Claire said. "I suspected a couple of weeks ago. But the last couple of days, I started getting sick. In the mornings. That's why I had to leave the counter the other day."

Katherine nodded and sighed. "And it couldn't just be something you ate or . . . ?" She raised her eyebrows and tipped her head.

"No," Claire said miserably. "I'm sure."

"Do you want a drink?" Katherine asked. "Something to steady your nerves?"

Claire nodded, and Katherine gestured toward the chair. Claire sat with her arms folded tightly against her body and rocked slightly. Katherine watched her for several seconds and retrieved the bottle of gin. As a rule, she preferred whiskey, but the gin was cheaper. She brought two glasses to the table and set them down.

"Single or double?" she asked and opened the bottle.

"Triple," Claire said with a weak smile.

Katherine poured the clear liquid into the glasses and slid one over to Claire who picked it up, drank heavily, and grimaced.

"Have you tried gin?" Katherine asked.

"Of course," Claire said. "You've seen me drink it a hundred times."

"No. For the . . ." Katherine gestured with her glass at Claire's midsection. "You know."

Claire blinked and recognition crossed her face. She lowered her eyes and nodded. "I tried it as soon as I was sure. You remember the other morning you said I looked like I'd had too much fun the night before? Well, it wasn't fun. I sat in the hottest bath I could stand for an hour and drank the whole bottle. It didn't do anything but make me sick."

Katherine nodded. "There are pills. You remember Rose Cochran in hosiery? I heard that she got some pills and—"

"Lenny asked around. They don't work." Claire held up her hand. "And don't even suggest throwing myself down the stairs. I'd be more likely to break my neck than lose it. And then I'd be paralyzed *and* pregnant." She shook her head. "This is the only way."

Katherine sat heavily down on the wooden chair across from Claire. It creaked with her weight and for a fleeting moment, she wondered about its stability. She sighed deeply.

"Who is this person that Lenny found to do the . . . ?" Katherine searched her mind for an appropriate word. "To get rid of it."

Claire took another large swallow of gin and shrugged. "I don't know. It's a doctor who does it out of his home."

Katherine gaped. "Is that safe? Does he know what he's doing?"

"Lenny said that a friend of his took his girl there," Claire said. "He isn't one of those butchers you hear about. Lenny says he knows what he's doing."

"As if he would know," Katherine muttered under her breath. She looked at Claire. "So when are you supposed to go?"

"Saturday night," Claire said tonelessly. "Lenny can't get the money until he gets paid on Friday."

She took Katherine's hand and squeezed tightly. Katherine felt as if the bones in her hand were being crushed. She looked down at their joined hands and saw that Claire's knuckles were white.

"I'm scared," Claire whispered. "I'm so scared."

Katherine nodded and placed her free hand over their clasped hands. "You don't have to do this." She kissed Claire's forehead. "You don't have to."

"But I'm going to," Claire whispered and rocked back and forth. "I'm going to."

THE DOCTOR'S RESIDENCE turned out to be less than a mile from their boarding house. Though it was already dark and not in the safest part of Near North, they walked there, knowing they would undoubtedly need to take a taxi cab home and Lenny, who had given Claire an envelope of cash the night before, hadn't included enough money for them to ride both ways.

"Is this it?" Katherine asked with a frown as she surveyed the building fronts. She flicked her lighter and squinted down at the smudged piece of paper in her hand. "There are no house numbers. It just gives the cross streets and a description of the building."

"I think this is it," Claire said dully. "Lenny said his friend said it was right in the middle of the block." She sighed and pointed toward the alley. "We're supposed to go in through the back. There's a towel hanging on the doorknob. Lenny said to knock twice, wait, and then knock three more times."

Katherine pressed her lips together, nodded tightly, and snapped closed her lighter. "You're sure you want to do this? You can still change your mind."

In the faint light shining from the buildings on either side of the street, she could see Claire's outline—a dark, shadowed form that shifted from side to side. Ghosts of the flame from her lighter floated across her vision.

"I'm not going to change my mind," Claire said. "I can't."

"All right," Katherine said. "Then, let's go around the back."

She stepped forward and linked her arm with Claire's. They walked around the corner to the alley that ran between the buildings. The air there seemed cooler, and Katherine could smell the dank odor of standing water and a strange sour aroma. Claire hesitated and then stepped resolutely forward.

"We're going to need some light," Katherine murmured and again flicked open her lighter.

The flame did little to cut through the darkness. They neared the middle of the alley, stopped, and Katherine swung the lighter to either side. Several feet forward and to their right, she saw a wooden door with a light-colored dish cloth hanging limply on the knob.

"Guess that must be it," Katherine murmured. Although her voice was low, the sound seemed amplified. Claire didn't answer and for several seconds, they stared at the dish rag. A dog barked in the distance and from somewhere nearby, Katherine could hear the faint strains of music being played on a radio.

Claire took a deep breath and stepped to the door. She clenched her hand into a fist, rapped twice, waited a second, and rapped three more times. Katherine could hear the sound of someone coming to the door, the sound of a lock disengaging, and the knob turning.

The door swung open, and Katherine could see a faint light from somewhere deeper inside the residence.

"Mrs. Wilson?" a man's voice asked.

"Yes," Claire said.

"Come in," the man said. "Quickly."

He pulled the door open, ushered them inside, and closed the door behind them. Katherine could hear the sound of the lock being reengaged. The man snapped on the light. Katherine blinked, momentarily blinded.

"So, which of you is Mrs. Wilson?"

Katherine studied the man. He was tall, thin, and had a kind face.

"I'm Mrs. Wilson," Claire said and stepped forward. She partially extended her hand and then hesitated and pulled it back.

The doctor was dressed in a white button-down shirt with the sleeves rolled to the elbows. His dark pants were held up by black suspenders.

He smiled kindly at Claire. "Nice to meet you." He inclined his head in a sort of bow. "I'm Dr. . . . Smith."

He turned his attention to Katherine and repeated the gesture. Without thinking, Katherine imitated his movement but didn't offer her name.

Dr. Smith returned his gaze to Claire and looked her up and down critically. "I'd say you're a couple of months along, then?"

Claire nodded. "Two or three, I'd guess."

"Which is it?" Dr. Smith asked, his eyes still appraising her midsection.

"Probably closer to three," Claire admitted and glanced in embarrassment at Katherine, who tried not to appear surprised at this new information.

Dr. Smith nodded and cracked each of his knuckles, his eyes still fixed on Claire. "Three might make it more difficult. Has the . . . ?" He cleared his throat. "Have you felt any quickening?"

Claire shook her head.

"All right," he said.

The slow, methodical *snap, snap, snap* of Dr. Smith working his knuckles made Katherine flinch. She looked at his hands. They were thin and delicate—the type of hands she would imagine belonging to a clarinetist or a pianist.

"You said difficult," Claire said faintly. "Difficult how?"

She looked ghostly in the harsh light of the kitchen.

"Nothing to concern yourself with," Dr. Smith said and ceased the pulling of his fingers. He turned his attention to Katherine and smiled again. "Moral support?"

Katherine nodded.

"Well." He returned his attention to Claire and raised his eyebrows expectantly. "Do you have the . . . fee?"

Claire nodded and pulled the folded envelope from her purse. "Lenny. My husband sent this to give to you."

Dr. Smith smiled apologetically and took the envelope. "Thank you. I'm sorry that I have to charge for this service, but given its illegal nature . . ." He shrugged. "Well . . . you understand."

He dipped his head, peered into the envelope, and shuffled through the bills with his thumb. "Well. Everything appears to be in order. If you'll just come with me to my office, we can proceed."

Claire turned and searched Katherine's face with pleading eyes. "Don't leave me?"

"No, of course not," Katherine said.

They followed him out of the kitchen and past a parlor where a woman and two young girls sat sewing. None of the room's occupants looked up as they passed, and Katherine wondered how many times they had seen this scene played out.

"After you," Dr. Smith said as he turned on a light and held the door open for them.

The room was a doctor's office with an exam table to one side, a screen on the other, and rows of glassed-in cabinets along the back wall. A paper-laden desk sat under the front window, which had the shade drawn and the heavy cloth drapes pulled.

"It's where I work during the day," Dr. Smith explained. "I only use it at night for . . . emergencies."

Claire took a deep breath and nodded. Katherine stared around the room.

"You can step behind the screen to disrobe," Dr. Smith said with professional courtesy. "Just your skirt and under things. There's no need to expose your upper body. You'll find hooks back there for your clothes and a sheet for you to wrap around your waist."

Claire nodded and disappeared behind the screen. Katherine followed and held out her hand for Claire's purse. She placed both of their purses on the seat of one of the chairs near the desk and watched Dr. Smith lay out his tools, which consisted of a three-inch round mask, several bottles of clear liquid, a syringe, and a long, curved piece of metal with a strange attachment on the end.

He looked up to see her watching him and smiled kindly. "Would you like to come closer? I would be happy to explain what everything is."

Katherine shook her head quickly. "No, thank you."

He nodded and turned to open a drawer. Inside were several neatly-folded sheets. He removed one and spread it over the examination table.

Behind her, she could hear Claire undressing.

"Kate?" she asked. "Could you help me?"

"Of course," Katherine said and stepped back behind the screen where Claire was fumbling with the closure at the back of her skirt.

"Let me," Katherine said as she leaned down to help.

Claire nodded gratefully and allowed Katherine to work the button and zipper. Once they were undone, Katherine slid the skirt down until Claire could step out of it. Katherine busied herself with folding the skirt while Claire removed her underwear. Katherine turned to see Claire standing awkwardly with her lower half completely exposed and slip bunched up around her waist, and looked quickly away. She took the folded sheet that was hung neatly on the back of the chair and handed it to her without looking.

"I'll just wait for you out there," Katherine said, still with her head turned away from Claire. Claire took the sheet, and Katherine stepped back out into the office.

Dr. Smith stood expectantly next to the examination table. He had pulled a white smock on over his clothing and was rubbing his hands together as if he again wanted to crack his knuckles.

He gave Katherine a small, distracted smile, and turned his attention to the screen. "Is she . . . ?"

Claire stepped into the office.

"Mrs. Wilson."

Claire stood like a statue, her lower half wrapped in the sheet, her eyes cast downward, her gloved hand clutching the metal frame of the screen.

The incongruity of the gloves struck Katherine, and she leaned toward Claire. "Your gloves," she whispered.

Claire looked at Katherine, then at her gloves, and then back at Katherine. She blinked several times.

"Do you want to take them off?" Katherine asked, still in a whisper.

Claire shook her head. Surreptitiously, she tapped her thumb against the third finger on her left hand.

Dr. Smith watched the exchange without comment, though he smiled when Claire turned her attention to him.

"I'm ready," she said.

He nodded and stepped backward, his body blocking the view of the carefully laid-out instruments.

"Please step this way." He gestured toward the examination table.

Claire walked toward him and gracefully, despite the sheet around her waist, climbed onto the examination table.

"All right." Dr. Smith patted her leg. "Now, if you could just slide backward and then lay back . . . Excellent." He went to the side of the table and pressed on her stomach.

Katherine again noticed his slender fingers. The gold of his wedding band caught the light as he pressed and prodded.

"All right. I'm going to wash my hands in an alcohol bath so they're clean and then we'll proceed with the internal examination." He turned away and dipped his hands in a bowl of clear liquid and wiped them carefully on a towel on the counter. "Now," he faced Claire, "if you could please put your feet up and slide down to the edge of the table we can get started." He sat on a stool in front of her bent legs. "And if you could relax your thighs."

Not wanting to see Claire in such a vulnerable position, Katherine went to stand in front of the bookshelf full of medical texts. They all appeared to be in good condition and several, she noticed, appeared to have been used frequently.

"All right," Dr. Smith said finally and stood. "Give me a moment and we can get started."

Katherine turned and peeked at the table. Dr. Smith had draped a second sheet over Claire's knees so that her most intimate parts were hidden from view. She went to stand at Claire's head. Despite the chill of the room, Claire was sweating.

She stared up at Katherine with fear in her eyes. "I'm scared, Kate."

Katherine winced at the use of her real name and glanced at the doctor to see if he had noticed. If he had, he didn't react.

"It's going to be all right," Katherine said and brushed the sweaty, auburn curls off Claire's forehead. "It's going to be all right."

"Stay with me?" Claire took her hand.

Katherine hesitated and nodded. "If Dr. Smith says it's all right."

"If I say what's all right?" he asked as he went to the other side of the table near Claire's head.

"If she stays with me," Claire said.

"As long as she stays where she is, I don't see a problem with that," Dr. Smith said and smiled down at her. "You probably won't know she's here, though."

He held up the cone and the dropper of ether.

"I'll know," Claire said.

"Of course," Dr. Smith said and put the cone over Claire's nose and mouth. "I'm going to place this here and put the drops on the cone. Just continue to breathe normally. You will probably feel strange for a couple of seconds and then you'll sleep. When you wake up, the procedure will be finished, and we can talk about what you need to do for the next couple of days so you'll heal properly."

Claire inhaled deeply and nodded. Her grip on Katherine's hand was so tight it felt as if the bones were being broken.

"Let's get started, then," Dr. Smith said.

He squeezed the rubber end of the dropper and several clear, fat drops of liquid fell onto the mask. Claire stared into Katherine's eyes and after only a couple of seconds she blinked heavily. Her eyes slid closed for the last time, her body jerked, and her hand relaxed.

"It's normal," Dr. Smith said to Katherine as he removed the mask and placed it on the counter. "There is a sensation of falling when the patient succumbs to the ether."

He returned to his stool in front of Claire's bent legs, eased them gently apart, and adjusted the sheet so it tented over her knees. With quiet efficiency, he dipped his hands again in the alcohol, dried them, and picked up a complicated-looking metal implement. Katherine averted her eyes and looked instead at the hand clasped in her own.

Dr. Smith hummed softly to himself as he worked. It took Katherine several minutes to determine that it was "Rock of Ages." She continued to stare at Claire's hand, sometimes glancing into her face. In her peripheral vision, she could see Dr. Smith occasionally turn to the tray on the counter for a particular tool.

The sounds coming from his work were moist and squishy. At one point, he cursed and grabbed a basin. Katherine could hear the wet splats as he filled it with the contents of Claire's womb.

After what seemed like an eternity, he stood, washed his hands, and dipped them again in alcohol. As he dried them, he turned to Katherine. She raised her eyebrows.

"It's done," he said and draped the used towel over the basin containing the bloody tissue.

"And everything's all right," Katherine asked.

Dr. Smith hesitated and nodded. "Yes. I think so."

"Think so?" Katherine asked.

He sighed. "The procedure didn't go quite as easily as I had hoped. I'm sure it's nothing to be concerned about. It was just a larger fetus than I had anticipated."

He picked up the basin, carried it to the counter, and placed it in front of the row of glass canisters that held cotton balls and other paraphernalia. He walked back to the table and peered under the sheet.

"She's going to be okay, though, right?" Katherine asked.

"There may be more bleeding than normal, but otherwise, I think it was a successful procedure," he said and glanced at the clock on his bookshelf. "She should be coming around."

Dr. Smith pulled out a retractable extension to the examination table and gently extended Claire's legs. Once she was prone, he covered her body with the sheet.

"As she becomes conscious, she might jerk and fight a little," he said. "It's normal. We just need to make sure she doesn't roll off the table."

As if she had heard him, Claire moaned softly and tossed her head.

Katherine looked down and squeezed her hand. "Sweetheart," she said in Claire's ear. "You're okay. I'm here."

Claire struggled to open her eyes and shifted on the examination table. The movement must have hurt because she winced and moaned.

"Claire," Katherine said, not caring that she was using Claire's real first name. "Sweetheart, it's okay. It's over. I'm here."

Claire's eyes fluttered open, and she looked wildly around the room. "Where . . . ? Is it . . . ?"

"It's over," Katherine said again. "You're fine."

Claire struggled to sit up.

"Oh, no, Mrs. Wilson," Dr. Smith said and pressed her back onto the table. "You need to rest for just a little while." He smiled kindly. "It's a fairly simple procedure, but it's important for you to rest for a bit and then, when you go home, stay in bed for a couple of days." He patted her arm and looked down at her, his expression serious. "Now, do you feel alert enough for me to discuss what you need to do for the next few days? Or should we wait a bit."

"You can explain it now," Claire said. "Ka—my friend will help me explain your directives to my husband."

"All right," Dr. Smith said and glanced at Katherine to make sure she was in agreement. "You should avoid any strenuous activities for the next few days. No hot baths. Get as much rest as you can and use a hot water bottle for cramps and pain. And no marital activity for several weeks."

Katherine and Claire nodded.

"You will have some bleeding for the next couple of days. And there will be cramping similar to what you experience each month during your menses." He paused for them to ask questions.

His eyes flicked to the screen where Claire's folded clothing and purse had been left and then back to Claire. "Did you bring your sanitary cloths and belt with you? I mentioned it to your husband."

Claire shook her head, looking miserable.

"Well," he said kindly, "I'll give you a cloth to put into your underwear until you get home."

Claire nodded.

"Do you have any questions?" he asked and glanced again at the clock. Katherine wondered if he had another appointment after theirs.

"I don't think so," Claire said.

"What if there are complications?" Katherine asked pointedly.

Claire jerked her attention to Katherine and then back to Dr. Smith. "Complications?"

"There shouldn't be, but if there *are* complications, you should, of course, get in touch with me," Dr. Smith said evenly to Katherine. "And in the event that you can't reach me and you have to go to the hospital, well . . . it would be best if you didn't divulge my name."

"Complications?" Claire asked again. "What sort of complications?"

Dr. Smith looked down at Claire and patted her shoulder. "The biggest concern is that the bleeding doesn't stop. Some bleeding is normal. But too much is dangerous—though I don't think that will be an issue." He smiled tightly. "You should be able to get up now, so I'm going to step out of the room and let you get dressed." He looked at Katherine. "Take your time. Just open the door when you're ready and I'll see you out."

He turned and quickly left the room.

Claire closed her eyes and breathed deeply. "I'm so glad it's over."

"How do you feel?" Katherine asked.

"Like I've been kicked in the stomach," Claire said.

"Oh, Claire," Katherine said. "I'm sorry."

"It's done," Claire said. "Thank God."

"Do you want to get up or do you need to rest more?" Katherine asked.

"I want to go home," Claire said. "I want to go home and lay down in my own bed. Will you help me?"

Katherine nodded and slid her hand under Claire's shoulder to help her rotate into a sitting position. She paused as Claire winced in pain.

"Okay?" Katherine asked.

"Yes," Claire said after a second and swung her legs to hang over the edge of the table. "Will you help me down?"

Katherine offered her arm, and Claire leaned heavily against it as she slid to the floor. She blinked and swayed slightly.

"All right?" Katherine asked.

"I will be in a second," Claire said. "I just felt a little light-headed."

She leaned back against the table for a few seconds. Levering herself forward, she slowly walked toward the screen. Katherine hovered at her side.

"I think I can get dressed by myself," Claire said wearily once she sat down on the wooden chair.

"I'll be just over there if you need anything," Katherine said and stepped back out into the office.

As Claire dressed, Katherine wandered around the room and examined the contents of Dr. Smith's cases. Most contained bottles of various colored liquids and containers of medications.

"I'm ready," Claire said.

Katherine turned to see Claire fully dressed and slightly hunched over. Her gloved hands were crossed over her abdomen.

"You look like hell," Katherine said.

Claire smiled wearily.

Katherine smiled back. "I'll get Dr. Smith." She opened the door and poked her head out. He was standing down the hall, looking into the parlor where his wife and daughters sat. "We're ready."

He nodded, said something to his family, and came to meet them. "How are you feeling, Mrs. Wilson?"

"I've felt better," Claire admitted. "But now that I'm up and about, I feel better. Just weak."

"Well, that's to be expected," he said and led them down the hallway, past his wife and daughters who again didn't look up, and into the kitchen.

As soon as they reached the door and Katherine put her hand on the knob, Dr. Smith turned off the lights. Katherine opened the door, and she stepped into the dank, sour alley with Claire.

"How are you doing?" Katherine asked as they paused on the sidewalk. "Better?"

Claire nodded and leaned heavily on Katherine's arm. "Yes. Though I would be happy to have a cab right about now."

"I'm not sure we'll find many here," Katherine said and looked around, worried. "How about we get you to a place where you can sit, and I'll go up to one of the main streets and flag one down? Then I can come back for you."

Claire pursed her lips in thought and shook her head. "I'd rather walk toward home than sit by myself. It's not that far."

"Several blocks," Katherine said dubiously. "Dr. Smith said not to do anything strenuous."

"I don't know as I'd consider that strenuous," Claire said. "And honestly, the sooner we get home, the better."

"All right," Katherine said and extended her arm. "But the minute you begin to feel badly, you'll let me know?"

Claire nodded.

IT TOOK FORTY-FIVE minutes to get back to their rooming house and at no time did a taxi cab pass them.

"God damn Lenny," Katherine muttered under her breath as she helped Claire climb the stairs to their rooms.

"It's not his fault there aren't any cabs on the street," Claire said weakly.

"No, but it's his fault that we're here in the first place," Katherine said. "And it's entirely his fault that he's too much of a coward to bring you here himself or at least arrange for a car to pick you up."

"I don't want to talk about that now," Claire said. "I'm just glad to be home. I know I'm not supposed to take a bath, but I could stand to wash off."

"You probably can do that much," Katherine said. "Do you want me to bring you some water?"

They stood in front of Claire's door, and Katherine fumbled with the key.

"Not yet," Claire said. "I think I'd like to lay down. I'll wash after I rest."

Katherine nodded and helped her to the bed where she gingerly sat and leaned down to unlace her shoes.

"Let me," Katherine said and knelt to help.

"I'm so tired," Claire said. "Do you think it's from the ether?"

"Perhaps," Katherine said. "Or maybe it's just the anxiety from the experience. Or loss of blood."

"Was there a lot of blood?" Claire asked.

"I don't know," Katherine said honestly. "I didn't watch. I couldn't."

Claire nodded and slowly swung her feet onto the bed. "Could you get me some aspirin?" She curled onto her side and closed her eyes. "They're in that tin on my dresser." Katherine brought her the aspirin and poured a glass of water from the pitcher on the table. Claire opened the tin, tipped five aspirin into her palm, and held her hand out for the glass of water. She swallowed the pills in a gulp and set the glass on the nightstand. "Wake me in an hour so I can change the cloth?"

Katherine nodded and put her hand on Claire's forehead. It was warm. "Would you like me to stay?"

"No," Claire said and closed her eyes. "I think, if you don't mind, I'd just like to be alone."

Katherine nodded, backed out of the room, and pulled the door quietly closed behind her. Her steps were heavy as she walked down the hallway to her own room. Once inside, she turned on the reading lamp and sank onto the bed, exhausted, numb, and oddly distanced from her own body.

"There but for the grace of God," she said softly and thought about Alex. Granted, the relationship had ended almost as soon as they had taken it to a sexual level, but still, the feeling of being with him stuck with her—so much so that it hadn't been uncommon to run into each other and fall back into bed. She thought briefly about those fumbled, clumsy meetings and felt almost as if she had somehow avoided a calamity. The feeling made her long for a drink. She wanted to blot out the images and sounds she had just witnessed. She found too, to her surprise, that she wanted to talk to Annie.

"Ridiculous," she muttered and rose to get the bottle of gin from the shelf. A glass she had used that morning sat on the table, and she picked it up. She poured several fingers-worth into the glass and, without putting down the bottle, tipped the contents down her throat. She sighed at the heat as it slid down her throat and into her empty stomach, and immediately poured a second glassful. This time instead of drinking, she placed the bottle on the table and grabbed her cigarette case.

Her fingers trembled as she took her first, deep drag and pulled the smoke into her lungs. She counted to ten before exhaling slowly. The action reminded her of Annie, and she picked up the glass. Within minutes, the combination of the gin and the cigarette began to work its magic. She felt calmer and her brain was finally slowing down. She took another, final pull off the cigarette and snubbed it out. Her limbs felt heavy, and she stretched back out onto the bed. Despite herself, She thought about Annie. What, she wondered again, would Annie say about the situation.

Katherine jolted awake with the unsettling sensation that she had left something undone. She looked frantically around the room before remembering that she had taken Claire to Dr. Smith and now, Claire was resting in her own room.

"Oh my God, Claire." She looked at her watch. It was well past two a.m. She jumped to her feet and hurried toward the door. The hallway was dark. She strode toward Claire's room. She could hear Dorothy snoring from her room down the hall. She paused for a moment at Claire's door and knocked softly.

"Claire," she whispered loudly. "Are you awake?"

When she heard no response, Katherine eased open the door and stepped inside. Claire had turned off the light, and in the dim light from the street, Katherine could see the dark shape on the bed.

"Claire," Katherine said again. "Sweetie, wake up. I'm here to check on you."

Careful not to disturb her, Katherine crept closer to the bed and put her hand on Claire's forehead. It was cool—almost too cool. She frowned and slid her hand down Claire's shoulder. Gently, she shook her. Claire didn't move. Katherine shook her again, this time harder.

"Claire?" she asked sharper and louder.

Claire still didn't respond.

Katherine turned the lamp on next to the bed. She stared aghast. Claire lay sprawled, her legs awkwardly splayed. Her hands and her dress were covered with blood. A deep crimson stain had spread across the coverlet beneath her body.

"Oh my God. Claire!" She shook Claire's shoulder hard. "Claire. Claire."

Claire made no response.

"I need to get help." She hesitated. She couldn't leave Claire, not like this. Perhaps she could get one of the other girls in the building to go for help. She looked around for Claire's purse. It lay on the table. She picked it up and dug around for the piece of paper with Dr. Smith's telephone number on it.

She raced down the hall to Dorothy's room. "Dorothy. Dorothy. Wake up." She knocked, softly at first and then louder. "Dorothy!"

The snoring stopped, and she knocked again.

"Dorothy!"

She heard the movement of feet padding to the door.

"Who is it?" Dorothy asked.

"It's Kate," Katherine said. "From down the hall. Open up. I need your help."

Dorothy opened the door and peeked out. She was wearing a long nightgown and her hair was in rollers, secured in place with a scarf. She blinked sleepily and rubbed her eyes.

"What's wrong?"

"It's Claire," Katherine said. "She needs a doctor. I don't want to leave her. Could you go downstairs and see if Mr. and Mrs. Andersen would let you use the telephone? It's an emergency."

Dorothy stared. "What's wrong with Claire?"

"Just call this number," Katherine said. "Ask for Dr. Smith. Tell him that there's been a complication with . . ."

To tell Dorothy to use the name Mrs. Wilson would immediately generate questions. But to not tell her would complicate the situation even more. She considered again going downstairs to call Dr. Smith herself, but somehow knew she needed to stay with Claire. She cleared her throat.

"Tell him that there is a complication with the procedure he performed earlier and that the patient is bleeding profusely," she said. "Can you do that please? Tell him he needs to come immediately."

Dorothy nodded. "Let me get my wrap." She disappeared into the darkness of her room.

Katherine hurried back down the hall and pushed open the door to Claire's room.

"Claire," Katherine said as she went to the side of the bed and touched Claire's face. It was still cool. Frowning, she placed her hand on Claire's chest. It moved only slightly as she breathed in and out and she could barely feel the slow, faint pulsing of her heart under her palm. Hoping she was doing the right thing, she went to the closet and searched for a blanket. When she was unable to find one, she went to her own room and grabbed the quilt her mother had insisted she bring back with her the last time she had visited Big Springs. Dorothy was coming up the stairs as she hurried out of her room.

"I called," she said as she met Katherine at Claire's doorway and looked in. She gasped when she saw Claire and the pool of blood. "Oh my God, Kate. What . . . ?"

"What did Dr. Smith say?" Katherine asked as she pushed Dorothy aside and entered the room.

"He . . . he said . . ." Dorothy began.

Katherine covered Claire with the blanket and turned to Dorothy. "He said what? What did he say?"

"He said to take her to a hospital," Dorothy said.

"What?" Katherine spun around to face Dorothy. "He didn't say he would come?"

"He said to take her to a hospital," Dorothy said.

"We can't take her to a hospital," Katherine said angrily. "We can't move her. She has lost too much blood. We need a doctor. Go call Dr. Smith back and tell him that he *has* to come. And if he can't, ask him to recommend someone who will."

Dorothy nodded and hurried back out of the room. Katherine returned her attention to Claire. Her breathing had become even shallower.

"Claire," Katherine said and lightly tapped her cheek. "Wake up, sweetheart. Can you do that for me?"

Claire still didn't move.

"Please, Claire," Katherine said. "We've called the doctor. We're going to get you help."

Time seemed to stand still as Katherine waited for Dorothy to return. She leapt to her feet as Dorothy hurried into the room.

"He gave me the name of a doctor and I called," Dorothy said as she craned her head to see around Katherine to Claire. "He's on his way."

"Oh thank God," Katherine breathed.

"How is she?" Dorothy asked. Her round face was flushed with excitement and the exertion of running up and down the stairs. "Kate, what happened?"

"It's a long story," Katherine said. "Did he say how long it would take to get here?"

"He said he'd come as soon as possible," Dorothy said. "Mr. and Mrs. Anderson are waiting for him. They wanted to come up, but I told them not to."

"It's probably best," Katherine said.

"Is there anything we can do?" Dorothy asked and went to the other side of the bed.

"I don't think so," Katherine said and knelt to stroke Claire's head. "I think all we can do is wait for the doctor and pray."

Chapter 13
Chicago, Illinois, 1933

KATHERINE KNOCKED SOFTLY on the door and waited. When no one answered, she raised her fist and knocked again. After several seconds, she heard footsteps and the door swung open. Annie, clad in a nightgown, her hair disheveled and eyes puffy with sleep, peered out.

"Kate?" she asked and blinked in confusion.

Katherine nodded, not trusting herself to speak.

Annie frowned and rubbed at her eyes. "Why are you here? Is everything all right?"

Katherine shook her head. She opened her mouth to speak and closed it. She could feel the tears burning the backs of her eyes and knew she was about to start crying again. She swallowed thickly and whispered, "Claire's dead."

Annie blinked twice and lowered her gaze to take in Katherine's blood-smeared dress.

"She's dead," Katherine said again, this time louder. She started to cry.

"Come in," Annie said quickly and opened the door wider. She stepped to the side and gestured Katherine into the apartment. "Sit down."

Katherine walked numbly to the small sofa and sank heavily down as Annie went to the foot of the bed for her robe. She studied Katherine with a worried expression as she knotted the belt and went to the shelves for the ever-present bottle. On her way back to the living area, she grabbed a coffee cup that was sitting upside down on a drying towel.

"Nothing else is clean," she said. "This okay?"

Katherine nodded. Annie filled the cup halfway and handed it to her. She unceremoniously gulped the contents, exhaled sharply, and extended her arm for a refill. Annie raised her eyebrows, shrugged, and poured a second shot into the cup. She pulled one of the wooden chairs over to the sofa, sat down, and picked up her pack of cigarettes. She offered one to Katherine who shook her head slightly.

"I've had several," she said.

Annie nodded, struck a match on the side of the chair, and held it to the tip of the cigarette, which glowed brightly as she inhaled. She held the smoke in her lungs as she shook out the match and exhaled as she leaned back.

"What happened?" she asked gently.

"She was pregnant," Katherine said, still staring blankly into her coffee cup. "Lenny didn't want her to have it so he made the arrangements."

"Arrangements?" Annie asked.

"With a doctor . . . to get rid of it," Katherine said. "An abortion."

Annie nodded slowly but didn't speak.

At the silence, Katherine raised her head. "I begged her not to do it. I told her that between the two of us, we could find a way to take care of it. Or she could take it to an orphanage. But, Lenny insisted."

Annie snorted. "Typical."

"It was horrible. The doctor wouldn't even come when she started to bleed." Katherine raised the cup to her lips again. "He said there would be some bleeding and cramping, but this . . ."

She shook her head, and tears flooded her eyes, her body shaking so hard the whiskey sloshed from the coffee cup. She took several deep, gulping breaths and shakily lifted the cup to her lips and drained the contents.

"There was so much blood, Annie. It wouldn't stop. It was everywhere. I was supposed to look in on her. But I . . . I fell asleep. By the time I woke up, it was too late." Katherine gave Annie a pleading look. "I couldn't make it stop. I didn't know what to do and then it was too late."

Katherine bent forward, her head cradled in her hands. Her body shook again.

Annie snubbed out the cigarette and went quickly to the couch. "Come here." She pulled Katherine into her arms. "It's okay. Shhh. It's okay." She gently rocked her.

"I should have left her and gone for the doctor," Katherine said into the cloth of Annie's robe. "This is my fault."

"This wasn't your fault," Annie said. "You did the best you could. If anyone is to blame it's Lenny and that God damned butcher of an abortionist. They should all be rounded up and shot."

"I didn't want to take her," Katherine said. "But she was going to go regardless and I didn't want her going alone." She snuffed noisily. "It was so awful."

"Don't think about it now," Annie said, still gently rocking her. Softly, she kissed the top of Katherine's head and tucked one of the longer loose strands of hair back behind her ears. Katherine's tears flowed again, and Annie pulled slightly away. "Look at me." She cupped Katherine's puffy, tear-stained face. "This was not your fault. Do you understand? There was nothing you could have done differently."

Katherine's eyes were filled with tears but she nodded.

"You couldn't have stopped her," Annie said earnestly. "And there was nothing you could have done to save her."

Katherine opened her mouth to protest.

"Nothing," Annie said.

They stared at each other for several seconds before Annie blinked, averted her eyes, and picked up Katherine's cup. She poured more whiskey into it, handed it to Katherine, and tipped the bottled to her lips.

"I think maybe we both need a drink," she said.

KATHERINE'S FIRST SENSE when she woke the next morning was that she wasn't in her own bed. Her second realization was that she couldn't open her eyes. They were puffy, sore, and crusted shut. She lifted a hand to rub them and became aware of the warm body next to her. She groaned and wondered how she had let herself end up in bed with Alex again. She had sworn last time that—and then she stopped, remembering.

Claire.

The heavy realization made her stomach ache. Claire was dead, and Katherine had come to Annie's apartment. That's where she was now. She had been crying, and Annie had given her whiskey—a lot of whiskey. And then she had washed her face, helped her out of her bloody dress, and helped her to the bed. She was in Annie's bed—which meant that the body next to hers must be Annie. Her stomach lurched and she tried to remember what had happened after they had gone to bed. Had they . . . ?

She sat up and rubbed at her eyes. They felt glued shut. She rubbed harder and the grit gave way. She turned her head to look at Annie. She was curled onto her side on the edge of the bed. She was still in her robe. She looked quickly down to see she was wearing a faded nightgown that was far too short.

She felt suddenly ashamed. She had come to Annie for support. And after all that had happened, Annie had let her in—had taken care of her. And her first thought upon waking was that Annie had taken advantage of her.

"Shame on you," she said aloud.

"Umm?" Annie muttered sleepily.

"Nothing," Katherine said. Her head throbbed from the whiskey, and she lay back down. As soon as she closed her eyes, she envisioned Claire, covered in blood, on her bed. The realization struck her again. Claire was dead. And it was her fault because she had fallen asleep. She raised her hands to her face and tears flowed through her fingers.

Annie rolled over. "It's okay," she said in a hoarse, sleepy voice.

"I just remembered what happened to Claire," Katherine whispered.

"Oh, sweetheart, come here." Annie lay on her back and pulled Katherine into her arms.

For once, Katherine didn't worry about what touching Annie might mean, but instead, turned into her embrace and rested her head on her shoulder. Annie sighed and murmured softly into her hair until Katherine fell asleep.

Katherine opened her eyes and blinked at the clock. She had slept for several hours and was surprised she was still curled around Annie's body, her arm draped across her stomach. She shifted, and Annie murmured softly and pulled her closer. It felt good, she thought sleepily. She buried her face into Annie's neck and inhaled the familiar scent of Breck shampoo. She felt safe. Loved.

The word echoed in her brain, and she stiffened, suddenly awake and fully aware of what she was doing. She jerked abruptly away and sat up, flustered. She glanced at Annie who blinked in confusion.

"I'm sorry," Katherine said. "I didn't mean to take up so much of the bed."

She looked down at her lap and back up at Annie who was studying her with a slightly amused expression.

"It's okay," she said finally. "I'm just glad you slept."

"Passed out, more like," Katherine said and rubbed her eyes. She pushed several strands of hair from in front of her eyes and, realizing how she must look, tried to comb the rest of her hair into place with her fingers. She looked up to see Annie watching her.

"It's no use," Annie said with a small smile.

"That bad?" Katherine asked, unable to look away from Annie's gaze.

Annie nodded. "But given what you've been through, you could look a lot worse."

Katherine blinked, remembering in a rush the trip to the abortionist and Claire's death. Her eyes burned.

Annie looked down at her hands, lips pressed together. "I didn't want to ask last night, but what's next? I assume they took the body . . . I mean, took Claire to the . . ."

Katherine nodded. Blinking back the tears, she swallowed the lump in her throat. "I'm sure her family will handle the arrangements. I will . . . when I know more . . . I'll . . ."

"I'd like to go to the funeral," Annie said. "If you don't mind."

"Of course not," Katherine said quickly. "We should go together."

"I'd like that," Annie said.

"Thank you for taking care of me last night," Katherine said softly, still looking at her lap. "After the way I've acted, I wouldn't have been surprised if you had turned me away."

"I'd never do that," Annie said. "We're friends."

Katherine lifted her eyes to meet Annie's. "I know that. And if I didn't before, I do now."

KATHERINE MET CLAIRE'S parents at the train station the next day.

"They were confused and disoriented," she told Annie later that evening as they sat in Annie's apartment and sipped tea. "Part of it was that they've never been to a city the size of Chicago. But more than that they just seemed . . . lost. I wanted to help more, but they didn't want me to."

"They're probably in shock," Annie said and leaned forward to look closely at Katherine. "How are you holding up?"

"I don't know. I feel mainly . . . numb." Katherine closed her eyes and shook her head. "It's like what happened wasn't real. I'm so tired. All I want to do is sleep. But I tried to lay down this afternoon and all I could see was Claire laying there with blood everywhere."

She pushed at her eyelids with her fingertips.

"And knowing that her room, her things, her bed is just down the hall," she said wearily. "It just makes the fact that she's gone seem all that much more real."

"What are her parents going to do about the funeral?" Annie asked.

"They're taking her home," Katherine said. "As soon as the coroner releases . . . her."

Annie nodded. "Will you go? To the funeral?"

Katherine shook her head. "Her parents have asked me not to go. And they've asked me to tell the man who did this to her that he's not welcome either." She sighed. "They blame the people she knew here in Chicago for what happened."

Annie raised her eyebrows.

"They're very religious. Catholic. Apparently they didn't approve of her life here." Katherine picked up her cup and, more for something to do rather than because it was hot, blew on it. She put it down without taking a sip. "I offered to pack up her things but they made it clear they didn't want my help. It's awkward."

"Why don't you stay here?" Annie asked.

Katherine blinked and looked up, startled.

"Just for a day or two," Annie continued. "Until they are gone. It has to be uncomfortable to have them down the hall from you."

"It is," Katherine admitted. "But I don't know about staying here."

"I'm not going to take advantage of you, if that's what you're worried about," Annie said and added playfully, "Unless you want me to."

Katherine blushed as she recalled waking up next to Annie, her arm draped across her midsection. Embarrassed, she looked down at her lap.

"I'm teasing," Annie said gently. "I'm just offering you a place to stay for a day or two so you won't have to interact with Claire's family. I don't even have to be here."

Katherine looked up sharply. "What do you mean?"

"I can stay with a friend and leave you my room," Annie said. "You could make yourself at home, relax—"

"But where would you stay?" Katherine interrupted quickly.

"With a friend," Annie repeated.

Katherine frowned as she remembered the woman who was leaving Annie's room the morning she had come to return the books.

"Margie?" Katherine asked. She could hear the edge to her voice.

"Yes," Annie said.

Katherine deepened her frown, and she shook her head, suddenly furious that Annie would suggest leaving her alone in her grief to go do . . . *whatever* with that woman.

"You're kind to offer," she said tightly. "But no thank you."

Annie frowned. "What's wrong?" Her expression was one of genuine concern. She leaned forward and lightly touched Katherine's arm.

"Nothing," Katherine said and pulled away. "I appreciate the offer, but I think I probably should just stay in my own room."

Annie tipped her head to the side and narrowed her eyes. "Does this have something to do with my going to stay at Margie's? Because—"

"I couldn't care less what you do," Katherine said with feigned indifference.

Annie pursed her lips thoughtfully and nodded again. "All right. But if you change your mind—"

"I won't," Katherine interrupted. "In fact, I probably should be going. I'm tired. It's been a long couple of days and I just want to try to rest."

"Kate . . ." Annie began.

"I'm fine." Katherine stood up.

Annie also stood. They looked at each other awkwardly for several moments until Annie pulled Katherine into her arms. At the contact, Katherine felt her anger disappear, and she allowed herself to lean into Annie's body. The tears came in huge, racking sobs.

"Oh, Annie," she managed finally. "I'm sorry. I don't mean to be short with you. You've been great. I'm just so tired, and I feel like this is my fault. If I hadn't fallen asleep, Claire might still be here."

"No, sweetheart, no," Annie murmured. "It's not your fault. There is nothing you could have done."

They stood that way for a long time, Katherine crying and Annie holding her and gently rocking her.

Katherine finally broke the embrace. "I've stained your dress." She gestured to her eyes and runny nose. "I'm sorry."

It will wash," Annie said. "And, even though it might not seem like it right now, you'll heal."

Katherine sniffed and swiped at her nose.

"Are you sure you want to go home?" Annie asked. "You really can stay here. I'll run over to your room and get your things."

"No, I need to go home," Katherine said. She turned, picked up her purse, and opened it. She pulled out a handkerchief and unceremoniously blew her nose.

Annie watched her with an inscrutable expression.

"I'll see you at work," Katherine said as she shoved the handkerchief back into her purse, snapped it closed, and walked to the door. "Thank you for the tea."

Annie followed her and, as Katherine stepped to the side, reached for the knob, though she didn't open it immediately.

"Are you sure you're all right?" she pressed.

"I'm sure," Katherine said.

Annie nodded, studied her for several long seconds, and rose up on her toes and brushed a light, chaste kiss on Katherine's cheek.

Despite her weariness, Katherine felt her cheeks warm.

"Why did you do that?" she asked as Annie opened the door.

"Because you looked so . . ." She shrugged. "Broken . . . and sad."

"I am," Katherine admitted and wished that Annie would hug her again. When she didn't, she stepped through the doorway and down the hall toward the stairs. Behind her, she heard the door softly close.

"WHAT ARE YOU doing here?" Katherine asked several days later when she opened the door and found Annie standing in the hallway. "Shouldn't you be at work?"

"I begged off sick," Annie said as she took in Katherine's rumpled clothing, bare feet, and unbrushed hair. "I was worried that you were missing Claire so I came to keep you company."

Katherine smiled ruefully. "You're right." She held up the book she still clutched in her hand. "I've been trying to read, but I think I've read the same passage about two hundred times and I still don't know what it says."

Annie reached into her bag and produced the familiar Walker's bottle. "I just might have the remedy for that." She grinned. "That is, if you invite me in."

Katherine widened her eyes, and she jumped backward, pulling the door open with her. "I'm sorry. I was just so surprised to see you. I didn't mean to be rude. I . . . please, come in."

Annie stepped inside and headed to the table where Katherine sat to eat and to write letters. As she passed, Katherine caught the whiff of one of the colognes they sold at the perfume counter. It was different than the scent Annie usually wore, and Katherine wondered absurdly if it had been sprayed on for her benefit. The thought made her blink. What was she thinking, she chastised herself? Why had that even occurred to her? She closed the door and with her back to Annie, tried to compose herself. The grief over Claire's death was making her thoughts unpredictable. They were making her needy.

Katherine turned around. Annie had set the bottle on the table and was unbuttoning her coat.

"Let me take that," Katherine said and stepped forward.

Annie slid out of her coat and pulled off her gloves. She handed both to Katherine. "You can just lay them over the chair. You really don't need to worry about hanging them."

"Nonsense," Katherine said and walked to the closet.

"Mind if I use these?" Annie asked.

Katherine looked over her shoulder. Annie was holding up two small jelly jars that Katherine had brought from home.

"Those aren't glasses," she said.

"I know, but I don't care," Annie said. "And they look clean."

Katherine shrugged. "Be my guest." She carefully hung the coat and returned to the table were Annie was pouring several finger's worth of whiskey into each jelly jar.

She handed one to Katherine and raised the other. "To Claire."

Katherine raised her own glass and touched it to Annie's. "To Claire." She raised the glass to her lips.

The whiskey burned warmly as it slid past her throat to her stomach, and she closed her eyes. She opened them. Annie was in the stuffed cloth chair under the window where the light was best for reading.

Katherine went to sit on the corner of the bed across from the chair and realized just how messy the room was. The bed hadn't been made in days. The ashtray was almost overflowing with the burnt remains of cigarettes and books were stacked in crooked piles. It looked more like Annie's room than her own.

"I'm sorry everything is such a mess," she said. "I haven't been interested in housekeeping the past few days."

Annie shrugged and leaned forward, her dark eyes full of concern. "So, how are you, really? You haven't been to work and, quite honestly, you look like hell."

"I'm all right," Katherine said with a shrug. "Tired. Sad. I'll be going back to work in a couple of days." She sighed. "I can't afford not to. I just needed some time . . . alone."

She looked around the room.

"Is it hard being here?" Annie asked. "With Claire's room just down the hall?"

Katherine nodded and felt the familiar sting of tears. She covered her face with her hands.

"Oh, Kate," Annie said and stood up. She put her glass on the window sill and went to the bed. "I'm sorry. I shouldn't have asked that."

She sat down and put her arms around Katherine, who still sat with her head in her hands.

"I'm sorry," she said, slowly rocking Katherine. "I didn't mean to say that. I shouldn't have reminded you."

Katherine's shoulders shook as she cried. "You didn't remind me. I can't seem to forget it. Every time I walk down the hall to the bath or try to go out, I pass her door and it's all I can think about. I just keep replaying it in my mind, thinking about what I could have done differently." She sighed miserably and lifted her face from her hands. She swiped at her nose, embarrassed. "She took care of me, you know—when I moved here. She made sure I was safe. And now she's gone. I feel so alone."

Her body shook with a fresh wave of sobs.

"It's okay," Annie murmured. "You're not alone. You have me and you have other people at work who care about you. And your family. You're not alone."

Katherine lifted her head, her teary eyes meeting Annie's. Her nose was running.

Annie laughed softly and pulled a handkerchief from her pocket. "You do need looking after." She blotted the tears. "Blow." She held the handkerchief to Katherine's nose.

Katherine laughed, despite herself. "I can do it myself." She took the handkerchief from Annie's fingers, wiped her nose, and crumpled the cloth in her hands. "I'll wash it and get it back to you."

Annie gave a tiny smile and nodded as Katherine took a deep, shuddering breath and leaned forward, her head down, her elbows braced on her knees. Annie put her hand on Katherine's back and gently moved it back and forth.

"I've never lost anyone close to me before." Katherine straightened and turned to Annie.

Annie smiled affectionately and tucked several strands of hair behind Katherine's ear. She let her fingertips linger on Katherine's jaw.

Katherine blinked and felt her heartbeat accelerate. She stared at Annie. Her expression had gone from one of gentle affection to something else—something Katherine had seen before. Her jaw twitched, and Annie pulled her hand away. She stood quickly and walked to the windowsill for her drink.

"So, it's strange knowing you're not at work," Annie said as she settled back into the chair. "Did Ansen give you a hard time about taking off?"

Katherine shook her head. "Not really. I don't think he knows how to deal with crying women."

Annie nodded. She studied the amber liquid in her makeshift glass and gently swirled it. "I stopped by a couple of times on my way home the last few days." She didn't look up. "You didn't answer when I knocked on your door. I wasn't sure . . . I didn't know if you just wanted to be alone or if you were upset with me." She seemed to choose her words carefully. "You seemed angry with me when I offered to let you stay in my room."

"I was upset about everything that had happened," Katherine said.

"So you weren't angry?" Annie asked.

"I just wanted to be alone," Katherine said.

"Ah." Annie glanced up at Katherine and raised the jelly jar to her lips and took a sip. "But, you didn't answer my question."

"I . . ." Katherine paused, unsure how to explain what had happened—unsure if even she understood it. She sighed. "Perhaps I was a little upset."

"Why?" Annie asked.

Katherine shrugged. "I don't know. I guess it felt like you were abandoning me so you could go to Margie's." She shook her head miserably. "It makes no sense. I know that."

Annie set her glass on the table and went to sit next to Katherine on the bed. "I was trying to help. I wanted you to have someplace to go, but I also know that you're uncomfortable around me because of my . . . because of the people I spend time with."

"The women you spend time with," Katherine said pointedly.

"The women I spend time with," Annie acknowledged. "And I didn't want you to worry about me . . . to think that I would . . ." She hesitated and chewed on her lower lip as her eyes darted around the room. She took a deep breath. "I didn't want you to think that I was going to do anything to make you feel uncomfortable."

Katherine nodded. "No, you made it clear that you were going to go someplace else to do that." She was surprised at the bite in her tone.

Annie pulled back, apparently surprised as well. "You asked me where I would go. I told you the truth."

"Um," Katherine said, her voice tight.

"Kate, what is this about?" Annie asked.

"Nothing," Katherine said.

"I don't believe you," Annie said. "I was—I *am* trying to be a good friend to you. But all I seem to do is make you angry."

"I'm sad about Claire," Katherine said.

"I know," Annie said. "But I think it's more than that."

"No, it's really not," Katherine said shortly. "I just would have liked to have had you offer to stay with me rather than running off to Margie's. That's all."

Annie pursed her lips and shook her head in exasperation. "What do you want from me? I want to help. But *every time* I think I'm doing what I'm supposed to—what you need—it's the wrong thing. I'm damned if I do and damned if I don't. So now I'm asking you. What do you want?"

"I want . . ." Katherine felt her eyes sting with tears. "I want . . ." Her throat constricted. "I want things back the way they were."

She leaned forward, buried her face in her hands, and let the tears flow.

After several seconds Annie pulled her into her arms. "Shhh," she murmured against Katherine's hair. "It's all right. I'm sorry."

They sat like that for several minutes until Katherine's sobs eased, and she pulled away from Annie.

"It seems like all I do is cry," she said and opened her clenched fist to reveal Annie's wadded handkerchief. She blew her nose loudly and wiped ineffectually at her eyes with the back of her wrist.

"You are kind of a slobbery mess," Annie said as she pulled at the edge of her sleeve and used it to blot the spots Katherine had missed. She gently touched Katherine's cheek with the backs of her fingers.

Katherine's heart stopped for a moment and her breath caught in her throat.

Annie heard it and froze. She looked intently into Katherine's eyes and in that moment, Katherine understood that Annie was about to kiss her. And more to the point, she realized with surprise, she *wanted* Annie to kiss her. She parted her lips in anticipation, her breath slightly accelerated.

Annie continued to gaze at her. "Oh, Kate," she said finally, her voice little more than a whisper.

She cupped the other side of Katherine's face and gently caressed the crest of her cheek with her thumb.

Katherine could see the internal struggle reflected in Annie's expression. She leaned into Annie's hands. Annie lifted Katherine's chin and, pressed her lips to her forehead for several seconds, and sat back.

"So, when was the last time you had a meal?" Annie asked, her tone neutral and businesslike. She stood and walked toward the table.

Katherine stared at her back in disbelief, her lips still parted in anticipation of the kiss that hadn't come. She blinked and closed her mouth, unprepared for the wave of anger that washed over her.

"I'm not hungry," she said.

Annie turned, and Katherine could tell from her expression that she not only sensed her anger, but also recognized the cause.

"Kate," she said simply, "you have to understand."

"Oh, I understand," Katherine said shakily as she stood and walked to the window. "I understand all too well."

She stood with her back to Annie, her arms crossed over her chest, her hands balled into fists. She felt stupid and confused. Outside, the gloom of the day was giving way to the gloom of dusk. She heard the soft creak of the wooden floorboards and felt Annie's presence behind her.

"You just lost your best friend." Annie put a gentle hand on Katherine's shoulder. "You're grieving and in shock. This is not what you need right now."

"Please don't presume to tell me what I need," Katherine snapped, aware that her words sounded like something from one of the novels Annie disliked.

"All right," Annie said evenly. "I won't. I'll tell you what I need. I need to be true to myself. You know how I feel about you, but I don't want you this way. You've just lost your best friend and you're vulnerable. You want to be comforted and I want to help if I can. But I don't want you making decisions that you're going to regret, Kate. And quite honestly, I'm not in a position right now to do more than be your friend."

"Fine," Katherine said dully.

"You know I'm right," Annie insisted.

"I think you should go," Katherine said shortly.

"And now you're going to punish me for doing what's right for you," Annie said as she dropped her hands to her side with a small slap.

"Is that what you're doing?" Katherine asked and faced Annie. "What's right for me?" She snorted in disbelief.

"You're dealing with a lot right now," Annie said. "You're sad and confused and you don't need to add me . . . to add this . . . to the mix."

Katherine laughed bitterly.

"I care about you," Annie said finally. "And I want to help you, but I'm not going to be treated like this. If you need me, you know where to find me. I'll never turn you away, but I'm not going to come to you again."

She went to the closet, yanked her coat off the hanger, and walked to the door.

"And for the record, I know why you're angry," she said as she turned the handle. "And if you were honest with yourself, I think you do, too."

CHAPTER 14
Chicago, Illinois, 1933

IT'S SO COLD it feels like the air could break, Katherine thought two days later as she trudged to the stop for the streetcar that would take her into downtown. The morning was brittle and cold. The wind nipped at her exposed skin and tore at her coat as she stomped her feet and waited with the other passengers. The streetcar was late again.

"It's never on time in the winter," a woman behind Katherine complained loudly.

"It's never on time in the summer, either," another woman replied.

Katherine stiffened at the sound of the familiar voice. It was Annie. She felt her earlobes grow hot as she caught snatches of her conversation. "Warmer . . . work . . . stayed in bed longer." Her voice was low and playful. The other woman laughed.

Katherine flushed, no longer cold. Her heart hammered in her chest, and she stared fixedly forward as they continued to murmur to each other. She wanted to turn to see who Annie was talking to. Was it Margie? She narrowed her eyes at the thought. How dare Annie come to this stop with that woman, knowing that she might encounter Katherine. Didn't Annie care about how it might make her feel? Or was she just trying to make her jealous?

The word stopped Katherine cold as she realized the truth of it— accepted the truth of it. She was jealous—plain and simple. But it was more than the jealousy of knowing that her friend liked another friend better. What she felt as she heard Annie and the woman talking was the type of jealousy one feels about a lover. She felt sick, and excited, and giddy all at once. The truth was unavoidable, despite what she had said or tried to convince herself.

"—make a fantastic casserole," the woman was saying. "Come to my place. Let me cook for you tonight."

Annie laughed. The sound was warm and throaty. She murmured something, and the woman chuckled in response.

They're going to have dinner together, Katherine thought, and again felt the blinding surge of jealousy. She couldn't stand to be around them any longer.

She looked up, startled by the clanging of the approaching streetcar.

"Finally," Annie's friend said.

As the growing cluster of people pressed forward in anticipation, Katherine stepped slightly to the side and let the people behind her move ahead and begin boarding. Annie and the woman—it *was* Margie—passed to her right. Katherine continued to keep her face turned toward the street. From the corner of her eye, she saw Annie step toward the car and then stop as she caught sight of Katherine. Katherine felt her stomach clench and without being able to stop herself, turned her head to fully meet Annie's gaze. They stared at each other. Annie frowned slightly, her eyes unreadable.

Katherine started to speak, but stopped, unsure what to say. She imagined scenarios.

"Good morning?"

"How are you?"

"Please forgive me? I only said those things because I'm in love with you."

The sudden realization that the words were true—that she *was* in love with Annie—pushed all other thoughts out of her head. She blinked, unable to move or speak as she watched Margie grab Annie's sleeve and pull her forward and onto the streetcar.

"After you," the man said next to her, his nose and cheeks ruddy from the cold. He swept his hand forward so she could board ahead of him. She blinked at him and after a second, he repeated both the gesture and the words.

Katherine shook her head. "I . . . thank you, but . . . I . . . um . . . I forgot something." Blindly, she turned and walked in the direction of the river. Behind her, the streetcar clanged its warning that it was about to leave and began its clattering, rattling departure toward downtown.

BY THE TIME Katherine made it to work, she was more than thirty minutes late. As she snuck to the back room to clock in, she passed the shoe department and saw that Annie was changing out a display. She blushed, aware that suddenly, everything and nothing made sense. She felt her heart beat faster and she forced herself to hurry past.

Once in the break room, she stowed her things in her locker, clocked in, and headed toward her department. As she passed the shoe department, she saw that Annie had been joined by Mr. Ansen who stood in the aisle gesturing toward the new display. Katherine smiled politely in their direction, forcing herself to resist meeting Annie's gaze. She wondered if Annie had watched her walk away.

"Thanks for covering for me," Katherine said when she arrived at the glove counter. Claire's replacement, a fleshy girl named Francine had transferred from housewares. She was pleasant, but nothing like Claire.

"Not a problem," Francine said brightly. "Anything I can do to help out. What happened? Oversleep?"

"No," Katherine said. "I missed my ride. It was one of those mornings."

"Oh, I know about those. My husband is always saying I'm a day late and a dollar short." She laughed and glanced sideways at Katherine. "You'd like Jesse. He's awfully funny." She paused. "Hey, you should come over for supper some night. You can meet him and we can play cards or dominoes. I'll make a meatloaf."

Katherine smiled politely. "Oh, that's really nice, but I don't . . ." She sighed. "Since my friend Claire died, I haven't much felt like going out."

Francine smiled and patted Katherine's arm. "Well, just know that when you're ready, you have a standing invitation. I make a great meatloaf. Or, if you'd rather, I could make a casserole."

The mention of casserole reminded Katherine of why she had been late, and she felt the slow flush of jealousy rising up her chest and neck. She looked in the direction of the shoe department. She needed to talk to Annie—that much was clear. And she needed to find out what was going on with Margie. Tonight, she promised herself as she bent to remove a box of gloves from beneath the counter. She would talk to her tonight if for no other reason than to apologize for her behavior.

ANNIE WAS STRUGGLING into her coat as Katherine walked into the employee room. Around her, other employees were collecting their things and talking about the day or their plans for the evening. Unsure of how Annie would react, Katherine didn't want to risk having the conversation in front of them, but she also knew she wouldn't have a chance to talk to her alone unless they left at the same time.

"In for a penny, in for a pound," she said softly as she took a deep breath and stepped forward.

Annie was tying her black woolen scarf around her throat, her back to the rest of the room. Katherine felt a surge of panic at the thought of what she was about to do. She lightly touched Annie's arm with a trembling hand.

"Can I talk to you?" she asked in a low voice so as not to be overheard.

Annie stopped and turned to look up at her. Her dark eyes were wary and guarded.

"Please?" Katherine asked.

Annie hesitated and nodded. She nudged the door to her locker shut and walked to the doorway where she waited for Katherine to get her coat and purse. Katherine could see the tight muscles of her clenched jaw as they walked through the store, nodding good nights to coworkers. Out on the street, the cold air caused her to gasp.

"I hate this time of year," she said in a rush. "It's dark when we get up and dark when we go home."

Annie nodded but said nothing. Katherine gestured toward the streetcar stop, and they walked toward it.

"So, do you want to go for a drink?" Katherine asked. "We could find something here or go someplace when we get closer to home."

"I actually don't have a lot of time," Annie said. "I promised a friend we would meet up for dinner."

"Margie?" Katherine said tightly.

"Yes," Annie said. "Margie."

Katherine glared angrily at the sidewalk. They were almost to the stop. She didn't want to have this conversation with so many people around but it was clear Annie was in no mood to indulge her desire for privacy.

"So are you . . . seeing her?" Katherine asked, hating herself for asking, but also wanting desperately to know. They were standing far enough from the other passengers that they couldn't be overheard, but close enough that when the streetcar came, they could be assured of seats.

Annie sighed, the gray cloud of her breath illuminated in the street light. "Kate, what do you want?"

"I'd like to talk in private." Katherine looked around. "Please. I'm sorry for the way I've acted and I want to explain." Annie didn't respond. "I can come to your apartment or we could go someplace for a drink. Any place. You can choose where."

"What do you want to talk about?" Annie asked.

"I want to talk about . . . us," Katherine said softly.

"Us," Annie scoffed. "Us meaning . . . what exactly?"

Katherine hesitated, unsure what to say or even how to begin.

The streetcar bell clanged, signaling its arrival. The sound was brittle and metallic in the cold night air. They silently lined up to board. The streetcar was crowded and there were no seats together.

Probably just as well, Katherine thought as the car jerked along. She needed time to think. From where she sat, she could see the back of Annie's head swaying with the rhythm of the car. She had acted impulsively, asking to speak to Annie, but not knowing what she wanted to say. By the time they reached their stop, she still was at a loss.

Annie disembarked first and waited as Katherine stepped from the car onto the pavement. Her usually full lips were pressed into a thin line, though Katherine couldn't tell if it was in annoyance or hurt.

"Please, just give me ten minutes," Katherine said. "Honestly, I don't know what I want to say, but if I can't express it in that amount of time, you can go."

Annie looked up and met Katherine's gaze. She sucked her bottom lip into her mouth and seemed to chew on it. She sighed. "Ten minutes. And then I have to go."

They walked in silence to Katherine's rooming house, through the entryway, and up the stairs to the third floor. Annie's gaze lingered on the door of the room that had been Claire's as they passed, though she said nothing. She waited as Katherine unlocked the door to her room and followed her inside. Katherine removed her coat and scarf as she crossed the room to turn on the small table lamp. Annie remained by the door.

"You can take off your coat," Katherine said.

"I don't think I'll be here all that long," Annie said.

"All right," Katherine said as she tossed her things over the back of the chair and faced Annie. She smoothed the front of her dress nervously.

Annie watched her, but said nothing.

She isn't going to make this easy for me. Katherine cleared her throat and looked down at the floor. "The other day when you were here, I was horrible to you. I didn't realize why at the time—or maybe I did, I don't know—but I . . ." She faltered and glanced up.

Annie was still watching her, her face impassive.

"I miss Claire desperately," Katherine said. "And although I'm grieving, that's not why I acted the way I did."

She took a deep breath and let it out slowly, steeling herself for what she knew she needed to say. "You were right about why I was angry. How I feel when I'm around you scares me. I've been trying to convince myself that I'm not like you—that we're just friends. But then today, when I saw you with Margie, I realized . . ."

She shook her head in confusion and turned toward the window, her back to Annie. She pressed her forehead against the cool glass of the window and took the time to compose her words.

"When I saw you with Margie, both that first time and then again today, I was angry. I was jealous." She turned and looked at Annie. "I still am."

In the dim light, Annie's eyes were dark and unreadable. She stared at Katherine for several seconds and dropped her gaze. Katherine could hear her soft, quick breaths as she seemed to study the floorboards.

"Please say something," Katherine said softly.

"What do you want me to say?" Annie asked, her voice flat.

Katherine looked at her plaintively, wanting to scream, "Tell me you love me. Tell me she means nothing to you. Tell me we can fix this."

Annie was silent for several seconds. "I need to go."

"I understand," Katherine said. "My ten minutes are up."

Annie nodded though she made no move to leave. Katherine studied her—her small frame still bundled in the coat and scarf, her dark hair made almost black by dim light, her long eyelashes. She remembered how those lashes had felt against her cheek the first time Annie had kissed her and felt a jolt in her stomach and chest.

"Annie," she said softly.

Something about her tone caused Annie to look up. Her dark eyes met Katherine's, and they stared at each other for several seconds. Without breaking the gaze, Katherine crossed the room and placed a palm on either side of Annie's face, tipping it gently upward. She could see the pulse throbbing in Annie's throat just above her black, woolen scarf and realized she was just as nervous as she was herself.

"I'm sorry." Katherine dipped her head and lightly, gently, firmly, kissed Annie's lips. It was like their first kiss, but in reverse. This time, it was Katherine who guided Annie's face. It was Katherine who gently parted Annie's lips with the tip of her tongue. It was Katherine who was the aggressor.

Annie exhaled deeply through her nose, but didn't pull away. At first, she just stood with her arms at her sides and let Katherine kiss her. But as the kiss lengthened and grew more intense, she raised her hands to gently rest on Katherine's shoulders. Katherine pressed her advantage and slid one hand from Annie's face to the back of her neck. Annie made a soft noise and pressed her body against Katherine's. The contact made Katherine's body tingle, and she groaned softly in response.

Annie smiled into Katherine's mouth and slid her lips to Katherine's cheek and to the hollow below her jaw. Katherine's breathing quickened, and she tipped her head slightly backward. Annie whispered something unintelligible against Katherine's neck and pulled her face down again. Katherine felt as if she couldn't catch her breath. She deepened the kiss and reached between them to the front of Annie's coat. She unfastened the buttons until she was able to slide the coat off Annie's shoulders. It made a muffled "whoosh" as it landed in a pile on the floor.

Annie froze.

"What?" Katherine asked, slightly breathless as she pulled back to look into Annie's eyes. "What's wrong?"

"I can't do this," Annie said. She looked shaken. "I have to go. I'm already late."

Katherine stepped awkwardly, unwillingly, backward. "Margie."

"Yes," Annie said. "I promised I would be home for dinner."

Katherine felt her body tighten in anger. "Home." The word seemed to catch in her throat.

"You know what I mean," Annie said and knelt to pick up her coat.

"So you . . ." Katherine didn't know what to say.

"Kate—" Annie began.

"Don't. Just, please . . . don't." Katherine turned and walked back to the window where she stood, arms crossed, and pretended to look out. She could see Annie reflected in the glass, her face a pale, blurred shape.

"You have to understand, I didn't think you would ever . . ." Annie said.

Katherine laughed bitterly. "Neither did I." She sighed. "I know. You need to go."

Annie's blurry face nodded. "Kate . . ."

Katherine turned. "What?"

Annie blinked and bit her lip as if she had more to say. "I'll see you tomorrow at work."

Katherine turned back to the window, closed her eyes, and waited for the soft click of the door closing before allowing herself to cry.

THE NEXT DAY, Katherine made sure to leave for work early enough that she wouldn't be on the same streetcar as Annie and Margie. She had spent the better part of the previous evening imagining the two of them together. Images of them laughing and having dinner—of Margie kissing and caressing Annie haunted her. Granted, she had no idea what two women did together, but given what she knew from her experiences with men, she could imagine.

Katherine sighed and rubbed her eyes. She had been up most of the night thinking about what had happened, trying to figure out what to do. She didn't feel rejected, she was surprised to realize. Annie's reaction made it clear she still had feelings for her. But she was also clearly involved with Margie. And, if Katherine's first meeting with Margie was any indication, had been so for quite some time.

Because she had left so early, she arrived at work too early to clock in. She walked down the street until she found the small diner she and Claire had frequented. Since Claire's death, she had come here often, imagining that she was waiting for her friend to get off work. Sometimes she conjured imaginary conversations in her head—recounting her day. Today, she simply wanted coffee and anonymity. The warmth of the diner was soothing, as was the aroma of frying eggs. She sat down at the counter and ordered coffee from the harried-looking waitress. As she sipped, she returned to thoughts of Annie. Kissing her had been as good as she had remembered—better, in fact. So much different from the kisses of the men she had dated. Softer, more—

"More?" the waitress asked.

Startled, Katherine looked up. The woman was holding a coffee pot aloft. Her pencil-thin eyebrows were raised in two perfect arches. She looked as exhausted as Katherine felt.

Katherine looked down at her watch and shook her head. "I've got to go to work. But thank you."

Katherine opened her coin purse, extracted a nickel and three pennies and put them on the counter. She felt jittery, though from the coffee or her emotions, she wasn't sure. The wind caught the hem of her coat as she turned onto State Street. The icy blast made her gasp. That was one thing she hadn't been prepared for when she came to Chicago— the wind. Her eyes watered, and she blinked away the tears. She neared the entrance, and was surprised to see Annie, her head bowed and her arms crossed and hugged to her body. A cigarette was scissored between two fingers. She seemed to be waiting.

Katherine stepped forward and walked briskly the rest of the way to the entrance. Annie looked up and caught her gaze. Almost by reflex, she lifted the cigarette to her lips a last time, took a long drag, and dropped it to the ground. She exhaled slowly.

"I wanted to talk to you," she said as Katherine drew near. Residual smoke came out with the words. "About last night."

Katherine nodded brusquely.

"I don't know what to say," Annie admitted with a sigh.

"I know," Katherine said quickly and pushed her hands deeper into her coat pockets. "I'm not sure I do either." She stepped closer. "Look, this is all new to me. These feelings, admitting how I feel about you— how I've felt about you . . ." She shook her head.

"What do you want, Kate?" Annie asked finally.

"I'm still trying to figure that out." She paused. "Are you and Margie serious?"

Annie raised her eyes to Katherine's face. "We've been seeing each other for a while now. I care about her."

Katherine pressed her lips together and nodded slowly. She exhaled the breath she hadn't realized she had been holding and cleared her throat. "Is it the same as what you feel . . ." She stopped, not wanting to hear the answer.

"For you?" Annie asked. "No. But with Margie, I know what I'm getting. She's been this way for a long time. I know she's not going to see this as an experiment or up and change her mind one day."

The words stung. "Like me."

Annie's jaw tightened, but she didn't answer.

"Fine," Katherine spat and started to brush past Annie.

"Kate," Annie said as she grabbed her arm. "Please. Listen. I wanted to talk to you about this like adults. I wanted to explain why—"

"Your explanation was more than clear," Katherine interrupted tightly.

"I want to be friends," Annie said.

Katherine laughed, a short, harsh bark. "Friends." She rolled her eyes. "Funny how things change, isn't it? Wasn't I the one saying this very same thing to you?"

Annie blinked and smiled wryly. "Ironic perhaps, but not funny."

Katherine sighed and considered. Friendship was better than nothing. And Annie had admitted that she didn't feel the same way about Margie that she did for her.

"We could spend time together," Annie continued. "Like we used to before all this."

"What about Margie?" Katherine asked pointedly.

Annie hesitated. "It wouldn't have to include Margie."

"Wouldn't that be wrong?" Katherine asked.

"No," Annie said. "She and I have a relationship and you and I have . . . a friendship. The lines are clear. Believe it or not, I understand the differences in the two. I won't do anything to jeopardize either."

"And you can be so sure of that," Katherine said, an idea forming in her mind.

"Yes," Annie said firmly.

Katherine looked at her for several seconds and then, as Annie had so long ago in the library, extended her hand to shake on it.

"Okay," she said. "I'm game if you are."

CHAPTER 15
Lawrence, Kansas, 1997

JOAN AWOKE THE next morning with a vague sense of unease and disorientation. It took her several seconds to realize she was in her mother's home—in her childhood room. She rolled onto her back and looked at the ceiling, blinking away the shadowy remembrance of her last dream. There had been a fight or an argument between her and Luke that had ended in angry, almost violent sex. It had been consensual, bruising and strangely, it had been good.

Joan rubbed her eyes with her fingertips. She and Luke had never had angry sex. They rarely had sex at all anymore, she thought wryly. So why had she dreamed something so out of character? It must have been her conversation with Mrs. Yoccum. She shook her head, trying to dispel the image of her father forcing himself on her mother. He had a temper, she knew. And he could be volatile. But would that extend to rape? Or, given that they were married, did he see it as a rape? Not an excuse, she reminded herself. Never an excuse.

The fact that Joan was the result of that act, though, explained a lot. As a mother, she knew it was impossible not to love your own child. But to have a daily reminder of such a violent act . . . was that why her mother always had such a hard time showing her affection? Perhaps. It certainly explained her mother's dislike of her husband. It made Joan's dislike of Luke seem ridiculous.

Luke.

Joan sighed and slid her hands down her body to her belly. Her stomach was still fairly flat, but she knew from experience that in a couple of weeks, she would begin to develop a pooch. Something needed to be done, and soon. She rolled onto her side and slid her hands up under the pillow. She wondered what Mark was doing. Was he with his wife? Did he miss her? What would he do if he knew she was pregnant with his child? Would he care if he knew that she was planning to have the pregnancy terminated?

The thought of having the procedure, of ending the one tie that would forever bind her to Mark, made her sad. She wasn't sure she believed in abortion, but, she didn't want another child, did she? She imagined the sleepless nights, the dirty diapers, the constant feeding—all of which would be on top of taking care of the two children she already had. And then there was the question of parentage. Even though she was fairly sure she could pass it off as Luke's, what if the child picked up some genetic throwback in Mark's family?

No. She wasn't like her mother. She wasn't going to have a child she wasn't convinced she really wanted. Besides, what kind of person brings an innocent child into the middle of a broken marriage with a woman who doesn't want to be a mother. Not one with a conscience.

"I've become a monster," she said aloud as she threw back the covers in disgust and swung her feet to the floor. She had a lot to accomplish today. First she would have coffee. Then she would call to get an appointment with the doctor in Wichita. Once she had that date, she would talk to the auctioneer to see if he could hold the sale while she was away.

As she waited for the coffee to brew, she went into the dining room and picked up the last letter and her pad of paper. In the living room, sunlight streamed through the front window and onto her mother's chair. Drawn to the warmth, she sank into the chair and unfolded the letter. It was dated 1959. The paper was the same as the others. She began to read.

> *My Love ~*
>
> *It's been five years and I'm no closer to being over the loss of you than I was the day you were taken from me. We had so little time together.*
>
> *I never told you this, but I think I fell in love with you that first day when you came over and asked me for a cigarette. There was something about you that made me nervous, but at the same time, you intrigued me. You were so bold—and so persistent. In fact, you would still be alive if you had never come back for me, do you realize that? Without your persistence, we would have had our "great love affair" and left it at that. It would have been a fond, cherished memory and I would have gone on with my life. I would never have gotten over you, but I could have gone on.*
>
> *I still remember the day I came onto the porch and found you standing awkwardly by your car. I thought it was the farmer from next door checking on me. But it was you. My heart stopped and I knew in that second that I had been foolish to think a life without you was possible. Just like that, you ruined me and saved me—all at once.*
>
> *I see now that I was wrong about so many things. I never should have let you leave that last day. I should have grabbed you and made you listen. I should have said the*

*words I can now only write—Annie, I love you and I cannot
live without you.*

Joan blinked and lowered the letter to her lap. "That can't be right,"
she murmured softly. Slowly, carefully, she reread the last line. It was
exactly as thought; her mother had indeed written the name "Annie."

Holy shit," Joan said as she sat back in stunned surprise. "My mother
was a lesbian."

"IT'S TRUE," MRS. Yoccum admitted.

Immediately after reading the letter, Joan had rushed over to Mrs.
Yoccum's house, pounded on the door, and demanded to know if "A"
was, in fact, a woman.

"How?" Joan asked, still shocked at the revelation. "When? I don't
understand."

"Come in," Mrs. Yoccum said kindly even as she looked anxiously
up and down the street. "It's too cold to stand outside talking about this.
Come in and have some tea."

"I . . ." Joan shook her head, still ready to do battle and then, with a
sigh, acquiesced.

Wordlessly, she followed Mrs. Yoccum through the house and into
the kitchen. The morning sun slanted sideways through the window,
brightening the room which smelled deliciously of cinnamon and homemade bread.

"I'm baking," Mrs. Yoccum said. "Your mother used to come over
every Thursday morning for my cinnamon rolls. Did you know that?"

"No, I didn't," Joan said.

"She had quite the sweet tooth," Mrs. Yoccum said.

"It was the only thing sweet about her," Joan muttered before she
could stop herself.

"Oh, Joanie," Mrs. Yoccum said. "You shouldn't be so hard on her."

Joan rolled her eyes and shrugged before dropping her gaze to the
familiar chrome and Formica kitchen table. She was surprised that Mrs.
Yoccum hadn't replaced it and gently ran her fingers over the scratches
from countless coffee cups, plates, and bowls. She smiled as she
remembered summer afternoons when she and Jason would rush inside
from whatever they were doing to sit at the table and eat cookies or slices
of fruit.

"Sit down," Mrs. Yoccum said as she shuffled to the counter next to
the stove. "Would you like coffee or hot tea?" She turned to Joan who
was standing with her fists clenched at her sides.

"Whatever is easiest," she said.

"Well, I prefer hot tea," Mrs. Yoccum said.

Joan nodded absently, her mind still reeling from the realization that the great love of her mother's life had been a woman.

"And, of course, I'll bet you'd like a warm cinnamon roll. I just finished frosting them." Mrs. Yoccum gestured at the pan. "Don't they smell delicious?"

Joan forced her attention back to the present. She looked at the pan. Steam rose lazily from the coils of pastry, and she had to admit, the aroma was wonderful.

"They do smell pretty good," she said.

"Well, then, you'll just have to tell me if they taste as good as they smell," Mrs. Yoccum said and turned to fill the kettle with water. "I know a lot of people use those microwave ovens, but they scare me with all their beeps and buttons." She lit the gas burner and put the kettle over the flame. "I prefer to do it the old fashioned way—cooking with fire."

She turned to Joan again and grinned impishly. Despite herself, Joan grinned in response.

"Sit down," Mrs. Yoccum said again and gestured toward one of the chrome and vinyl-covered chairs. "Take off your jacket, and I'll answer your questions."

Joan looked down at her clothing and grimaced. She was still in her pajamas. After reading the letter, she had hurried out the door, pausing only to pull on a pair of hiking boots she had left in the foyer and an old barn jacket of her mother's that she used for yard work. She shrugged off the jacket, hung it over the back of the chair, and sat down.

"So, tell me about Annie," Joan said.

Mrs. Yoccum pulled two plates out of the cupboard and set them on the counter next to the stove. She stood with her back to Joan for several seconds before facing her.

"Your mother was a complicated woman," she said.

"I'm beginning to realize that," Joan said tightly.

Mrs. Yoccum nodded slowly and studied Joan's face. "You look like her, you know."

Joan pressed her lips together and gave a small shrug.

"You're angry," Mrs. Yoccum said as she turned back to the counter and cut into the pan of cinnamon rolls. "But you shouldn't judge her until you know the whole story."

Mrs. Yoccum's gnarled hands shook with the effort of holding the heavy knife, and Joan felt her anger fade. It wasn't Mrs. Yoccum's fault that her mother had secrets.

"Can I help?" she asked.

Mrs. Yoccum laughed. "Oh, no, dear. I can do it. Everything just takes a little longer when you get to be my age."

Joan nodded and watched Mrs. Yoccum free two of the rolls and, using a fork, spear them and plop them onto the waiting plates.

"There now." Mrs. Yoccum carried them to the table, placed one in front of Joan, and the other in front of the empty chair across from her. She returned to the stove just as the kettle whistled and, using both hands, lifted the kettle off the burner and poured hot water into two cups. She tore open the tea bags, and Joan could hear the clinks of glass and metal as Mrs. Yoccum prepared the tea.

"Do you take sugar or lemon?" she asked.

"Neither, thanks," Joan said.

"Just like your mother," Mrs. Yoccum said with a soft laugh as she brought the cups to the table.

With a flourish, she pulled two forks and two spoons out of her apron pocket and eased herself into the chair.

"There now," she said and raised the steaming cup to her lips. "Tea and cinnamon rolls on a fall morning. What could be better?"

Joan smiled and picked up her own cup. She smelled the whiskey in the tea before she parted her lips to take a sip. She glanced sharply at Mrs. Yoccum who nodded knowingly.

"That's the something special," she said.

Joan nodded and blew on the liquid as if to cool it. As upset as she was, whiskey at nine-thirty in the morning was not the solution. "So. My mother."

"Your mother," Mrs. Yoccum echoed.

"Who was Annie?" Joan asked.

"Annie was . . . oh, where to begin," Mrs. Yoccum said. "She was your mother's friend."

"Friend or lover?" Joan asked.

"Both," Mrs. Yoccum said after several seconds. "They became friends in Chicago. They both worked as counter girls for Sears."

"And that's where they . . . ?" Joan asked.

Mrs. Yoccum nodded.

Joan closed her eyes and tipped back her head. She sighed deeply and reconsidered the spiked tea. "How much of the story do you know?"

"Most of it, I'd expect, though I didn't know about the letters," Mrs. Yoccum said.

Joan opened her eyes and studied Mrs. Yoccum. "Did you ever meet Annie?"

Mrs. Yoccum shook her head. "When she was here, it was out on the farm. I came later, after your parents moved to Lawrence."

"What do you mean, out on the farm?" Joan asked.

"During the war," Mrs. Yoccum said. "She was your mother's boarder when your father was away at the war."

"Wait. *Annie* was the boarder?" Joan laughed without humor. "Unbelievable. So, if Mom was gay, why did she marry Dad?"

Mrs. Yoccum smiled sadly. "There was no such thing as 'gay' back then. At least not the way the word is used today. Back then the word 'gay' meant full of life and fun. What you're talking about is something quite different. Back then, there was natural and unnatural. And it was a distinction your mother struggled with. I suspect she married your father to prove she wasn't unnatural. But in the end . . ." She shook her head sadly. "It just brought misery to everyone involved."

Joan snorted. "So, how did Annie end up as a boarder?"

"She refused to give up," Mrs. Yoccum said. "Your father was off for the war effort and she showed up and . . . stayed."

"And I assume they resumed their . . . relationship?" Joan asked.

Mrs. Yoccum nodded.

Joan sat back in her chair and shook her head in disbelief. "Did anyone know what was going on?" She thought about Bud's comments about Katherine being a whore.

"Oh no," Mrs. Yoccum said quickly. "They were discrete. Your father found out, of course, but it was much later. After it had ended."

Joan stared at Mrs. Yoccum and lowered her eyes to the cinnamon roll. Idly, she poked at it with her fork. "When did Dad find out?"

"It was—"

They jumped as the phone on the wall rang.

Mrs. Yoccum pushed herself to her feet and picked up the receiver. It was, Joan noticed, much like her mother's rotary phone except Mrs. Yoccum's was harvest gold.

"Hello," Mrs. Yoccum said into the receiver. "Oh, hello . . ." She paused. "All right . . . Yes . . . Of course . . . I'll be waiting outside."

She replaced the receiver and turned to Joan, her face pale. "Jason's been in a car accident. He's in the hospital, and I need to go there."

"Oh, my God," Joan said. "What happened? Do you need me to take you?"

"I don't know the details." She gestured toward the phone. "That was my daughter-in-law. She's on her way to the hospital now and is going to pick me up." She looked around the room as if unsure what to do next. "I need to get ready. We . . . can we discuss this later?"

Joan nodded vigorously. "Of course. I'm so sorry. If there's anything I can do, please know—"

"You're a sweet girl," Mrs. Yoccum said. "Right now I just need to get ready. You can see yourself out?"

Joan nodded and walked to the doorway. Outside, she stood on the porch and looked up and down the street. From some place in the distance, she could hear a leaf blower. She looked at her mother's house and then in the direction of campus. *A walk would be nice*, she thought as she headed toward her mother's house to change clothes. She stepped outside ten minutes later dressed in jeans, a T-shirt, and a light jacket. She paused to let the crisp air caress her face and hair and looked next door. Mrs. Yoccum's house appeared to be empty, which meant she was probably on her way to the hospital.

"Poor Jason," Joan murmured as she turned and began to climb the long, curved hill that led to campus.

As she walked, she tried to push all thoughts from her mind, though, try as she might, the realizations of the past two days swirled in her head. Her mother had been involved in a long-term affair with another woman. She had been raped by Clyde. Her mother had lost her lover over . . . what? Over Joan's birth? Clyde's claim on his wife? The cultural norms of the time? And then Annie had died, and her mother was left with a child, a husband, and her regrets. It was almost unbearably sad.

Joan tried to imagine what Annie must have looked like. Perhaps she had seen pictures in her mother's things and hadn't realized her identity. She wondered if Mrs. Yoccum could help.

Joan breathed heavily as she crested the hill. The stretch just before the peak was always the hardest part. The irony that it was much like life wasn't lost on her as she stopped, hands on her hips, to catch her breath. Students rushed along the sidewalks, their faces arranged in varying degrees of self-absorption. Joan felt suddenly old. *Was I ever this young?* She knew she had been. She also knew that once, before marriage and kids, life had been fairly uncomplicated.

"I want to be like you," she said to no one in particular. A young woman in headphones paused and pulled one of the speakers away from her ear.

"Sorry, did you say something?" she asked.

Joan blushed and laughed self-consciously. "I . . . no."

"Oh, okay," the woman said with a shrug as she returned the headphone to her ear, dipped her head so as not to make eye contact with anyone else, and continued in the direction of the library.

Joan watched her go as people continued to hurry past. It felt strange and exhilarating to be still in such a flurry of movement—as if she was invisible. She considered the thought. What if she *were* invisible? Or more to the point, what if she disappeared? What if she sold her mother's house and possessions, packed her bags, and rather than going back to Chicago, simply disappeared? It was possible to do, she knew—or at least, not *impossible*. The idea made her giddy.

"I can't believe I'm even thinking about this," she said under her breath as she turned and trekked back down the hill. Still she mulled over the possibilities. If given the choice, where would she go? Who would she become? What would she do? She thought about the children. She could leave Luke with no problem, but the children? And Mark . . . well, Mark wasn't hers to lose anyway. But the children. Could she do that? Could she actually leave them? And more to the point, why would she want to? Was she really so unhappy that she just wanted to abandon her life?

"Jesus," she said and laughed uncomfortably. "I sound like my mother."

The realization stopped her in her tracks. *This is how Katherine must have felt.*

She looked up and realized she was within half a block of her mother's house. She stared at it as a stranger might see it. She thought again about the night she saw her mother crying over the contents of the suitcase, the annual commemoration of Annie's death, the fact that she had stayed in a life that made her miserable because it was the right thing to do.

Joan forced herself to walk the rest of the way to her mother's house, but rather than going inside, she sat down on the top step. The neighborhood was silent aside from the skittering of blowing leaves. So much suddenly made sense. Her mother hadn't hated her. She had hated her life—what she had allowed herself to become because she chose to live a lie.

"But I don't have to do that," Joan murmured. "I can make decisions and take control."

It was, she realized with a start, the first step in forgiving her mother.

CHAPTER 16
Chicago, Illinois, 1934

AS WINTER GAVE way to spring, Katherine's life settled into a routine that wasn't quite as bleak as the months immediately following Claire's death. Though she still missed Claire terribly, she had come to accept that there wasn't anything she could do to change the past. She simply had to accept it.

Truly alone for the first time in her life, Katherine spent the majority of her time at work or at the library. She occasionally went out with people from work and once had even gone to dinner with Francine and her husband. The only person with whom she spent any significant amount of time was Annie. As before, they spent their time together talking, window shopping, and discussing books. But instead of the camaraderie that existed before, their dynamic now was stilted and awkward, their interactions often underscored by an awareness of each other.

As if by mutual agreement, they chose not to talk about Annie's relationship with Margie. Katherine knew they were still seeing each other and could only assume that the vague activities Annie mentioned doing when they were apart, were done in Margie's company. But Annie never offered details, just as Katherine never asked. She really didn't want to know. Just the thought of them talking, making dinner, or going out for drinks was upsetting—but only slightly less so than the excruciating thought of what they did when they weren't doing those things.

Katherine was considering this one Sunday afternoon as she and Annie walked on the path that ran alongside Lake Michigan. The breeze off the water was brisk, but the sunlight and the budding trees had inspired them to look for a place to sit and read. To their left was the giant Ferris Wheel from the 1893 World's Fair and to their right was the soon-to-be reopened grounds of the previous year's World's Fair. The event had been such a success that the producers were going to try for a second season.

"What are you thinking?" Annie asked, shaking Katherine out of her reverie. "You're awfully quiet."

Katherine felt her cheeks flush. "I was thinking about last year's fair."

"Ah," Annie said without asking her to elaborate.

In the silence that followed, Katherine remembered that it had been after their day at the fair that Annie had first kissed her. She wondered if Annie was thinking about the same thing.

"I was wondering if it will draw as many people this year," Katherine added quickly.

"I'm sure it will," Annie said distracted.

"Maybe we should go," Katherine said.

Annie squinted up at her from under the brim of her hat and smiled. "But no lemonade."

Katherine grinned. "No lemonade."

"So, where shall we sit?" Annie asked.

Katherine considered and pointed to the domed top of the Planetarium. "There are some benches over there. And even if we go near the water, it shouldn't be too cool."

Annie nodded, and they walked across the grass to the Planetarium grounds. On the incline that sloped toward the water, several people with the same idea sat talking, laughing, and eating. A dark-haired woman about Katherine's age sat on a blanket, staring thoughtfully at the lake. An open book lay in her lap.

"I hope we're not intruding," Katherine said as they chose a spot nearby and spread their jackets on the ground.

The woman glanced in their direction and then back out at the water. "Not at all," she said and smiled broadly. Her voice was low pitched and warm. "I was just looking out at the water and thinking."

"It's beautiful here," Katherine agreed. "It's one of the things that surprised me most when I moved from Kansas—all this water. It's what I imagine the ocean looks like."

The woman turned, her expression one of surprise. Her eyes were a deep, almost smoky green. "You're from Kansas? Me, too. Where?"

Katherine laughed and rolled her eyes. "No place you've heard of. It's a tiny town in the northeastern part of the state."

"I'll bet I have," the woman said. "I'm from Lawrence."

Katherine grinned in disbelief. "You're not going to believe this, but I'm from Big Springs."

"Imagine that," the woman said with a laugh. "I know exactly where it is. What a small world."

"I'm Katherine," Katherine said as she approached the woman and extended her hand. "And this is my friend, Annie."

"Lillian." The woman shook Katherine's hand and smiled a greeting to Annie, who nodded and gave a slight wave, though she didn't come over. Lillian raised her eyebrows slightly and returned her attention to Katherine.

"So, do you live here or are you visiting?" Katherine asked.

"Oh, I live here," Lillian said. "I work at Marshall Field's."

"What a coincidence—we work at Sears," Katherine said in delight and gestured to include Annie. "I work in gloves and Annie is in shoes."

"Women's dresses," Lillian said with a grin. "Today is my day off. It was simply too gorgeous to stay inside so I grabbed a book and here I am."

"That was exactly our thought," Katherine said. She gestured at Lillian's novel. "So, what are you reading?"

Lillian flipped over the book so Katherine could see the cover. "Sherlock Holmes. I love British mysteries."

"Me, too," Katherine said enthusiastically.

Annie sighed in displeasure. Surprised, Katherine turned to see her staring fixedly at the grass in front of her, a look of irritation on her face.

Katherine returned her attention to Lillian. "I love a good mystery, although Annie, here, prefers more *avant garde* subject matter."

"Oh, really?" Lillian said pleasantly and leaned forward to address Annie. "What do you like?"

Annie shrugged and raised her gaze to meet Lillian's. Katherine could see a defensive set to her jaw.

"I like a variety of genres and authors," she said, seeming impatient with the conversation. "It's hard to choose just one."

"Well, I'm sure my tastes are boring in comparison," Lillian said easily and returned her attention to Katherine.

She had beautiful teeth, Katherine thought as Lillian smiled up at her.

"Well, we should let you get back to your reading," Annie said after several seconds of silence.

Lillian looked at where Annie was sitting. Katherine's jacket was spread out next to her.

"But you shouldn't sit on your jackets. You'll ruin them." She patted the space next to her. "There's plenty of room on the blanket for both of you if you'd care to join me."

She looked at Katherine and raised her eyebrows in invitation.

Katherine felt a small tingle run through her body and her face warmed.

"That's kind of you," Annie said, her tone suggesting the opposite. "But I'm actually a little chilly." She stood, shook out her jacket, and slipped it on. "In fact, I think I'm going to walk some more—to warm up."

She looked pointedly at Lillian. Something seemed to pass between them, and finally Lillian nodded almost imperceptibly.

Annie turned to Katherine. "Ready?" Her posture indicated impatience.

Katherine nodded and smiled politely at Lillian. "Looks like we're going to keep moving, but it was a pleasure to meet you."

"And you." Lillian extended her hand again. "Maybe I'll come look you up when I need some new gloves."

"Please do," Katherine said and returned the handshake.

Annie cleared her throat and turned to walk away. Katherine bent, scooped up her jacket, and followed.

"What was that about?" Katherine asked angrily once they were out of earshot. She was out of breath from rushing to keep up with Annie. "That was horribly rude."

"She was flirting with you," Annie said angrily. "Or maybe you didn't notice. 'Maybe I'll come look you up when I need some new gloves.'" Her imitation of Lillian's words, though accurate, was bitter and catty.

"You don't know what you're talking about," Katherine said.

"Don't I? And it's not like you weren't flirting right back." She clasped her hands together. "Oh, I like mysteries, too. And I'm from Kansas, too. Of course I know where Lawrence is."

"Annie," Katherine said. "Please. Slow down so we can talk."

"And the way you were looking at her," Annie continued. "It was nauseating."

"I have no idea what you're talking about," Katherine said. "We were having a conversation."

"A conversation. Like hell you were. Standing there watching the two of you was . . ." Annie shook her head and walked faster. "Maybe you should go back and get her address. See if she's free for dinner."

"Annie, stop." Katherine grabbed her arm.

Annie stopped and faced Katherine. Her face was flushed, and her eyes blazed in anger. "Leave me alone, Kate." She jerked her arm away and turned on her heel. "Just leave me the hell alone."

ANNIE WASN'T AT work the next day. Nor was she there the day after.

By the third day, Katherine had had enough. Instead of heading back to her room after work, she walked to the market and purchased several cans of chicken noodle soup and a fresh-baked loaf of bread. She slipped them into her empty lunch bag and walked to Kenzie Street. As she stood in front of Annie's building, she could see the soft light from her lamp glowing in the window. She considered for a moment what she would say if Margie was there. The thought made her stomach tighten but she took a deep breath and reminded herself that all she was doing was checking on a friend who had been absent from work.

"It's now or never," she said softly and pushed open the front door to the building. Outside of Annie's door, she paused and listened for several seconds, straining to hear the sounds of conversation or music playing on her radio. Nothing. Resolutely, she raised her fist and knocked. In the silence of the hallway, the sound seemed ridiculously loud.

"Who is it?" Annie asked, her voice muffled.

"It's me," Katherine said softly.

She could hear rustling and Annie's soft footsteps as she padded bare-foot to the door. She waited in silence for several seconds before Annie opened the door and peeked out. Her eyes were red rimmed.

"I came to see if you were all right," Katherine said. "The woman filling in for you said you were sick."

Annie pursed her lips and nodded. "Just a spring cold."

"You look awful." Katherine took in the mussed hair, the disheveled bed clothes, and red eyes.

Annie snorted ruefully. "I feel awful."

"I brought you soup." Katherine held up her bag. "It's in a can, but I thought we could heat it up on your warmer."

Annie stared at her for several seconds before finally opening the door wider and gesturing for her to come inside.

The room was a mess with papers covered in Annie's untidy hand-writing strewn across the small table and stacked haphazardly on one of the wooden chairs.

Annie followed, quickly collected them, and shoved them into one of the half-open dresser drawers. She pushed the drawer closed and turned, looking self-conscious.

"Soup?" Katherine asked.

Annie nodded. "Sounds good. I haven't had much to eat the past couple of days. I've just been sleeping and . . ." She shrugged.

"I'm sorry you're sick." Katherine walked to the table and removed the cans from her bag. "Where is your opener?"

Annie padded to the shelves and rummaged through a small box of utensils.

Katherine took off her sweater and rolled up her sleeves. "It's going to take a little while to heat. Why don't you go take a bath and I'll get this ready."

Annie hesitated.

"Let me put it this way," Katherine said. "You're not eating until you've bathed."

Annie glanced down at her nightgown and back at Katherine. "All right." She went to the closet to collect some of her things. "I'll be right back."

Once Annie was gone, Katherine busied herself with opening the cans and pouring the contents into a small pan. As she waited for it to heat, she rummaged through Annie's utensils for a knife. The bread was still warm and the aroma as she cut off several thick slices reminded her of home.

As she waited for Annie to return, Katherine went around the room, picking up clothes and tidying the stacks of books. Her gaze returned several times to the closed dresser drawer, and she wondered what Annie had been writing that she felt it necessary to hide. It was none of her business, she reminded herself as she opened the window. The spring air felt cool on her face, and she closed her eyes. She was still standing there when Annie returned five minutes later.

Katherine turned around. "Better?"

Annie's scrubbed face was flushed from the bath. Her hair was damp, and she was clad in an old, but clean nightgown and robe that made her look very young. Katherine smiled affectionately, and Annie nodded.

"I was going to put fresh sheets on your bed." Katherine gestured toward the bed which she had tried to straighten. "But didn't know where you kept them and didn't want to look through your things."

Annie glanced at the dresser. "I changed them a couple of days ago. And honestly, I haven't been sleeping in them much anyway."

"Oh." Katherine suddenly realized that perhaps Annie had been at Margie's all this time. "Would you like a toddy or something—for your throat?"

"No," Annie said and smiled ruefully. "That's the last thing I need." She sat down on the small sofa and looked at Katherine. "I've had quite enough lately."

"So it wasn't a cold?" Katherine asked.

Annie shrugged, but didn't answer.

"Well, at least you look better after your bath," Katherine said.

"I feel better, actually," Annie said. "And the food smells delicious. I haven't really eaten much the past couple of days."

Katherine carefully poured soup into two bowls and set them on the table where she had already laid out spoons and a plate with the bread.

Annie came to sit down. She ate slowly at first, then ravenously. Katherine kept up a chatter about the weather and what was going on at work. When Annie finished her soup, Katherine slid her own, untouched bowl across the table. Annie raised her eyebrows.

"Not hungry," Katherine said. "Eat some more bread."

She cut up the remainder of the loaf and passed another piece to Annie who dipped it into her bowl.

"So, what caused the bender?" Katherine asked. "Out with Margie?"

"Something like that," Annie said.

In the silence that followed, Katherine debated whether or not to press for more details.

"So, did you go back and talk to that woman? Lillian?" Annie asked.

Katherine looked up from studying the crumbs on the bread plate, startled. Annie's large, dark eyes studied her intently.

"No," she said softly. "I didn't."

"Why not?" Annie asked. "You had the perfect opportunity. And she was interested."

Katherine shrugged and picked up her cigarette case. She took her time lighting a cigarette and sat back in her chair. "I . . . I don't know. I just didn't."

"You were flirting with her." Annie's voice was tinged with anger.

Katherine felt a twinge of satisfaction at Annie's obvious jealousy. "We were having a conversation. That's all."

"That wasn't all." Annie narrowed her eyes. "I saw the way you were looking at her. You thought she was pretty. Admit it."

Katherine thought about how she had noticed Lillian's teeth, her smile, her eyes. She sighed. "Yes, she was pretty."

Annie snorted and stabbed her bread into soup. "I knew it."

Katherine considered pointing out that Annie was seeing Margie, and who she, Katherine, talked to and yes, perhaps enjoyed the attention of, was none of Annie's business. She considered seeing how far she could push Annie's jealousy.

"But not as pretty as you."

Annie's hand stilled, though she didn't raise her head.

"And I'm not attracted to her the way I am to you," Katherine continued.

Still hunched over her bowl, Annie flicked her eyes upward and met Katherine's gaze. After several seconds Katherine slid her hand across the table and opened it, palm upward.

Annie hesitated and lightly touched it with her fingertips, first the fingers, then the palm and then the wrist. She traced the veins that ran along the underside of Katherine's wrist with her finger, and Katherine could see the tiny throb of her pulse as it accelerated.

The corner of Annie's mouth twitched in a small smile as she noticed, too. "I'm sorry. I was jealous. Even though I have no reason to be and am in no position to feel that way, I was jealous. I'm sorry." She looked up to see Katherine's reaction.

"I understand," Katherine said.

Annie nodded, stood, and walked around the table. She put her hands on Katherine's shoulders and pulled her into a hug. Katherine could feel Annie's heart thudding rapidly beneath the thin robe and nightgown. She wrapped her arms around Annie's narrow torso and put her head against her chest. They stayed like that for a long time; Annie cradling Katherine's head and gently stroking her hair.

Finally, Annie stepped back and yawned. "I feel better."

"Me too." Katherine nodded. "Well, I should let you rest," she said after several seconds of silence. "I'll just—"

"You could stay," Annie said quickly.

Katherine hesitated. She thought about what that would mean—what it *could* mean. "What about Margie?"

Annie smiled. "I'm just talking about sleep. It's late and I don't think you should be walking home in the dark."

Katherine felt both relieved and disappointed. "All right. But I don't have anything to sleep in."

"I'll loan you something. Or you could sleep in your slip." Annie grinned. "I promise not to look."

Katherine laughed. "Fair enough."

She felt awkward as she went down the hall to the communal bathroom, returned to the room, and slipped out of her street clothes. She crawled into bed while Annie did her bedtime ablutions.

Annie returned to the room, locked the door, turned off the light, and went to the bed. Katherine could see her dark form silhouetted against the light from the window as she removed her robe and slid beneath the covers. Neither spoke as they lay stiffly next to each other.

Katherine was sure Annie could hear her heart pounding and was about to say something, to make a joke, when she realized that Annie's breathing had become slow and regular. She really *had* just wanted to sleep, she thought in disappointment. She turned onto her side and studied Annie's profile. She was on her back, one arm over her head, the other on her chest. She smiled. She had forgotten that Annie slept like this, loose-limbed like a rag doll.

Carefully, so as not to wake her, Katherine touched Annie's cheek. Her skin was warm, and she marveled at its softness. She trailed her fingers down Annie's cheeks to her lips. She remembered with a jolt how they had felt pressed against her own, and her body tingled in response. She jerked her hand away and turned onto her side, her back to the now softly snoring woman next to her. Annie was with Margie, she reminded herself as she scooted to the edge of the bed and closed her eyes. Nothing was going to change that.

Katherine awoke several hours later, and it took her a moment to remember where she was. The light from the street shone through the window, and she saw the familiar shapes of Annie's furniture—which meant that the warm body curled up against her, head on her shoulder, arm draped across her stomach, was Annie. Katherine smiled and squeezed her gently, enjoying the chance to hold her without restriction. As if in response, Annie made a contented noise in the back of her throat and pressed herself closer, sleepily moving her leg so it lay across and between Katherine's. The sensation made her gasp, and she struggled to control her breathing.

Against her shoulder, Annie sighed deeply and nestled her face into the crook of Katherine's neck, gently kissing along the underside of her jaw. She murmured indistinct words against Katherine's skin as she lazily moved her hand from where it lay across Katherine's stomach, up her chest and to her face. Katherine held her breath as she felt gentle fingers turning her chin and pulling her lips downward in a sleepy, yet somehow urgent kiss.

Katherine froze, wanting to respond, but unsure if Annie was intentionally kissing her or if she thought she was kissing Margie. There was a small part of her that honestly didn't care *who* Annie thought she was kissing if it meant that she would continue to touch her this way. But the larger part of her knew it wasn't right. She forced herself to pull back.

"Annie," she whispered softly.

"Shhh," Annie said and rolled so that she was partially on top of her, her thigh now firmly between Katherine's legs, almost, but not quite pinning her to the bed. Slowly, she began to move her hips. Katherine moaned softly and arched upward. Against her lips, she could feel Annie's smile. Annie dipped her head and kissed her deeply. This time, her lips met no resistance. Annie groaned, slid her hand down Katherine's neck to her shoulder, and to her breast. At her touch, Katherine made a noise somewhere deep in her throat.

They stayed like that for several minutes, kissing and touching, until finally, Annie slipped her hand back beneath the covers and pushed up the hem of Katherine's slip. Katherine gasped at the softness of Annie's touch. She arched into each stroke, each kiss, as the pressure between her legs intensified. It didn't matter that it was a woman doing these things to her. What mattered was that it was Annie who was making love to her. Katherine felt suddenly desperate to feel Annie's skin against her body. She reached down and began to tug at her nightgown.

"I need to feel you against me," she murmured. "Take this off."

At the sound of her voice, Annie froze.

Panting softly, Katherine opened her eyes to see Annie staring down at her, her face a mask of confusion.

"Annie, what's wrong?"

"I can't do this," Annie said softly. She rolled away and shifted to sit at the foot of the bed. Quickly, Katherine pulled her slip back into place and tried to sit up as well. She took a deep breath and tried to collect her thoughts.

"Because of Margie?"

Annie nodded, the movement barely visible in the dim light. "That's part of it."

"But you want to be with me." Katherine's body still throbbed. "I know you do."

Annie rubbed her eyes and dropped her head into her hands. "This is so much more complicated than you realize."

"So explain it to me," Katherine demanded.

She waited for more than a minute before swinging her feet over her side of the bed and going to crouch in front of Annie. In the dim moonlight, she could see Annie's dark eyes, round and almost hollow-looking.

"I'm in love with you," Katherine said.

Annie tried to look away, but Katherine grasped her face with both hands and forced her to meet her eyes.

"Kate," she said softly. "Don't."

"Don't what?" Katherine asked.

They stared at each other for several seconds before Katherine leaned forward and gently pressed her lips against Annie's. At first, Annie didn't respond. But as Katherine increased the pressure of the kiss, Annie pulled her forward.

"Are you sure?" Annie asked.

Katherine stood and pulled her slip up and over her head. Annie exhaled softly as she studied Katherine's body. She reached out and gently ran her fingertips over Katherine's stomach and across to the sharp edge of her hip bone. She looked up to see Katherine watching her intently.

"I'm sure." Katherine stretched out next to Annie. Together they inched backward until they were able to slide back under the covers.

"You're going to have to show me what to do—what you like." Katherine fumbled with the buttons on Annie's nightgown.

"We shouldn't be doing this," Annie said again.

"Shhh."

THE NEXT DAY as she stood behind the counter watching women look at gloves, Katherine felt both exhausted and exhilarated. Annie had been asleep when she had crept out of bed at daybreak to return to her own rooming house. They had seen each other as she walked past the shoe department, but hadn't spoken.

Katherine felt a warm thrill in the pit of her stomach every time she thought about being with Annie. She also felt strangely aware of her own body—the way her clothes fit, the energy in her arms and legs as she moved. She felt powerful and, she realized as she smoothed the front of her skirt, perpetually aroused. It had been so different than the times she had slept with Alex—softer and slower, though no less urgent. Katherine felt herself throb at the memory.

"Do you have this in black?"

Katherine blinked and looked up to find a tall, familiar-looking woman speaking to her. She smiled, and Katherine was struck by what beautiful teeth she had.

"Lillian," she said in surprise. "How are you? What are you doing here?"

"I told you I'd come to see you if I needed gloves." Lillian laughed and spread her hands wide. "And here I am."

Katherine smiled and looked down at the display. "We don't have them in black—at least not now. We have more ordered but they won't be in until next week." She paused in thought. "But they might have them at Marshall Field's."

Dimples appeared in Lillian's cheeks. "They might, but then I wouldn't have the chance to see you again, would I?"

Katherine jerked her eyes up from the glass counter and met Lillian's gaze. She realized now what that smile meant and despite herself, imagined Lillian naked beneath her. She felt her face redden. Was that what her night with Annie had done to her—changed the way she saw women?

Lillian leaned over the counter and spoke in a tone just low enough that Katherine had to lean forward to hear her. "So, I know this may seem forward, but I often find myself missing Kansas—not that I want to go back, you understand. But I thought it might be nice for us to get together for coffee or a meal and talk about home. I'm willing to bet we have a lot in common."

Katherine hesitated, remembering what Annie had said about Lillian flirting with her. Was Lillian asking her out or was she simply looking for a friend? She considered the invitation and then wondered what Annie would say. She wouldn't be pleased. But then again, she had no idea what their relationship was. Technically, Annie was still seeing Margie. The thought made her feel sick. The reaction must have shown because Lillian touched her arm.

"I've upset you, haven't I?"

Katherine was about to answer when she saw Annie standing by one of the round glove displays near the aisle. Her eyebrows were knit in a frown as she watched the interaction. Katherine quickly pulled her arm from Lillian's touch and smiled in Annie's direction.

"Annie," she said loudly and waved her over. "You remember Lillian, don't you? From our walk last weekend?"

Lillian turned and smiled at Annie. "Hello. I decided I needed some gloves."

Annie's gaze flicked to Lillian and then back to Katherine. "Sorry to interrupt. I just wanted to see if you wanted to walk home together."

"Well, what good timing," Lillian interrupted. "Katherine and I were just making plans to have dinner. You should join us."

"That's kind of you," Annie said, the chill in her tone suggesting the opposite. "But I don't think I can. I have to meet a friend later this evening." She looked pointedly at Katherine. "But you should go. We can talk some other time, Katherine."

"Annie—" Katherine began.

Annie turned and hurried back to her department.

"Is she always so gruff?" Lillian asked.

"No." Katherine watched Annie disappear into the crowd of noonday shoppers. "She's just . . . it's hard to explain."

Lillian leaned closer. "Well maybe you can tell me about it over dinner." She grinned. "My treat."

Katherine met her gaze and smiled. "I appreciate the offer, but I think I need to talk to Annie."

Lillian turned to look in the direction in which Annie had disappeared and then back at Katherine. Her expression changed from intimacy to understanding. "So it's like that, then. I wondered, but you can't blame a girl for trying."

"I'm flattered." Katherine grasped her arm. "Really, I am. But I can't."

A small smile played at the corners of Lillian's lips. She stood straighter. "Maybe some other time. Or if circumstances change?" She let the question hang in the air, and Katherine nodded. "Well, then." She graced her with a last, brilliant smile. "You know where to find me."

"ANNIE, LET ME explain," Katherine said in a low voice as they stood in front of the lockers in the employee room. It was the end of the day, and Katherine had just barely intercepted her before she left for the evening.

"Kate, there's nothing to say," Annie said sullenly.

"But there is," Katherine insisted. "Don't you see?"

"Oh, I *saw* all right." Annie closed her locker, turned, and walked out the door.

Katherine grabbed her purse and sweater and rushed to catch up with her. She waited until they were outside before continuing the conversation. "Will you just listen? Whatever you think you saw . . . well, it wasn't what you thought."

Annie continued walking. "Fine. Now, if you'll excuse me, I'm late. And I'm guessing so are you."

"Where are you going?" Katherine asked even though she was pretty sure she already knew.

"It's really none of your business," Annie said.

Katherine grabbed her arm and yanked her to a stop. "I think it is." She swallowed and rushed on before she lost her nerve. "I want you to end it with her."

"Really?" Annie asked. "And are you sure about that given that you have so many other enticing offers?"

Katherine struggled to keep her tone even. "You know I don't want Lillian. Or anyone else for that matter. I want you." She softened her grip on Annie's arm. "Annie, I love you."

Annie closed her eyes and sighed. "You say this now, but have you even thought this through?"

"What do you mean?"

"Have you seriously considered what you're letting yourself in for? Have you thought about what you're going to tell your family . . . or Albert . . . or the people in Big Springs when they ask why you aren't married and aren't seeing anyone? What are you going to say when men ask you to dinner? Have you even thought about these things?"

"Where is this coming from?" Katherine asked.

"You said yourself that this . . . *perversion* is unnatural," Annie said. "How do I know that you're not going to change your mind when things get difficult? I don't want someone who is just trying out the way I live my life."

Katherine stared at Annie, unable to believe that she would discount the significance of their night together. "Is that what you think?" She waited for Annie to answer and when she didn't, Katherine threw her hands up in surrender. "Fine. If that's what you think, then there's nothing I can to do change your mind. Maybe you and Margie belong together after all."

Without waiting for a reply, Katherine spun on her heel walked away.

KATHERINE WOKE UP with a start. She heard a knock on the door and fumbled with the switch on the bedside lamp.

"Kate? It's Annie. Are you there?"

Katherine picked up the alarm clock and squinted at the numbers. Two-thirty. "I'm coming."

She threw back the covers, hurried to the door, and opened it.

Annie stood in the hallway, her dark hair disheveled, her clothing rumpled and creased. Her left cheek was swollen and red, as if she had been in a fight. "Can I come in?"

Katherine stepped back and pulled the door fully open. "Oh my god, of course." Annie shuffled inside, and Katherine closed the door and guided her to the bed. "Sit down."

She tipped Annie's face upward so she could examine the injury in the light. "What happened?"

Annie flinched as Katherine gently touched the crest of her cheek. "Margie."

Katherine gasped in surprise. "She hit you?"

Annie shook her head. "Slapped me. Twice. In the same spot."

Katherine frowned. "We need to see if we can bring down the swelling." She walked to the cupboard for a bowl and a hand towel. As an afterthought, she also grabbed the bottle of Walker's whiskey and one of the small jelly jars Annie preferred to a glass. She placed everything on the table and turned on the desk lamp. "I'm going to get some cold water for compresses. Help yourself to a drink."

Katherine crept down the hallway to the bathroom where she filled the bowl with water as cold as she could get it. When she returned to her room, Annie was sitting in one of the wooden chairs at the table. A generous shot of whiskey sat in front of her. She looked up and tried to smile when Katherine came into the room.

"I hope you were serious." She picked up the jelly jar and took a sip. "What you said before . . . about being together."

Katherine put the bowl of water on the table and grasped Annie's hands. "Of course I was serious."

Annie studied her face as if looking for a hint of doubt. After several seconds, she swallowed and dropped her gaze to the whiskey glass. "There's something I have to tell you. I didn't plan on telling Margie it was over when I went over there."

Katherine nodded, released Annie's hands, and picked up a neatly-folded towel. As she waited for what she was sure she didn't want to hear, she submerged the cloth into the cold water, wrung it out, and submerged it again.

"I slept with her." The words were low and almost inaudible.

Katherine exhaled sharply, pressed her tongue against the inside of her cheek, and shook her head slightly. "What do you expect me to say?" She wrung out the cloth and handed it to Annie, who pressed it against her cheek.

"I was angry," Annie said. "But all I could think about . . . during . . . was you and last night."

Katherine raised her eyebrows and snorted in disbelief.

"I told her afterward about you—about what happened," Annie said.

"And that's when she slapped you," Katherine said.

Annie nodded.

"Serves you right," Katherine said softly and held her hand out for the compress.

Wordlessly, Annie handed it to her and then reached for her drink.

Katherine pushed the towel back into the cold water. She heard Annie take a sip, swallow, and set the glass back on the table.

Katherine looked up. Annie was staring at the amber liquid, her brows knit into a frown.

Seeming to sense Katherine's scrutiny, Annie looked up and met her gaze. "Are you angry?"

"Honestly, I don't know," she said and poked at the towel with her finger. "I don't know as I have any right to be." She pulled the cloth from the bowl, wrung it out, and handed it to Annie. "Technically, I'm the other woman." She smiled ruefully.

Annie pressed the compress to her cheek. They sat in silence for what seemed like several minutes—Annie frowning into her drink and Katherine fingering a deep nick in the wood of the table. She could hear the alarm clock on her nightstand ticking off the seconds. Annie dropped the compress back into the bowl, and Katherine looked up. Water splattered onto the table. Katherine used the sleeve of her nightgown to dab at the droplets.

"Is this really what you want?" Annie asked suddenly. "Have you really stopped to think about the consequences? You'll be giving up a normal life."

Katherine pursed her lips and shrugged. "I thought a lot about what you said earlier."

"And?" Annie asked.

"And," Katherine said, "I'm conflicted."

Annie closed her eyes and sighed. "I knew it."

"No, hear me out. I was raised to believe that this," she gestured to the two of them, "is a sin. That we are an abomination. But I don't believe that. I can't help how I feel about you. I denied it for a long time. But since Claire died, I've realized a lot of things about myself. And one of those is that I am in love with you. Seeing you with Margie all those months—imagining what you were doing when you were with her . . . It made me crazy."

Katherine took a deep breath and reached across the table for Annie's hand. She waited until Annie looked up at her. "This isn't easy for me. And I'm scared. I'm scared of what people will think if they find out—

what my family would think if they knew. And I can't say that sometimes that fear won't get the better of me. But I'm also in love with you. It's as simple as that."

Annie still watched her, her eyes serious and very dark. "So, where do we go from here?"

Gently, Katherine raised her hand and touched her injured cheek. "We take it one day at a time and figure it out together. But I think the first thing you should do, if you're not in too much pain, is to kiss me."

CHAPTER 17
Chicago Illinois, 1935

"I DON'T UNDERSTAND why I can't come along," Annie said as she lay across the foot of the bed. "They know we're friends. Hell, I even spent Christmas at their house."

Katherine went to stand in front of the mirror and held a green-and-white dress in front of her.

"Yes," she said absently as she eyed the outfit critically.

"Yes, what?" Annie pressed.

Katherine lowered the dress and turned to Annie who was on her stomach, hands propped under her chin, eyes wide as she watched Katherine.

"Yes, they know about you," Katherine said in exasperation. "But when I say they know about you, it's that they know you exist. They know you're my friend. They don't know that we sleep together naked. And believe me, if you were there with me, that's exactly what I'd want to do."

Annie rolled her eyes and flipped onto her back. "I'm not suggesting that we tell them we're lovers. I just mean . . . they know we spend a lot of time together, that we work together. I don't think they would find it strange if I came home with you."

Katherine picked up a dark blue dress and turned back to the mirror. "I disagree."

"Why?" Annie persisted.

"Because when you came home with me for Christmas, it was because you had no family to go home to. But to come home with me now, when I'm going to visit old friends and spend time with family, well . . . I just think they would think it was strange." She shifted her gaze from her own reflection to Annie.

Annie was picking at a cuticle on her thumb. "I think they would be glad to see me. Your mother liked me. She told me to come back any time I wanted."

Katherine turned and looked at Annie. "That was before you were sleeping with her daughter." She grinned. "I don't think she would be quite as welcoming if she had that bit of knowledge."

Annie held out her hand. Katherine walked to the bed and interlaced her fingers with Annie's.

"I want to be more a part of your life," Annie said as she idly twisted the tiger's eye ring she had given Katherine after seeing her admiring it in a shop window. "I want this to be permanent."

Katherine squeezed Annie's fingers. "You *are* a part of my life and we *are* permanent. Just because I'm going home alone doesn't mean we're not—"

"I want us to live together." Annie sat up and regarded Katherine with a serious expression. "It's been more than a year. Isn't it time we began to build a life together?"

"We *have* a life together," Katherine said.

"Not really," Annie pressed. "I want to see you every morning when I wake up and every night before I go to sleep."

"You already do," Katherine said.

"I'm tired of having two places. I want us to have one place. Together."

"Annie—" Katherine began.

"I know, I know." Annie pulled her fingers from Katherine's grasp. "What would people think? Wouldn't they find it strange? I'm tired of that argument."

"That's only part of it," Katherine said. "I'm just not ready. Not yet."

Annie sighed. "You're never going to be comfortable with this." Katherine could hear the irritation in her voice. "I knew it that first night. You're still clinging to your old idea of yourself as a heterosexual woman. You're still not sure." Her face was flushed with anger.

"I *am* sure," Katherine said. "I love you."

"But not enough to move forward," Annie said.

"Please don't be like this." Katherine grasped Annie's hands again. "Look. I know you're concerned about me going home. But you've got no reason to worry. I want to be with you. And just because I'm not ready to live together, doesn't mean I'm not committed to you or to us. I'm just not ready to give up my independence."

Annie studied her for several long seconds and then smiled ruefully. "Lean down."

"I've got to pack," Katherine insisted.

"Lean down," Annie said again and pulled her onto the bed. She kissed her lightly on the lips. "I'm tired of you telling me no."

Katherine sighed and slid down so that her head rested on Annie's shoulder. Annie kissed the top of her head and was silent for several seconds.

"You probably couldn't get off work anyway," Katherine mumbled. "Shhh."

"And honestly, I think if you went home with me, it would be obvious."

"Shhh."

"I don't think I could hide it," Katherine said. "Nor, do I think you could either."

Rather than try to silence her again, Katherine felt Annie's arms around her tighten. She snuggled closer. Annie's heart thudded steadily in her ear.

"I just know you'll be around people who don't know about us and who have an idea of who they think you are," Annie said. "And I worry if I'm not there, you'll be tempted to listen to them and their ideas about how you should get married and have children and leave Chicago." Katherine felt the light kiss on the top of her head. "I couldn't stand it if I lost you."

"You're not going to lose me." Katherine raised her head to look up at Annie.

Annie smiled weakly. "I worry that I will. I imagine you going to church, seeing *Albert* and deciding that the pressure of doing what's expected of you to do is too much."

"Oh, sweetheart," Katherine said quickly. "That's not going to happen. I'm in love with you."

"You care what people think about you." Her tone was matter-of-fact.

"That's not fair," Katherine said. She felt the anger welling up in her chest. "I told you from the beginning that I would struggle with this. But I also promised you that I would figure out a way through it." She sighed, collecting her thoughts. "You just have to trust in me and know that just because I go home, just because I go to church or see Albert—who's married by the way—that I'm no less committed to you or what we have. I don't need you there to remind me of how much I love you."

Annie studied Katherine's face for several seconds. Katherine wondered what she was searching for.

At last, Annie smiled. "I believe you."

She lay back and opened her arms. Katherine grinned and slid down next to her, her head on Annie's shoulder. Within minutes, they were asleep.

KATHERINE STEPPED OFF the train in Lawrence and was reminded not for the first time, of just how different her life in Chicago was from that of the rest of her family. Chicago was a constant, ever-changing noisy hive of activity. But Lawrence, with its small town atmosphere, was like an old friend who never changed. She felt simultaneously relaxed and claustrophobic.

"Well, ain't you a sight for sore eyes."

Katherine looked up to see Bud hurrying over to her. He was dressed in dirty overalls and thick work boots. Sticking from his side pocket were worn, black cloth gloves.

"Bud!" Katherine dropped her suitcase onto the platform and rushed to hug him.

"Careful." Bud tried to hold her at arm's length. "I'll get your dress dirty if you're not careful."

Katherine brushed off his concerns and pulled him into her arms. "I don't care. It's good to see you."

"It's good to see you, too, Katie-doodle," he said somewhat awkwardly and broke the embrace. He looked around her at her bag. "Just the one?"

She grinned. "Just the one." She turned to walk back to where it sat.

Bud hurried forward. "I got it."

Katherine opened her mouth to protest.

"Maybe it's okay in Chicago for a lady to carry something like that," Bud said as he lifted it. "But here, carrying things for ladies is the man's job."

Katherine fought back the desire to insist that he relinquish the bag. "Well, then, thank you."

Bud nodded but didn't reply. Instead, he gestured toward the gravel parking lot on the side of the train station and walked toward it. Katherine followed him down the steps and into the lot where his dusty farm truck sat. It was yet another reminder that she was back in the country.

"The seat's kinda' dirty," Bud said as he yanked opened the passenger door and extracted a neatly-folded quilt. He grinned as he unfolded it and spread it across part of the seat. "Emily made sure I brung this so you wouldn't get dirt or grease on your clothes."

Katherine smiled. "You married a good woman."

He nodded his agreement and stepped back so Katherine could get into the truck. As she was settled herself, he put her suitcase in the bed and walked around the back of the truck to the driver's side door. The door groaned as he pulled it open and again as he pulled it shut with a heavy, metallic slam. The odor of the oil and dirt, combined with the acrid smell of the train made Katherine's throat constrict, and she cranked down the window.

They pulled out of the parking lot and onto 6th Street.

"So, how is everyone?" Katherine asked.

"Good," he said, his gaze fixed on the road.

Katherine waited for several seconds to see if he was going to elaborate. She tried a different tact. "And how are the crops looking?"

Bud frowned and rubbed his hand across his chin. "Well, we ain't got it as bad as the folks out west, but the dust blowin' round is making it hard." He shrugged. "But it also makes the prices of what we can harvest higher."

"Times are hard all over," Katherine agreed. "Everything is so expensive in the city. A lot of people are struggling to get by."

Bud nodded.

"Do you remember my friend, Annie—the girl I brought home for Christmas a couple of years ago?" she asked, wanting somehow to include Annie in the conversation. "Well, she and I pool a lot of what we earn and cook dinners together to save money."

Bud nodded again. "Good thing about being a farmer is that you grow your own food. We don't got much else, but we got that."

Katherine nodded, unsure if he was simply making an observation or if he was trying to make a point. Rather than reply, she stared out the dirty windshield at the well-tended fields that bordered the road. They had already passed through Lawrence and were on their way to Big Springs. She saw a hawk circling overhead in the distance. She craned her neck to get a better view and pointed it out to Bud, who nodded.

"You probably already heard Albert got married," Bud said after several minutes of silence. "Got drunk as a skunk the night before. Was talkin' 'bout you."

Katherine frowned and turned to look at Bud. "What do you mean he was talking about me?"

Bud shrugged. "Said he got tired of waitin' for ya. Said there was somethin' wrong with ya that you'd rather live in the city alone than get married."

"And what did you say?" Katherine asked.

"I wasn't here. I heard it down at the store couple of weeks ago. Just thought you should know 'cause it's got Mama all riled up. She's probably gonna' be pushin' for you to come home for good."

"Well, I'm not going to," Katherine said forcefully. "I'm happy in Chicago. I have friends and a job and . . . I have a good life there."

Bud shrugged and pulled off onto a gravel county road. As they neared the first of several washboard sections, he slowed the truck to a crawl. "Just thought you should know what to expect."

Katherine sighed. "Thanks. I guess I'm not surprised. I was sort of expecting it."

He grinned. "Just listen to what she has to say and then make up your own mind. I don't know what you see in livin' there, but if it makes you happy . . ."

"It does," Katherine said passionately and impulsively touched his arm. "It does, Bud. I *like* making my own money and doing what I want, when I want. I don't want to come home and marry Albert."

"Albert's already married," Bud reminded her.

Katherine sighed. "Yes. But you know what I mean, don't you?"

Bud nodded.

"So you'll back me up?" Katherine could hear the pleading note in her voice. "If Mama starts in, you'll support me?"

Bud maneuvered around a pothole, his eyes focused on the road. "I didn't say that. But I won't speak out against you. And neither will Emily."

Katherine tried to hide her surprise. "You two have talked about it?"

Bud nodded. "She was the one who convinced me. I'm not sayin' it's right, but I can't quite say it's wrong either."

Katherine smiled, though she knew better than to say something to embarrass him. They bumped along in silence until Bud slowed and turned onto the rutted drive that led to their parent's house.

"You'd best find the time to come visit Emily while you're around," he said. "Maybe one afternoon? I know she'd like to see you and she'll be wantin' to show off the baby."

Katherine nodded and looked almost hungrily at the familiar trees and fences. She smiled in pleasure as they rounded the final curve, and their parent's angular farmhouse swung into view. She was about to tell Bud how nice it was to be home when she saw her mother open the front screen door and step out onto the porch. She was wiping her hands dry on the front of her apron.

"She musta' heard the truck," Bud said. "She's been strung tighter than a fiddle since she got your letter sayin' you was comin' home."

Katherine grinned and rolled down her window, not caring if dust got all over her clothes.

"Hello, Mama," she yelled as she leaned out of the cab and waved her arm in greeting.

Her mother waved in return and watched as Bud pulled the truck into the dirt turnaround next to the house. She waited for the dust to settle and hurried down the steps toward them.

Katherine flung open the truck door, clambered to the ground, and rushed forward for a hug. Her mother squeezed her tightly against her chest and rocked her back and forth. "You're so thin." She thrust Katherine away from her so she could study her. "You're nothin' but skin and bones. You're not eating enough up there all alone, are you?"

Katherine laughed. "I'm eating, Mama. I eat three squares a day."

"Well," her mother said reproachfully, "it's not enough, I can tell you that."

"Give her a chance to say hello before you start in on her, Mama,"

Bud said as he walked past them carrying Katherine's suitcase. He jerked his chin in the direction of the house. "I'll take this on upstairs."

"That boy," her mother said as he climbed the steps and let the screen door bang shut behind him. "It's just a good thing he has that sweet Emily to look after him." She looked pointedly at Katherine, who ignored the unspoken message and linked her arm with her mother's.

"I'm so thirsty," Katherine said dramatically. "What do you suppose the chances are that I might be able to get some homemade lemonade?"

"Well," her mother said with a grin. "I think they might just be pretty good. Come sit down and I'll get you a glass. I'll get one for Bud, too, and then we can all sit down and catch up."

THE DAY PASSED quickly and by evening, Katherine was more than ready to go to bed. She pulled her nightgown over her head and heard a soft knock on her bedroom door.

"Do you have everything you need?" Her mother bustled into the room, a glass of warm milk in her hand.

"I do," she said. "Thank you."

Her mother smiled. "I thought you might like this." She handed Katherine the glass. "So, I meant to ask earlier, how's your little friend? The one you brought home that time—Annie?"

Katherine felt the heat rush to her cheeks and hoped it wasn't noticeable. "She's fine. Still working in the shoe department."

Her mother nodded. "She seemed like a nice girl. She'll make some man a good wife someday."

Katherine smiled politely.

"Speaking of that," her mother continued, "do you have someone special in Chicago?"

Katherine raised her glass of milk to her lips and sipped in an attempt to buy time before answering. Should she lie or tell a vague half-truth?

"I spend most of my time working or with Annie." It was not a lie, exactly, though it wasn't entirely the truth either.

"But no young man you're interested in?" her mother asked.

Katherine walked to the dresser and picked up her hair brush. With her back to her mother, she pulled it through her hair and tried to appear nonchalant. "Not really. I'm awfully busy."

Her mother made a sympathetic noise. "So, does that mean you're too busy for visitors?"

Katherine turned. Her mother was smiling broadly.

"What do you mean?"

"Well, your daddy and I been talking about it and we were going to wait to surprise you, but I'm just too excited." Her mother clapped her hands together. "I'm going to go back to Chicago with you."

Katherine blinked, unsure how to react. Part of her was excited to show her mother around the city. But a larger part suddenly realized that she would have to completely change her lifestyle. She had to find a way to get word to Annie so she could make sure to get all of her things out of Katherine's room. And, she realized with a sinking feeling, with her mother in tow, she would be unable to spend any time with Annie— no homecoming celebration and no time together for however long her mother was planning on staying. Her heart sank, but she put the hairbrush down and hurried to hug her mother.

"Oh, Mama, that's wonderful. We'll have such a good time. I'll show you all around the city and introduce you to people at work. How long do you think you'll be staying?"

"Well," her mother said. "Your daddy can't be left alone for too long on his own, so we're thinking no longer than a week. I thought I'd just ride back with you, see the sights and then come home before too much damage could be done here."

"That's wonderful." Katherine grabbed her mother's hand and pulled her to the bed. "Is there anything you would like especially to see? It's too bad you didn't come when the World's Fair was there."

"Oh, sweetheart," her mother said. "I just want to see your life."

Even as she half-listened to her mother, Katherine began a mental list of what she needed to have Annie remove from her room. The cigarettes, the whiskey, Annie's clothing, and any books or letters the two had written each other would need to be moved. The trick would be sneaking away to contact Annie. She had no way to get into town to send a wire— nor could she explain why she needed to send something so urgently back to Chicago or to whom. She could, she supposed, send a letter, but it would have to be mailed immediately and tomorrow was Saturday.

" . . . excited to see all the big buildings," her mother was saying. "I wouldn't want to live there, but I have to admit I am looking forward to seeing it."

"We'll make sure you see everything you want to," Katherine promised. "Lake Michigan and the downtown area . . . I'll show you everything."

AS SHE LAY in bed, Katherine considered how to get a letter to Annie. If she could get Bud to take it into town for her, it would reach Annie in time. And if for some reason Bud asked why the letter was so important, she would say that she had left her room a mess and wanted to make sure it was tidy for their mother's visit. That certainly wasn't a lie.

The next morning, Katherine hurried downstairs and found her mother in the kitchen making a pie crust. She tried to appear casual. "Mama, could I borrow a sheet of paper? I need to write a letter."

Her mother turned, a small frown on her face. "Who do you need to write a letter to? You just got here."

"I need to write my friend, Annie," Katherine said. "I left in such a hurry. My room at the boarding house is a mess. I wanted to ask her if she could tidy it up."

Her mother dipped her sticky fingers into the tin of flour and sprinkled a liberal amount on the counter. She put the dough in the center of the mess and then dusted the rolling pin. She glanced over her shoulder at Katherine. "There's no need for that. I know how you are. And besides, I'm sure it's not that bad. We can clean it when we get there."

"It's important to me," Katherine said quickly. "I want everything to be nice for you. This is your first visit. I want it to be perfect. And I don't want to have you help me clean. I want you to enjoy yourself."

"Well," her mother said as she rolled out the crust, "if you're sure, there's paper in the desk in the sitting room and everything else you need. We can send it with Bud. He's going into town tomorrow for seed. But really, you don't have to go to all that trouble."

"I really do," Katherine said and kissed her mother's cheek. "Trust me. I do."

CHAPTER 18
Chicago, Illinois, 1935

"OH MY WORD," Nedda exclaimed as she and Katherine stepped from the train and onto the platform at the terminus in Chicago. "It's so busy."

Katherine looked at the people rushing around with suitcases and boxes. Railroad personnel helped people onto and off of the trains and ladies in travel suits and dresses, and men in suits and shirt sleeves milled around. She closed her eyes and listened to the noise of the trains. The air smelled of exhaust, cologne, and cooked food. She smiled. She was home—or at least almost home.

"—can't imagine how you get around," Nedda was saying as she tried to look in all directions at once. "So many people."

Katherine opened her eyes and tried to see the scene as her mother might—as she herself once had seen it with its six train tracks and the steel and glass structure called simply "the train shed."

She grabbed Nedda's arm and squeezed it. "Welcome to Grand Central Station, Mama. From here, we'll take another train that will drop us very close to my rooming house. Or, if you would like and don't mind carrying your suitcase, we can walk. It's about fifteen minutes from here."

Nedda craned her neck upward as she tried to take in the glass and steel. "It's just so big."

Katherine patted her arm. "Wait until you see the waiting room. The ceilings are twenty-six feet tall and the floors and columns are made of marble."

Nedda gawked as they left the train shed and entered the waiting room. She spun slowly, taking in the walls, the ceilings, the stained-glass windows, the giant clock. "It's so fancy and big. I feel so out of place."

"You're fine." Katherine slid her arm through her mother's and looked around the waiting room. "It *is* amazing though, isn't it? So, would you like to take the train or the streetcar? If we take the streetcar, you'll get more of a chance to see the city."

"I don't even know how to answer," Nedda admitted.

Katherine smiled and felt suddenly bad for her mother. "There will be plenty of time to see the city. Let's stick with the train. Stay here with our bags and I'll take care of everything."

Katherine left her mother for a few minutes to purchase their tickets. As she strode back across the terminal, she saw her mother standing in exactly the same place she left her, anxiously scanning the faces of the passing people. She grasped her mother's arm. "Mama, what's wrong?"

"I was just . . ." Nedda shook her head and shrugged awkwardly. "I just was worried that you got lost or that you weren't coming back."

"Well, I did my share of getting lost at first. It's a big change. But you'll get used to it." She paused and looked at the clock. It was four o'clock. She hoped that Annie had received her letter and had cleared everything out of her room. Either way, she couldn't stall any longer. She picked up the suitcases and gestured toward the train shed. "Let's go home."

"It's pretty straightforward," Katherine said once they were settled in the car. "We just take the Loop train downtown and across the river and get off not far from the rooming house."

The train jerked forward, and Nedda turned to watch out the window as they pulled out of the station and onto the tracks. Katherine kept up a running commentary, pointing out landmarks as they wove through the city, all the while imagining what she would say if Annie hadn't received her letter. She would say she had borrowed several things from Annie for her trip, had tried them on, but none had fit so she left them in piles around the room. As for the cigarettes and alcohol, well, she would just have to think about how to handle that later.

They arrived at their stop in what seemed like no time at all.

"This is us," Katherine said as she gestured for Nedda to stand.

They stepped onto the platform with the rest of the people disembarking, but Nedda moved much slower than the rest of the throng.

"Are you okay, Mama?" Katherine grasped her mother's suitcase. "It's a lot to take in at first."

"It is." Nedda lifted her hand to her chest and took a deep breath. She looked up at the buildings that surrounded them. "How do you breathe? With so much . . ." She wrinkled her nose and gestured at nothing in particular. "The smell and everything is so close together?"

Katherine shrugged and tried not to smile. "You get used to it, I guess. How about we go home and get you unpacked?"

As they walked the two blocks to her rooming house, Katherine chattered about the city, the shops, and the neighborhood. She could tell immediately that her mother wasn't impressed with the red brick building she called home.

"Now, I know it's not much," Katherine said as she pushed the door open and stepped back to let Nedda step inside. "But for the money, it's actually quite nice."

Katherine led Nedda up the creaky stairs and down the darkened hallway to her room. She fiddled with the keys to her door. Behind her, she could hear Nedda's breath, labored from the exertion of the stairs. *It's now or never*, she thought as she inserted the key into the lock and pushed open the door.

The room was cleaner than she had ever seen it. Annie had done more than a quick cleaning. She had scrubbed everything until it shone. On the reading table were yellow tulips—no doubt stolen from the gardens of one of the nearby parks. Katherine gave a quiet sigh of relief as she stepped into the room and set the suitcases down. Nedda followed.

"I know it's not much, but, it's mine." Katherine swept her hand outward. "What do you think?"

"It's so small," Nedda said as she took in the sparse furnishings. "All these buildings and then a room so small." She looked sadly at her daughter. "Oh, Katie."

Katherine took a deep breath and tried not to be defensive. "Actually, it's all I need. There's room for my books and all my things. I have a hot plate for cooking and a bath down the hall. It's really quite perfect for me."

"Well, I suppose it would be easy to keep clean," Nedda conceded. "And how sweet of Annie to put fresh flowers on the table for us." She shifted her attention from the flowers back to Katherine. "Will I get to see her while I'm here?"

The thought of seeing Annie made Katherine tremble. To cover her nervousness, she picked up her mother's suitcase, walked to the chair closest to the closet, and set it down. She took a short, deep breath and tried to compose herself. She turned to see Nedda standing in front of the window looking out onto the street. "So, what would you like to do first?"

Nedda looked at her and smiled tiredly. "To tell the truth, I'm pert near tuckered out. I suppose I'd like to unpack and then maybe lay down for a spell."

Katherine nodded. "Would you like something to drink? Coffee? Tea? Water?"

"No." Nedda waved her hand. "Just a little time to get settled." She looked around. "Where would you like me to put my things?"

"Well, here's the closet." Katherine walked to the door and pulled it open. From inside she took out three wooden hangers. "And, if you need a drawer . . ." She grasped one of the bureau handles and pulled. Inside were stacks of papers, her letters from Annie and the copy of *Well of Loneliness* that Annie had inscribed and given her on their six-month anniversary. Katherine quickly pushed the drawer closed.

"I don't need a drawer," Nedda said. "I can keep my folded things in the suitcase. I just need someplace to hang my dresses."

"My place may be small, but I won't have you living out of a suitcase." Katherine went to the closet and removed an empty shoebox from the shelf. "I'll just clean out one of these drawers." She was careful to stand so Nedda couldn't see the contents of the drawer as she transferred everything into the box. She then slid the box to the very back of the closet—well beyond Nedda's reach. "Voila."

They stared at the open drawer for several seconds before Katherine awkwardly stepped out of Nedda's way and went to sit on the edge of the bed.

"We could go to a restaurant for dinner," she said as Nedda opened her suitcase and maneuvered her bulk in the small space between the dresser and closet. "There's a little place down the street that I go to sometimes."

Nedda shook her head. "I don't want you spending your money on fancy dinners for me. We'll just eat here." She glanced at the hotplate and cleared her throat. "That is if you can cook on this thing."

"You'd be amazed at what you can do with it," Katherine said. "I usually just fix simple things, but still . . . I get by."

She heard a knock on her door. She looked at Nedda, raised her eyebrows, and tried to appear calm even though she knew it had to be Annie. She crossed the room, and the knock came again.

Katherine took a deep breath and opened the door. Annie stood beaming up at her, a grocery sack cradled in her arms. Katherine felt her heart thud wildly. She wanted to laugh and cry and hug Annie all at once. More than anything, though, she wanted to kiss her.

Annie grinned. "Welcome home," she said loudly as she laid her hand against Katherine's sternum.

Katherine felt her face flush and her body tingled in response. Even though the action couldn't be seen by Nedda, she stepped quickly away from Annie's touch.

"I thought perhaps you were tired from your trip, so I brought over some food for dinner," Annie said with a wink and then stepped into the room. "Welcome to Chicago, Mrs. Henderson." She set the bag on the table. "You were so kind to me when I visited, I wanted to return the favor. I thought I should bring dinner and welcome you properly."

Nedda hurried to Annie and pulled her into an enthusiastic hug before thrusting her back and studying her with careful scrutiny. "You're still skinny as the day you were born. We need to have you out to the farm this summer and fatten you up."

"I'd like that," Annie said pointedly and turned to smile at Katherine. "I need to be fattened up."

Katherine raised an eyebrow, but said nothing.

"Thank you for cleaning up for Katie," Nedda said. "She was fit to be tied when she found out I'd be coming back with her and she hadn't had a chance to pick up."

"It was my pleasure." Annie smiled. "I wanted it to be nice for your stay almost as much as Kate did." She gestured at the open suitcase. "You must have just gotten here."

"We did. The train was a little late." Katherine walked over to the bag and peered inside.

"It's nothing much," Annie said. "Just hard-boiled eggs, cheese, and pickle sandwiches. And a couple of cans of soup."

"Apparently, that's all you girls eat," Nedda muttered as she transferred clothing from the suitcase to the dresser.

Katherine waited until Nedda's back was turned. "Thank you for the food," she said, softly. "You really didn't have to."

Annie grinned. "I wanted to."

Katherine looked at her and again fought back the desire to kiss her. She glanced at Nedda and then back at Annie. "How about I run down the hallway and get some water for the soup."

"I'll help," Annie said and hurried to the shelves for the saucepan and the pitcher. She handed one to Katherine, but held onto the other.

"We'll be right back, Mama," Katherine said and stepped out into the hallway. Annie followed and closed the door behind them. They walked in silence down the hallway, close enough that Katherine could feel the heat of Annie's body, but not touching until they were in the bath. Katherine opened the door and stepped inside.

"Oh my god," Annie whispered as she put the pitcher in the sink and pushed the door closed behind them. "I can't believe you're finally back." She walked quickly to Katherine, backed her up against the wall next to the tub, and pulled her face down, kissing her hard. She pressed her body into Katherine's and deepened the kiss, breaking it only long enough to murmur Katherine's name.

Their breath came heavily, and Annie wasted no time in sliding her hand from Katherine's neck to the curve of her breast. Katherine exhaled sharply.

"God I've missed you," Annie murmured as she fumbled with the buttons on the front of Katherine's blouse.

Katherine grabbed Annie's hands and tried to still them. "Annie, stop. We can't."

"Of course we can." Annie pulled her face down and silenced her with another kiss. Katherine felt her resistance weaken until she remembered that Nedda was down the hall.

"Annie." Katherine's voice shook as she tried to still Annie's hands. "We need to stop. My mother is waiting for us. We could get caught."

Annie smiled wickedly, freed one of her captured hands, and slid it to Katherine's waist and then lower.

"Annie, stop," Katherine said, though she didn't remove her hand. "We can't. Not now." She felt her hips involuntarily arch into Annie's palm and gasped as Annie slowly rubbed. "Maybe I can walk you home or something." She closed her eyes and despite herself, moaned softly. "Annie, we're supposed to be getting water."

"Kate." Annie pressed harder and buried her face against Katherine's neck. "Please. You've been gone for a week. All I want is a little time alone with you."

"That's not all you want and you know it." Katherine exhaled slowly and then forced herself to push Annie's hand away. She laughed shakily. "We need to fill these with water. We've already been gone too long."

"Say you'll walk me home." Annie stood between Katherine and the sink. "Say it or you're not leaving this room without a scene."

"Annie," Katherine said softly. "Don't threaten me."

"It's not a threat." Her grin was sly. "It's a promise. Just say you'll walk me home."

Katherine wanted to say "no" but she couldn't. Instead she nodded.

"There." Annie leaned up and kissed the tip of Katherine's nose. "Was that so hard?" She smiled sweetly and stepped back so Katherine could get to the sink.

Katherine set the pitcher in the sink and turned on the spigot. "I'm not joking when I say we need to be careful. My mother may be from a small town, but she's not stupid. She doesn't miss a thing."

"Except what she's not looking for, Kate." Annie slid her arms around Katherine's waist and pulled her backward against her. "Seriously, do you really think it's going to occur to her to think that we might be lovers?"

Katherine pulled the pitcher from under the flow of water and turned sideways so that Annie could slip around her to reach the sink. "She wants me to get married. And she's going to be looking for any clues she can find about my life here. She wants me to have grandchildren and settle down close to home. You have no idea the pressure I've been under this week."

"And you," Annie said sharply, "have no idea how hard it's been for me to be here alone, wondering what they're trying to convince you to do—worrying that you're going to change your mind."

Katherine blinked in surprise. Annie turned away from her and stood stiffly at the sink, her face tense, her expression serious. Katherine touched Annie's arm. She could feel the slender muscles of her bicep shift as she changed her grip on the pan of water.

"I'm not going to change my mind," Katherine said softly. "I love you and I want to be with you. Nothing is going to change that." She paused. "I'm scared, too."

Annie faced Katherine and studied her. After several seconds, she sighed. "I know. And that's part of what worries me most."

Katherine set the pitcher down on the lid of the toilet, took the pan from Annie's hands, and balanced it in the sink, then pulled her into her arms. She could feel the warmth of Annie's body against hers and the slow thudding of her heart as they leaned into each other. She put her head against Annie's and inhaled the smell of her shampoo.

"Oh, sweetheart," she murmured into Annie's ear. "You don't—"

"You girls okay?" Nedda asked from what sounded like down the hall.

Katherine jerked away from Annie and reached clumsily for her pitcher. "We're in here, Mama." She jerked open the door.

Nedda stood in the hall, halfway between Katherine's room and the bathroom.

"We got to gossiping about some of the girls at work and lost track of time." Katherine felt her face flush at the lie and hoped that Nedda couldn't see it in the dim light of the hallway. She stepped out of the bathroom and walked toward Nedda. Annie followed.

"It was my fault, Mrs. Henderson," Annie said. "It was just too juicy a story not to tell."

The three walked back to Katherine's room. Nedda sank heavily into one of the chairs as Annie and Katherine prepared the makeshift meal. Annie handed the pan of water to Katherine and went to sit next to Nedda.

Katherine opened the cans of soup and poured the contents into the pan with the water. As she stirred, she watched Nedda and Annie. They were talking about the weather in Big Springs, and Nedda was relating the details of their train trip.

Nedda's face was animated. " . . . just can't get over how big and dirty everything is."

Annie laughed. "It's a shock the first time. But you get used to it."

"I'm not sure I ever would," Nedda said. "But I want to see what it is about the city that makes Katie want to stay."

Annie smiled and glanced at Katherine who smiled back and raised her eyebrows. Katherine was surprised and pleased to see Annie blush slightly in response.

"I'm so glad Katie has you, though, dear." Nedda patted Annie's hand. "I would hate to think of her here all alone with no one to spend time with."

Annie laid her hand on top of Nedda's and squeezed gently. "We take care of each other. You don't have to worry about that."

Nedda smiled and sat back in her chair. "So, Annie, tell me about you. Do you have a fella—someone special?"

"I . . . uh . . . well," Annie began and then dropped her eyes to the table. "There is someone." She looked up to meet Nedda's gaze.

Katherine coughed a warning. Annie and Nedda looked at her.

"You okay, Katie-doodle?" Nedda's expression registered concern.

Katherine thumped her chest and coughed again. "Just swallowed wrong." She looked pointedly at Annie. "I need to be *more careful*." Nedda gave her a strange look, and she wondered if she had been too obvious in her warning to Annie. She coughed once more for effect and tried to adopt a casual tone. "Soup should be ready in a second. Would one of you set the table?"

Both rose. Nedda went to get the dishes and silverware, Annie moved the flowers from the table and pulled the stuffed chair over so there would be three seats. Nedda set the table while Annie unpacked the eggs and sandwiches and put them on a place in the middle of the table. When they were done, Katherine brought the pan to the table and poured soup into each of the bowls.

"It looks real tasty." Katherine could tell Nedda was trying to be complimentary for Annie's sake. "Thank you for being considerate."

"It's my pleasure." Annie slid into the stuffed chair.

Katherine set the empty pan on the warmer and hurried back to the table. She pulled out the wooden chair between Nedda and Annie and sat down.

"Who will say the prayer?" Nedda asked just as Annie picked up her spoon and dipped it into the bowl.

"I will," Katherine said quickly and nudged Annie's foot under the table.

Nedda nodded and extended her hands—one across the table to grasp Annie's and the other toward Katherine. Annie coughed, replaced the spoon, and grasped Katherine and Nedda's hands.

Katherine closed her eyes and prayed.

"SORRY ABOUT THE prayer," Annie said later as she and Katherine walked the few blocks to her own residence. "I completely forgot that your family does that."

Katherine leaned toward Annie. "It's fine." They walked slowly, arms linked, swaying together.

"Do you think your mother likes me?" Annie asked suddenly.

"Of course she does," Katherine said. "But you need to be careful about talking too much about your 'someone special.' You can bet she'll ask about it again."

"I know. I shouldn't have said anything. I just couldn't lie or hide that there *is* someone I'm madly in love with." She squeezed Katherine's arm. "It's too big to keep inside."

Katherine smiled. "Imagine how hard it was for me the week I was home. Everyone kept asking me when I was going to settle down—if I had a sweetheart in the city." She squeezed Annie's arm. "I hate the lies."

"Me, too," Annie said and then, suddenly, "What if we just told them the truth?"

Katherine stopped abruptly and dropped Annie's arm. "Please tell me you're joking."

"I'm not joking," Annie said. "Though I'm not serious either. It was more of a 'what if.'"

"It's a bad idea and there's no 'what if' about it," Katherine said hotly. "Most people believe what we have is unnatural. If we were found out, we would lose our jobs, our homes, our lives."

"And are you one of those people?"

"You know I'm not," Katherine said with a sigh. "Do we really have to go into this now? It's been such a long week—such a long day. Can't we just . . . walk?"

"Fine. I just . . . ." Annie shrugged and slipped her arm back through Katherine's. "Fine."

The silence was uncomfortable as they walked the rest of the way to Annie's rooming house. When they reached the entryway, Annie turned and slid her arm around Katherine's waist.

"Come up."

Katherine glanced up at the window to Annie's room, tempted. She wanted to, but she knew what would happen if they were alone together. She shook her head. "I can't I have to get back. Mama will wonder. And worry."

"She's bathing and getting ready for bed. That will take a while." Annie pulled Katherine closer. "Come up. We can be quick."

"Annie, I can't," Katherine protested.

Annie sighed dramatically, grasped Katherine's hand, and pulled her into the entryway. "You can. Just for just a second so we can have a proper hello."

Katherine let Annie pull her into the building and up the stairs to her room.

"All right," she murmured as Annie pushed the door closed behind them and pulled her head down for a kiss. "But just for a second."

KATHERINE SLIPPED INTO her room much later than she had intended.

Her mother was sitting up in bed, her open Bible in her lap. "I was beginning to worry."

"I'm sorry," Katherine said quickly. "I . . . we just got to . . . talking and lost track of time."

"Well, I'm just glad you're home safe." She peered at Katherine in the soft light of the reading lamp. "You okay? Your face is red."

"I'm fine." Katherine raised her hands to her face. It was hot. She could smell Annie's perfume on her fingers. "I just walked back quickly."

Katherine fidgeted under her mother's scrutiny. She looked at the table and then turned and went to the dresser for her nightgown. Finally, she picked up the basket she used to carry her soap and lotion to the bathroom. "I'm just going to get changed for bed." She headed quickly for the door.

"You're going to need a towel," her mother said.

Katherine stopped. She laughed self-consciously. "You're right." She returned to the closet to pull the towel from the hook inside the door. "I almost forgot. Travel always wears me out. By the end of the day, I'm just useless."

Nedda's gaze softened. "Go get cleaned up and come to bed. I reckon we could both use a good night's sleep."

Katherine smiled and left the room. By the time she returned, Her mother was snoring softly.

"Thank God for small favors," she thought tiredly as she settled onto her side of the bed. "Let's just hope it holds out for the rest of the week."

KATHERINE'S PRAYERS WERE answered until the second to last day of her mother's visit. She had been able to take time off work but couldn't find anyone to cover her Friday shift.

"I'll be fine," her mother said that morning when Katherine asked for the hundredth time if she would be all right alone. "I'm just going to walk down to that park. Seems funny to walk someplace so you can sit and look at trees, but when in Rome . . ." She shook her head and laughed. "Wait till I tell folks back home how city folk experience the outdoors."

Katherine laughed with her. Though she loved her mother, secretly, she was relieved to have a day away—even if it was only to work.

"I'll be home by six," Katherine said as she opened the door to leave. "And then we'll go out to dinner to celebrate your last night here. We'll go someplace nice. Perhaps we could find someplace downtown."

The day passed quickly, and Katherine was reminded of how much she enjoyed her life away from the scrutiny of her mother.

"I love her," Katherine said as she and Annie walked home across the Franklin-Orleans Street Bridge. "But I'm ready to have my life back."

"Amen," Annie said with a grin. "So, tonight is . . . ?"

"Dinner out." Katherine slowed their pace so they could have a little more time.

"Can I come along?"

Annie had asked several times to do things with Katherine and her mother. And each time, Katherine had found an excuse not to include her. She shook her head. "I wish you could, but it's Mother's last night in the big city. It should just be the two of us."

Annie abruptly stopped and went to stand against the bridge's railing.

Katherine stopped, too. She could tell from Annie's expression that she was upset.

"She's going home tomorrow and then things can get back to normal," she said quickly.

Annie nodded slowly. "Normal meaning that you won't have to pretend like I don't exist anymore? Normal meaning that we continue to live in two places and act like we're nothing more than friends? Normal meaning that you don't have to be ashamed of being found out by your family?"

Katherine narrowed her eyes. "Listen Annie, I know you're frustrated—"

Annie snorted. "I'm more than frustrated. I'm angry. I'm tired of being excluded from the important aspects of your life. It's been over a year, Kate. When are you going to stop being so scared of what people might think? Jesus, you won't even let me spend time with your mother under the guise that we're just friends. How do you think that makes me feel?"

Katherine sighed. "Do we really have to have this conversation right now? Mama is expecting me."

Annie threw up her hands. "Case in point. Heaven forbid that you're late and you had to explain that you were spending time with me. She might suspect."

"You're not being fair," Katherine said.

"Neither are you," Annie said tightly as she turned and walked in the direction of her boarding house. Katherine followed, and they walked in silence until they reached the Merchandise Mart where they parted without saying goodbye.

Katherine watched Annie until she turned the corner and disappeared from sight. Their conversation bothered her. She fought the urge to run after Annie and talk to her immediately. Deep in thought, she entered the boarding house, climbed the stairs, and opened the door to her room.

Her mother's head jerked up in surprise as Katherine stepped into the room. She was sitting on the bed which was strewn with sheets of paper. Her eyes were red and her expression was stricken.

"Mama?" Katherine asked with a frown.

"How dare you use those lips to say my name after what you've been using them for," her mother hissed.

"I . . . I don't . . ." Katherine began and then looked down at the papers. She recognized Annie's handwriting. She raised her hand. "It's not what you think."

"All this time." Her mother thrust out a handful of paper. "All this time I thought you were just headstrong. I thought you wanted to find a man better than what we got in Big Springs. And now I know you never wanted a man at all, did you?"

"Mama . . ." Katherine shook her head. She held out her hands. "It's not like that."

"Oh, I got eyes," her mother said knowingly. "I read what you and that girl do together. It sickens me, Katherine. It sickens me to think you're doing those things. And to think I lay in this bed." She looked down at the mattress in disgust.

"Mama, please, let me explain." Katherine felt the tears sting her eyes. "Annie and I . . . we're . . . it's . . ." She shook her head, unsure what to say.

"I always thought there was something odd about the two of you," her mother said. "You was too . . . comfortable with each other. And now I know why and it breaks my heart."

Her mother dropped her chin onto her massive chest and sobbed. She squeezed her fist and crumpled the sheets of paper in her hand. Katherine resisted the urge to rush forward—though not to comfort her, but to save the letters from Annie.

"Why have you done this?" her mother cried with renewed anger. "Why have you forsaken God and his plan for you?" Her tear stained face was red and swollen. Her lips twisted into a sneer and when she spoke, flecks of spittle flew from her lips. "You will burn in hell if you don't stop."

"I can't stop," Katherine cried.

Her mother scowled. "Can't or won't."

Katherine shook her head miserably and tears rolled down her cheeks. "Both. I love her." She dropped her head into her hands.

"You might not be able to, but I can."

Katherine jerked her eyes upward, her stomach tight. Her mother's expression was defiant. "What do you mean?"

"You're coming home with me," her mother said. "You're leaving this city full of sin and you're coming home. Once you're away from that . . . woman . . . and this *life* you can settle down and lead a good, godly life."

"I won't go back." Katherine shook her head. "You can't make me."

"You can and you will," her mother said resolutely. "You have a choice. It's either her or your family because I can tell you right now, if you choose to live this . . . unnatural life . . . you will not be welcome in my home. You will no longer be my child."

"Mama," Katherine cried. "Please. No. You don't understand. I love her."

"It's wrong," her mother spat and threw the letters on the floor. Katherine rushed to pick them up but her mother stood and placed her feet on them. "No!"

"Those are mine!" Katherine cried.

"They need to be destroyed."

Katherine's fear was replaced by anger. "Those are my letters and you will *not* destroy them." She barely recognized her voice as her own. "You had no right to read them in the first place. You had no right to go through my things."

"I knew something was wrong here." Her mother was talking as much to herself as to Katherine. "I knew in my bones there was something wrong with that girl. I knew it when she came to the house for Christmas and I knew it when she didn't pray before dinner. She is leading you down her dirty, unnatural path." She clenched her now-empty fists. "And I won't have it!"

"It's not your decision," Katherine spat.

"You're coming home with me." Her mother looked distastefully around the room. "You will pack your bags tonight and get on that train with me tomorrow. And you can leave all of this here. I don't want any of it in my home." She looked down at the bed. "And as for these . . ." She grabbed a handful of letters and began to rip them apart.

"Mama, no!" Katherine rushed forward and grabbed her mother's hands in an attempt to stop her.

"Don't you dare touch me," her mother said sharply as she pulled away from Katherine's grasp and slapped her across the face. Bits of paper flew from her hand and fluttered to the floor.

Katherine stood in stunned silence and slowly lifted her hand to her cheek. The skin burned.

"I will not let you ruin your life with this disgusting activity." Her mother's voice rose as she kicked at the papers under her feet, trampling and tearing them. "You will not be like this!"

Katherine leapt forward. "Mama, stop. Please, stop."

"How could you do this to me?" her mother asked as she collapsed on the bed and sobbed.

Katherine stared, unsure what to say or do. "Mama, please don't cry. Please."

Her mother looked up at her and her face twisted into a sneer. "I can't even stand to look at you."

The words stung. Katherine hesitated for several seconds and then, both ashamed and furious, turned and walked purposefully to the door.

"You're going to her, aren't you?" her mother said. "You should be going to church to pray for your soul."

"There is nothing wrong with my soul." Katherine yanked open the door, not caring if anyone heard her words. "And there is nothing wrong with loving Annie."

She stepped into the hall, slammed the door closed behind her, and hurried down the hall to the stairs and out the front door. All she could see was the pavement in front of her and the tops of her shoes as she walked. She had to get to Annie. She had to see her—to hold her and be reassured that there was nothing wrong with their love. She turned in front of Annie's building and collided with someone coming down the steps.

"Oh," Katherine cried. "I'm so sorry. I didn't see you. I—"

"My god, I'm sorry," the woman said at the same time. "I—"

They stopped and stared at each other.

"Katherine," Margie said finally. "How awkward."

Katherine blinked and stared at Annie's former lover. "What are you doing here?" She glanced up at Annie's window. The curtains were drawn.

"I . . ." Margie began and then stopped. She, too, looked up at Annie's window and then took a deep breath. "I . . . well, I guess it's good that it's finally out in the open now, isn't it."

"What's out in the open?" Katherine asked. Her throat was tight, and she felt as if she knew what Margie was going to say before she spoke.

"Well . . ." Margie said. "While you were gone Annie and I . . . oh, how should I say this? We reconnected."

"No," Katherine said and shook her head quickly. "That's not true. You're lying. Annie loves me, not you."

"Katherine," Margie said with a condescending smile. "I'm so sorry to have to be the one to tell you, but, well . . . that's not what Annie says. Or at least, that's not the whole of what she says. She loves you, yes, but you're not giving her what she needs."

Katherine shook her head slowly. "Annie would never . . ."

"Never, what?" Margie laid a hand on Katherine's arm. "Cheat on you? Like she did on me with you?" She smiled. "Darling, she not only would, she did. She's not entirely convinced you're really one of us. And neither am I, for that matter."

"No," Katherine said. "No, that's not true. She wouldn't."

"She was convinced that when you went home, you weren't coming back," Margie said. "We met for drinks, one thing led to another and . . . oh, Kate, I'm so sorry."

"No, you're not," Katherine said tightly. "You're taking a great amount of pleasure from this, I think."

Margie pressed a hand to her chest. "I'm not."

"I don't believe you," Katherine said.

"Well, then, you should go upstairs and ask Annie yourself," Margie said. "Mind you, she's still in bed so it might take a little while for her to come to the door." She leaned forward and whispered conspiratorially, "You know how she is . . . after."

"I hate you," Katherine spat.

"I couldn't care less," Margie said with a shrug. "Especially in light of everything that's happened. I'm just glad that Annie has finally decided to be with someone who truly is a lesbian and not just playing at it."

"You don't know anything about me." Katherine straightened and squared her shoulders.

"Don't you think it's time you stopped this charade and let her fall in love with someone who isn't ashamed of who they are—someone who doesn't hide her away?"

"I'm not . . . I don't." Even as she spoke the words, Katherine knew she was lying. She sighed, deflated.

"That's what I thought," Margie said with a tiny smirk. "Well, I've

got to run. I just stopped by for a quick chat, if you know what I mean."
She studied Katherine for several seconds. "Listen, if you don't mind the
advice, you might want to tidy up just a little before you go up. You look
like hell."

"You're a horrible, spiteful bitch," Katherine said.

"Yes," Margie said and made a show of stepping around Katherine. "I
am. You'd do well to remember that in the future."

She walked away without turning, and Katherine fought the urge to
rush after her and tear her hair out. Instead, she took a deep breath and
looked up at Annie's window. The room was still dark. *Is Annie really
asleep*, she wondered? Had she and Maggie really reconciled?

She shook her head. Annie wouldn't do that to her. She wouldn't do
that to their relationship. But then, she recalled how she had pushed Annie
away when she had come home—how she had kept her at a distance.
Annie had wanted to sleep together several times during her mother's
visit and each time Katherine had rebuffed her advances. Margie's words
echoed in her ears. "Don't you think it's time you stopped this charade
and let her fall in love with someone who isn't ashamed of who they
are—someone who doesn't hide her away out of shame?"

Katherine put her hand on the stone banister and started up the stairs
to the front door. She needed to talk to Annie—to find out the truth. But
halfway up, she stopped. What, she wondered, did she intend to say? She
had come to Annie because her mother had found out that they were
lovers. Her mother had said to choose. And she came here because she
was choosing Annie. But what was she choosing?

She thought about the number of times Annie had begged her to move
in together—to build a life. And she had said "no" every time. *Why?*
What was holding her back? Was it because she was scared or ashamed?
Was Margie right in her suggestion that Katherine really wasn't like her
and Annie?

Katherine slid down the banister to sit on the steps. Annie's frustration,
her fears about Katherine's commitment to their relationship—none of
it was an issue for Margie because she knew who she was. Unlike
Katherine, she was able to give Annie what she wanted and needed at
any time without all reservation.

"It's true," Katherine murmured with sudden realization. Even if
Annie wasn't being unfaithful, the core of what Margie had said was
true. She felt the tears sting the back of her eyes as she realized that she
could never fully give Annie what she wanted. And because of that, she
was being selfish and unfair.

Katherine rose and slowly descended the stairs to the sidewalk. She
looked up again at Annie's window and considered what to do—not just

at this moment, but in a general sense. She couldn't be the lover Annie needed, just as she couldn't be the daughter her mother expected. As she contemplated what to do, she saw a flare of light in Annie's room. She was lighting one of her candles or her kerosene lamp. She watched the glow of light brighten and then dim as Annie lowered the wick.

She realized she needed to move—to go somewhere before Annie looked out and saw her. She looked in the direction of her boarding house. She couldn't go back yet. She decided to go downtown. There was a church there she had attended when she first came to the city. Perhaps they would take her in. And if nothing else, she could stand before God, ask for forgiveness and pray for the strength to do what needed to be done.

"Good bye, Annie," she whispered as she took one last look at the softly-glowing window. Before she could change her mind, she turned and walked away.

CHAPTER 19
Lawrence, Kansas, 1997

JOAN SAT IN the car and stared at the water. Lake Clinton was small—just a pond compared to Lake Michigan—but still she found it calming. There was something about the water that, even when she was younger, had soothed her. She remembered how often, after she had fought with her mother, she would drive out to the dam and sit and stare at the water. Back then, she had thought her mother was a bitch. Now she realized that she was simply unhappy and struggled with issues that Joan, as a teenager, couldn't possibly have understood. She wasn't sure that she could even now.

Joan tried to imagine what it must have been like to have been raped and then to have had a child that she hadn't wanted in the first place. Mrs. Yoccum was right in that it wasn't that her mother hadn't loved her. It was just that she was a daily reminder of what had happened.

Joan closed her eyes and tipped her head back against the headrest. What if it had been her, she wondered suddenly? She tried to imagine the situation as her mother would have experienced it. The 1950s had been such a different, repressive era. She would like to think that she would have handled the situation differently, but would she have? She didn't live in those times. And she had never loved the way her mother had loved Annie.

Annie.

The sound of her name still gave Joan a bit of a shock. It wasn't that she disliked lesbians—far from it. She had several friends in Chicago that were gay. That wasn't the point. The point was, the woman she thought she knew had been someone else entirely—a woman who had loved so deeply that even after Annie's death, she continued to write her love letters so filled with passion and regret that it made Joan's heart ache in sympathy. The knowledge also made her heart ache in jealousy—not just that Annie had commanded all of her mother's love, but also that she had never had that kind of love of her own. She had never had an Annie.

Joan sighed and opened her eyes. The setting sun glinted off the water, and she suddenly wanted more than anything to be near it—to bathe herself in the deceptive rays of warm-colored light. She pulled the keys from the ignition and opened the door. The air was cool.

Carefully, she swung her legs over the guard rail and picked her way down the rocks to the edge of the water. She reached the shore and raised her hand to shade her eyes. The slap of water against the large, flat rocks at her feet was rhythmic and soothing. Near one of the far banks, two fishermen in a small rowboat cast their lines, slowly reeled them in, and then cast again.

"Why?" she wondered suddenly. "Why *haven't* I loved like that?"

She thought about the men in her life. She hadn't loved Luke—or at least not like her mother had loved Annie. And Mark had just been a distraction—a vacation from the predictable monotony of working, cooking, and hauling the kids from lesson to practice to activity. Mark had been an opportunity to feel something—anything, she admitted.

She sighed and looked out again at the water. The sun had almost dropped beneath the horizon and everything around her, the air, the trees, the water, was tinged with shades of honey, purple, and sienna.

"I spent so many years resenting Mom because she didn't love me the way I wanted her to," she said softly. "And come to find out, she didn't hate me as much as she hated herself."

The moment she said the words, she realized they were true. It was ironic. And it was sad. She wondered again if there were any pictures of Annie. What would she have looked like? Tall? Short? Heavy? Slender? Was she masculine? And how had she died?

Joan glanced down at her wristwatch. It was five-thirty—time for dinner. She wondered if Mrs. Yoccum was back from the hospital and if her son was all right. Joan hadn't seen Jason Yoccum in several years. They had played together as children and had attended the same schools, but because he was three years younger, they had never socialized outside the privacy of their yards.

She smiled as she remembered that Jason had been her first kiss. It was the summer of 1966. She had been eleven and Jason had been eight. They had been under Mrs. Yoccum's house looking for bugs for Jason's collection. Joan still remembered the musty odor of stale dirt and the sting of grit in her knees and palms as they crawled around. Dirty, broken spider webs clung to the lattice that ran from the bottom of the porch to the ground.

"Look at that one." Jason pointed to a large spider putting the finishing touches on the center of its web.

"Ugh." Joan cringed. "It's gross."

"No. It's beautiful. Look." Jason's voice was soft with wonder and appreciation.

Joan looked, but not at the spider. Something about his tone made her look at him. His dark curls were plastered to his head with sweat. Even in the dim light under the porch, she could see his long eyelashes.

"You're beautiful," she said without thinking.

Jason turned to her and smiled. It was such a sweet smile that Joan leaned forward and kissed him lightly on the lips. He didn't pull away or respond. He simply accepted it. She sat back, and he smiled at her.

"Why did you do that?" he asked softly.

"I don't know. I just . . . you were so . . ." She shrugged. "Do you mind?"

Jason shook his head. "No. It was nice. You can do it again if you want."

Joan studied him for several seconds before leaning in and kissing him again. This time he puckered his lips and kissed her back.

"What did you think?" Joan asked when they pulled apart.

Jason shrugged. "It was okay. But I don't get the big deal of it."

Joan nodded in agreement. "You're right. Maybe when we're older we can try it again."

They hadn't, of course. By the time Joan started dating, her attention was focused on boys her own age and Jason had seemed too much like a child. But now, as she sat by the lake and Jason was in the hospital, she thought again about that kiss. She considered going to see him. But how strange would that be, she wondered. She envisioned the scene— her showing up with his wife and family there. "Oh me?" she imagined saying. "Oh, I used to live next door. I was just feeling nostalgic about my first kiss with your husband. And how *is* Jason?"

Joan shook her head. It was a silly thought. She would simply go over to Mrs. Yoccum's later tonight to find out how he was doing. And while she was there, perhaps she would have the opportunity to ask more questions about her mother and Annie. In fact, she thought as the sun slid fully beneath the horizon, if she left now, she could run by the grocery store and get something for herself and Mrs. Yoccum for dinner. And maybe, she thought, she should also stop at the liquor store.

IT WAS FULLY dark by the time Joan returned to her mother's house, and she was glad for the motion-sensor lights. Mrs. Yoccum's house appeared to be dark, which was fine given that Joan still had to bake the premade lasagna she'd purchased from the organic grocery store. With a groan, she hefted the grocery bag higher on her hip, transferred the plastic bottle of whiskey from her free hand to the one supporting the bag, and fumbled to insert her key into the lock.

Once inside, she put away the groceries, stuck the bottle of wine she had bought for herself in the refrigerator, and preheated the oven for the lasagna. While she waited for the oven to heat, she ran next door and left

Mrs. Yoccum's whiskey and a card on the front porch where she would be sure to see it. Even if she didn't come home in time for dinner, she knew Mrs. Yoccum was too polite to not stop in and thank her—which could be the opportunity she was looking for to find out what had happened with her mother and Annie.

The oven beeped five minutes later, and Joan put the pan of lasagna in the oven and then stood back, unsure what to do with herself. The clock on the wall indicated that it was almost seven. She sighed. She knew she should call home, but if she were honest, she really didn't want to. She remembered her earlier thoughts of simply disappearing and again felt guilty.

She thought instead about the wine in the refrigerator. She'd bought it on a whim when she was getting Mrs. Yoccum's whiskey, but the more she thought about it, the more she wanted a drink. The realization made her cringe. It was wrong to drink while pregnant. She knew that. But still, she reasoned, one glass wouldn't hurt it, would it? Women in France did it all the time. And anyway, what did it matter? She was going to go to Wichita. She was going to have an abortion. She had already made that decision. So why was she worried about having a glass of wine? Hell, she should have the entire bottle. Still, she hesitated.

"Fuck it," she said after several long seconds. She had purchased the wine, which meant she knew that ultimately, she was going to have some. She should stop pussyfooting around and just open it.

Before she could change her mind, she strode to the refrigerator, took out the bottle, and used the cheap corkscrew she had bought at the market to pull the cork from the bottle. The aroma was deep and buttery. She poured herself a glassful and took a large swallow. It tasted wonderful, and she pushed away any guilt before she could think about it too much. What was done was done. She sighed, took another sip, and wandered out into the darkened living room. Her mother's chair beckoned.

Slowly, she rocked. The wine and the rhythm relaxed her as she let her mind quiet for several minutes of precious calm.

A sudden noise—knocking—cut through the silence. She almost jumped out of the chair in surprise.

She hurried to the door, flicked on the porch light, and saw Mrs. Yoccum. In her hand was the card Joan had left with the whiskey.

Joan pulled open the door. "Hi. I see you got my note." She gestured at the card.

"I did. Thank you." Mrs. Yoccum grinned. "And thank you for the gift. I'm sure I'll put it to good use."

Joan laughed. "I'm glad." She gestured toward the kitchen. "I have a lasagna in the oven. I thought maybe you'd like some company for dinner. I was thinking I could bring it over when it's finished baking."

Mrs. Yoccum smiled wearily. "Oh, that would be lovely. It's been such a long day." She grimaced. "I haven't had anything to eat since our cinnamon rolls this morning."

"So, what happened to Jason?" Joan asked. "Is he all right?"

"Oh, some man was fiddling with his radio and drove through the intersection and hit Jason's car." Mrs. Yoccum ticked off his injuries on her fingers. "He's got four broken ribs, a broken arm, and a concussion—which is why they're keeping him."

"Well, I'm glad he's all right." The timer on the oven beeped. "Sounds like the lasagna is done. How about you go home, get comfortable and I come over in say . . . ten minutes? Will that give you enough time to get settled?"

Mrs. Yoccum nodded and turned toward the steps. "I'll leave the door open, and you can just let yourself in, all right?"

"That sounds great, Mrs. Yoccum," Joan said

"Oh, and call me Lettie," she said over her shoulder. She grasped the railing and carefully stepped down. "You're too old to still call me Mrs. Yoccum."

"All right, then, Lettie," Joan said with a nod. "I'll see you in about ten minutes."

"I DON'T THINK I could eat another bite." Joan wadded her paper napkin into a ball and dropped it onto the empty dinner plate.

"It *was* good, wasn't it?" Mrs. Yoccum said. "I don't know as I've ever had eggplant lasagna before."

"I got it at The Merc," Joan said. "It was either that or spinach and I thought this would be more up our alley."

"It was a nice change." Mrs. Yoccum smiled sweetly. "And it was so thoughtful of you to bring it over. Thank you."

"It was my pleasure." Joan leaned forward and picked up the juice glass that held her wine.

"I'm sorry I don't have proper wine glasses," Mrs. Yoccum said. "I don't usually drink it."

"It's fine." Joan raised the glass to her lips and took a sip. "It tastes the same regardless of what it's served in."

"Well, yes, I suppose so." Mrs. Yoccum chuckled.

"I'm so glad that Jason is going to be all right. You must have been so worried when his wife called."

"Oh, Susan isn't his wife," Mrs. Yoccum said quickly. "Well, not anymore. She's his ex-wife. I still call her my daughter-in-law because . . . well, that's what she still feels like. They're still good friends."

"That's nice." The wine made Joan philosophical. "Hard to do, though, I would imagine—being friends with your ex."

Mrs. Yoccum nodded and pushed her plate of half-eaten lasagna away from her. She saw Joan watching her and said quickly, "It's not that it wasn't good. I just don't seem to eat much these days."

Joan looked at her own empty plate and grinned. "Well, that's not really a problem for me." She arranged and then rearranged her silverware as she considered how to broach the subject of her mother and Annie. When nothing occurred to her, she decided just to ask. "Mrs. Yoccum, I was—"

"Lettie," Mrs. Yoccum corrected.

"I'm sorry, *Lettie*," Joan said quickly and grinned. "I've just called you Mrs. Yoccum for so long that it's ingrained."

"I understand. It's nice that your mother raised you to be respectful." Mrs. Yoccum smiled fondly. "Katie was a stickler for propriety."

"Or maybe not so much," Joan said wryly. "Having a lesbian lover in the 1930s wasn't quite the norm."

"No, I don't expect it was." Mrs. Yoccum laughed.

Joan looked around the kitchen. It hadn't changed since she and Jason were kids.

"Mom has that same wall phone," Joan said with a little laugh. "Different color, but the same phone. How long have you lived here?"

"We moved in . . . well, goodness, it must have been . . ." She paused and gazed thoughtfully into the distance. "Not quite forty years ago. You were five or six and Jason was two."

"I kind of remember that," Joan said with a small smile. "There was a truck with all of your things in it. And the men were like worker ants taking things from the truck into the house."

"You were just a little thing," Mrs. Yoccum said, her eyes faraway. "I remember you standing on your porch watching everything."

"Mom wouldn't let me come over. She said I would just get in the way."

"She just didn't want you to get hurt is all. But I could tell you were itching to come over. You were such a strong-willed little thing."

Joan smiled at the memory. "I was so curious about you. You were so nice. And you seemed so glamorous. I don't remember your husband, though."

"You wouldn't have," Mrs. Yoccum said. "He died shortly before Jason was born."

"I'm sorry," Joan said quietly.

Mrs. Yoccum waved away her condolences. "We didn't know about this post-traumatic stress disorder back then. We just knew he hadn't adjusted to civilian life after the war. He had insomnia, nightmares, depression. He drank to numb the pain and finally, I came home one day to find him dead. He had shot himself in the head."

"Oh my god," Joan murmured. "I had no idea."

"It was a long time ago, dear." Mrs. Yoccum reached across the table and patted Joan's hand reassuringly. "But after it happened, I just couldn't stay in San Francisco anymore. There were too many memories." She paused and swirled the whiskey in her glass. "After Jason was born, I moved a couple of times. But no place felt like home. Eventually we settled here. Lawrence has been good to us."

"It must have been hard raising Jason on your own," Joan said. "Single mothers weren't very common in those days."

"Sometimes," Mrs. Yoccum agreed. "But John—that was my husband—left us well-provided for. He came from money. And then once Jason was in school, I got a job doing secretarial work for one of the construction companies in town."

She took a sip from her tumbler and smacked her lips appreciably.

"So, you never met Annie," Joan said, picking up where their conversation had ended that morning.

Mrs. Yoccum took another sip and shook her head.

"But you *do* know what happened to her, right?" Joan placed her elbows on the table and leaned forward. "I mean, you know how she died. Mom's letters don't give any indication, but you know, don't you?"

Mrs. Yoccum leaned back in her chair. A tiny smile played on her lips as she studied Joan. "You're so much like her—the way you worry problems to death and the way you stew about things." She smiled more broadly. "It's not a criticism even though it might seem like one." She paused and seemed to search for words. "You want to know about your mother and Annie." She met Joan's gaze and nodded as if she had made a decision. "You should know that your mother loved Annie, but she was *never* comfortable with that part of herself—at least not socially. She *cared* what people thought of her—of her reputation. Especially here in Kansas. In Chicago, she was free to be whomever she wanted. But here, she was always Clyde's wife, Nedda's daughter, *your* mother. Does that make sense? She chose social acceptance."

"But at a price," Joan said. "It made her bitter and angry." She shook her head. "You have no idea what it was like to grow up in that house. And regardless of what you say—" She held up her hand to stop Mrs. Yoccum from contradicting her. "Regardless of what you say, I know that every time she looked at me, she resented me. At least now I know why."

"You're right," Mrs. Yoccum agreed. "I didn't have to grow up in that house. But I saw what went on. And I know how she talked about you—how much she loved you. She just had a hard time showing it."

Joan pursed her lips and raised an eyebrow.

Mrs. Yoccum laughed. "She used to make that face, too."

"So, help me understand this." Joan was determined to find out what had happened to Annie. "Annie was the boarder while my father was at the war."

Mrs. Yoccum nodded. "She lived out at the old homestead with your mother while your father was down south building boats for the war effort."

"And no one thought it was strange?" Joan asked. "My father didn't think it was odd?"

"Everybody was doing what they needed to do to get by. People were taking in lodgers, families were moving in together to save money. It was such a different time. Young people today don't understand. And your father was relieved, I think, to have someone at the homestead with your mother. A woman alone . . . well . . ." Mrs. Yoccum raised her eyebrows meaningfully.

"So, what happened when he came home?"

"The war ended in '45, and when they got word he was coming back, Annie moved out,"

Joan nodded and picked up her wine, though she didn't take a drink. "Where did she go?"

"Well, she and Kate knew they couldn't be near each other and not be together, so Annie left," Mrs. Yoccum said. "She'd come into some money when her parents died, so she just traveled around the United States."

"And their relationship ended? Again?"

"Oh, I don't think you could say their relationship ever *really* ended," Mrs. Yoccum said. "Even when they weren't together, they weren't with anyone else—not really anyway. I expect the closest they came to that was when your mother left Chicago and married Clyde. It was the one thing she could do that would drive Annie away."

Joan frowned. "What do you mean? Why did she want to do that if she loved her so much?"

Mrs. Yoccum stared down into her glass as she considered the question. "Your mother thought she couldn't give Annie what she wanted—that in the long run, she didn't have what it took to go against social convention. So she decided she would set Annie free. And the only way to do that was to move back here and marry your father. She had to sever their connection completely." Mrs. Yoccum raised her eyes to meet Joan's gaze. "Your mother once compared Annie to a drug. She said the only way she could stay away was to quit cold turkey."

Joan stared at Mrs. Yoccum, amazed that they were talking about her mother.

"You seem surprised," Mrs. Yoccum said.

"I am, a little. And overwhelmed. I don't know what to think." She paused, wanting to ask about Bud's confession that there had been a murder, but unsure if she should bring it up. Barbara had said that he tended to fabricate things. But then there *was* the bullet casing. She chose her words carefully. "Did my mother ever mention somebody getting shot—a murder of some sort?"

Mrs. Yoccum stared down into her drink. "Why do you ask?"

"It's probably nothing." Joan waved her hand. "It's just that when I went to see my uncle Bud, he said something about helping my father kill somebody. And there was a bullet casing in my mother's box . . ." She shrugged. "I'm sure he was just talking nonsense, but . . ."

"What did your uncle say happened?" Mrs. Yoccum asked.

"Keep in mind, he rambles a lot, but he said that my mother couldn't forgive my father or him for what they had done to protect her reputation. He wouldn't elaborate beyond that and he won't talk to me now."

"Your mother said he had Alzheimer's," Mrs. Yoccum said thoughtfully. "It's a horrible disease, but a part of me thinks it serves him right for what he did."

Joan leaned quickly forward, her gaze intense and unwavering. "What do you mean?"

"The story of the murder is true," Mrs. Yoccum said finally. "But it's complicated. Very, very complicated."

CHAPTER 20
Big Springs, Kansas, 1942

FROM INSIDE THE kitchen, Katherine heard the car's engine cough, sputter, and then die. She frowned as she plucked the faded dish towel off the table and wiped the flour from her hands. Visitors were rare—especially at this time of the afternoon. As she passed from the kitchen into the hallway, she glanced in the mirror to make sure she didn't have flour on her face. Her hair, she saw, could use a brush, but there was no time for that. She hurried to the screen door and gasped as she recognized the figure standing next to the dusty car.

Annie.

She stared at her for several seconds. Annie was wearing dark trousers and a cream-colored silk shirt, her hair was longer than last time she had seen her and pulled back into a clip at the base of her neck. She looked thinner than Katherine remembered.

They stared at each other for several long seconds. Something deep in her stomach seemed to flutter, and she clenched the dish towel to keep her hands from trembling.

"What are you doing here?" she asked finally, sounding frail and tight in her own ears.

Annie shook her head and smiled ruefully. "I don't know, actually." She looked down at the ground and shuffled her feet before licking her lips and looking almost shyly back up at Katherine. "I've left the city. I've decided to go west. But before I did, I had to see you." She looked around the yard and then back at Katherine, who stood as if frozen, her hand on the handle of the screen door. "You have a nice place. Lots of . . . space."

Katherine nodded, not trusting herself to speak.

Annie squinted up at her. "So, are you coming out? I won't bite."

Katherine swallowed and then slowly pushed the door open. The dust stirred up by Annie's car hung in the still summer air. She stepped onto the porch and faced Annie for the first time in five years. Her pulse throbbed in her wrists, in her throat, in her temples, and she tried to steady her breathing. She noticed that Annie seemed to be carrying on the same struggle for composure.

"How is Margie?" Katherine asked finally.

Annie blinked twice and looked back down at the ground. She took a deep breath and looked back up at Katherine, her gaze defiant. "We're not together. We haven't been for more than a year."

"Ah." Katherine nodded a little. "Well, that's . . . I'm sorry it didn't work out."

"Kate," Annie said softly, "you know it was never going to work out. She was just someone I turned to after you left me. You were the one I loved." She hesitated. "You still are."

Katherine pursed her lips and nodded tightly. "What do you want? Why are you here?"

"I'm here because . . ." Annie began and then stopped. "Where is Clyde?"

"He's not here right now," Katherine said quickly. "He's in town."

Annie took a step forward. "Can I come in?"

"What do you want?" Katherine asked again.

"I want to talk," Annie said and went to the bottom of the porch steps. "I want to have the talk that you've been refusing to have for five years."

Katherine felt the adrenaline course through her body and tried not to tremble. "I . . . can't." She half-turned toward the house. "I've got to get dinner ready."

"I'll help."

Katherine shook her head. "I don't need your help."

"I'll help and then I'll leave," Annie continued as if she hadn't heard Katherine's refusal. "We can cook and talk. And then, if you never want to see me again, I'll go."

Katherine stared down at her, but said nothing.

"Kate," Annie said. "You owe me this. You owe me a conversation. Now, come down here so we can talk."

"We've already—" Katherine began.

"No, we haven't," Annie interrupted loudly. "You accused me of running around on you with Margie, you moved back to Big Springs with your mother, and you got married—all without giving me a chance to explain. You've rebuffed me at every turn, and I think I deserve to know why."

"You know why." Katherine looked nervously in the direction of the road and hurried down the steps to stand in front of Annie. "And could you please lower your voice?"

"We're in the middle of the God-damned country," Annie yelled. "There is no one within ten miles to hear me. Or to see me. Or to guess at your dark little secret."

Katherine set her jaw and glared. Once again Annie was spinning the situation out of her control.

"You know why," she repeated.

"No. I don't," Annie said in a normal tone, though no less exasperated. "All I know is that you said you were in love with me—that we were planning a life together. And then you accused me of cheating on you and ended our relationship in a fucking letter." Her voice grew louder with each word. "You didn't even give me a chance to defend myself. For Christ's sake, don't you think I deserved better than that?"

"I know," Katherine said weakly without meeting Annie's eyes.

"So tell me why," Annie demanded. "Because I can't get on with my life in any meaningful kind of way until I know why you've done this."

Katherine swallowed. "Margie—"

"There was nothing going on there and you know it," Annie said. "Or at least you should. You used what she said as an excuse. So tell me the real reason why you just picked up and left. Was it your mother?"

Katherine thought back to that last day in Chicago when she returned home from work to find that her mother had gone through her letters— the disgust and disappointment in her mother's face as she issued her ultimatum. She closed her eyes and pinched the bridge of her nose.

"What we had was never going to last," she said finally. "I'm not like you. I never was."

"Could have fooled me."

Katherine opened her eyes to see Annie studying her, her dark eyes cold.

"I seem to remember very clearly what you were." Annie's voice was low and seductive. "Or do you want me to remind you?" She smirked nastily. "Does your *husband* know?"

Katherine stiffened in anger and pointed to the road. "I think you should leave now."

"Does he know what you used to do with me?" Annie asked softly as she stepped forward. "How you used to kiss me? And touch me? Does he know that?"

She continued her slow steps toward Katherine and stopped in front of her.

Willing herself not to give Annie the satisfaction of making her step back, Katherine stonily stood her ground, though she could feel her pulse throbbing wildly in her throat. She knew Annie saw it, too, because she slowly raised her hand and gently brushed her fingertips across the spot at which she had been staring.

Katherine inhaled sharply but didn't pull away.

Annie blinked and flicked her gaze upward. Katherine forced herself to look down. Annie's eyes were no longer angry. They were sad. For several long moments, they stared at each other.

Annie pushed an errant lock of hair back behind Katherine's ear. "Do you really want me to leave?" she asked softly.

"I . . . Yes." Katherine forced herself to take a step backward, away from Annie. "It would be best if you did." She turned toward the stairs and the safety of the porch.

Annie caught her arm and pulled her back. "No. I've waited five years to have this conversation. This time you'll listen to what I have to say."

Katherine dipped her head, closed her eyes, and faced Annie. "Fine. Say whatever you have to, but please make it quick. I have to make dinner. Clyde will be hungry."

Annie smiled slightly. "Kate, I know Clyde isn't here. I had to ask for directions. I talked to people in town."

Katherine pressed her lips together, but said nothing.

"What Margie said to you wasn't true," Annie said. "None of it was true. She came up to see me that evening, but only to return some of my things." She watched for a reaction. Katherine refused to respond. "I ran into her one night while you were still out of town. She said she still had several of my books and some clothes and wanted to know what to do with them. I told her I would come get them, but she said she could just drop them off."

Katherine nodded. "All right. I believe you."

"What I don't understand is why you didn't tell me what she said," Annie said. "Why didn't you come up that minute and confront me? Why didn't you give me a chance to defend myself? Why didn't you fight for us?"

"It was complicated," Katherine said.

"Or maybe you wanted to believe her," Annie said. "Or at least pretend to believe her. Maybe you wanted an easy way out."

"You don't understand," Katherine began.

"Then explain it to me. Explain to me why you bought some half-baked story about my infidelity and then left with nothing more than a letter saying that you had changed your mind and that you couldn't give me what I needed?" Annie roughly grabbed Katherine's shoulder. "Tell me."

"She found your letters," Katherine said dully.

"What?" Annie asked in confusion.

"Mother," Katherine said. "She went through my things while I was at work. She read your letters. She went crazy. She told me it was either my family or you."

Annie stared at her.

"I ran away. I was coming to you when . . ." Katherine shrugged.

"When you saw Margie," Annie finished hollowly.

They gazed at each other for several moments.

"She was right, though," Katherine said finally. "She may have lied about your . . . relationship, but she was right about the fact that I could never have given you what you wanted. Not in the long term. You wanted to live together—to have a life together. You needed someone who was . . . who is . . . like you."

"You're—" Annie began

"Don't. I'm not." Katherine stood erect with her head bent forward.

"Fine," Annie said finally and took a tentative step toward the car. "Maybe I shouldn't have come. I just . . . I had to know." She shrugged.

Katherine willed herself not to respond.

Annie sighed. "I'll go."

Kate nodded, keeping her head down, not wanting Annie to see her tears. Her shoulders shook.

"Kate," Annie said gently. "Oh, Katie. What are we doing?"

Katherine shrugged and shook her head. She cleared her throat. "I don't know."

Annie took a tentative step toward her. "Do you want me to leave?"

Katherine stared at her. "I . . ." She shook her head in confusion.

"I'm not suggesting anything but sitting down and talking. There are so many things that weren't said." Annie took a step closer, though she didn't try to touch her. "Don't you think we should?"

Katherine swallowed and nodded again. Annie laid her hand gently on her arm. She stiffened, but didn't pull away. Annie tipped her head to look up at her with a hint of a smile.

Katherine softened her gaze and cleared her throat. "Would you like to come inside? I was getting ready to make a pie. You could help."

Annie grinned and nodded. "I'd like that. Or . . ." She hesitated. "We could go for a ride in my car."

Katherine slid her gaze to the automobile and then back at Annie. "Oh my god. You have a car. When did you learn how to drive?"

Annie grinned, looking relieved. "When I got it. I had to have the salesman show me how to drive it off the lot."

Katherine laughed softly. "Why am I not surprised?"

"So, would you like to?" Annie asked. "Go for a ride, I mean."

Katherine wiped at the tears that still clung to her lashes and looked from Annie to the car and back. It seemed like the safest alternative. To go inside the home she shared with Clyde seemed wrong—and far too private, if she were honest with herself. But in the same vein, to sit on the porch seemed too public.

"A car ride sounds nice. Let me just . . ." Katherine began and then realized that there was nothing in the house that she needed or needed to do before they could leave. She had only gotten as far as measuring the flour into the bowl for her pie crust and that would keep. She had no one she had to account her actions to or anything that prevented her from simply getting in Annie's car and taking a ride.

Annie was a good driver, Katherine was surprised to realize. She drove confidently with one hand on the steering wheel and one arm in the window, a cigarette pinched between the knuckles of her index and middle fingers.

"I'm so surprised that you have a car," she said again, more for something to say than anything else.

"When I made the decision to leave Chicago, I realized that I would need it," Annie said. "I've decided to take some time—travel around the West Coast."

Katherine felt a stab of envy. Unlike her, Annie did what she wanted, *when* she wanted. "But what about your job? How can you afford that?"

"My parents died," Annie said simply.

Katherine touched her shoulder. "Oh, Annie, I'm sorry."

Annie glanced at Katherine and then back at the road. "Me, too." She shrugged. "But, I guess even a queer daughter is a better heir than none at all. They left me everything." She laughed bitterly.

"How did they die?"

"That's the irony." Annie smiled ruefully without taking her eyes from the road. "They were in a car accident on their way to see me." She shrugged. "It's no surprise, though. My father was three sheets to the wind—as usual. I'm sure it was liquid courage for his meeting with his immoral heathen of a daughter. He took a bend in the road too fast and smashed into a tree."

Katherine gently squeezed Annie's shoulder. "What a shock. And just when you were reconciling."

"Story of my life. But they left me well off." Annie glanced quickly at Katherine. "I never told you, but my parents both came from money. And my father managed to improve on the fortune during Prohibition." She grinned. "There's always money in alcohol."

"You mean your father was . . ." Katherine searched for the least offensive word.

"It's not something we talked about," Annie said. "But he had friends that were of a . . . questionable nature, yes."

"You never gave any indication," Katherine said.

"What was there to say? We were estranged. They didn't approve of me and weren't a part of my life. But after I ended things with Margie, I wrote my mother and," she shrugged, "things went from there."

"And so now you're . . . what are you doing?" Katherine asked.

"I'm taking a trip," Annie declared. "I'm taking a long trip that will end in California. And from there, who knows?"

"And Big Springs, Kansas, just happened to be on your route."

"No." Annie raised what was left of her cigarette to her lips and inhaled deeply. She held the smoke in her lungs and then slowly exhaled.

Katherine watched the familiar movement and felt her throat tighten. She turned to stare out the windshield.

"I'm sorry about your mother," Annie said finally. "How is your father?"

"He still lives on the farm," Katherine said without looking at Annie. "I take him meals every few days just to make sure he is getting something decent to eat." She gestured at a narrow dirt road to the right. "Turn here. There's a really pretty spot over that hill."

Annie turned the car down a road which quickly became nothing more than two parallel lines where truck wheels had worn away the prairie grass to expose the hard brown earth. Annie slowed the car to a crawl.

"So, no children?" she asked finally.

"No," Katherine said simply.

"Why not?"

"It's a long story," Katherine said and continued to stare out the window at the pasture. As they crested the hill, she could see the cottonwood trees that shaded the pond. She pointed. "Over there."

Annie maneuvered the car to a spot close to the water, set the parking brake, and shut off the ignition. Out of the corner of her eye, Katherine could see Annie running her fingertips lightly over the top of the steering wheel. She pretended to stare out at the water on the pond.

"At some point we're going to have to talk about this," Annie said.

"I know, but not now," Katherine said tiredly. "Let's just—"

"It has to be now." Annie turned to Katherine and fumbled for her hands. She inhaled deeply and said in a rush, "I want you to come with me to California."

Katherine turned in her seat and stared at Annie.

"I know it sounds nuts, but just hear me out. We never got our chance. But we can still be together. If you're brave enough to come with me, we can still fix this."

Katherine shook her head in disbelief. "Are you insane? Do you realize what you're asking? I can't just leave. I have responsibilities. Clyde is at the war. My father needs me. I have—"

"Bullshit." Annie glared angrily at Katherine. "Those are just excuses and you know it. You don't love Clyde." She sneered. "You only married him because that's what your mother convinced you to do. I know you,

Kate, and believe me, I know better than to think you want to stay here and rot in this incestuous little town."

Katherine jerked open the car door and climbed angrily out of the car.

"Oh no you don't," Annie said as she pulled on the handle of her own door and leapt out. "You are *not* running away from me this time."

"Leave me alone," Katherine yelled over her shoulder as she walked quickly in the direction of the pond.

"We are going to have this conversation whether you like it or not," Annie said as she hurried after Katherine, stumbling on the uneven terrain. "Come back here."

"No!" Katherine said without stopping. "Why are you doing this to me? I'm settled. I have things in order."

"You aren't happy!" Annie rushed to catch up. "Jesus, I could see how miserable you are the moment you stepped onto the porch."

"You don't know anything," Katherine said shortly.

"When it comes to you I do," Annie said as she reached Katherine and grabbed her arm. "Will you just stop?"

Furiously, Katherine spun to face Annie. Her eyes blazed, and she pulled back her fist as if she meant to hit her.

Looking startled, Annie stepped back two paces. Her heel caught in a rut, and she stumbled. She twisted her body in an attempt to right herself and fell to the ground with a soft cry.

"Annie," Katherine exclaimed, her anger forgotten as she knelt next to her. "Are you okay? What's hurt?"

"My ankle." Annie thumped her fist against the ground and muttered, "Fucking country."

"Well . . ." Katherine began. "Can you walk on it?"

"What do you think?" Annie growled up at her.

Katherine pulled up the leg of Annie's trousers and looked at her ankle. It was red and a little puffy, but nothing serious. She raised her eyes to meet Annie's. "It actually doesn't look too bad. Can you make it back to the car?"

Annie looked down at the injury and gingerly probed the skin with her fingers. "It hurts like hell."

Katherine sighed and gently touched Annie's ankle. "I know, sweetheart. Let me help you back to the car. At least there you'll be off the ground."

Annie turned her upper body, gauged the distance to the automobile, and nodded. "I should be able to make it that far."

"Here." Katherine stood and bent down to grasp Annie's upper arm and help lift her. Balancing on her good ankle, Annie slowly stood and draped her arm over Katherine's shoulders. Katherine slid her arm around her waist. Slowly they hobbled back to the passenger's side of the car which was still open.

Katherine helped Annie slide back in the seat so that her legs were extended out the passenger-side door.

Once she was situated, Annie grabbed her purse and rummaged around. "Thank god," she murmured as she pulled out her cigarette case, unsnapped it, and fished out a cigarette. Almost as an afterthought, she offered one to Katherine.

"I quit," Katherine said.

Annie raised an eyebrow, pulled a second cigarette from her case, and put both between her lips. With a practiced flick, she lit both cigarettes and snapped the lighter shut. She handed one to Katherine who looked at it for several seconds and then stuck the end into her mouth and inhaled deeply. She closed her eyes as she held the smoke in her lungs. When she couldn't hold it any longer, she tipped her head back and slowly exhaled.

"Tastes good, doesn't it?"

Katherine opened her eyes and smiled. "It does. I stopped when I moved back. Mama didn't think it was appropriate."

"Ah," Annie said and turned to flick ash from the tip of her cigarette. "She refused to let me see you—when I came here after I got your letter." She took a drag from the cigarette. "I didn't know she had found the letters, but that would explain why she was so hateful."

Katherine nodded. "I know. I was upstairs. I heard everything."

"Ah," Annie said again. "Did you get any of my letters?"

Katherine shook her head. "Mama destroyed them."

Annie snorted softly and used her forefinger and thumb to pick a sliver of tobacco off her tongue. "So, aside from the fact that your mother didn't want you to see me, why didn't you give me a chance to talk to you—to understand what had happened?"

Katherine considered her answer. "Because the reasons why didn't really matter. And, I knew that if I saw or talked to you, I would lose my resolve."

"To cut me out of your life," Annie said.

"To set you free so you could find someone who could give you what you wanted—what you needed," Katherine said.

"You could have, though, Kate."

"No," Katherine said. "I realized that when Margie said all those things."

Annie touched Katherine's shoulder over the back of the seat. "Sweetheart, that was just on the heels of the confrontation with your mother. You were upset. She put you in a horrible situation. Of course you were going to think that. But you don't still . . . do you?"

Katherine said nothing, choosing instead to study the ashy tip of her cigarette.

"Tell me you're happy." Annie scooted forward so she could lean over the seat toward Katherine.

"I'm happy," Katherine said, still not looking up.

"I don't believe you," Annie said quickly.

Katherine rolled her eyes and shook her head in frustration. "Why did you make me say it if you are just going to tell me you don't believe me?"

Annie's lips curled into a smile, and she shrugged. "Sorry." She hesitated and then grasped Katherine's hand. "I was serious about what I said before. I came here to try one last time to fix things—to ask you to go with me."

"I know," Katherine said softly. "I think I knew it the minute I saw you."

"So, will you?" Katherine could hear the pleading in Annie's voice. "Please? If you're worried about money, don't. I have enough money to support both of us for the rest of our lives."

"Annie—"

"No, hear me out," Annie interrupted. "Your mother is dead. Your father can learn to cook for himself and Clyde . . . well, Clyde is Clyde. I'm not even going to guess why you married him but I know it wasn't for love. You love me. I know you do."

"I do," Katherine said softly. "But I can't love you the way you want me to. And I made a commitment to Clyde. He's my husband. To leave him would embarrass my family—embarrass him. It would be a huge scandal. I can't."

Annie wrinkled her nose. "Leave him. We could run away together. We could have the life we were meant to lead. Together."

"I can't," Katherine said. "And more to the point, I won't. I made a commitment."

Annie's expression grew hard. "You made a commitment to me."

"It's different."

Annie snorted and narrowed her eyes.

"It is and you know it is," Katherine insisted.

"So your answer is 'no,'" Annie said.

"It has to be," Katherine said.

"Fine." Annie raised the remainder of her cigarette to her lips, inhaled deeply, and flicked it onto the road. "We should get you back, then."

"Annie," Katherine began as Annie swung her legs around and slid into the driver's seat.

"Kate, please." Annie held up her hands in surrender. "Just let it go. I can't make you do something you don't want to."

"You don't understand—"

"I don't need to," Annie interrupted. "This was a stupid idea, and I should have known better."

She started the engine. "Are you going to ride back there or move up into the front?" she said without looking at Katherine.

Kate slid out of the back seat and climbed through the passenger-side door. Annie stared stonily forward.

"What about your ankle?" Katherine asked.

"It's fine," Annie said as she put the car into gear and pulled off the track onto the grass in a wide circle that ended with them back on the track facing the direction in which they had come. She scowled as they bounced along the rutted track toward the main road.

Katherine stared out the windshield, stealing glances at Annie's stony profile. "Annie–"

"Don't," Annie said. "I shouldn't have come."

Katherine closed her eyes, summoning her courage to admit what she knew was the truth. "I'm glad you came. And you're not wrong about how I felt . . . how I feel . . . about you. That hasn't changed."

Annie blinked though she said nothing.

"I'm just not like you," Katherine said. "I'm not bold or brave or able to rebel against convention. I'm not strong in the way it would take to do what you want me to do." She sighed deeply and looked down at her lap. The end of a thread poked from the seam, and she picked at it.

Annie looked sidelong at her and then back at the road. "What if you didn't have to leave your life?"

Katherine frowned. "What do you mean?"

"Just that," Annie said. "What if you didn't have to leave your life here? I have plenty of money. I could take a room in Topeka or Lawrence. I could get a job doing secretarial work or something like that."

Katherine felt her heart leap. To have Annie close. To have the opportunity to see her whenever she wanted. It seemed too good to be true. She envisioned dinners together, conversations about books, walks by the river. And then there was the possibility of other things. She felt her face flush at the thought of kissing her, of holding her, of undressing her. She felt the familiar pressure in her stomach . . . and lower. She closed her eyes and shook her head. Having Annie that close would only lead to disastrous consequences.

"It wouldn't work," she said numbly.

"Why not?"

"Because if you were that close . . . ." Katherine imagined Clyde finding out. "If you were so near . . . it would just be too difficult."

"Difficult how?" Annie pressed.

"Think about it. I'm married."

"Realization of that fact hasn't escaped me." Annie shrugged and lifted her chin. "Besides, where I choose to live isn't really your decision."

Katherine felt her temples throb. She had forgotten how exasperating Annie could be. "Why are you doing this to me? Do you have any idea how hard—?"

"How hard?" Annie pulled into the driveway that led to Katherine's house and slammed on the brakes.

The force of the stop threw Katherine forward. She thrust her hand out to avoid hitting the dash.

"You want to talk about hard?" Annie turned, her face flushed with anger. "What's *hard* is watching the woman that you love run away from you and marry a man she doesn't even like. What's *hard* is having her rebuff you at *every* turn. What's *hard* is repeatedly putting yourself in a vulnerable position simply because you can't imagine—*refuse* to imagine—your life with someone else. So don't you *dare* talk to me about what's hard."

She made a derisive noise in the back of her throat, shook her head in disgust, and put the car back into gear. She pulled down the drive and parked in almost the exact place she had been before. Still refusing to look at Katherine, she set the brake and killed the motor. They both stared out the windshield.

"Annie . . . ." Katherine sighed and turned to look at Annie. Rather than meet her gaze, Annie tucked several curls that had escaped their pins back behind her ears. Katherine stared at her slender fingers in rapt fascination, remembering the sensation of those fingers touching her. The memory made her shiver, and she shifted in her seat.

Annie looked at her, and Katherine knew she could see her vulner-ability—her desire. Annie blinked twice and frowned slightly. Her anger seemed to dissipate. "Sometimes I think I hate you just as much as I love you. Do you know that?"

Katherine nodded. "I do." She lightly touched the crest of Annie's cheek. She meant it to be a gesture of tenderness, but the moment her fingertips made contact with Annie's warm flesh she trembled. Annie saw her reaction and, before Katherine could protest, leaned swiftly forward and pressed her lips firmly to Katherine's.

Katherine tried not to respond, but as Annie increased the pressure and intensity of the kiss, her body reacted. Familiar longing flooded her limbs, and she felt herself become so aroused that she knew making love to Annie was a foregone conclusion.

"God, I've missed you," she murmured as Annie slid her lips down her neck to her collarbone.

Annie exhaled against the tender skin of her neck as she impatiently pulled Katherine's blouse free from her skirt and slid her hand up her warm stomach to her breast. Katherine moaned softly. Seconds turned into minutes as they kissed and touched and pressed their bodies into each other. Annie tugged at her skirt, and Katherine realized that anyone coming down the drive could see them. She pulled back and tried to catch her breath.

"We need to go inside," she said, her words coming in small pants. "Somebody could see us."

Annie blinked and looked dazedly back down the drive. "You're not going to change your mind, are you?" she asked, her voice hoarse. "If we stop to go inside, you're not going to think yourself out of this are you?"

Katherine shook her head and took a deep, steadying breath. "Even if I wanted to, I couldn't."

Annie stared at her in silence for several seconds and traced a fingertip across Katherine's slightly swollen lower lip.

"Come inside," Katherine said, her voice low and urgent.

Annie jerked her gaze upward and met Katherine's eyes. "If I come inside, I'm not leaving."

"I know." Katherine extended her hand. "I won't ask you to."

CHAPTER 21
Big Springs, Kansas, 1945

"DON'T FORGET THE blanket," Katherine called to Annie as she carried the picnic basket out to the car.

Annie leaned out of their upper-story bedroom window. "There are at least five in here. Which one do you want?"

Katherine looked up and smiled. "Grab the green one—the one we used last time."

Annie disappeared back inside the house only to reappear a minute or so later. "It's dirty. What about the yellow one?"

"I'd never be able to get any stains out of it," Katherine said. "What about the tartan one in your room? I think it's still at the foot of the bed. Or maybe in that trunk."

Annie nodded and disappeared from view. Katherine thought about where the blanket might be if it weren't in either of those places. Neither she nor Annie had been in that bedroom since they set it up to look like Annie's rented room.

Katherine had been surprised at how easily everything had fallen into place. After that first night, they had agreed that it would be simplest if they told everyone including Clyde that to make ends meet, Katherine had taken in a boarder. Many women whose husbands were in the war were doing it. And, they reasoned, that way they could live together and no one would be any the wiser. Katherine wondered if her sister-in-law, Emily suspected, but she had never said anything and Katherine was content not to discuss the arrangements.

"Found it," Annie said as she bounded out the front door, the folded blanket in her right hand. The screen banged shut behind her. "So, where are we going?"

Katherine grinned. "It's a surprise."

"Is it somewhere we've been before?" Annie asked playfully.

Katherine nodded.

"Potter's Lake?" They often went to the small pond on the University of Kansas campus. Although it wasn't private, it was beautiful and it was the perfect place to spread out their blankets and read.

"Nope," Katherine said. "Get in."

She opened the door to the driver's side and slid into the seat. Annie had taught her how to drive and, although she would never be as comfortable with it as Annie, she felt proficient enough behind the wheel. Annie grinned happily and went around to the passenger's side. She tossed the blanket into the back seat next to the picnic basket Katherine had packed and the cloth bag from which the whiskey bottle Annie had procured the week before stuck out.

"I see you brought something to drink." She gestured toward the back seat.

"Well, I thought it might be fun to celebrate," Katherine said.

Annie frowned. "Celebrate what?"

"Don't tell me you don't know what today is because I know better than that." Katherine glanced sidelong at Annie who was pretending to think.

"What today is," Annie mused thoughtfully. "What today is . . ." She shook her head. "I can't think of anything except for it being three years to the day that I showed up on your doorstep and asked to rent a room." She grinned. "Or did you think I had forgotten?"

"I never know with you," Katherine said as she started the engine and put the car into gear. "But I thought a picnic by our favorite out-of-the-way field might be a nice way to celebrate."

"I know a better way to celebrate." Annie slid closer and placed her hand on Katherine's thigh.

Without taking her eyes off the road, Katherine smiled and reached down to squeeze Annie's hand and to stop its exploration. "I'm sure that can be arranged."

"I like your style." Annie returned the squeeze and leaned her head back against the seat. "So what's on the menu?"

"Fried chicken," Katherine said. "And pickled vegetables. And cake."

"Umm," Annie said happily and closed her eyes. "Cake."

Annie had been wearing her hair loose recently, and the warm air that blew through the windows as they drove down the road tossed her curls wildly around her face. Katherine glanced at Annie and was again struck by how foolish she had been to think she could live without her.

"It's hard to believe it's been three years," Annie said, almost as if reading her thoughts. "It's gone by so quickly." She again squeezed Katherine's hand.

"I was thinking about it yesterday, and it occurred to me that most of the world is struggling and sacrificing because of the war. But for me, it's been one of the happiest times of my life."

Annie smiled and opened her eyes to see Katherine looking at her.

"You should pay attention to the road." She shifted to lean her head on Katherine's shoulder. "I don't want to wreck before we have our cake."

"You and your sweet tooth," Katherine said affectionately and slid her hand into Annie's lap where it stayed until she turned the car off the road and started down the rutted path to the pond. She grinned as they passed the spot where Annie had fallen and turned her ankle.

"What made you smile?"

Katherine hadn't realized Annie was watching her. "I was thinking about that day—how you tried to stop me and ended up turning your ankle."

"And you had to stop running away from me to help me," Annie said.

"Funny how it never really swelled up, though."

"Yeah, that is funny, isn't it?"

Katherine gave Annie a sidelong glance and was rewarded with a guilty grin. "In fact, now that I think about it, it didn't really hinder you in any way. After we went inside, it seemed to be fine."

"Huh," Annie said, still grinning.

"I've always wondered," Katherine said. "How injured you really were."

"What do you mean?" Annie asked innocently.

Katherine parked the car next to the pond, pulled the brake, and cut the engine. She turned to Annie and raised her eyebrows. "I've just always wondered if you played up your injury to get me to stop and then worked that to your advantage."

"Never," Annie said cheerfully as she opened her door and hopped out of the car. "It was just your excellent care that caused me to heal so fast."

"Uh huh." Katherine stepped out of the car and opened the door to the back seat to remove the picnic basket.

Annie reached in from the other side and pulled out the blanket and the bottle. "But you have to admit, it worked out well in the long run."

"It did." Katherine gestured toward the large tree next to the water. "There?"

Annie nodded. They strolled to the shady spot, and Katherine waited as Annie spread out the blanket. The leaves of the cottonwood tree slapped together in the light breeze.

"God, it's already hot and it's only the first week of May." Katherine sat down and began to unpack the picnic basket.

"I think it's going to be a hot summer." Annie flopped backward and closed her eyes. "But not as hot as it used to get in the city. Remember?"

"I remember one day riding home with Claire," Katherine said. "It was right after you had kissed me that first time and it was so hot and I was so upset and distracted."

Annie rolled her head to the side. "I was such a wreck. I was so in love with you and wanted you so badly."

"You just wanted to sleep with me," Katherine said.

"Well, there was that," Annie admitted with a laugh. "But it was so much more. From the first moment I saw you at work, I wanted you."

Katherine smiled at the memory of Annie with her delicate features and dark, dark eyes. "Mr. Ansen was showing you around and you were just standing there, taking it all in, nodding."

"I was trying not to stare at you," Annie said. "Honestly. You have no idea how carefully I watched for my chance to catch you alone. Thank god you were a smoker."

Katherine chuckled. "You overwhelmed me. Asking about my books. Trying to shock me with your feminism. You were so—"

"Persistent," Annie interrupted.

"Aggressive, I was going to say. You were aggressive."

"I knew what I wanted." Annie shrugged. "And I knew what you wanted, too, though you were too scared to admit it."

"It was all so new to me. You made me feel . . ." Katherine shook her head, at a loss for words.

Annie rolled onto her side and propped her head up on her elbow. She lightly touched Katherine's leg with her other hand.

"I love you, Kate," she said softly.

Katherine looked at her, her dark hair still tousled from the car ride. She gently twined one of the curls around her finger. "I love you."

Annie stared at her for several seconds. "Enough to leave him?"

Katherine flinched and pulled her hand away, the magic of the moment ruined. "Why do you do that?" She grabbed her cigarettes. "Why today of all days?"

"Because I'm tired of dancing around the issue," Annie said.

"Can't we just leave it?" Katherine lifted a cigarette to her lips and lit it. "Just for another time? Another day?"

"Kate, the war isn't going to last forever." Annie sat up and faced her. "You've heard the news reports. Germany is about to concede. Clyde is going to come back. You're going to have to make a decision."

"But not today," Katherine said tightly as she took another drag from the cigarette. "Not now."

"Then when?" Annie pressed. "Let's really make this a real anniversary. Let's make this the day that we decide to be together for good."

"Annie—"

Annie leaned back and fumbled in her pocket. Katherine had the absurd feeling that Annie was going to propose.

"I wrote you a letter." Annie extended her hand. A folded piece of paper was pinched between her thumb and forefinger. "It says all the things you won't let me say."

"Annie—" Katherine shook her head.

"I want you to come away with me," Annie said. "Now. Today. Or tomorrow even. I want us to be together. I have money. I can support us. We can go to California or New York or Chicago—wherever you want. We can go and be together. We can get jobs and build a life." She paused and took a deep breath. "Kate, the war is going to end soon. And when it does, I can't share you." She shook her head. "More to the point, I *won't* share you."

Katherine held up her hand. It shook perceptibly. "I can't make this kind of decision right at this moment. Can't we just enjoy our day? Please? I promise I'll think about it."

Annie stared at her in disbelief and looked down at the paper she still clutched in her hand. She gave a sharp snort of disbelief and shook her head.

Katherine touched Annie's wrist. "Please?" In the distance, two bobwhites called to each other. "Look, it's not like I haven't thought about this—I have." She sighed. "It's all I think about. And when the war is over, I *am* going to leave Clyde." Annie blinked and jerked her eyes upward to meet Katherine's gaze. Katherine nodded. "But it's not going to be immediately. I'm not going to sneak away before he comes home. He deserves to hear it from me. After he's back and settled, I'll tell him."

"Tell him what?" Annie asked. "Not the truth about us."

"No," Katherine said quickly. "God no. I'll just tell him that I'm in love with someone else and that I want a divorce."

Annie beamed. "Really? You're really going to do it?"

"Yes." Katherine tried to smile convincingly. "I'm really going to do it."

Annie studied Katherine and her look of elation turned to one of apprehension. "You don't seem very happy about it."

"It's going to be hard," Katherine said. "I'm not looking forward to it."

"But you're not going to change your mind," Annie pressed. "You're not going to chicken out."

"No," Katherine said shortly. "I just don't relish the thought of having to have the conversation, that's all."

Annie nodded and squeezed Katherine's hand. They were silent for a long time. Katherine looked out at the water, and Annie looked at their clasped hands. Finally, Annie sighed and reached behind them for the bottle of whiskey.

"Well, then I guess we have a real reason to celebrate," she said. "Did you bring glasses?"

Katherine smiled, relieved to have the discussion behind them, and rummaged through the picnic basket for the two jelly jars she had managed to sneak back to Big Springs from her room in Chicago when her mother had forced her to leave most of her things behind. Annie smiled when she saw them.

"A toast." She poured several fingers of whiskey into each jar. "To us and what is now our doubly significant anniversary."

"To us." Katherine clinked her glass against Annie's.

They drank and looked at each other expectantly.

"And now," Annie said with a grin, "let's have some cake."

"KATE, WHAT'S WRONG?" Annie asked several days later as she climbed the steps of the front porch and sat down on the porch swing where Katherine rocked listlessly forward and back. In one hand was a creased piece of paper. In the other was a sweating glass of iced tea.

"Huh?" Katherine jerked her gaze to meet Annie's concerned face.

"What's wrong?" Annie repeated.

"It's a letter," Katherine said. "From Clyde. He's going to be home in a couple of weeks. They don't need ships now that the Japanese have surrendered. They're finishing out this last one and then he's coming home."

"Well, that's good news, isn't it?" Annie said excitedly. "We can finally start our lives together."

"Yes," Katherine said distractedly.

"Kate." Annie laid her hand on Katherine's leg. "You haven't changed your mind, have you?"

"No," Katherine said and then again, more strongly, "No. I just . . . it's all suddenly so real."

"What is?" Annie asked slowly.

"This," Katherine said and gestured limply at nothing in particular. "What I'm about to do. Leaving Clyde."

Annie narrowed her eyes. "Of course it's real. It's always been real." She squeezed Katherine's leg tightly. "Sweetheart, you're not in love with him. You never were."

"I know." Katherine nodded.

"You're in love with me," Annie said. Something in her tone made Katherine look up.

"I know." She said the words more sharply than she had intended.

"Then act like it."

Katherine felt her jaw tighten, and she struggled to bite back an angry response. "You don't understand. This is difficult for me. I am about to leave my life—to end everything I've ever known to take a chance on you—on us."

"Leave your life," Annie echoed dully. "I don't believe you just said that."

"You know what I mean," Katherine said quickly.

"No, actually, I don't," Annie snapped. "In fact, I think that if you were as committed to me—to us—as you say, this would be a cause for relief, not distress. You would be happy to have it resolved."

"I *am*," Katherine said angrily and then softer, "I am. But there are other considerations—things you don't understand because you're not in my position."

"And what about *my* position, Kate?" Annie said bitterly. "Have you ever thought about that? I have put my life on hold for three years to play house with you—to pretend we're together—in your *husband's* house, for Christ's sake!"

"Annie, calm down."

Annie stood quickly and paced the length of the porch. "Calm down? You want me to calm down?"

"You're overreacting."

"I don't think so," Annie spat. She spun to face Katherine. "I think I've just had a glimpse of the future."

"Where is this coming from?" Katherine stood, walked quickly to Annie, and pulled her into her arms. "Why are you so angry? Nothing has changed. I'm still going to tell him. We're still going to be together."

Annie snorted and pulled away. "Look at me. Look into my eyes."

Katherine reluctantly met her gaze.

Annie studied her for several seconds and sighed. "I don't believe you. Honestly, I don't know as I've ever believed you—not really. I wanted to, but to see the way you're reacting to his letter . . ." She shook her head. "I see this now for what it is."

"*What* are you talking about?" Katherine asked.

"I thought I could carry this for both of us," Annie continued almost to herself. "I thought my love for you would be enough to make this work until you could commit." She raised her eyes to meet Katherine's. "But as long as you see this as leaving your life instead of starting your life we don't stand a chance." She laughed bitterly.

"Annie, stop," Katherine pleaded. "You're making far too much out of this."

"Am I?" Annie asked tiredly. "I don't think I am."

"I'm going to tell him," Katherine insisted. "Once he's home, once he's settled in, I'm going to tell him."

Annie shook her head. "And what am I supposed to do while you're breaking it to him gently? Wait in Lawrence? Go to Kansas City? Go back to Chicago?" She gave a short shake of the head. "No."

"What are you saying?" Katherine clutched Annie's hand. "You're scaring me."

"I'm saying that you're not going to leave Clyde. And even if you do, it's going to be the thing that breaks us because you will never be able to reconcile your decision."

"That's not true," Katherine said quickly. She tried to pull Annie into her arms, but Annie pushed her away.

"Kate, it *is* true," Annie said tiredly. "And I think I probably knew it all along, I just haven't wanted to admit it to myself."

"It's not," Katherine said. "I can make myself do this."

"But don't you see? If you have to make yourself do it . . ." Annie pressed her lips tightly together and sighed deeply through her nose. "I need to leave."

"No!" Katherine cried. "No, you can't."

"I'm going to Lawrence—to check into the Eldridge for a couple of days." Annie's voice was calm and carefully controlled. "I don't want you to come after me. I need time alone to think about this. I think you do, too."

"Don't leave." Katherine knew she was begging, but she didn't care. "I love you. I'll do whatever you want to be with you."

"But see, that's the problem. It has to be what *you* want."

"I want you."

"But not enough." Annie gave a small shrug of defeat and turned to walk toward the screen door.

"Annie." Katherine sobbed. "Please. Don't do this."

Annie hesitated. Her fingers rested lightly on the handle. Katherine knew that if she went inside, it was over. She waited, praying that Annie would turn and pull her into her arms.

"I'm sorry," Annie said finally as she pulled open the screen and quickly stepped inside. "But I can't stay."

CHAPTER 22
Big Springs, Kansas, 1946

"KATIE?" KATHERINE HEARD Clyde's voice followed by the slam of the front screen door.

"In the kitchen," she called as she closed the stove door and set the pan on the cooling rack. The smell of baking bread filled the room.

His footsteps thudded heavily on the wooden floor of the hallway as he walked back to the kitchen. Katherine turned as he stepped into the room.

"I can't tell you how much I missed the smell of freshly-baked bread," he said.

Katherine smiled tiredly at him. Although he had gained back some of the weight he'd lost while working in the shipyard, he still looked gaunt. He walked slowly to the kitchen table and settled into one of the creaky wooden chairs.

"How was town?" Katherine asked.

Clyde leaned forward and rested his forearms on the table. "Good. I stopped in at the feed store. Saw your dad. He said he might stop by for supper."

Katherine took a pot holder and nudged one of the tins of bread toward the back of the counter.

"I told him you was makin' a roast," Clyde said.

Katherine nodded and resisted the urge to correct his grammar. She set the pot holder on the counter and turned to watch Clyde as he flipped through the mail.

"Anything good?" she asked more for something to say than because she cared.

"Just bills," Clyde said with a sigh. He slid the stack into the middle of the table. "I'll look at them tonight. Any coffee left?"

Katherine nodded and went to the cupboard for a cup and saucer.

"Ran into an old friend of yours in town."

Katherine froze in mid-reach for the coffee pot. *Had Annie changed her mind?* She picked up the coffee pot.

"Really?" She forced her voice to remain calm. "Who?"

"Albert," Clyde said. "He's back from Kansas City visiting his family. Said the car dealership was doing well. They're opening a second lot."

Katherine felt her stomach sink in disappointment. She hadn't heard from Annie since the letter she found wedged in the screen door the day after their confrontation on the porch. In it, Annie had professed her love, but said that she needed more from Katherine than Katherine was able to give. *I want to be wildly, bodily, fully in love and to have that returned,* Annie had written. Katherine had rushed to the Eldridge Hotel only to find that Annie was gone. She had checked out before dawn.

"Well, that's good," Katherine said as she filled the cup and set it on the table in front of Clyde.

"He turned out to be real successful." Katherine could hear the resentment in his voice. "You ain't sorry are you?"

"Sorry?" Katherine asked, puzzled.

"That you didn't marry him."

"No, of course not," Katherine said quickly.

"Or that you married me?"

"No," Katherine lied.

Clyde nodded thoughtfully and then picked up the coffee cup. He took a sip and made a face. "Cold."

"I could heat it up," Katherine offered.

Clyde shook his head. "No need. 'Sides, I'd better get out to the field and get a little work done before your father gets here." He pushed the chair back with a squeak and stood. "Speaking of your father . . ." He reached into the front pocket of his overalls and pulled out a folded envelope. "Your dad sent this with me. It got sent to his house by mistake."

Katherine looked at the letter clutched in Clyde's massive hand. "Who's it from?"

"Dunno," he said with a shrug. "Probably one of your Chicago friends who didn't know you was married."

Katherine took the letter and looked down at the envelope with her name—her maiden name—written in Annie's bold hand. Her hand trembled, and she quickly dropped it to her side to hide her reaction.

Katherine raised her eyes to see Clyde thoughtfully watching her. After a second, he jerked his head toward the barn. "Well, I'm gonna get to work. You can tell me all about it tonight."

He turned and pushed open the back door. Katherine could hear his off-tune whistling and the retreating crunch of his work boots on the gravel as he headed toward the barn. She walked to the doorway and waited until she was sure he was in the barn before she went to the table and sank down in the abandoned chair.

With trembling hands Katherine laid the envelope on the table and smoothed it out. The postmark was from Los Angeles. She traced the letters of her name. Just the shape of Annie's letters made her heart race. Part of her wanted to rip the envelope open and read what Annie had written. Another part of her was terrified. It had taken six months before she had been able to think about anything else but Annie. She had told Clyde it was just the shock and happiness of having him home again that had made her so scattered, but she suspected he didn't believe that was the case.

Katherine pulled her fingers back from the letter and, after taking a deep breath, touched it again. Annie had held this paper in her hand just days before. She picked it up and carefully slid a shaking finger under the flap. As she pulled out the folded sheets she realized she had been holding her breath. She forced herself to exhale and unfolded the letter. Annie had written on unlined paper that looked as if it had been ripped from a notebook or journal.

Dear Kate:

Hopefully this finds you well. As you can probably see from the postmark, I'm writing from Los Angeles. They call it the city of angels, although to be honest, I've met more devils than angels here. You wouldn't believe the weather or all the movie stars. They're everywhere. The ocean is amazing! I've made several friends here and am happy with my life—at least as happy as can be expected.

But that's not why I'm writing. I'm writing to let you know that I'm well and that I am going to be passing through Kansas City on my way to Chicago. It's a long story and I won't bore you with it, but I have something of yours that I want to return to you. It's something I've had since—well, for a long time. I arrive in Kansas City on September 20th. I could meet you in Lawrence if you would rather, though if you came to Kansas City, perhaps we could take in a play or go to a musical. Just a thought.

I will be there for two days most likely. If you could meet me, I would very much like to see you. I'll be at the Quarterage. If you could send a letter there, addressed to me, with your answer and when/if to expect you, I would appreciate it.
Best Regards,
Annie

Katherine stared sightlessly at the words and remembered the afternoon they had fought over Clyde's letter announcing his return. Annie had gone inside, packed her bag, and carried it out to her car.

"Please don't do this," Katherine had pleaded and tried to grab her suitcase. "You're overreacting."

Annie had turned, her face stony, her mouth a tight, straight line. "I'm not overreacting. I'm just finally seeing what I didn't want to acknowledge. We were just playing house. And now, it's about to end. I can't change that. But I *can* change the part I play in it." Katherine started to speak, but Annie held up her hand and continued in a louder, stronger voice. "I can sit back and wait and watch you struggle with telling Clyde. And I can be jealous and angry and sad." She smiled sadly. "But in the end, I'm the one who will get hurt. And that hurt will come slowly. I'll see it coming and I will wait for it. But, Kate, I don't want to do that. I can't. So, I'm making this decision now. For me—for both of us really."

Katherine shook her head in protest.

"But that's not—"

"It *is* what is going to happen. And I don't want to hate you—which I would in the long run." She sighed and cupped Katherine's cheek in her hand. "Sweetheart, I can't change the situation. Your reaction to his letter has made me realize that. But I *can* control what I do about it."

"Don't." Katherine grasped Annie's hand. "It doesn't have to be like this."

"Doesn't it?" Annie smiled sadly and rose up to kiss Katherine gently goodbye on the lips. It was, Katherine realized only in retrospect, much like their first kiss—just a light brushing of lips. Annie pulled back and lightly caressed Katherine's cheek. "I've got to go."

And she had—though not just to stay at the hotel. She had disappeared and for the past year, Katherine had struggled to get up every morning, to make it through the day, and at night to lay down beside a man she didn't love. Her life had become a blur of survival. But now, she thought with a jolt, Annie was back. And now was her chance. All she had to do was go to her.

Katherine stared out the back door in the direction of the barn. She wondered if she could get to Kansas City without explaining her reasons for going. But, she thought suddenly, why *shouldn't* she explain why? Why *shouldn't* she tell Clyde that her friend from Chicago was going to be in town, and she wanted to go visit? The fact that she was going shouldn't be a secret. The secret was the fact that she was running away.

She began to formulate her plan. She could ask Clyde or perhaps Bud to drive her to Kansas City. She would pack her suitcase with as much as she could carry. She would tell them that Annie would bring her back before she left for Chicago. And then, she would simply write a letter from the road explaining that she . . . what? Was dying in her life? Was in love with someone else?

"It doesn't matter," she murmured as she climbed the stairs to the bedroom she now shared with Clyde. A hot breeze fluttered the curtains as she opened the door and went to stand in front of the full-length mirror. She tipped it slightly in its stand to get the best light and stepped back so she could see herself as Annie might. She realized with a start, that she hadn't looked in a mirror for months. The woman who stared back looked much older than thirty-five. Her face was tired and there were gray hairs sprinkled in amongst the brown. *When did I become so thin?*

I look like a scarecrow," she murmured as she touched the sharp edges of her cheekbones and leaned in to study the fine lines that creased the corners of her eyes.

She wondered what Annie would think. She imagined her, now, tanned and happy in California. She was used to seeing movie stars and beautiful people. Katherine feared that she was a pale facsimile to the smart, glamorous women of Los Angeles. Still, she had a couple of weeks to try to make herself presentable. She needed to take in a couple of dresses—that would be her first priority. And she needed to force herself to eat more. If she could put on just a little weight—enough to at least fill out her face—she would be satisfied.

"Salvageable," she murmured as she nodded once at herself and turned away from the mirror. She walked to the closet and began to take inventory of her clothing. There were several dresses she would take. And her underthings, of course. She would take two pairs of shoes. The rest, she would leave. Perhaps when she got settled, she could ask Clyde to send them to her. She knew he loved her, but she also knew he understood their marriage was one of obligation and friendship. They had agreed upon that when he had asked her to marry him.

It had been five months after she had returned to Big Springs. Clyde had been to the house several times for dinner, and they had gone for a walk down the same lane she used to walk with Albert.

"That was good ham," Clyde had said as he hurried to keep up with Katherine's quick pace. His scuffed boots kicked up tiny puffs of dust.

"It was," Katherine agreed.

"Your mama is a good cook. Do you like to cook?"

Katherine shook her head. "Not really. I didn't have much opportunity when I lived in Chicago and now . . ." She shrugged. "I help Mama, but she does most of the cooking."

"But you *can* cook."

Katherine stopped walking and turned to face him. "Yes, Clyde. I *can* cook."

He nodded, ignoring the sharpness of her tone. "How do you like living at home?" Katherine narrowed her eyes, and Clyde blinked. "I just figure it must be hard after being on your own for so long."

Katherine blinked and drew slightly back, surprised to find his tone was one of genuine concern. "It's been an adjustment."

"I can tell you're not happy," he said softly. "Whenever I see you, you just seem so sad. And lonely."

Katherine pressed her lips together and shrugged. "Most of my friends here are married with families. And I'm stuck on the farm with Mama and Daddy with no job, no money, no means of doing anything on my own."

She was surprised at her honesty.

"What if you didn't have to be here?"

"I can't go back to Chicago—" Katherine began.

"No," Clyde said quickly. "What I meant was, what if you didn't have to be at your mama's house?"

"There aren't any jobs here that would pay me enough to live on my own," Katherine said bitterly.

"What if you got married?"

"Married." Katherine scoffed. "That's really the last thing I want to do."

"What if it weren't a real marriage?"

Katherine looked at him in confusion. "What do you mean?"

"Well," he drawled. "I know you love someone else."

Katherine opened her mouth to ask how he knew.

He held up his hand to stop her from interrupting. "And I ain't never gonna' love nobody but Wilma—not really. So, what if we was to get married—not because we love each other, but because it would be good for both of us?"

Katherine realized her expression must have been one of disbelief because Clyde said, "Just . . . hear me out."

Katherine sighed, nodded, and stepped back so she could lean against the rail fence.

"I know you don't love me," Clyde said. "But I know you like me well enough. And I'll treat you right. I won't drink much or beat you. And we would be good company for each other. I get lonely and I need someone to take care of my house—to cook and clean."

"So get a housekeeper," Katherine snapped before she could stop herself.

Clyde looked sternly at her for several seconds. "It would get you out of your mama's house. And it would give you respectability." He glanced fearfully at Katherine. "Now, I know everyone thinks you're an old maid, but you don't have to be. I could fix that for you. And, you would have a place of your own."

"I'm not an old maid," Katherine spat. "It's not necessary for women to marry if they don't want to. I could have married. I chose not to."

"And you can choose again," Clyde said. "I would give you your freedom as long as you were faithful to me."

Katherine sighed and shook her head. "I really do appreciate the offer, but I don't love you. And I don't want to be married to someone I don't love."

"It don't got to be based on love," Clyde insisted. "We get along. We could be friends."

"And what about . . . the other?" Katherine asked, not because she was considering this offer, but because she was curious.

"Other?" he asked with a frown.

"*Other*," Katherine said more meaningfully.

"Oh." He grinned self-consciously. "That. Well . . ."

"I don't want children." Katherine had a flashback to the day she and Annie stood in front of the Macy's display window and Annie had teased her.

"Neither do I." Clyde pushed his hat back on his head. His brow was sweaty. He glanced at Katherine. "I'm not going to say that I don't have needs, but if you was to say yes, I wouldn't exercise my rights all that often—just enough to keep things in working order. And I could make sure that there was no babies."

Katherine stared, trying to imagine Clyde as a lover, envisioning his sweaty body on top of hers. She remembered what it had been like with Alex. And Annie. She felt sick.

" . . . could be good for both of us," Clyde was saying. "If you was just to think about it."

"But I don't love you," Katherine said again, softly this time.

"You don't need to love me to marry me," Clyde said. "I'll take whatever you give."

And he had.

They had married, quickly consummated the marriage, and set out on a life based on companionship. Katherine hadn't been happy, but she hadn't been unhappy, either. She was out of her mother's house, around family, and Clyde was true to his word about his sexual demands. It wasn't pleasant, but it wasn't horrible either. It simply *was*. And it had been enough—or at least it had been until that day that Annie had shown up and made her listen, made her feel, made her admit the truth.

Katherine studied the clothes she had chosen to take with her to Kansas City. She had no idea why Annie was going to Chicago, but when they got there, she would get a job. She would earn money and she would buy herself the things she needed. It would be like it was before, although this time she would get a place with Annie. They would live together and build a life.

"AND YOU'RE SURE you don't need me to come back and get you?" Clyde asked as he pulled the truck to a stop in front of the hotel.

"I'm sure." Katherine picked up her purse from the seat between them. Clyde placed his hand upon hers.

"I'm glad you're going to see your friend," he said softly, "But I'm going to miss you. There are some things I want to talk to you about when you get back."

Katherine looked up at him warily. They never spoke of their feelings, and his words made her uncomfortable. She swallowed, cleared her throat, and forced a tight smile across her lips. "Drive safely back."

He studied her for several seconds and removed his hand. Katherine could tell he wanted to say more, but instead he nodded. She put her hand on the door handle.

"I'll miss you," he said again as she opened the door.

Katherine hesitated almost imperceptibly and made a loud show of opening the squeaky door and pretending she hadn't heard. She stepped quickly out of the truck and pulled her suitcase from the bed, careful not to get her dress dirty. She deposited the suitcase on the sidewalk and turned to push the door closed with a hollow, metallic clang.

"I'll see you Sunday." She knew it was a lie but she felt like she had to say something. Clyde nodded and started the engine. Katherine waited until he was about to pull away before raising her hand in goodbye. Even as she did it, she wondered if Annie was inside, watching.

"Thank god," she murmured under her breath as she watched him drive away from the hotel. She waited until he was out of sight before picking up her suitcase and stepping into the foyer of the hotel. Her legs trembled with anticipation, and she had to take several deep breaths to force herself to calm down.

The reception area was much nicer than she had anticipated— especially given Annie's frugality. Katherine looked around the room, her eyes skipping over the polished wood, the shiny reception desk, the clusters of chairs in which people sat talking. Nowhere did she see Annie's dark head, and her excitement and nervousness gave way to apprehension. She spun around and found herself looking up into the wide, eager face of a hotel porter.

"May I help you?" he asked.

"I . . . no," she said quickly. "I mean, yes."

He smiled and tipped his head slightly to the side.

"I'm looking for someone. A guest. She's staying here."

He nodded and gestured toward the front desk. "I'm sure if you asked—"

"It's all right," Annie said from behind her. "I'm who she's looking for."

Katherine felt her entire body go numb. Her heart thumped wildly in her throat as she forced herself to take a deep breath and slowly turned to look down into the face that had haunted her for the past year.

Annie smiled kindly at her and looked over Katherine's shoulder at the porter.

The young man gestured to Katherine's suitcase. "Shall I take this up to your room?" he asked Annie. "Or are you checking in?" He looked at Katherine.

"I . . ." Katherine looked at Annie for direction.

"We'll take care of it ourselves," Annie finished and nodded to the porter.

"Of course," he said and backed away.

"Hello," Katherine said softly once he was gone. She stared down into Annie's dark eyes and felt her legs weaken.

"It's good to see you, Kate," Annie said slowly.

"You look . . . amazing," Katherine said as she took in Annie's sun-kissed skin and dark hair which was pulled back into a bun. "California agrees with you."

Annie stared at Kate. Her gaze, though veiled, was appraising and hungry. "You look good, too—though your mother would say you're too thin."

Katherine laughed softly. "My mother had an opinion on every-thing." She touched Annie's arms, which were folded across her stomach. "There's so much I want to say to you—things I didn't get a chance to say last time."

Annie nodded, but rather than respond to Katherine's touch, looked down at her suitcase. "I guess you decided to stay for a day to take in a show?"

Katherine frowned at the diversion. "I have. But I'd rather talk first. Can we go to your room?"

Annie blushed. "I actually have already reserved a room for you. "Just in case you wanted to stay over."

"Oh," Katherine said. "I guess I thought . . ."

"You're in Room 307." Annie unfolded her arms and produced a room key with the diamond-shaped tag. "It's down the hall from me."

"Okay," Katherine said slowly.

"Let's go up." Annie turned in the direction of the elevators. "We can talk there."

Surprised and slightly confused, Katherine followed.

They rode in silence to the third floor though Katherine snuck glances at Annie several times during the ride. Once off the elevator, Annie led her down a wide hallway to the door numbered 307 and inserted the key into the lock. Katherine noticed that her hand trembled slightly as she struggled to turn it.

"Let me." Katherine reached out, her fingertips brushing Annie's as she turned the key and pushed the door open.

The room, though small, was well-appointed. Katherine gestured for Annie to go ahead of her. Once inside, Annie placed the suitcase on the stand and turned stiffly to face Katherine, who stood next to the bed.

"It's a nice room," Katherine said finally.

Annie gave the room a cursory look and lowered her eyes to study the carpet in front of her.

"This is ridiculous," Katherine said finally. She walked quickly to Annie and pulled her into her arms. The physical contact made her body tingle. The effect on Annie seemed to be different. At first she stood stiffly in Katherine's embrace. But after a minute, she sighed, lifted her arms, and circled Katherine's waist. At her acquiescence, Katherine pulled her tighter against her body, and Annie responded by nestling her face into the warm hollow of Katherine's neck below her jaw.

They stood that way for several minutes, neither speaking, neither moving except to breathe in each other's scent.

Annie finally broke the embrace. "We need to talk." For the first time, she met and held Katherine's gaze.

Katherine nodded. "I know."

"How about a drink?" Annie asked. "I have a bottle in my room."

"Of course you do," Katherine said teasingly.

Annie hesitated and then grinned begrudgingly. "Of course I do." She stepped toward the door. "I'll be right back."

As soon as Annie was gone, Katherine sank down onto the bed and exhaled heavily. Her head throbbed, and she pressed her fingertips to her temples in an attempt to alleviate the pain. She didn't hear Annie come back into the room and was startled when she looked up to see Annie standing there watching her.

"One of your headaches?"

Katherine nodded. "I . . ." She shrugged rather than explain. "I've been a nervous wreck ever since I got your letter." She tried to smile.

When Annie didn't respond, she stood and went to her suitcase. "I brought our jelly jars."

Katherine felt Annie's scrutiny as she opened the case and pulled out the jelly jars. "It's strange to have you be so quiet. You're usually full of things to say." She walked to the small table, set them down, and held out her hand for the bottle.

"I can do it," Annie said as she unscrewed the cap. Katherine saw her hands shake slightly as she poured healthy shots into the makeshift glasses. Carefully, she set the bottle on the table and turned to hand one of the glasses to Katherine.

"What should we drink to?" Katherine asked.

Annie shrugged. "To . . . change." She waved her glass in Katherine's direction and gulped down the contents in two swallows.

Before Katherine could take a sip, Annie poured herself another drink.

"What?" Annie asked as she looked up to see Katherine watching her.

"I guess I'd like to know what's going on?" Katherine sat in one of the two upholstered chairs. "I know you're angry . . . or that you were. But why are you being so formal? I'm nervous, too, but it doesn't have to be like this."

"Actually, it does," Annie said and settled into the chair across from her.

"No," Katherine said and took a deep breath. "It doesn't. We can fix this." She started to reach for Annie's hand and stopped herself. "What happened at the farm . . . I was wrong, I should have gone with you."

Annie started to interrupt but Katherine held up her hand. "No, I need to say this. You can say what you want when I've finished, but you've got to let me say this." She inhaled and then exhaled deeply. "When you left, I thought my life was over. You made up your mind, and you didn't give me a chance to say anything or to prove you wrong. Despite what you might have thought, I wasn't going to stay with Clyde. But then you left, you took that option away from me."

Annie stared at her, and Katherine forced herself not to look away. "I was so angry with you. And hurt. But never, not for one instant, was I not in love with you. I have never, not from the day I first saw you, not been in love with you." She paused and took a deep breath. "I am leaving Clyde. Today. Right now. What's in that suitcase is all I'm taking with me. You're all I've ever wanted and I don't care what anyone thinks. I want to build a life with you."

She paused, gauging Annie's reaction to her words. She was surprised to see that Annie looked dumbfounded and . . . something else. She took Annie's hands and gently interlaced their fingers.

"I'm saying it without reservation. I will go with you wherever you want—do whatever you want. I'll get a job. We'll get a place together. We'll cook each other breakfast and walk to the park for picnics on Sunday afternoons." She squeezed Annie's fingers and gazed into her eyes. "I love you and want to be with you. Only you. I can do this. I can give you what you need and what you want. I can love you the way you deserve."

Annie sat in stunned disbelief, her mouth open. She closed it and then opened it again as if to speak. She jerked her gaze down to their clasped fingers and squeezed Katherine's to the point of pain. She looked up. Tears streamed down her cheeks.

"Oh, sweetheart." Katherine gathered her into her arms. "Shhh, don't cry. What's wrong? I thought you would be happy. I thought . . . What's wrong?"

"I can't," Annie said as she sobbed violently. "That's what I came to tell you. I . . . Oh, Kate . . ."

Fear trickled coldly through Katherine's body, and she struggled not to pull away. She hadn't even thought to ask the question that now seemed obvious. "You're seeing someone else."

Annie nodded but didn't speak.

"A woman you met in Los Angeles?"

Annie nodded again and sniffed. "Her name is Doris. She's a dancer. That's why we're going to Chicago."

CHAPTER 23
Lawrence, Kansas, 1997

"SO, MOM TOLD you the story?" Joan leaned eagerly forward.

Mrs. Yoccum raised her glass to her lips, tipped it backward, and drained the contents. She set the glass on the table and looked at the bottle of Evan Williams.

"Would you like me to get it for you?" Joan asked.

Mrs. Yoccum smiled and nodded. "I suppose one more won't hurt. Especially for this story."

"That good, eh?" Joan asked as she went to the table and poured several fingers of liquor into Mrs. Yoccum's glass.

"Oh, it's a doozy, if I do say so myself," Mrs. Yoccum said.

Joan went to the refrigerator and refilled her own glass. "I'd like to hear it." She corked the empty bottle and tossed it into the trash can.

Mrs. Yoccum studied the whiskey in her glass for several seconds. "Your mother had made the decision that she was going to leave your father for Annie. What she didn't realize was the reason Annie wanted to see her was to tell her that their relationship was over."

"But I thought that when Annie left after the war ended that it *was* over," Joan said

Mrs. Yoccum held up a finger. "Yes and no. Annie left because she thought your mother would never leave your father. Annie was an all or nothing kind of person. So, when she decided that your mother wouldn't leave your father, she chose nothing. And she moved on—not just geographically, but physically as well."

"A woman," Joan said.

Mrs. Yoccum nodded. "A dancer. Doris."

Joan repeated the name softly. It was the name her mother mentioned in one of the letters.

"That's why Annie was passing through Kansas City," Mrs. Yoccum said. "They had been living in Los Angeles. Doris couldn't find work in movies, so she took a job in Chicago dancing on the stage there. The coincidence was that she was originally from Kansas City and so they stopped so she could visit her family."

Joan sat back, stunned.

Mrs. Yoccum raised her glass to her mouth and swallowed.

"So, Annie was moving to Chicago with this woman, Doris," Joan said. "And they stopped in Kansas City so she can see her family and Annie could . . . what? Rub it in? Put closure to it?"

"Probably more the latter," Mrs. Yoccum said. "She said she needed to return something to your mother. But I think in actuality, she wanted to say good bye."

"What did she want to return?" Joan asked quickly.

"A ring," Mrs. Yoccum said. "A tiger's eye ring that Annie bought for your mother when they were in Chicago. Your mother saw it in an antique shop on one of their walks, and Annie snuck back and bought it for her. When your mother left Chicago with her mother, she mailed it to Annie in a letter."

"Why didn't she give it back to her when they were in Big Springs?"

"Why do people do any of the things they do?" Mrs. Yoccum raised her eyes to meet Joan's and shrugged. "Maybe she wanted to give it to her as something symbolic after Kate left Clyde. Or, maybe, secretly she knew it wasn't going to work out and wanted something to hold on to." She looked pointedly at Joan. "It's hard to let go of something you love so much—even if it's just an idea."

Joan shifted uncomfortably at the parallel to her own life. "So, she met with Mom to give her back her ring and to tell her it was over." She imagined her mother's disappointment and sadness when she realized that she had been too late. "And then what happened?"

"Well, your mother was emotionally devastated, of course," Mrs. Yoccum said. "She had gone there determined to start a new life and instead, was relegated back into her old one with no hope of salvaging what she had lost."

Joan picked up her wine glass. "It just seems so sad."

"It is," Mrs. Yoccum said. "But hopefully it explains more about why your mother was the way she was."

Joan sipped her wine and thought about Mrs. Yoccum's words. It *did* explain a lot about her mother. Suddenly, a thought occurred to her.

"But you said that my father found out about the affair," she said. "You said that he . . . that there was a murder."

"Yes." Mrs. Yoccum glanced up at the wall clock.

Joan followed her gaze and was startled to realize it was past ten o'clock. Although she wanted to know more about what had happened, she also recognized that the stress of the day, Jason's accident, and the alcohol had taken their toll on Mrs. Yoccum.

"I should go."

"I'm sorry, sweetheart," Mrs. Yoccum said. "I forget sometimes that I'm an old lady until it smacks me in the face."

Joan smiled. "Maybe we could continue this conversation tomorrow? If you're going to see Jason, I could take you. I'd love to see him again. It's been years."

"That would be wonderful. I'm sure he would enjoy that."

Joan looked around the kitchen. "I should let you get to bed. How about I help clean up first? You don't want to wake up to these dishes in the morning."

"So like your mother," Mrs. Yoccum said with a laugh. "I couldn't care less about the dishes. I'm just going to rinse them off, and I'll wash them tomorrow."

"How about I wrap the lasagna for you," Joan suggested.

"Oh no." Mrs. Yoccum waved her hand. "You should take it home with you. I won't eat it. It was a treat, but . . . you take it."

"All right." Joan picked up her plate, silverware, and the juice glass and carried them to the sink. "So, I'll be by tomorrow morning? Around ten or ten thirty?"

"Perfect," Mrs. Yoccum said.

BACK IN HER mother's house, Joan sank down on the porch steps and looked out at the darkened street. What must it have been like to love someone so deeply, so fully, that you would give up everything to be with them, she wondered? What had her mother felt when Annie told her it was over? It had stung when Mark had ended their relationship, but it hadn't really hurt her—not deeply. Yes, they were planning to leave their spouses, but it wasn't true love—not like what her mother had with Annie. For Joan, what had hurt more was the recognition that nothing in her life was going to change. She was going to remain married to Luke and muddle through her days just like she always had. The fact that she was pregnant didn't even really change things because she never seriously considered keeping it.

She wondered yet again why her mother hadn't aborted her. It wasn't unheard of, even in the 1950s.

Penance.

The word came to her just as clearly as if it had been spoken aloud by someone else. Her mother had given birth not because she wanted a child. Nor had she stayed in a loveless marriage because it was the right thing to do. She did both of those things as penance. She had, Joan realized with a start, been punishing herself. *But why*? For loving a woman? After reading the letters her mother had written to Annie, she wasn't convinced that was the case. For having an affair? She shook her head. Not likely either. For hurting Annie? Perhaps, but all indications pointed to the fact that Annie was the one who ultimately ended their relationship. It had to have been for the murder.

Joan stared thoughtfully into the night and resisted the urge to go back to Mrs. Yoccum's house, knock on the door, and demand to know the full story. She looked at Mrs. Yoccum's house. The light was still on in the kitchen and, as if summoned, Mrs. Yoccum suddenly walked into view. It was voyeuristic, Joan knew, but she watched in fascination as Mrs. Yoccum disappeared from view and then reappeared. Her lips moved as if she were talking to someone—or to herself. Perhaps she was singing, Joan thought as she resisted the urge to sneak across the yard and peer more closely into the window.

She forced herself to look away from the house. Instead, she looked up at the stars. They offered no answers. She glanced back at Mrs. Yoccum's and jumped when she saw Mrs. Yoccum standing in the window staring out at her, a tiny figure silhouetted by the light of the room.

Though she couldn't see Mrs. Yoccum's face, Joan raised her hand in a silent wave, and Mrs. Yoccum, after a moment's hesitation, returned the gesture. They stayed like that for several seconds until Joan put her hands on her knees and, with a soft grunt, pushed herself into a standing position. As she reached her front door, she looked back at Mrs. Yoccum's house. The light had been turned off, but even as she put her key into the lock, she had the sense that Mrs. Yoccum was still there, still watching.

MRS. YOCCUM ANSWERED the door the next morning before Joan had a chance to knock.

"I'm almost ready," she said as she turned and hurried back into the kitchen. "I've put a chicken in the crock pot and I just need to turn it on."

Joan stepped into the entryway. Something about the play of light or the smell of Mrs. Yoccum's house made her remember a summer afternoon when she and Jason were young. They had been outside playing in the sprinkler and had raced into the house, their bodies wet and muddy with bits of grass stuck to their legs and arms. Her mother had been sitting in the kitchen with Mrs. Yoccum drinking iced tea and talking when Jason slipped on the hardwood floor and smacked his head against the sharp edge of the steps leading upstairs. Both had rushed into the room at the sound of Jason's sobs and Joan's worried cries.

"Oh, sweetheart, are you okay?" Mrs. Yoccum crouched down beside her son and examined his injury.

"Joan, what have I told you about running in the house," Katherine scolded as Mrs. Yoccum rocked Jason and murmured softly into his ear. "And look at you, you've gotten grass and mud all over Mrs. Yoccum's clean floor. You're as bad as your father."

The sharpness of her tone and the unfavorable comparison to a man that Joan, even at that young age knew her mother hated, made her cry even harder.

Mrs. Yoccum craned her neck to look at Joan and turned to Katherine. "Kate. Could you go get some ice for this bump on his head?"

Once Katherine was out of earshot, Mrs. Yoccum removed one arm from around her son and gestured for Joan to kneel beside her. Joan crouched down, and Mrs. Yoccum slid her arm around her and pulled her wet body close to her.

"It's okay, sweetie. I don't mind a little grass or dirt on the floors. A house is supposed to be lived in, right?" Mrs. Yoccum grinned and kissed the top of Joan's head. "What's important is to have fun. We can clean up the mess later."

Joan leaned into Mrs. Yoccum's warmth, reveling in being held close. "Am I really like my dad?" Images of him spanking her or snapping nastily at Katherine filled her head.

"No," Mrs. Yoccum said soothing. "No. You're tall like him, but that's a good thing." She smiled. "You're a good girl. Don't ever think any different."

Joan thought about those words now as she waited for Mrs. Yoccum to turn on her crock pot and collect her things.

"How long has it been since you've seen Jason?" Mrs. Yoccum asked as she hurried back into the room. She was carrying a dark jacket and woven silk scarf.

"I was thinking about that this morning as I was getting dressed," Joan said. "The last time must have been just before I got married."

"You probably won't recognize him, then." Mrs. Yoccum slipped into the jacket and wrapped the scarf around her neck. "Especially now that he does all that bike riding."

"Motorcycles?" Joan asked.

"Oh, goodness no." Mrs. Yoccum laughed. "Bicycles. He has this group he goes out with, and they ride their ten-speeds all over the country. They spend all weekend riding around." She shook her head. "And then they all ride to Free State Brewery and drink beer." She laughed. "All those fancy bikes . . . My idea of a bicycle has fat tires and a basket on the front—not these newfangled things you can lift with two fingers."

Joan laughed. "I haven't been on a bicycle in years. Not since college."

"Well, Jason will probably talk about it, so be prepared." Mrs. Yoccum glanced at her reflection in the mirror and grimaced. "Getting old is hell. I'm always startled to see the old woman looking back at me from the mirror."

Joan shifted so she was standing behind Mrs. Yoccum. She tipped her head as she took a quick inventory of her own reflection. "I know what you mean."

"You look wonderful." Mrs. Yoccum met her gaze in the reflection. Her eyes were sad. "You look like your mother."

"You said that earlier." Joan scowled and tried to look severe. "I don't see it unless I do this."

"Maybe you don't want to see it," Mrs. Yoccum said.

Joan said nothing and turned toward the door. She waited until they were in the car and headed for the hospital before she broached the subject that had been nagging her since their discussion the previous night.

"Can you tell me about the murder?"

Mrs. Yoccum glanced at Joan and returned her attention to the road.

"There was a bullet casing in the box with Annie's letters. I know from the letters that Annie died, and I know that Uncle Bud thinks he helped kill someone." Joan swallowed and pressed on. "I've got to know the truth, Lettie. Did Uncle Bud and my father kill Annie?"

CHAPTER 24
Big Springs, Kansas, 1954

KATHERINE HURRIED INTO the darkened house. It seemed to her that choir practice had been running later and later as time went on. And by the time everyone mingled and talked after and she drove Emily home and talked with Bud, well . . . the evening just slipped away.

"Kate?" Clyde's voice drifted from out of the kitchen.

"It's me," she said tiredly as she removed her hat and walked back to where he was likely sitting at the kitchen table paying bills. "Sorry I'm late. Practice went a little over and then I got to talking to—"

She stopped abruptly as she entered the room and stared. Clyde sat slouched in one of the kitchen chairs. A half-empty bottle of whiskey sat on the table next to a partially-empty glass.

"What's wrong?" she asked. His expression was one of thinly-masked fury. He held a crumpled piece of paper in one of his massive hands. "Clyde, what it is? Has someone died? Are you okay?"

"What's wrong?" he slurred and thrust the paper toward her. "Why don't *you* tell me what's wrong."

"I don't know," she said in genuine confusion as she stepped closer to see what had upset him.

"Bullshit," he said as he slapped the paper onto the table and smoothed it with his hands. "You know exactly what it is."

Cold fear flooded Katherine's body as she looked down and recognized her own handwriting. It was a letter—one of many she had written but never mailed to Annie after their meeting in Kansas City. *How,* she wondered, *had he found it?*

"Clyde," she began. "That's an old letter that—"

"I don't fucking care how old it is," Clyde snarled. "What I want to know is if it's true."

Katherine stared, unsure as to what to say.

"Is . . . it . . . true?" His eyes were hard and angry. "Were you whoring around while I was in the war?" He quickly rose to his feet. "Were you seeing someone else? Is it really true you can't stand to be with me?" He loomed over her menacingly.

"Clyde, sit down," Katherine said tightly. "If you'll just let me explain—"

"I should have known," he said with a snort of disgust. "Frigid bitch." He turned, went unsteadily toward the table, and dumped himself back into his chair. He picked up his glass and tipped the contents into his mouth with one swift movement. Before he even swallowed, he picked up the bottle, and refilled the glass.

"You don't understand," Katherine said. "It's not what you think."

"Ain't it?"

"No," Katherine insisted.

"Kate, I know." He swung his head back and forth miserably. "I've always known. Your mother told me before we got married. I guess I just thought it would pass—that it was puppy love or something." He looked glumly into his glass and spoke almost to himself. "But I should have known better."

He gulped down the contents of the glass and gave her a sharp look.

"All this time, I thought you were happy. I thought you cared for me. But now . . . Now I know you hate your life and you hate who you are. You've never been faithful to me." He shook his head angrily. "All those nights I lay there beside you, wanting you, and you was just laying thinkin' 'bout . . . it turns my stomach."

Katherine straightened her back and pressed her lips together. "When we got married . . ."

"I been waiting for you to want me," he interrupted, a strange glint in his eye. "But no more waiting. I'm taking what I want and what is my right as your husband. You're my wife." He thrust a thick finger into his chest. "*My* wife."

He stood, tipping the chair backward with a crash, and advanced on her.

Katherine turned to run into the other room, to run upstairs to their bedroom where she could lock him out.

Clyde grabbed her arm and yanked her painfully around to face him. "Tonight you're gonna' act like my wife," he snarled and bent his head toward her.

"No!" she said angrily and turned her face from his. "You're drunk."

"Yes!" he snarled and slapped her across the face with the back of his hand. "Tonight you're mine and you're going to give me what I want or I swear to God I'll kill you."

"No!" she screamed. "We agreed—"

He grabbed her hair and yanked her head back. She struggled and tried to turn away as he forced his lips roughly against hers.

"Hold still," he growled as he held her head more firmly and thrust his tongue into her mouth.

"Stop!"

She tried to scream, but he continued to cover her mouth with his, kissing her brutally. She could feel his hardness as he ground himself against her. He moved one of his hands to her breast and roughly squeezed it, pinching the nipple hard through the thin cloth of her dress and brassiere.

"Please, don't," she begged as he pushed her against the wall and moved his hand down to undo his fly. "Please, no."

He grunted deep in his throat but said nothing.

"Clyde—"

"I told you to shut up!" he yelled as he ceased fumbling with his fly and slapped her again.

"Aghhh!" she cried.

He grabbed her by both shoulders and shoved her like a rag doll onto the floor. "Just shut up!"

Katherine sobbed but said nothing as he climbed between her knees, pushed up her skirt and ripped away the crotch of her underwear.

"You're mine," he growled as he pulled himself out of his pants and shoved himself savagely into her. "Mine."

He said the word over and over with each painful, dry thrust until finally, he pushed himself deeply into her, gasped in release, and collapsed in a heap on top of her.

Katherine waited for several minutes before trying to extract herself from beneath him.

"No," he muttered as he kept her pinned beneath him. "I'm not done."

"KEEP HER HERE," Clyde told Emily the next morning.

Katherine stood by the window in the upstairs bedroom. She had barricaded herself up there after Clyde had passed out and now, stood out of sight of the people outside in the front, but where she could still peek out and watch what was going on. The best she could tell was that Clyde had summoned Emily to come watch her while he and Bud went away.

"I don't care what she tells you, keep her here. She's my wife and what I say goes. Understand?"

Katherine peeked out to see Emily nod and then look at Bud.

"Do as he says," Bud said in a tone that left no doubt that she was to follow his directions without complaint.

"Should be easy enough," Clyde said. "She's locked herself in the bedroom, but still . . ." He looked at Bud who nodded. "There's plenty of food in the house. We should be back in a couple of days."

Emily looked from Clyde to her husband and then back. "Where are you going?"

"None of your business," Bud said tightly. "Just make sure she don't leave."

Emily frowned but said nothing. After several seconds, she crossed her arms over her stomach.

"It may seem nasty, but it's for her own good." Clyde paused and glanced up at the second-story bedroom window. Katherine ducked back out of sight. "She tried to hurt herself," she heard him say. "She even threw herself down the steps. She's not right, if you know what I mean. She's been making up stories about people trying to get at 'er. She even started yelling the other night that I'm trying to hurt her."

Katherine craned her neck to look down on the yard. Clyde had turned his attention back to Emily.

"We're going to try to get a doctor in Kansas City to come here and help her," Clyde said.

Next to Emily, Bud nodded.

"But shouldn't you take her there?" Emily asked. "I mean, wouldn't that make more sense?"

"She's not well enough to get in the truck," Bud said. "Clyde's scared she'll hurt herself."

Katherine frowned, hurt that her brother would so easily accept such nonsense.

"Just watch over her," Clyde said. "We'll be back in a couple of days and hopefully will have the doctor with us."

"Is it really going to take so long?" Emily asked.

"Probably not, but we might have to do a lot of talking before one of them doctors will come all the way out here," Clyde said.

Clyde placed his hand on Emily's shoulder and smiled tiredly. "Thank you, Emily. You don't know how hard it's been. I been so worried but I know you'll take good care of our girl."

"I will," Emily said. "Nothing bad will happen to her. I promise you."

CLYDE AND BUD returned four days later looking haggard and exhausted. From her upstairs window, Katherine watched them climb out of the truck and walk toward the house. Neither man looked as if they had slept the entire time they had been gone.

Emily rushed out in the drive. "Any luck?"

"No. We tried all the doctors in Kansas City but nothing. We even went to St. Louis and Chicago. All they wanted to do was put her in the nut house." Clyde shook his head sadly. "I won't do that to her. She needs to be here with me—with us. She needs her family now more than ever."

"You two look exhausted," Emily said.

"It was a lot of driving for not a lot of good. But we tried." Clyde paused. "How is she?"

Emily shrugged and then sighed. "She hasn't come out of her room except to pee. I've been taking her food, but she hasn't done more than nibble at it."

Clyde lowered his head dramatically and sighed. His show of worry only made Katherine angrier. "Thank you for staying with her." He turned to Bud. "I don't know about you, but I need some sleep. Thanks for all your help."

Bud nodded and stepped forward to pick up Emily's suitcase. "You know where we'll be if you need us." He started toward his pickup parked under one of the large cottonwood trees in the yard.

Clyde waited until they pulled out of the yard and turned to look up at the bedroom window. Rather than duck out of sight, Katherine forced herself to stand straighter and stare down at him. He blinked several times and rubbed his hand along the back of his neck. He stood there for several seconds as if considering what to do. Finally, he walked toward the house.

Katherine heard his footsteps as he climbed the stairs and walked to stand in front of the bedroom door.

"Katie? I know you're in there."

Katherine refused to answer.

He knocked.

"Go away," Katherine said.

"Katie."

Katherine crossed her arms in angry defiance.

"Don't matter anyway. I just came to give you something."

"There is nothing you have that I could ever want," Katherine spat.

"I think you're wrong," he said. "Let me in."

"Go away," Katherine said miserably.

"You will let me in or I will tear down this door." Clyde's words were tight and precise.

Katherine stared at the door for several long seconds, then stepped forward and turned the key in the lock. She opened the door a crack and peered out.

"Open it all the way," he said softly as if he were trying to calm a wild animal. "I'm not gonna' hurt you. You're my wife. I love you."

"What do you want?" She resisted opening the door any farther.

They stared at each other for several seconds. Clyde reached into his pocket of his trousers and held out his closed hand, palm side down. His knuckles were swollen and bruised.

"Hold out your hand," he said.

She glanced up at his face and saw nothing to indicate he was going to hurt her. Slowly, she extended her hand. Clyde hovered his fist over hers and slowly, slowly, opened his fingers. A bullet casing fell into her palm. It was warm from his pocket. Katherine looked at it in confusion and then back up at Clyde's stubbled face.

"I just wanted you to know that your goddamned *lover* is dead. Bud went with me and can vouch that what I'm sayin' is true. And I'm tellin' you this because this is the last time we're ever gonna' talk about it. But know this." He grabbed Katherine's chin and roughly tipped it upward so she was forced to meet his eyes. "You *ever* cross me again, next time it will be you."

Katherine watched as he turned, walked down the hall, and down the stairs. She looked down at the bullet casing in her hand and felt her heart contract. She had thought perhaps he and Bud had gone out drinking, but it had never occurred to her that they would go to Chicago and track down Annie.

Surely he's bluffing. There was no way Clyde would kill a woman, was there? She felt her body go cold at the realization that five days ago she wouldn't have thought he was capable of rape, either—or any kind of violence for that matter. She studied the bullet casing and realized she didn't know the man she was married to or what he was capable of. Slowly, she pushed the door closed and twisted the key in the lock.

Katherine went to the mirror and studied her face. The bruises from where he had slapped her had turned a sallow yellowish-green. She touched her fingertips to the angriest bruise and knew in that instant what Clyde had said was true. Fresh tears stung the back of her eyes. Her heart felt as if it were about to burst. She stumbled to the bed and curled into a ball. She hugged her legs to her chest and sobbed.

"Annie," she said softly as she rocked back and forth. "Annie. Annie. Annie."

"DID DAD AND Uncle Bud kill Annie?"

The question hung in the air, and Mrs. Yoccum stared straight ahead without answering.

Joan waited. She promised herself she wasn't going to speak until Mrs. Yoccum told her what she wanted to know. They were silent for several minutes; Joan driving and Mrs. Yoccum considering.

Finally, Mrs. Yoccum sighed deeply and turned to Joan. "Out of respect for your mother, I haven't been completely honest with you. But I thought about it last night and despite what your mother thought, I don't think it's fair to keep all this from you. I'll tell you anything you want to know."

The hospital was ahead. Joan turned on her left turn blinker and pulled into the visitor's parking lot. As she put the car in park and turned off the engine, she realized that despite her desire to know the whole truth, she was suddenly scared.

She turned her body to Mrs. Yoccum. "Within the last week, I've found out that my mother was a lesbian, my father was a rapist, and that he and my uncle were quite possibly murderers." She shook her head. "Is it any wonder I've got the problems that I do?"

Mrs. Yoccum frowned. "What problems do you have?"

The concern and genuine caring Joan saw reflected in Mrs. Yoccum's eyes threatened to break down the front she was trying so hard to maintain. She looked at her lap as tears burned the backs of her eyes. She cleared her throat. "I can't tell you. If I do, I'll start crying. And I'm not sure if I start I'll be able to stop."

Mrs. Yoccum reached out a gnarled hand and gently gripped Joan's wrist. The veins bulged beneath the papery skin. "That bad?"

Joan nodded.

"Sweetie, tell me what's wrong," Mrs. Yoccum said softly. "Maybe I can help."

"I don't even know where to begin," Joan said thickly. She threw her hands up in exasperation. "I don't love my husband. I have been having an affair and now I'm pregnant with this other man's child. I'm scheduled to have an abortion, and all I want to do is run away from my life. I'm no better a mother than Mom was. I'm just like her." Tears rolled down her cheeks.

"Oh, sweetheart." Mrs. Yoccum unfastened her seat belt. "Come here." She held open her arms and pulled Joan into her frail embrace. "Shhh. It's okay. There is nothing wrong with you. And your mother, well . . . there was just so much you didn't know . . . couldn't know. But I think it's time." She sighed and looked in the direction of the hospital. "I need to go inside now, but if you're available tonight, I'll tell you anything you want to know."

Joan sat upright and wiped at her eyes with the heel of her hand. She stared out the windshield at the gray van parked in front of them and nodded quickly.

"Okay," she said and then hesitated. "Listen, I know I said that I wanted to see Jason, but I'm just not sure I'm up to it after all. But I can come pick you up after or—"

"No," Mrs. Yoccum said as she pulled on the plastic door handle. "I can call a cab or I'm sure Susan will drive me home." She stepped slowly out of the car and then bent to speak. "We'll talk when I get home. I promise."

She pushed the door closed, waved, and walked slowly toward the hospital. Only after she was inside did Joan start the car and pull out of the parking lot. For a while, she simply drove aimlessly around Lawrence, looking at the buildings and businesses that had emerged in the years since she had left. But finally, as if it had been her ultimate destination all along, she turned and headed east toward the cemetery.

She drove along the curved roads that ran through the grounds until she arrived at her mother's grave. Katherine had been adamant that she not be buried in the family plot in Big Springs, which was where Clyde had been buried. Instead, she had insisted in purchasing a plot in the Lawrence Cemetery.

Joan sat in her car and studied her mother's gravestone. It, too, had been pre-purchased, though this was the first time she had seen it since it had been set. The engraving was simple and to the point: Katherine Henderson Spencer, December 27, 1912—September 20, 1997. The dark brown earth was still mounded over her mother's grave and hadn't yet had the chance to settle. As she studied the headstone, she realized that a second headstone, exactly like her mother's, was set in the adjacent grave.

Joan climbed out of the car and studied the plot. The ground was still a solid sheet of grass. As far as she could tell, no one had been buried there, although the upturned earth around the headstone suggested it had been set in the ground at about the same time as her mother's. "I wonder if . . ." She frowned at the thought. "Could she have purchased this for me?"

Joan studied the plot more closely. There was nothing to indicate the identity of the owner or the intended occupant. Perhaps she should ask at the main office. If nothing else, she could pretend to be interested in purchasing it for herself. It would make sense, wouldn't it? What daughter wouldn't want to be buried next to her mother? And if it turned out that her mother had purchased it for her, then she wouldn't have to feign surprise.

Joan walked back to her car and drove to the cemetery's administrative center. The woman behind the heavily-polished wooden desk greeted her as she stepped inside. She seemed to be about Joan's age with dark blonde hair pulled back into an intentionally messy bun.

"Good morning," she said cheerfully. "How can I help you?"

Joan blinked as her eyes adjusted to the office's ambient lighting. "I was interested in purchasing the plot next to my mother's."

"Of course," the woman said smoothly. "And what was your mother's name?"

"Spencer," Joan said. "Katherine Spencer."

The receptionist wrote the name on a piece of scratch paper and spun her chair to face her computer screen. Her perfectly-manicured nails clicked lightly on the keys as she typed in Katherine's name. "And which plot were you interested in purchasing?"

"The grave is immediately to the right of hers," Joan said.

The woman entered more information into the computer. The screen blinked. "Oh, I'm sorry, but that plot isn't for sale." She used the spin wheel on the computer mouse to scroll down the screen. "There is an open plot a little further down. I know it's not right next to your mother, but—"

"I'd really like the plot next to Mom," Joan interrupted. "Could you tell me who the other owner is? I'd like to contact them about purchasing it."

The receptionist turned to Joan and smiled apologetically. "I'm sorry, but I can't do that. It's confidential."

"Isn't it public information, though?" Joan said quickly. "I mean, technically, isn't it land ownership?"

"Well, yes, but . . ." the woman said.

Joan pushed her advantage. "Is there someone you could ask?" She forced herself to tear up. "My mother and I were very close. We couldn't stand to be apart from each other and . . . well . . . we would want to be together in death as well." She leaned forward and put gentle fingers on the woman's arm. "Please."

The receptionist looked at her for several seconds. "Let me ask my supervisor and see if it's all right. Can you wait here for just a moment?"

"Of course."

The woman rose and disappeared into the back of the building. Joan counted to five, crept out of her seat, and leaned over the woman's desk to peer at the computer screen. She could hear the muffled conversation between the receptionist and another woman as she scanned the information on the screen. It was about her mother's purchase. She could see a second window open behind her mother's. Joan glanced quickly at the doorway through which the receptionist had exited and clicked on the other window.

She blinked in disbelief at the name that popped up on the screen.

"Holy crap," she murmured. "It's Mrs. Yoccum."

JOAN HURRIED OUT of the administrative offices in a daze. Not surprisingly, the receptionist had told her she couldn't release the information. Joan had murmured something about understanding and excused herself quickly.

"Mrs. Yoccum," she said as she walked to her car. "Why in the hell would she have the plot next to Mom's?"

She got into her car and started the ignition. They had been best friends, she knew, but that didn't explain the decision to buy joint gravesides, unless . . . *had her mother and Mrs. Yoccum become lovers?*

She pulled out of the cemetery. Her ears filled with a sickening crunch, and she flew toward the passenger's side. She gasped as her head snapped sideways and smacked against the dash. She cried out as her body twisted and her side and chest slammed forward into the steering wheel. For what seemed like several minutes, there was absolute silence.

"Jesus, lady, are you okay?" a man asked.

She turned and frowned up at the figure peering in the broken driver's-side window. His wide, anxious eyes stared in at her. Dazed, she blinked and felt her left eye sting. She raised a shaking hand, wiped away the tears, and stared at the blood on her fingers.

"Are you okay?" the man asked again. "I'm so sorry. I couldn't stop. You just pulled out . . . Jesus, are you okay?"

Joan nodded and winced at the pain. She grabbed the door handle and clumsily yanked. Nothing happened.

"You're not going to be able to get out that way," he said. "The door's crushed in. You're going to have to get out the other way. Are you okay to move?"

"I'm . . ." Joan felt drunk. "I need to get out of here."

"Why don't you just wait," the man said. "The police are on their way. The people across the street called for an ambulance. Just stay there."

"I can't stay in here." Joan painfully began to crawl toward the passenger's door. She realized she hadn't been wearing her seat belt. "They're going to give me a ticket."

"Lady, just stay there," the man said.

Joan heard the sirens in the distance. She pulled herself the rest of the way across the passenger's seat and pushed open the door. Her entire body ached as she forced herself into a sitting position and then stepped out of the car. The sirens were getting closer.

"I'm okay," she told the man who had hurried around to the other side of the car. "I'm fine. I just need to . . ." She looked at him plaintively. "I need to . . . lie down." She reached blindly in front of her, fighting off the white noise that filled her mind and clouded her vision.

"It's okay," the man said as he caught her. "I got you."

"JOANIE?"

The voice seemed to come from very far away. Joan tried to open her eyes, but found that her eyelids were extraordinarily heavy.

"Joanie? Sweetheart, wake up."

Joan felt sudden panic. She didn't know where she was. She wanted to move, to sit up, to struggle, but couldn't. Her arms and legs were thick and leaden.

"I think she's coming around." This time it was a male voice. "I'll get the nurse."

"Joanie, it's all right, dear. You're safe. We're right here."

It was a familiar voice. An older woman's voice. Her mother? Somehow that didn't seem right, but . . . She forced her lips to move.

"Mom?"

"It's okay, sweetheart," came the voice again. "We're here. You're in the hospital. Luke is here."

"Luke?" Joan murmured. The words were coming easier now, although she still couldn't seem to open her eyes. "Mama?"

She heard a soft laugh.

"No, sweetie," came the voice. "It's Lettie. Lettie Yoccum. From next door."

"Mrs. Yoccum," Joan repeated. The name nagged at her. She had needed to talk to Mrs. Yoccum about something—something important. She struggled again to open her eyes. They felt glued together. She felt her eyes roll back in her head before she forced her lids apart.

"Welcome back. My name is Sally."

The speaker was a woman she had never seen before, though judging from her blue scrubs, she was either a doctor or a nurse. She smiled kindly and then turned her attention to the beeping, clicking machine next to the bed.

Joan opened and closed her eyes several times before holding them open and looking around.

Luke stood on one side of the bed slightly behind Mrs. Yoccum, who sat in the chair next to the bed holding her hand. She turned her head to gaze fully at them, and both smiled. The movement caused her head to pound painfully, and she grimaced.

" . . . your name?"

Joan forced herself to slowly turn her head to look at Sally. She had asked for her name.

"Joan," she said hoarsely.

"And your last name?"

"O'Connor." Joan tried to swallow. "Could I get some water?"

"Of course," Sally said. "I'll get you some chipped ice in just a second. Just let me ask a couple more questions, okay? Do you know what day it is?"

Joan closed her eyes and tried to concentrate. "My head hurts."

"I know," Sally said. "You banged your head up pretty good. Do you know what day it is?"

Joan thought for a second. "Is it still the same day I had the accident?"

Sally nodded.

"Tuesday"

"Excellent," Sally said. "Now, what's the last thing you remember?"

Joan frowned and tried to recall what had happened. She had been at the cemetery. And she was leaving when a car crashed into her.

"I was pulling out into the street and another car hit mine," Joan said. "There was a man who helped me out of the car."

"That's right. Very good." Sally patted Joan's leg under the thin hospital blanket. "I'll just go see about that ice." She turned, pulled aside the curtain, and disappeared from the room.

"Hi, baby," Luke said softly as he came around to the empty side of the bed and took her hand. "How are you doing?"

"Sore," Joan said. "My head hurts."

He nodded and gave her a halfhearted smile. "You're lucky. From what I've heard, the car looks like shit. But that's okay," he added quickly, "we'll get a new one."

"How badly am I hurt?" Joan asked.

Luke glanced at Mrs. Yoccum. "You've got a concussion, a broken nose, several broken ribs and . . ." He looked again at Mrs. Yoccum who nodded. "And you lost the baby."

"The . . . baby." Joan closed her eyes.

"Joanie, why didn't you tell me you were pregnant?" Luke asked.

"I . . . I didn't have a chance with everything that was going on and Mom's death . . ." Joan stopped—her mother's death, the cemetery, the grave. She opened her eyes and looked at Mrs. Yoccum. "You own the grave next to Mom's."

Mrs. Yoccum looked at Luke and then back at Joan. "I should leave the two of you alone," she murmured and pushed herself unsteadily to her feet.

"No," Joan said. "I need to know why—"

"Joan," Luke interrupted. "You can talk to her about that later. Right now you need to rest. You've . . . you should rest."

"But . . ." she said helplessly as Mrs. Yoccum left the room.

Luke waited until they were alone before sitting on the edge of her bed and leaning forward. "Joanie, why didn't you tell me you were pregnant?"

Joan closed her eyes, wanting nothing more than for the conversation she knew was coming to not take place. "I don't know, Luke. It just . . ." Tears pushed against her eyelids.

"But you knew, right?" he asked softly.

Joan considered lying to him but finally, sighed. "I knew."

Luke rose silently from the side of the bed and walked toward the window. "The doctor said you were three months pregnant."

Joan watched him but said nothing. It was clear he had done the math.

"I was out of town most of that month. And when I was back, we didn't . . ." He sighed and rubbed his hand across his face. "That's why you didn't tell me, wasn't it?"

"Luke—" Joan began.

Sally walked into the room. "Here we are." She set a blue plastic pitcher and two Styrofoam glasses on the stand next to the foot of Joan's bed. "Water or ice chips?"

"Ice chips," Joan said, thankful for the diversion.

Sally handed one of the cups to Joan. "I'll be back in a few minutes to check your vitals. Until then, just rest."

Joan nodded her thanks, leaned back against the pillow, and closed her eyes. When she opened them, Luke was still standing with his back to her, staring out the window into the darkness.

"I just need to know if it was mine." His voice was tight with anger.

She didn't answer for several seconds, then cleared her throat. "No. It wasn't."

"That guy from work?" he asked finally.

"Yes." Joan admitted.

Luke snorted angrily and tensed his shoulders. "Are you in love with him?"

"No."

He spun around and glared at her. "Then why—?"

"Look," Joan said more harshly than she intended. "It wasn't about you. Or us. It was about me." She gingerly touched her head with her fingertips. "It was about what I wanted for a change. Not you. Not the kids. Not work. What I wanted."

Luke's eyes blazed in anger as he studied her. "So, what do *you* want me to do now?"

"I don't know. There are some things I have to do here—things I have to figure out." She met his gaze apologetically. "This wasn't about you."

"So . . . ?"

"I need some time," she said and then added more softly, "I think you should go home."

"Go home," he said with a snort. "So just go home and leave you here."

"Yes."

"Is this about Mark?" She could hear the jealousy in his voice. "Is he here or . . . Is he staying with you at your mom's? Is that why you don't call or . . . check in?"

"No. It's been over for a while." She sighed. "I just need . . . time—time to figure out who I am and what I'm doing."

"You're a wife and mother," Luke said. "You're a paralegal. You have a life in Chicago . . . with us."

"I know." Joan closed her eyes. "But I may not want that anymore."

"Which?" Luke asked.

Joan opened her eyes, met his gaze, and shook her head. "I don't know."

"Unbelievable. That's just fucking unbelievable." Luke stomped to the chair, grabbed his jacket, and rushed to the door. "Don't call me or the kids until you have this figured out. You have one week." He held up his index finger. "And if I don't hear from you by then, don't bother coming home."

He turned and strode out the door.

JOAN AWOKE AND found Mrs. Yoccum sitting beside the bed.

"You're back." Mrs. Yoccum patted her arm. "You were sleeping like a child."

Joan tried to sit up and winced at the pain.

"Do you want me to get the nurse?"

Joan shook her head. "I think I'd prefer to do it on my own." She shifted again and finally settled into a more comfortable position.

"I'm sorry about the baby," Mrs. Yoccum said finally.

Joan pursed her lips, nodded, and closed her eyes. She didn't want to talk about the baby. "Why do you have the grave next to my mother's?" She opened her eyes. Mrs. Yoccum stopped picking at a thread on her pants and looked up. "Were you lovers?"

Mrs. Yoccum stared down into her lap and blinked several times. She looked up with tears in her eyes. "We found happiness together late in life. I loved your mother dearly."

"And that's why you know so much about what happened with my father and Annie and all of it," Joan said. "Mother told you."

"There's more to it, but yes. I begged her to tell you herself, but . . ." She shrugged.

Joan stared at her for several long seconds, trying to imagine her mother and Mrs. Yoccum together.

"I don't understand," she said finally. "When did it begin? Was it going on when Jason and I were kids?"

"It was," Mrs. Yoccum said.

"So, what . . . it was some sort of rebound thing for Mom?" Joan asked. "You were mourning your husband? You were both lonely?"

Mrs. Yoccum smiled. "No, nothing like that."

"Then what?"

Mrs. Yoccum looked past Joan at the machines pulsing and beeping on the other side of the bed. She took a deep breath. "Jason's not my son. Not biologically, anyway."

Joan frowned, unsure what Jason's parentage had to do with anything. "I don't understand."

"Jason's mother died shortly after he was born," Mrs. Yoccum said. "I promised her that if anything ever happened, I would take Jason and raise him as if he were my own."

CHAPTER 26
Chicago, Illinois, 1959

ANNIE STOOD IN the entryway of the apartment and sorted through the mail—not that she expected anything to actually be for her. The only person who might possibly write her would be Doris and that was unlikely given that she was on her honeymoon.

"Nancy, are you here?" she called down the hall.

There was no answer, though Annie thought she heard soft gurgles coming from Nancy's bedroom.

"Nancy?" Annie took several steps down the hall. She could definitely hear Jason making the little noises he did when he was entertaining himself in his crib. She walked the remaining steps to the bedroom and tentatively pushed open the door.

Nancy lay on the bed, asleep. In his crib, Jason was sitting up, chewing on a wooden spoon that he had recently decided was his new favorite plaything. Annie smiled at the little boy, crept softly to the crib, and gently brushed back his dark curls. He looked up at her with large brown eyes and held out the spoon.

"No thank you," she whispered and shook her head in an exaggerated motion. "No thank you, baby boy."

She glanced at the bed where Nancy lay and then back into the crib. Nancy had been sleeping a great deal over the past few months. She had become depressed after Jason had been born. For her part, Annie had tried to step in and take over as much responsibility as possible.

"Is your mama sleeping again?" she whispered. "How about you come out in the living room and play with me?" With a grunt, Annie lifted the baby from the crib. He giggled in delight, and Annie turned quickly to see if the noise had awakened Nancy. She hadn't moved. In fact, Nancy wasn't moving at all—not even to breathe.

"Nancy?" Annie said loudly.

She could hear the panic in her voice.

"Nancy. Nancy, wake up!" She carefully put Jason back in his crib and hurried to the edge of the bed. She touched Nancy's shoulder and knew she was dead. She recoiled.

"Oh my God," she gasped. "Shit!"

She scanned the room for an explanation. Nothing seemed out of place until she looked down and saw the bottle of gin and the small glass prescription bottle. It was empty. She glanced back up at Nancy's slack face. Behind her, Jason babbled nonsensically.

Annie knew she should call the police, but she was worried about what would happen to Jason if she did. She glanced in his direction. They might let her take care of him, but what if they didn't? She frowned as she remembered the conversation she and Nancy had had the week before. She had been cooking dinner and Nancy was sitting at the Formica kitchen table. They had been talking about the weather when Nancy said suddenly, "Annie, I need you to do something for me."

Surprised by the urgency of her tone, Annie had put down her knife and turned to look at her. "Of course. What's wrong?"

Nancy sighed and idly traced the metal edge of the tabletop. "I don't know." She gave an embarrassed laugh. "It's probably nothing. I'm just so tired. I think something is wrong with me."

Annie went to the sink, rinsed her hands, and sat down next to her. "Sweetheart, what is it?"

Nancy glanced sidelong at Annie and then back down at her fingers. "Ever since the baby was born . . ." She shrugged helplessly. "Life seems to have worn me out."

"I know." Annie squeezed Nancy's hand. "But it's normal. You just need to go see the doctor. He'll get you squared away."

Nancy gave an unconvincing laugh. "I'm sure you're right." She paused. "But what if it turns out to be something?" She raised her eyes to meet Annie's. "Promise me that if anything ever happens to me, you won't let him grow up without a mother."

Annie blinked. "Don't talk like that." She squeezed Nancy's hand again. "You're fine."

"I'm not fine," Nancy said dully. "And I need to know that you'll take care of Jason."

"Nancy," Annie said quietly as she looked into Nancy's face. "You took care of me when I had no one else to turn you. You have accepted me for who I am, and you've never once judged me. You two are my family, and I promise that if anything should ever happen, I won't let Jason be an orphan." She smiled. "But that's not going to happen. You're just a little blue is all."

"And promise me you'll never let Ed know he has a son," Nancy continued.

"I won't." Annie shook her head.

"Promise me." Nancy's expression was stricken.

"I promise," Annie said.

"Thank you," Nancy said softly and closed her eyes. "Thank you so much."

"Is there something you're not telling me?" Annie asked.

Nancy opened her eyes and smiled. "No. Not at all."

But there had been, Annie thought as she nudged the empty pill bottle with her toe. Nancy had been planning her death even then. Behind her, Jason's soft gurgles turned into full-fledged cries. She hurried to the crib. The small boy reached out his chubby arms, and she picked him up.

"Shhh," she whispered and kissed him on the head. "It's okay. It's all going to be okay. We just need to figure out what to do."

She bounced him gently in her arms as she paced the room. As she walked, an idea began to form. Quickly, she returned Jason to his crib and went into the living room where she knew Nancy kept her stationery. She removed a sheet of paper and an envelope. Nancy's fountain pen lay in the drawer next to the remaining sheets of paper. If she was going to do it, she needed to do it before she called the authorities—before she could change her mind. She went into the kitchen and sat down at the table. She paused in thought before uncapping the pen.

> *To Whom It May Concern:*
>
> *I, Nancy Louise Yoccum, being of sound mind and body, do hereby make this my last will and testament. In absence of any remaining blood relatives, I bequeath the following:*
>
> *To Charlotte Annette Bennett, I leave, in your care, as we have agreed upon, my son, Jason Allen Yoccum. He is a good boy and I know that you love him as much as if you were his real mother. I have no other family and I know that you will take care of him better than I ever could.*
>
> *To Jason Allen Yoccum, I leave all of my worldly possessions including and especially my father's St. Christopher medal. He wore it in the war and it kept him safe. It is my hope that it will do the same for you. I love you, my son, and want you to know that in the event that you are reading this, I will regret every day I am not able to see you grow up and become the man I know you will be.*
>
> *To anyone else who reads this, please honor my wishes in this matter.*
>
> *Nancy Louise Yoccum*

Annie dated the document to more than nine months earlier. Next she found a different pen and signed her own name as a witness and added the illegible signature of a man named Andrew Stratton. Finished with her task, she sat back and looked at the document. She had tried to make it look like Nancy's handwriting although she wasn't sure how successful she had been. She shrugged. It was all she could do. Carefully, she folded the letter, slid it into the envelope and took it into the bedroom where she laid it carefully on Nancy's night stand. Jason, who had stopped crying, watched her curiously.

"Well," Annie said, as much to him as to herself. "That about does it. Now it's time to call the police and do the best we can." She walked to the crib and picked up the toddler. He squirmed in her arms, and tears welled up in her eyes. "It's just you and me now, buddy," she whispered and squeezed him tightly. "Two orphans. But we're not alone. As long as I'm alive, you will never be without family."

"I KNEW SHE had been concerned about her health," Annie told the police detective. "Just last week she told me she was going to the doctor. She had been so tired lately. Giving birth to Jason had exhausted her."

The detective, a man who had identified himself as Lawrence Riddle, nodded and jotted some notes in his notebook. "And you knew Miss Yoccum . . . how?"

"We worked together," Annie said. "And then, when I needed a place to live, she offered to let me move in here. She was about to give birth, so I helped her before and then after she delivered."

Annie looked at Nancy's body and forced herself to cry. Riddle shifted uncomfortably and looked anywhere but at her. "Had she seemed sad to you?"

"She . . ." Annie swallowed and shifted Jason from one hip to the other. "She had been. She talked to me just last week and reminded me of my promise to adopt Jason if anything ever happened to her. She said she was tired. She said she thought there was something wrong with her."

Riddle nodded and wrote again in his notebook.

"She committed suicide, didn't she?" Annie tried to make her voice sound disbelieving.

"That's what it looks like, yes," the detective admitted. "Between the empty pill bottle and the alcohol . . . well." Annie cried fresh tears, and he touched her shoulder. "She made sure her will was in plain sight."

"Her will?" Annie looked up at him.

"On the nightstand. You probably didn't notice it but it was in plain sight so it would be found. Lots of people leave notes. She didn't, but the will made it pretty obvious what she had done." He reached into the inside breast pocket of his ill-fitting jacket and removed the envelope containing Annie's hastily-composed forgery.

Annie nodded when she saw it. "She asked me and a friend of hers to witness it. A man named Stratton or Stanton. I hadn't met him before that day."

"Did she have any enemies you knew of?" Riddle asked. "I don't think this is murder. We just have to be thorough."

"I understand," Annie said and kissed Jason on the top of his head. She pretended to think for several seconds and then shook her head. "I can't think of any, no."

"And what about the baby's father?" Riddle asked.

"I don't think she knew who the father was," Annie lied.

Riddle nodded. "And Miss Yoccum's parents?"

"Both dead," Annie said. "She was an only child. We shared that in common."

Riddle made another note and turned to look at Nancy's body on the bed. The men from the coroner's office were preparing to move it.

"Fellas . . ." Riddle said.

The men straightened and stepped back from the bed.

He turned to Annie and smiled kindly. "You're not going to want to see this. How about we go into the kitchen to finish up?"

Annie glanced at Nancy's still form and the men hovering next to the stretcher and nodded tightly.

"What about Jason?" she asked when they were seated at the kitchen table.

"Well, it's really not a matter for us to decide, but it seems like everything is in order in terms of what she wanted done with the boy. We'll have to wait for the official ruling for cause of death, but as far as I can see, it looks like a case of suicide. There is a witnessed will giving you custody and no one to contest it." Riddle held up the envelope containing the will and shrugged. "And you want the child?"

Annie nodded vigorously. "I've been here since the day he was born. I consider him my own son—if that makes sense."

"Of course it does," Riddle said kindly. "I don't think there will be any trouble in that regard."

Annie sighed in relief and dipped her chin to again kiss the top of Jason's head. He was dozing, despite all the activity in the apartment, and she slowly rocked him back and forth. Riddle closed his notebook and laid it on the table on top of the forged will. He extracted a business card from his jacket pocket and slid it across the table to her. Then, for lack of anything better to do with them, he folded his hands on the table in front of him. He watched Annie and Jason.

"Well . . ." he said finally.

Annie met his gaze and he smiled sadly at her.

"I'm terribly sorry for your loss." He picked up his notebook and got awkwardly to his feet. "I'll be in touch."

"Thank you," Annie said hoarsely and fought back a new wave of tears. She swallowed several times, cleared her throat, and stood as well. Riddle, who had watched her with a mixture of discomfort and pity, clumsily patted her shoulder.

"I'll show myself out," he said and turned quickly before she could respond one way or the other.

The men had already removed Nancy's body, and with Riddle's departure, the apartment was quiet. Annie looked around the kitchen and then wandered aimlessly through the living room and back into Nancy's bedroom. She was gone, and Annie was once again alone.

CHAPTER 27
Lawrence, Kansas, 1960

KATHERINE STOOD IN front of the sink, looking out the window and vigorously scrubbing at the baked-on residue of the casserole dish. Outside, she could hear Joan talking to herself as she ran back and forth along the side of the house in a game that seemed to involve sprinting as fast as she could from the back of the property to the front and then walking slowly back, only to do the same thing over again.

Ever since the next-door neighbors had moved two months ago, Joan had had no one to play with and had taken instead to making up her own games—games with complicated plots that often seemed to include running or creeping along the ground with a long stick that she referred to as her Brown Bess Kentucky long rifle. It was a reference from one of her favorite stories about Daniel Boone. Katherine smiled at that. Joan was a smart child—that much had been clear from the beginning, and Katherine had gone out of her way to read to her often. As with the details of the Daniel Boone book, Joan had committed many of the stories to memory.

Though it might not have been obviously apparent, Katherine was proud of her daughter. She knew that people thought she was a hard woman—a cold mother. And perhaps she was. But something had changed after the rape and Annie's murder. It was as if she had lost the ability to feel. She had tried to love Joan. She did love Joan. But as hard as she tried, every time she looked at her daughter, she was reminded of the night she had been conceived and what had been taken from her.

At first, Katherine hadn't believed that Clyde had murdered Annie. She didn't think he had it in him. Of course, she hadn't thought he was capable of rape either. If anything, she thought it was a trick to punish her. But her conversation with her sister-in-law changed her mind.

Katherine had gone to see Emily in the middle of the afternoon when she knew Bud would be gone. Her knock had been answered after several minutes by a reluctant Emily who stepped out onto the front porch rather than invite her in and had looked at her with a mixture of disgust and disbelief. She held a baby on her hip.

"What are you doing here?" She glanced nervously up the road. She bounced the little boy, Seth, and murmured soft words in his ear.

"Emily, I don't know what Bud told you—" Katherine began.

"Bud told me everything," Emily said tightly.

"Then please, tell me what happened while they were gone," Katherine pleaded. "I need to know if it's true. Did they really kill—?"

"I don't know how you can stand to look at yourself," Emily interrupted. "Clyde is a good man and you just . . . Katie, how could you?"

"You don't understand," Katherine began.

"Oh, I understand all right," Emily spat. "You couldn't just let the past go, could you? No, you had to go and shit on the one man who would marry you to save your reputation." She shook her head in disgust. "They did what they had to do. Nobody's ever going to find the body." She looked disdainfully at Katherine and said in a low, angry voice, "I hate what you made my husband do—what he's going to have to live with on his conscience until his judgment day. Now please go away. You're not welcome here. Clyde might keep you around, but we don't want nothin' to do with you."

With that, Emily turned on her heel and walked back into the house, pushing the screen and the front door closed behind her.

Katherine stood, frozen in amazement. After several seconds she turned and walked blindly back to the truck. The glimmer of hope she had been nursing—that this was all one big trick—faded. Annie was dead.

Three weeks later, she discovered she was pregnant.

She hadn't wanted Joan. But having an abortion had never really been an option. After what had happened with Claire, the idea terrified her. And then when Clyde—who after the rape had taken to demanding his marital rights—had realized she was pregnant, she had no option but to have it. None of it was Joan's fault. Katherine knew that. But the situation and the fact that she was forced to have the baby, made her resent her. She wanted to love Joan, but something in her had been broken. Love was just another word to her.

Katherine stepped back from the sink, tired of scrubbing and even more tired of the dark thoughts that seemed to plague her today. She grabbed the dish towel and started to dry her hands and then stopped as she realized she hadn't heard Joan run past the window in quite some time.

She peered out the back and then toward the front. She could hear Joan's voice coming from the front yard. She hurried to the front door and saw Joan standing on the sidewalk talking to a woman holding a wriggling, dark-haired toddler. The woman had her back to her, though Katherine could see her nodding at something Joan was animatedly explaining.

The woman said something to Joan and then walked toward a car parked across the street. Joan watched them walk away and waved back when the little boy waved goodbye. When they were in their car Joan turned and saw Katherine standing in the doorway. Realizing she was likely in trouble, she walked slowly to the house and up the porch steps.

"What have I told you about talking to strangers," Katherine snapped the minute Joan stepped into the house. "You didn't know that woman from Eve. She could have snatched you up in a heartbeat."

"Sorry," Joan said meekly.

Katherine sighed and then said in a gentler tone, "So, what did she want?"

"She wanted to know who I was and why I was playing by myself," Joan said. "I told her that Julie and Sarah used to live next door but they moved away."

"Joanie, you can't just share that kind of information with people you don't know." Katherine tried to keep her tone from being too harsh. "Was that her son?"

"His name is Jason. He's two years old."

"And that's all she wanted?" Katherine asked suspiciously.

"She asked how old I was." Joan grinned widely. "And she asked if my mama was as pretty as I am."

Katherine narrowed her eyes and glanced out the door. The car still sat under the tree across the street. "Joan, you need to listen to me. I don't want you talking to her or anyone else you don't know. Do you understand?"

Joan nodded her head. "Yes."

"Yes, what?" Katherine asked.

"Yes, ma'am."

ANNIE SAT IN the car and watched the little girl run up to the house. She felt something in her stomach flutter at the sight of Katherine's unmistakable form silhouetted in the screen door. It was all she could do to hold herself back from rushing up to the house and throwing herself into Katherine's arms. Instead, she looked down at Jason who smiled sweetly up at her.

She had been surprised to find out that Katherine had a daughter—surprised and a little sickened at the thought of how it came to be. Still, she reasoned, she'd had her chance and she had gone to Chicago with Doris. It stood to reason that Katherine had gone on with her life. It seemed, incongruous however, that both she and Katherine had children. The little girl, Joan, had seemed high-spirited as she explained her game

Sandra Moran

and why she was playing by herself. Her friends had moved away. Annie looked again at the house next to Katherine's. It seemed almost too good to be true that it was unoccupied and likely for sale.

"How would you like to live in a real house?" Annie asked Jason, who stared up at her, not understanding what she was saying, but wanting to please her.

"Tree." He pointed out the car window at the large maple in front of the unoccupied house.

Annie grinned. "Yes. Tree. Our tree. As soon as we find out who owns this house and how much they want for it."

"Tree," Jason said again.

Annie pressed her lips to the top of his head before turning the key in the ignition. The engine roared to life, and she quickly put the car into gear and pulled away from the curb. There were details to work out, but first and foremost, she knew, she had to find a lawyer and make arrangements to buy that house.

"MAMA!" JOAN CALLED.

Katherine heard the screen door bang shut. Scowling, she hurried from the kitchen.

Joanie skidded to a halt in the hall. "Mama, guess what! Guess what?"

"Joanie, how many times have I told you not to run in the house and not to let the screen door slam?" Katherine asked tiredly.

"I'm sorry." Joan dropped her chin to her chest.

Katherine sighed and tried to remind herself that Joan was just a little girl with lots of energy. It wasn't her fault Katherine was tired and developing one of her headaches. She forced a less severe expression on her face.

"So, what was so urgent that you had run in here like a wild Indian to tell me?" she asked.

"Oh, Mama," Joan said, suddenly excited again. "There are men moving things into the house next door. I saw them. And I saw the woman again—and the little boy."

Katherine craned her neck to look out the front door. There was indeed a moving van. "Did you talk to her or her husband?"

Joan shook her head. "You told me not to."

Katherine blinked and looked at her daughter in surprise. "Good girl." She patted Joan on the shoulder.

Joan beamed at the attention. "Can I go watch them? I'll stay out of the way."

"It's lunchtime," Katherine said. "Maybe after lunch."

"But I want to play with Jason," Joan said. "Please?"

"Joan." Katherine felt herself quickly losing her patience. "Go wash your hands for lunch."

In an expression that almost mirrored Katherine's, Joan narrowed her eyes and crossed her arms. Despite her irritation, Katherine almost smiled. She studied her daughter for several seconds and then softened.

"What if I read to you this afternoon?" she asked. "We could read a Nancy Drew mystery."

Joan shrugged noncommittally.

"Either way, you need to eat your lunch." She pointed to the kitchen. "Ham sandwich and a pickle. And be careful about crumbs. I've already swept."

Joan disappeared into the kitchen, and Katherine stepped to the screen and looked at the movers. The same slender woman she had seen before stood on the porch of the house next door. She still wore sunglasses, but this time her dark hair was pulled back in a ponytail.

Katherine could only see her in profile as she said something to one of the men and gestured at the sofa being carried up the sidewalk, but something about the way she stood and moved made Katherine think about Annie. Her heart skipped several beats. It had happened before, this case of mistaken identity. Shortly after Annie's murder, Katherine couldn't leave the house without seeing women who, for an instant, made her heart leap with joy and then plummet into her stomach when she realized the woman wasn't Annie—was, in fact, nothing at all like Annie. At first it had given her hope, but now it caused nothing but pain. She forced herself to look away and return to the kitchen, where Joan babbled on and on about the furniture, the woman, and her son.

Joan shoved the last bite of pickle in her mouth and stood up. "Can I go outside now?"

Katherine was inwardly amused at her daughter's persistence, though she tried not to show it. "Yes. But stay on the porch or in the back yard and do *not* bother the new neighbors or the movers." She pointed her finger at Joan in warning. "I mean it."

Joan nodded, pushed her chair in, and walked sedately out of the kitchen. Katherine heard her running down the hall and out onto the porch. The screen door banged shut. Katherine flinched and pressed her fingertips to her temples. Noises were too sharp today—always an indicator of one of her headaches. At this rate, she knew she would be locked in her room with a cool rag over her forehead by nighttime. Clyde would have to cook dinner for Joanie.

The thought of her husband made her frown. In the years since Annie's murder and Joan's birth, Katherine had spoken to him only the words necessary to run the household. Their dislike for each other bound them together just as surely as she needed his financial support, and he needed someone to take care of his daughter. Even when they had moved into Lawrence from the country, they spoke only enough to arrange the move. Dinners were spent in cool silence until Joan was old enough to speak and then she carried the conversation for all of them, babbling on and on about her day.

Katherine continued to massage her temples. *It's going to be a bad one*, she thought. She might even need to take the medicine Dr. Thompson had given her for when the pain became intolerable.

She sighed and pushed herself into a standing position. Perhaps she should just go to her room now. She started down the hall and stopped on the steps to tell Joan to come inside. She craned her neck and looked out onto the porch. Joan was nowhere to be seen.

"Damn it," Katherine muttered angrily as she stepped out onto the porch. Joan was playing in the grass with the dark-haired boy. "Joanie. What did I tell you about leaving the porch?"

"Don't blame her, it's my fault."

The voice was unmistakable.

Katherine jerked her head in the direction of the woman standing on the neighboring porch. For the first time she saw the woman's face. Sheepishly, the woman smiled, removed her sunglasses, and slid them into the pocket of her dungarees.

Katherine felt the blood drain from her face and raised a trembling hand to her mouth. The woman looked exactly like Annie. She stared as the woman hurried down the stairs and across the grass to the bottom step of Katherine's porch. The unmistakable dark eyes searched hers as the woman climbed the steps and stood in front of her.

"Hi, Kate," she said softly.

Katherine stepped clumsily backward and swayed slightly. "What is this?" She looked anxiously from the woman's face to the street and back. "Who are you?"

"It's me," Annie said.

"You're not real," Katherine stammered. "This . . . this is a cruel joke. Clyde hired you to punish me, didn't he?" Annie frowned and reached out her hand. Katherine slapped it away. "Don't touch me." She stared at the woman who looked like Annie and her entire body trembled. The pain in her head hummed and she felt nauseous.

"Kate." Annie looked at her strangely. "I know this is unexpected, and I can only imagine that you're angry but—"

"Who *are* you?" Katherine asked again.

"It's me," Annie said and then, in a much lower voice, added, "Annie."

"It can't be you." The hum in Katherine's ears was an insistent buzzing. She swayed slightly, fighting the darkness pushing at the sides of her vision. "You're dead."

Annie's mouth twitched. "Dead? Not hardly—though you might have wished it was the case after the last time we saw each other, but no." She shook her head. "I'm very much alive."

"No." Katherine shook her head almost violently. "Clyde killed you. I have the bullet shell to prove it."

Annie studied Katherine with a confused expression. "I haven't seen Clyde since that time we went skating in '32." She frowned.

"No," Katherine said, her voice shaky. "He found out about us. He found a letter I had written to you. He and Bud went to Chicago. They killed you."

Annie again reached out to touch Katherine. Katherine flinched, but let her. She knew that touch. It was Annie. The buzzing in her head receded slightly.

"Sweetheart, listen to me. No one came to find me or kill me. I'm fine." She looked at Jason and Joan playing together, and then at the house next door. "I know I should have told you—should have contacted you before I just moved in. But I thought if you knew it was me, you'd say 'no.' I thought you wouldn't let me be near you, so . . ." She shrugged and grinned.

Katherine stared at her. Annie shifted uncomfortably and stepped closer. Katherine could smell the familiar shampoo and the scent that belonged only to Annie.

"Listen, I know this isn't the time or place, but there are some things I need to say." Annie's grin faded, and she became serious. "I love you, Kate. I always have. And I can't be without you anymore. I know you're married to Clyde. I know you have a daughter and I won't disrupt that." She swallowed and took a deep breath. "I don't expect to be your lover. I just want . . . I need . . . to be close to you. You and Jason are all I have for family and I'm not going to give you up again. I will let you set the terms. All I ask is that you let me be a part of your life."

Katherine blinked and then realized the dangerousness of the situation. "You can't stay here. If Clyde sees you, he won't just trick me into thinking he's killed you—he'll actually do it. You've got to go away. Go someplace safe." She looked anxiously up and down the street. "Annie, you can't live there. If he sees you he'll—"

"Kate, stop." Annie grasped both of her shoulders and shook her gently. "Listen to me. No one is going to kill anybody."

"But Clyde knows about us," Katherine said. "He will—"

"Clyde won't even know who I am. He's only seen me once and I was bundled up in winter clothes. Besides—"

Katherine stared in numb fear as Clyde's battered truck pulled slowly into the narrow driveway.

Annie looked at Katherine with wide eyes.

"You've got to hide," Katherine said urgently.

"No," Annie said. "I'm not going to hide and I'm not going to leave—not again. I'll handle this."

Clyde climbed out of the truck and ambled up the sidewalk. He was dressed in overalls and a dirty John Deere hat. In one hand he carried a dented, black metal lunch box. He squinted up at the porch as he climbed the steps.

"Hello there," Annie said brightly.

Clyde stared at her for a moment and then glanced at Katherine.

"I'm your new neighbor," Annie said and extended her hand. He gripped it in his and shook it quickly. "I'm Lettie Yoccum and that is my son, Jason." She pointed over to where Joan and Jason were playing.

"Ma'am," he said and dipped his head in greeting. "Nice to meet you. I'm Clyde Spencer and it looks like you've met my wife, Kate."

"I have," Annie said smoothly. "And your daughter, Joan. She's lovely."

"Thank you." Clyde chuckled. "She's a handful, all right." He looked at the uniformed men moving the last of Annie's things into the house. "Husband too busy to help with the move?"

"I'm a widow," Annie said.

"Oh, well . . . that's too bad. I'm sorry." He looked down at his worn work boots and then back up at Katherine. "I just stopped by to get a couple of things. The hydraulic hose on the plow blew out. Got to go to the implement store and get a new one." He looked back at Annie and dipped his head. "So . . . ah . . . Nice to meet you."

"And you."

He smiled, pulled open the screen, and stepped inside the house.

Katherine stared at Annie.

"See?" Annie said softly and grinned. "He didn't even recognize me."

Katherine blinked and whispered, "You're absolutely insane. It's only a matter of time before he figures it out."

"Kate, listen to me." Annie grabbed her arm and pulled her away from the door. "I let you go once, and it was the biggest mistake of my life. I'm not doing it again. I don't care if he recognizes me or tries to kill me or . . . anything. I want to be near you and there is nothing you can do to stop me. You can ignore me. You can pretend I'm not here, but I'm not going anywhere." Before Katherine could argue, she turned and went down the steps. "You know where I am when you want to talk," she said over her shoulder.

KATHERINE LAY ON her bed with the cool cloth pressed to her forehead. The headache was gone but the pain had been replaced the swirl of thoughts and emotions that came too quickly for her to process. Only one word made sense: Annie. She felt her heart beat faster at the thought of her. Annie wasn't dead. She was very much alive and still loved her—still wanted her. She trembled with elation, numbness, excitement.

For the first time in years, she allowed herself to think about the night of the rape. Clyde had said he had known about her—that her mother had told him, and he had married her anyway to save her reputation. For the first time, she wondered just what exactly her mother had told him. She suddenly realized that he hadn't seemed upset when Annie became her boarder while he was away at the war. In fact, he had welcomed the extra money. He had also taken her to meet Annie in Kansas City that day— the day that she had planned to leave him and run away with Annie. And then today, he clearly hadn't recognized her.

"He didn't kill Annie because he didn't know about her," Katherine murmured. "Why didn't I realize this before? How could I have been so stupid?" So, who then, if anyone, had Clyde and Bud murdered? Had that been made up just to hurt her? She shook her head as she remembered her conversation with Emily and her allusion to the fact that no body would ever be found.

Katherine stood and walked to the window. A light shone from one of the upstairs windows of Annie's house. She was probably unpacking. Or, she thought, perhaps she was waiting for her. She looked at the clock on her nightstand. It was well after midnight. Clyde and Joan would be sound asleep by now. She quietly went to her closet and pulled on a pair of dungarees and a blouse. Silently she tip-toed barefoot down the stairs and out the front door. She reached the steps to Annie's house.

"I was beginning to think you wouldn't come," a low voice came from the shadows of the porch.

Katherine squinted into the darkness and could just make out Annie's form on the porch swing. "I . . ." She paused. "I'm sorry about earlier. So much has happened that—"

"Come here," Annie said.

Katherine slowly climbed the steps.

Annie stopped the softly rocking motion of the swing.

Katherine stood in front of her. "I can't believe it's really you."

Annie took Katherine's hand and held it lightly, her thumb gently caressing the back of her fingers. Katherine felt the warmth of her touch and gently caressed Annie's cheek with her other hand. She cupped her jaw and ran her fingertips down to the corners of her mouth.

Annie sighed, and Katherine felt the familiar response. She stepped closer just as Annie stood. Their bodies were inches apart, and Katherine could smell the whiskey on Annie's breath. It was sweet and achingly familiar. She smiled.

They stood that way for several seconds, just breathing in each other's breath until Annie pulled Katherine's face down to hers. Katherine closed her eyes as Annie lightly kissed her forehead, her cheek, and then, finally, her mouth. Katherine gasped at the contact and deepened the kiss. She opened her lips slightly at the touch of Annie's tongue and sighed as the interaction became more demanding.

"Oh my God," Annie murmured when they pulled apart. She gently stroked Katherine's back and slid her hands up to her shoulders. "I've missed you. I—"

Katherine pulled Annie to her in an almost violent kiss.

"Later," Katherine murmured softly. "We'll talk later." She ground her body against Annie's and was rewarded with a soft groan. She dipped her head to kiss her again but Annie stopped her.

"Inside," she said. "Let's go inside."

Katherine nodded and allowed herself to be led into the darkness of the first story.

"Your son—" Katherine said.

"Sleeps like a log." Annie pulled her toward the stairs. "And even if he didn't, we're locking the door. Nothing is stopping us tonight."

CHAPTER 28
Lawrence, Kansas, 1997

JOAN STARED INCREDULOUSLY at Mrs. Yoccum.

"You're Annie?"

Mrs. Yoccum nodded.

"And all this time, all these years, you . . ."

"Yes," Mrs. Yoccum said softly.

"And that's how you know so much." Joan shook her head in disbelief. "And my father never suspected?"

"No. I'm convinced he had no idea who I was or my relationship with your mother—past or present." Mrs. Yoccum shook her head. "I don't know what your grandmother told him that made him think he needed to marry your mother, but I don't think it had anything to do with our relationship. I'm willing to bet it had to do with what he thought—or was told—was unrequited love for Albert Russell. He was a boy your mother dated."

"And you two just . . . how did you . . . I don't understand," Joan asked. "When she found out you were alive and still loved her, why didn't she leave him? Why did she stay with him when she hated him and was in love with you?"

"Because I wouldn't let her." Mrs. Yoccum chuckled. "Ironic, isn't it? After all of those years of insisting she ignore social conventions, I was the one who insisted she stay married to your father until you were grown and out of the house. The same with Jason. It wasn't just about us anymore. We had children. You had to be our priority."

Joan shook her head in amazement.

"She loved you," Mrs. Yoccum said. "And she was proud of you."

Joan leaned back into the pillow and closed her eyes. "I don't think she would be right now, Mrs. Yoccum. My life is such a mess."

"Lettie," Mrs. Yoccum corrected.

"Lettie," Joan echoed hollowly and opened her eyes. "Why not Annie?"

Mrs. Yoccum smiled slightly. "When I moved next door to your mother and father, I thought it would be best to start with a clean slate. The name Annie might have raised some flags with your father. Lettie is short for my given name—Charlotte. Charlotte Annette Grayson Bennett."

"And you were the great love of my mother's life," Joan said softly.

"And she was mine," Mrs. Yoccum said. "We didn't have an easy row to hoe, but we made the best out of it in the end."

Joan swallowed and studied the woman who had been her mother's lover and her own next door neighbor for so many years. Mrs. Yoccum looked back at her with dark, solemn eyes.

"So, if Daddy and Uncle Bud didn't kill you, who did they kill?" she asked. "Bud said they murdered someone."

"I don't have any proof, mind you, but I think they killed Albert Russell."

"The guy my mom dated?" Joan frowned. "That's who you think my grandmother told my dad about?"

Mrs. Yoccum nodded. "Your mother and I talked about it a lot. And it just so happens that Albert Russell disappeared at exactly the same time your father said he killed her lover."

"Disappeared?" Joan repeated.

Mrs. Yoccum nodded. "Albert owned a couple of car dealerships in Kansas City. He was very successful but he also was connected with some of the seedier elements in Kansas City. There were rumors that his business was somehow associated with Nick Civella and his group—that and he had a gambling debt. When he disappeared, a lot of people thought it was mafia related."

"But you think my father did it?" Joan asked incredulously.

"I do," Mrs. Yoccum said. "And only because of a conversation your mother had with your aunt Emily. After I moved next door, your mother went to talk to Emily. She pretended to feel remorse for what she did and said that she wanted to make amends. Eventually she found out that a body was buried some place on Clyde's family's homestead. Some of the property was heavily wooded. My guess was that it was out there."

"And how did you figure out it was Albert?"

"Emily never said the name, but she did use the pronoun 'he' and it all makes sense," Mrs. Yoccum said. "Clyde was always jealous of Albert. And if your grandmother spun the tale that your mother had been in love with him . . . well . . ." She shrugged.

"Did you and Mom ever look for the body?"

Mrs. Yoccum shook her head. "Oh, no. It just seemed best to leave well enough alone. And, honestly, if the rumors were true, even if your father and Bud hadn't gotten to him first, I'm convinced Civella would have done it eventually."

Joan sat in stunned silence.

"Well, dear, I should let you rest." Mrs. Yoccum stood and started toward the door. "I know it goes without saying, but I'm here if you need anything."

Joan nodded. "Thanks, Lettie. How are you getting home?"

"Taxi," Mrs. Yoccum said. "With maybe a stop at the liquor store. I'll get you a bottle of wine for when you come home."

Joan laughed and watched as she slipped out the door. As soon as she was alone, she laid her head back on the pillow and closed her eyes. So much had changed in the span of just a few hours. Luke knew about the affair. The baby was gone. Mrs. Yoccum was Annie. And her father quite possibly murdered an innocent man.

"I guess all secrets get exposed one way or another," she murmured softly to herself. "Now then all that's left is dealing with the consequences."

LATE THE FOLLOWING afternoon Joan stepped carefully from the back seat of a cab in front of her mother's house and thanked the driver who had jumped out and rushed to open the door. She waited until he pulled away before shuffling up the sidewalk to the porch steps. She glanced at Mrs. Yoccum's house and saw her standing in the window watching her progress. Joan raised her hand in a vague wave, but didn't stop. Mrs. Yoccum didn't come out of her house.

Once inside, Joan stood in the foyer, closed her eyes, and, like her first night back, inhaled the scent of her mother. This time the smell of the house didn't make her angry as much as it made her sad—sad for her mother and sad for herself.

"I'm so sorry, Mama," she said softly as she ran her hand along the top of the polished banister. "There was so much I didn't know."

She sighed and slowly climbed the stairs to the bathroom. She needed a shower. She turned on the taps and studied her body in the mirror as she waited for the water to get hot. She was bruised in several places, had several cuts on her face and hands, and it hurt to breathe. Otherwise, she looked exactly the same as she had before the accident. She placed a hand on her flat belly and turned to the side. Nothing. It was as if it had never happened—as if she had never been pregnant. She waited for the sense of loss. Or guilt. When neither came, she stepped into the steaming water and began to wash.

Twenty minutes later, clean and dressed in a faded T-shirt, jeans, and a sweatshirt, she made her way slowly downstairs. She was on the second to last step when she heard the soft knock on the door. She could see Mrs. Yoccum through the lace curtains.

Joan opened the door.

"I thought you could use this." Mrs. Yoccum held out a bottle of white wine. "I was going to just leave it on the porch, but then I thought someone might steal it if I did that." She smiled and turned to leave. "I don't want to bother you. I just—"

"Would you like to come in for a drink?" Joan interrupted quickly.

Mrs. Yoccum looked startled, but also pleased. "Well, I suppose I could stay for one."

Joan stepped awkwardly backward so Mrs. Yoccum could enter. They walked to the kitchen. Joan opened the wine and poured two glasses. She handed one to Mrs. Yoccum and gestured toward the living room.

"How are you feeling?" Mrs. Yoccum asked as they settled into the chairs that still sat in front of the picture window.

"Sore," Joan said. "And overwhelmed."

"It's a lot to take in."

Joan nodded. "So, were you and Mama happy?"

"As happy as we could be, I suppose." Mrs. Yoccum took a sip of wine and relaxed into the chair. "It took us a long time to get it right. It was better once your father died, though, I would have liked to have had a home together."

"Why didn't you?" Joan asked.

"We talked about it." Mrs. Yoccum stared into her glass. "But your mother didn't want you to know, and I wasn't about to hide it. And honestly, we were both pretty set in our ways by the time we could have lived together without raising suspicion. It worked out just fine staying at one or the other's place."

She took another sip and set her glass on the small table with a trembling hand.

"She died in my arms." Mrs. Yoccum's voice was thick with emotion. "We were upstairs, asleep in bed. We had stayed up late talking. We laughed a lot that last night. And when I woke up, she was gone." Her brown eyes filled with tears. "Leaving her here was the hardest thing I ever did. But I knew that's what she would have wanted. So I kissed her goodbye, got dressed, and made it look as if she had died alone in her sleep. Then I went downstairs and called the police. I said I had gotten worried about my next door neighbor so I used her spare key to check on her and found her upstairs in her bed." Her shoulders shook as she broke down, sobbing.

"Oh, Lettie . . . Annie." Joan stood and despite her injuries, pulled her into her arms. "I'm so sorry."

"I loved her," Mrs. Yoccum sobbed. "I know she was difficult, but I loved her more than you could imagine. Those last years we had together weren't perfect, but I wouldn't have traded them for anything."

Joan held her mother's lover until she stopped crying. "Let me go get you a tissue."

Joan rose painfully to her feet and moved slowly into the dining room for the tissues she had left there the other day. The box sat on the table next to the stack of letters her mother had written Annie when she thought she was dead. Carefully, she folded each one and slid them back into their envelopes and carried the stack, along with the tissues, back into the living room.

"Oh, thank you dear." Mrs. Yoccum tugged a tissue from the box. "Nothing worse than an old woman's tears."

Joan waited until Mrs. Yoccum composed herself before laying the stack of letters in her lap.

Mrs. Yoccum looked up into Joan's face.

"She wrote them to you," Joan said simply. "I'm sorry I read them before you got a chance to."

Mrs. Yoccum ran a knobby finger across the edge of the top envelope. "Thank you. She never told me about them. You don't know how much—"

"I think I do." Joan struggled to hold back her own tears. "I have never loved anyone or anything the way you and my mother loved each other." She shook her head. "Never. And I want that for myself."

Mrs. Yoccum nodded. "Luke?" she asked after several moments of silence.

"No," Joan said. "Not if I'm honest. I don't love him. He says he can forgive me for the affair, but honestly, I'm not sure I want him to."

"And your children?"

"I love my children," Joan said almost fiercely. "If nothing else, this experience, finding out about you and Mom and Dad makes me realize that being a mother means making mistakes. And, being the child means forgiving those mistakes." She shook her head and closed her eyes. She opened them and gazed at Mrs. Yoccum, who was watching her.

"So you're going back to Chicago."

Joan could hear the disappointment in her voice. She nodded. "There are things I need to do there. But I don't see myself staying there." She smiled slightly. "Lawrence has good schools. And KU has a pretty good law school." She shrugged. "I still have a lot to figure out, but the one thing I do know is that I can no longer settle."

"I think your mother would be proud." Mrs. Yoccum smiled. "You're taking control of your life. That's all she ever wanted for you."

"I don't know as she'd be proud," Joan said finally, smiling fondly. "But let's just say I don't think she'd be entirely disappointed either."

CPSIA information can be obtained at www.ICGtesting.com
Printed in the USA
LVOW08s1612161214

419117LV00003B/729/P

9 781939 562104

ABOUT THE AUTHOR

Sandra Moran is a teacher, writer, and international woman of intrigue—though mainly a writer. When she's not running around Kansas City (literally) or torturing college students with the fundamentals of anthropology, she can be found in her lair listening to Pandora and making up stories.

To learn more about Sandra, to send her an e-mail, or to read her blog, visit her website at www.sandramoran.com.

Joan rose painfully to her feet and moved slowly into the dining room for the tissues she had left there the other day. The box sat on the table next to the stack of letters her mother had written Annie when she thought she was dead. Carefully, she folded each one and slid them back into their envelopes and carried the stack, along with the tissues, back into the living room.

"Oh, thank you dear." Mrs. Yoccum tugged a tissue from the box. "Nothing worse than an old woman's tears."

Joan waited until Mrs. Yoccum composed herself before laying the stack of letters in her lap.

Mrs. Yoccum looked up into Joan's face.

"She wrote them to you," Joan said simply. "I'm sorry I read them before you got a chance to."

Mrs. Yoccum ran a knobby finger across the edge of the top envelope. "Thank you. She never told me about them. You don't know how much—"

"I think I do." Joan struggled to hold back her own tears. "I have never loved anyone or anything the way you and my mother loved each other." She shook her head. "Never. And I want that for myself."

Mrs. Yoccum nodded. "Luke?" she asked after several moments of silence.

"No," Joan said. "Not if I'm honest. I don't love him. He says he can forgive me for the affair, but honestly, I'm not sure I want him to."

"And your children?"

"I love my children," Joan said almost fiercely. "If nothing else, this experience, finding out about you and Mom and Dad makes me realize that being a mother means making mistakes. And, being the child means forgiving those mistakes." She shook her head and closed her eyes. She opened them and gazed at Mrs. Yoccum, who was watching her.

"So you're going back to Chicago."

Joan could hear the disappointment in her voice. She nodded. "There are things I need to do there. But I don't see myself staying there." She smiled slightly. "Lawrence has good schools. And KU has a pretty good law school." She shrugged. "I still have a lot to figure out, but the one thing I do know is that I can no longer settle."

"I think your mother would be proud." Mrs. Yoccum smiled. "You're taking control of your life. That's all she ever wanted for you."

"I don't know as she'd be proud," Joan said finally, smiling fondly. "But let's just say I don't think she'd be entirely disappointed either."

ABOUT THE AUTHOR

Sandra Moran is a teacher, writer, and international woman of intrigue—though mainly a writer. When she's not running around Kansas City (literally) or torturing college students with the fundamentals of anthropology, she can be found in her lair listening to Pandora and making up stories.

To learn more about Sandra, to send her an e-mail, or to read her blog, visit her website at www.sandramoran.com.

CPSIA information can be obtained at www.ICGtesting.com
Printed in the USA
LVOW08s1612161214

419117LV00003B/729/P

9 781939 562104